Maya Blake's hopes
when she picked up
Little did she know h
she still pinch herself
sure it's not a dream? Yes, she does! Feel free to
pinch her, too, via Twitter, Facebook or Goodreads!
Happy reading!

Jackie Ashenden writes dark, emotional stories, with
alpha heroes who've just got the world to their liking
only to have it blown wide apart by their kick-ass
heroines. She lives in Auckland, New Zealand, with
her husband, the inimitable Dr Jax, two kids and two
rats. When she's not torturing alpha males and their
gutsy heroines she can be found drinking chocolate
martinis, reading anything she can lay her hands on,
wasting time on social media or being forced to go
mountain biking with her husband. To keep up to date
with Jackie's new releases and other news, sign up to
her newsletter at jackieashenden.com.

AN HEIR FOR THE WORLD'S RICHEST MAN

MAYA BLAKE

CLAIMING HIS ONE-NIGHT CHILD

JACKIE ASHENDEN

MILLS & BOON

First Published in Great Britain 2019
by Mills & Boon, an imprint of HarperCollins*Publishers*
1 London Bridge Street, London, SE1 9GF

An Heir for the World's Richest Man © 2019 by Maya Blake

Claiming His One-Night Child © 2019 by Jackie Ashenden

ISBN: 978-0-263-27354-0

MIX
Paper from
responsible sources
FSC™ C007454

This book is produced from independently certified FSC™ paper
to ensure responsible forest management.
For more information visit www.harpercollins.co.uk/green.

Printed and bound in Spain
by CPI, Barcelona

AN HEIR FOR THE WORLD'S RICHEST MAN

MAYA BLAKE

To Dad.

For passing your love of books to me.

For setting me on my path to my true self.

For making me what I am today. An author.

I miss you. I thank you. Always and for ever.

CHAPTER ONE

SAFFRON EVERHART STARED at the obscenely large, hideously expensive bouquet of flowers on her desk and her heart dropped into her stomach. This was going to be much more difficult than she'd ever imagined.

Over the years she'd learned to decode the levels of hell associated with the gifts that arrived on her desk on any given day.

Flowers meant prepare not to sleep for the next seventy-two hours. Flowers and a gift certificate to the most exclusive spa in Switzerland meant pack a bag and have someone water your plants because you won't be going home for a week. The last circle of hell was reserved for flowers and *jewellery*. These days the sight of precious gems made her shudder. She had three diamond bracelets, a Harry Winston pink diamond necklace with matching earrings, and a diamond and sapphire brooch she absolutely hated the sight of simply because of the blood, sweat and tears they'd wrung from her.

So, in a way, the flowers, as breathtaking and stomach-hollowing as they were, were a blessing simply because they had no accompaniment.

Still…

She set the Waterford crystal vase down at the farthest corner of her desk, curbing the urge to caress the soft petals of the hothouse lilies she knew had come from a florist who catered to a handful of exclusive A-list clientele. Just as she resisted the urge to lean forward and inhale their bewitching midnight-breeze scent, or be bowled over by the knowledge that each of the thirty long stems in the gigantic vase cost over a thousand pounds.

She rose from her desk, ignoring the sensational view of London spread out in rare sun-splashed splendour below her, and pivoted to face the double doors of the office adjoining hers.

The breath she took was shaky and weak, her clammy hands and churning gut a world removed from the image she strove to achieve. The image her straight spine and impeccable clothes projected.

More and more, that set of doors had seemed like the summit of Everest, fraught with dangers that screamed at her to turn back. Except she couldn't.

Not just yet.

But she'd delayed enough. Two whole months to be exact. It was time to take the final step.

Time to put that one night, that astoundingly risky dive into temptation that had set in motion events that made her heart dip each time she allowed herself to think of it, behind her.

Time to take back control of her life before it was too late.

Before she could compel her feet to move, a knock on the outer door stopped her. She turned, her stomach dropping to her toes at the sight of the smartly dressed courier heading purposefully towards her. Bicycle couriers and messengers weren't allowed above the fifteenth floor. She was on the forty-ninth, one step from the highest floor in the building owned by the richest man in the world.

And the man who was heading her way reverently clutching a black velvet briefcase with the logo of the Queen's jeweller proudly emblazoned on it was the furthest you could get from an ordinary courier.

'No.' The word was ripped from her throat, accompanied by several self-preserving steps backward, because, unlike the tennis bracelets and the other priceless gifts, this jeweller, this *delivery* signalled a whole new playing field.

The kind that warned you to kiss your soul goodbye. That clammy hands and an inability to breathe properly would be the least of her worries if she gave into what was unfolding.

'No, no, *no.*'

The courier paused halfway to her desk, his gaze befuddled. 'Beg your pardon, miss? Do I have the wrong floor? I have a delivery for a Miss Everhart. Can you redirect me if this isn't the right office? I'm afraid I'll need a signature from her.'

She shook her head. 'No. I mean, yes, you're in the right office but, no, you don't need a signature. You won't need one because you won't be making a delivery.' She was aware her voice bordered on hysterical but she couldn't help it. 'The gift is being returned,' she added for complete and undeniable emphasis.

His nervousness increased. 'I'm afraid that won't be possible. There's a non-returnable, non-refundable condition attached to the gift.'

'That's not true,' she stated firmly. 'I'm Miss Everhart, and I've dealt with your establishment before. I know for a fact that's not the case.'

Sweat beaded on his forehead. Saffron almost felt sorry for him. 'Well…yes, miss, in most cases it is. But not this time.'

'Why not?' she demanded, but deep down, she knew the answer.

'Because the client specifically requested it.'

She resisted the urge to squeeze her eyes shut in panicked exasperation because…*of course he did.* The man could outthink the shrewdest opponent without breaking a sweat, could execute a dozen chess moves in a dozen games simultaneously while lounging behind his desk with his eyes shut. Why she'd think he wouldn't use such a contingency on this occasion was almost laughable.

But Saffron wasn't in the mood to laugh.

Her gaze dropped to the case, her stomach knotting tighter. If it'd held a nest of deadly scorpions, she would've been more welcoming.

The courier cleared his throat. 'If I may say so, Miss Everhart, this is no ordinary piece. I believe permission was sought, and given, by Her Majesty for her necklace to be replicated. It's one of the most exquisite pieces our establishment has had the privilege of creating.' His tone bordered on reverence, his bewilderment at her reaction evident.

She didn't doubt him. But the reason for its appearance in her life was blaring thunderously in her ears, blocking everything save for the fact that if she didn't refuse this, if she delayed taking control of her life, she would be lost for ever. She'd already given four years of her life. Lived on the edge of her emotions. She couldn't give another day. *Another minute.*

The man in front of her wasn't the problem, though. The man seated on his throne-like chair behind the grey steel doors twenty feet from her was.

With brisk efficiency that disguised the churning mix of panic and dread inside her, she signed the delivery document and took possession of the package, knowing in her heart that she was making a huge mistake.

The door shut behind the courier. Saffron remained rooted in place, the box growing heavier with each second. When she could bear it no longer, she returned to her desk, sat down heavily and opened it.

The tiered diamond and ruby necklace was flawless.

Breathtakingly beautiful in a way no blatant bribe from a ruthless, coldly dismissive man had the right to be. At least it wasn't a choker. That symbolism would've been a step too far.

She suppressed a hysterical laugh and stared, awed despite herself, at the most stunning piece of jewellery she'd ever seen in her life. Her fingers itched to caress the precious stones, to experience their sparkling beauty through touch as well as sight.

She snapped the box shut before temptation took hold, and, just like the flowers, set it out of arm's reach.

She couldn't…*wouldn't* be swayed.

For far too long she'd given herself a pass, let the irresistible enticements of her position, specifically her proximity to the most charismatic man she'd ever encountered, lead her towards that one final act of insanity.

Well…never again.

Jaw gritted in a futile effort to stop the electricity that zapped through her every time she recalled that fateful night in Morocco, she read through the document she'd redrafted a dozen times and hit print.

The whirring sound of the printer spitting out the single sheet was both reassuring and terrifying. She was finally doing this, taking the ultimate step. Soon, she would be in complete control of her life. But first, there was the small problem of getting over this last monumental hurdle.

Saffron had no doubt that it would be a formidable battle.

She picked up the paper, folded it in two and rose.

With a cursory knock, she entered the lion's den. Just in time to hear the exclusive phone reserved for super-VIP clients ring.

She froze in the doorway, her breathing nosediving as her gaze landed on the man reaching for the silver phone.

Joao Oliviera.

Her boss.

The richest man in the world with looks far outmatching that awe-inspiring title.

Despite the innumerable times she'd entered his domain, Saffron had never quite mastered the awe that possessed her in his presence. She'd just learned to disguise it to the point where she could appear almost dismissive of the endless layers of the powerful, magnetic aura he exuded, the breath-stealing vitality of his six-foot-four frame, his innate ability to strike the most influential leaders dumb with a few well-placed words.

And the feverish electricity of his touch.

No amount of training or self-denial could disguise the fact that Joao Oliviera, with his obscene wealth and good looks, was Midas, Croesus and Ares rolled into one sublime package.

Thick dark brown hair, longer than conventionally acceptable and tipped with the faintest gold, gleamed in the May sunlight slanting through the glass window behind him.

Chiselled cheekbones drew immediate, captivating attention to the olive vibrancy of his face, the uncompromising line of an upper lip neatly counterbalanced by the sinful, sensual curve of his lower lip, and the rugged outline of his faintly shadowed jaw that no amount of shaving could completely smooth.

Startling whisky-gold eyes framed by long, spiked eyelashes completed the magnificent picture.

Those eyes flicked up at her entrance, studied her for a piercing second before he beckoned her with long, elegant fingers. As was his habit, he'd shed his jacket shortly after his day began, leaving the pristine white shirt and Italian-made silk vest that emphasised his racehorse-lean physique on full display.

It was early, barely eight o'clock on a Monday morning, so he hadn't got around to undoing his cuffs and folding back his shirtsleeves to reveal his brawny forearms. In the giant scheme of breathless hellishness, she took that as a blessing in disguise.

'Lavinia, I've been waiting for your call,' he drawled into the phone.

And just like that, Saffron was lashed by another whip

of her most sinful craving. Over the years she'd battled to suppress her base reactions to almost everything about Joao—save for that one searing night in Morocco. His impressive mental dexterity, his jaw-dropping physique, his superhuman energy, the breathtaking ruthlessness wrapped around a core of unwavering integrity. But the one thing she'd never conquered was her reaction to the deep, intensely sexy, accented voice.

It shot arrows of flaming lust into her during her waking hours, and, with alarming frequency lately, invaded her dreams just as shamelessly. It'd reached the point where she almost dreaded walking into his office.

With any luck, she wouldn't have to suffer it for much longer.

Saffron shut the door behind her and tuned into the conversation. Regardless of her primary reason for coming into Joao's office, she had work to do. This morning—and, she suspected, countless more to come—that work involved Lavinia Archer.

At seventy-four, the head of the renowned Archer Group, an empire that comprised Archer Hotels, Archer Brewery, Archer Cruise Liners, Archer Airlines and several more offshoots, had been in control for over three decades.

When rumours had surfaced that Lavinia intended to sell her company to one buyer before her seventy-fifth birthday, Saffron had known it would be catnip to her boss. She'd been proved right when Joao had immediately set out to add the entire Archer empire, valued at thirty-one billion dollars, into his already staggering portfolio.

For the last three months, he'd woven an intricate web around Lavinia Archer, one involving a game of mental chess and charm that the older woman, despite courting several buyers, hadn't been able to resist participating in.

'I know you take pleasure in making me wait, Lavinia,' Joao continued, the timbre of his voice smooth, dark and potent like the special blend of coffee his handpicked aficionados cultivated for him exclusively in his native Brazil. Every word oozed effortless charisma as his dark golden gaze tracked Saffron across his office. 'I hope when the time comes, you'll let me make the climax worth your while.'

Saffron stumbled, briskly caught herself on the edge of the sectional sofa that graced the office, and dragged her gaze from his coolly mocking one before she compounded her rare clumsiness by blushing.

Sultry laughter flowed from the phone. Saffron curbed the irrational jealousy that welled inside her and attempted to maintain her composure.

Even though she'd given him four years of her life, when it came right down to it, she had no rights where Joao was concerned. He didn't care about her beyond her excellent organisational skills.

Not once had he asked her what her interests were outside the office—not that she had much time to pursue any of them. Her last two birthdays had passed her by because she'd been so engrossed in making Joao Oliviera's life problem-free that she'd missed them.

And the fact that there'd been no one else to remind her—no family, friends, nor even acquaintances—and that her boss hadn't known to treat those days differently from any other work-hard-and-then-even-harder days, had been just one of the many things that had bruised her deep inside when she'd finally girded her loins and taken stock of her life.

Unsurprisingly, all the things wrong with her life had been down to one man.

Joao Oliviera.

So, no, she wasn't going to waste a moment's energy on being jealous. And when she was done with her task here, he could charm the birds from the trees for all she cared.

She wouldn't be around to see it. Wouldn't experience that stressful little pull in her chest when he arranged an assignation with the next supermodel or socialite.

Thankfully he hadn't done that since Morocco. Not to her knowledge anyway, which in no way proved conclusively that he hadn't—

Enough!

Interrupting her own spiralling thoughts, she refocused to find Joao's gaze raking over her body, lingering for a moment on the document in her hand before rising to meet her eyes.

Her heart lurched.

For the last eight weeks, he'd treated her with cool indifference. He'd watched her when he'd wanted to and ignored her when it had pleased him.

Saffie was forced to admit it was that detachment that had finally triggered her actions. That knowledge that she couldn't endure much more of this, couldn't pretend that her life hadn't boiled down to being an insignificant satellite that orbited around his brilliance.

That Morocco hadn't happened.

She pressed her lips together, fighting the chaotic sensations in mind and body as Joao let out a low, deep laugh.

'*Sim*, I'll respect you in the morning. You'll leave satisfied that your legacy is in the best hands possible.'

Long fingers tapped the smooth surface of his glass desk, drawing her attention to its graceful elegance, its subdued power. From there it was a mere skip to unlocking memories of when those fingers made firm, deliberate contact with her skin. Stroked and teased and branded, leaving an indelible mark on her.

She watched his arm rise, his fingers stretching out in silent command for the document.

While Joao's ability to multitask was another skilful feather in his cap, she hadn't anticipated executing this task while he conducted one of the biggest deals of his company's history.

But…the order of things didn't matter. She was here to take her life back.

So, do it.

Lips pressed firmly together, she handed over the paper.

Perhaps her expression gave her away. Perhaps the poker face that had seen her through four long years but had begun to crack after Morocco had finally let her down.

Seconds breathlessly ticked by as he continued to recite facts and figures to Lavinia in his deep accented voice, all without taking his eyes off Saffron's face. A full minute later, his gaze finally dropped to the sheet.

Shrewd eyes skimmed the document with lightning speed. Then his breathtaking face tightened.

Her insides jumped as those hypnotic eyes rose to lock on hers.

'*Sim,*' he murmured smoothly to Lavinia, although Saffie heard curt edginess wrapped around the word. 'But remember I'm not a patient man. I want your company, and I will play your games for now. But eventually one of us will grow bored and resort to…other measures. Prepare yourself for that scenario, too, *meu querido*. Until the next time.'

The words might have been directed into the phone but Saffie felt their impact deep inside.

With a casual flick of his hand, he ended the call. Then chilled, narrowed eyes rose from her carefully crafted resignation letter to her face.

'What is the meaning of this?' he breathed in a low, deadly voice.

Saffron called on every last crumb of composure and held his stare. 'It's exactly as it says. I'm tendering my resignation.'

His gaze flickered with a hint of disbelief, then dropped to the page. 'For *"personal reasons"*? You do not have a personal life, therefore you cannot have personal reasons. *Therefore*—' he flicked a disdainful finger at the sheet '— this is a blatant lie.'

She didn't want to be hurt by the caustic words. By now, she should be immune to his brand of ruthless disregard for any impediment that stood between him and whatever goal he pursued. And yet that mysterious pang that had sprung up the morning after their fateful night burrowed deeper into her heart.

'Thank you so much for pointing that out. And while I'm at it, thank you for the flowers and jewellery, although I won't be accepting them. I'm assuming you're about to step things up with Lavinia, hence the need for that outrageous bribe?'

Not by a flicker of an eyelash did he acknowledge any wrongdoing in commissioning a necklace most monarchs would give an eye tooth for. 'You're building up to a point, I expect? Some sort of negotiation perhaps?' he mused.

'You're not going to give me the courtesy of an answer?'

'I believe one of the first things we discussed at the start of your employment was not to ask questions you already know the answers to. Would you like me to repeat mine? Because you haven't given me a satisfactory answer.'

'Every answer you need is in that letter. I'm resigning for personal reasons. Effective immediately after the requisite notice period.'

The gaze he flicked at the letter was filled with such singeing disdain, Saffron was surprised it didn't catch fire.

'You're not flighty. You're supremely efficient. Dependable. Level-headed. One of the most hardworking people I know. In the past four years, there hasn't been a single task you haven't executed to my satisfaction,' he drawled, angling his body back to lounge in the high-backed, throne-like chair a vaunted French furniture designer had fashioned exclusively for him. The stance threw his gladiator-like frame into high-definition relief, the sunlight doing its part to showcase his perfect body.

Saffron's thighs snapped together as heat singed her feminine core and burrowed deep, sensuously, into her pelvis, reminding how it'd felt to have that body up close, personal...*naked*.

Inside her.

'Thank you. I'm glad you noticed.'

Her sarcasm went over his head. As with most things he thought beneath his regard. Why was she even surprised?

'Which is why I'm puzzled by your need to couch your so-called resignation in such...whimsical, flowery prose. You're *"honoured by the opportunity"* to have worked with me? You wish me *"the brightest of futures"*? Your experience with me will remain *"an unforgettable experience"*?' he recited.

Fine, so she'd let her nerves run away with her in the early hours of the morning when she'd redrafted the letter *yet again*, but did he really need to repeat it in such mocking tones? 'Believe it or not, everything on there is true—'

'Everything on here is nonsense!' His deep voice was a merciless scythe through her response. 'Your resignation is not accepted. Especially not at such a crucial point in my dealings with Lavinia. We've been going about this all wrong. It's time to flip the script. To win her over we have to show her what she *doesn't* know she's missing. Let's take her out of her comfort zone, in the most enticing way. You think you can handle that?'

Saffron fought the urge to clench her fists and stamp her foot. That would achieve absolutely nothing. Besides, as Joao had so coldly categorised, she wasn't flighty. She was dependable. Level-headed. Hard-working. *Obedient*.

Qualities she'd striven for as an orphan. Everything the nuns at St Agnes's Home For Children had assured her would secure foster parents and eventually parents who would adopt her, only for her to be passed over time and again in favour of others. She'd shed silent tears—because it wouldn't have done for Sister Zeta to hear her crying and be disappointed in her—when bratty Selena had been chosen instead of her that week before Christmas when she was seven.

She'd been overwhelmed with sorrow when eight months later another smiling couple had walked away with a child that wasn't her.

Through every heart-rending repetition of those events, she hadn't shown any outward sign of distress or, even worse, thrown a tantrum like some of the other children. Eventually when her moment had finally arrived at the ripe old age of fourteen, she had refrained from exhibiting any outward signs of elation, lest it be misconstrued.

She'd maintained that self-possession through the two happy years she'd spent with her foster mother, and then through the harrowing eighteen months when her health had rapidly declined. Saffie had kept tearless vigils by her bedside, made the solemn promise that, no, she wouldn't succumb to loneliness, that, yes, she would seek another family for herself when the time came, no matter what.

When, a week before her eighteenth birthday, Saffron had buried her foster mother, she'd buoyed up everyone at the small funeral gathering, recounting her fondest memories of that wonderful woman and drawing smiles to everyone's faces. And she'd made sure she was completely alone before shedding a single tear.

It was near enough with that same composure that she pivoted away from Joao's desk and returned to her desk. Where she placed a call to a number she knew by heart.

Once the call was done, she reached for the velvet box with not quite steady hands and returned to her boss's office.

'Are you coming down with an ailment?' Joao demanded, a healthy dose of that Brazilian temper melting away a layer of indifference. 'Would you like me to summon the company doctor for you?'

'That won't be necessary. I'm absolutely fine. In fact, I'm more than fine. I'm seeing things a little more clearly for the first time in a long while.'

He tensed, his eyes probing deeper. 'And those things include resigning from a job that you stated in your last evaluation was *"the most fulfilling thing"* in your life?'

She bit the inside of her cheek, regret for those exposing words drenching her. But again, it was one of the many faults in her life she intended to rectify sharpish. 'Yes.'

Tense seconds ticked by as he eyed her. 'You do realise you could've stated a number of reasons for resigning besides this *personal* excuse you're holding so preciously to your chest?'

The observation stopped her short.

Had it been deliberate? Did she, on some subliminal level, wish him to see beneath her façade, to the heart of her single, deepest desire? To that yearning that had started with a deathbed promise and blossomed soon after her foster mother's passing, when Saffron had realised she was once again alone in the world, and had known she wouldn't feel whole again until she fulfilled it? A yearning that had momentarily faded against the brilliant supernova that was Joao, only to re-emerge invigorated, viscerally demanding fulfilment?

No.

One night had been enough. The last thing she wanted was to reveal any more of her vulnerabilities to a man like Joao Oliviera. A man who breathed and bled commerce. A man who dropped his lovers swiftly and without mercy the moment they harboured the barest notions of permanence. A man without a family and a blatantly stated anathema towards ever encumbering himself with one.

'I was hoping you'd respect my privacy and leave it at that.'

'We have never deluded one another, Saffie. Let us not start now.'

Her breath caught at the accented way he pronounced her shortened name. *Saahfie.*

Each time it sent electric shivers down her spine, made her breasts tingle and her belly flip-flop in giddy excitement. This time was no different despite the volatile tension arcing between them.

But his statement made her breath catch for different, more terrible, reasons.

She had lived through months, perhaps even years of delusion.

Ultimately, *that* shameful realisation that she was chasing dreams, and wasting precious time doing so, was why she stood before him now.

'Your letter threw up red flags. I'm acknowledging those flags and demanding to know what's going on. Especially since we parted company only a few hours ago and you gave no inkling of pulling this stunt.'

'Firstly, it's not a stunt. Secondly, did it occur to you that I might not want to do this for ever? You might imagine you have immortal blood flowing through your veins and are therefore going to live for ever. Some of us are more cognisant of our mortality. So pardon me if I've realised that I don't want to work until two a.m. on a Monday morning only to turn around and return to the office at seven-thirty to put in another eighteen hours.'

A dark frown descended over his brows and something like disappointment shot through his eyes. For whatever reason his anger didn't grate as much as his disappointment. 'That's the problem? You're complaining about your workload? You have my permission to hire yourself another assistant.'

She eased her grip on the box, breached the last few steps to his desk and set it down. 'I can't accept this. Even if I weren't leaving, it would still be too much. I've donated the flowers to the gala organisers for the charity dinner you're attending this evening. Prepare for Lady Monroe's effusiveness when she sees you tonight. She believes they'll easily fetch twenty thousand pounds if they're auctioned off—'

'*Pelo amor de*—enough with this lifeless performance. Tell me what you want and let's get it out of the way so we can get back to work! Give away the flowers if you wish but the necklace is yours.'

'Joao—'

'It cannot be money. I already pay you ten times more than your closest rival. I'd offer to triple that salary but I suspect you'd say—'

'It's not money.'

He gave a brisk nod. '*Bom*, we're getting somewhere. What is it, then?'

Her heart stuttered. She couldn't tell him. Not everything and certainly not what had triggered her decision to walk away. His indifference since their night in Morocco had said everything.

At best, that disappointment on his face would deepen. At worse, he'd mock her for letting emotions get the better of her.

But she wasn't a robot.

Her life was flashing past before her eyes and she'd already given him more years than she'd originally planned. And with every day she sacrificed her innermost needs on the altar of Joao's newest business obsession, she despaired a little more.

And perhaps even hated him a fraction, too. For that indifference she knew would never change. For his inabil-

ity to step down from his god-like throne and deign to acknowledge the needs of mere humans.

Her needs.

'You want to know why I'm leaving? It's simple. I've
decided you're not the answer to my every problem.'

His eyes narrowed into dark gold slits. 'What is that
supposed to mean?' he snapped. 'Stop playing games and
speak plainly!'

Irritation bristled through her. 'Or else what? You're
going to stop me from walking out?'

Silence throbbed between them.

Slowly he rose, his impressive height dwarfing hers even
from across the desk as he removed the cufflinks from his
shirtsleeves, and meticulously folded them back.

She didn't want to watch, didn't want to acknowledge
that extra dose of virile masculinity that made him impossible to ignore. But she couldn't help herself. Her gaze
dropped to follow every inch of silky-hair-dusted forearms
that was exposed. Tiny lightning bolts fired through her,
blazing her already aggravated libido as she wondered
how those strong arms would feel banded around her waist
again, drawing her close to the towering perfection of his
hard, muscled body.

'What is going on, Saffie?' The low-voiced demand,
wrapped in power and authority, jerked her from her lust-
ful reverie.

Her fingers gripped the straps of her handbag. At no
point had she deluded herself that resigning as Joao's executive assistant after living and breathing the role for four
full-on years would be easy. But she hadn't anticipated it
being this *hard* either. If he'd shown zero interest in her
life outside the walls of his existence before Morocco, he'd
been a million times more detached since.

He didn't know about her childhood in the orphanage,

about her short, happy spell with her foster mother. About her devastation when she'd been orphaned once again.

About the promise she'd made.

Her heart thundered as she panicked that he wouldn't let go until she gave him something. She didn't realise she was slicking a nervous tongue over her bottom lip until his gaze dropped to her mouth.

For a single moment, detachment vanished.

Then it returned full force, bruising her with its severity.

'Do you remember how I came to be your assistant in the first place?' Saffie asked, needing temporary relief from this quagmire.

His frown intensifying, he dropped the cufflinks in a drawer and slammed it shut. 'I fail to see how that's relevant.'

'It's relevant to me. I was supposed to be here temporarily, while my old boss, Mr Harcourt, was on holiday. You'd just fired your own assistant, remember?'

'Barely. I'm still not seeing how this is material—'

'My point is, I was supposed to be here for *two weeks*. I've been here for four years. And by the way, is it true you offered Mr Harcourt early retirement so you could keep me here?'

Again, he didn't so much as blink. '*Sim.* I knew by the end of your first week that you were far more suited to me. Your talents were wasted creating company retreat spreadsheets so I made him an offer he couldn't refuse,' he said with zero remorse.

'Well… I'm glad that's out of the way.'

His jaw gritted but a wary gleam entered his eyes. A gleam that said he was realising that this wasn't a tantrum or a stunt. That she might actually mean it. 'Now that we've wandered uselessly down memory lane, can we get back on track? What would it take for you to end this? Name your price and I'll make it happen.'

Name your price.

If only she could.

If only she didn't know the futility of naming her *actual* price.

She stared at him, her heart hammering as it had every time she'd contemplated taking this final step.

Granted, the thought that she would one day soon wake up and not be in his presence left her bereft. But then she forced herself to think of what else she would be replacing that experience with. The fulfilment her heart and soul yearned for. A true connection. A life-affirming purpose. 'My price is my freedom, Joao. I gave you two weeks, then I added four years to that. Now I want out.'

Leisurely he leaned forward, his bronzed forearms rippling as he resettled his weight on his hands, brought that red-hot sensuality dangerously closer, and glared at her across the desk. 'You have one last chance to give me a clear, concise reason for this absurdity, Saffie.'

The urge to tussle with him sizzled bright and urgently within her. What did she have to lose? In a few short weeks, she'd be out of his life. He planned to conquer the world, while she planned to retreat from his orbit, hopefully to embark on a lifelong project her soul had screamed for since she was a child. Since she'd tasted loneliness and vowed to make her life more meaningful.

Once she was done with Joao, she highly doubted their paths would ever cross again.

Ignoring the twinge in her chest, she boldly stepped forward, placing both feet on the battle ground. 'Very well. You want the unvarnished truth? You're a brilliant businessman, Joao. But you're also a ruthless vampire. You take and you take, and you think throwing diamonds and flowers and unimaginable perks grants you automatic authority over my life. Well, it doesn't. I mapped out a path for myself when I joined your company. I put my plans on hold and now I'm making them a priority again. I'm re-signing because I want more. More from *life*. I want free-dom from being *consumed* by you. Freedom to dream of other things besides the acquisition of your next *Fortune 500* company. Freedom to dream of a family. A baby. Of turning that dream into a reality.' She paused, her insides shaking at the thought of taking that last, intensely ravaging but *necessary* step. 'I want freedom from *you*.'

CHAPTER TWO

SILENCE PULSED IN the aftermath of his executive assistant's terse monologue. Joao, stunned into uncharacteristic silence, coldly ticked off the myriad sensations zipping through him.

Shock. Banked fury.

Hardened disappointment.

Perplexity.

It was to that last one that he returned. That feeling of being caught off guard when he'd believed them to be perfectly in sync.

He stared at her, wondering whether this was her idea of a joke. But then his level-headed, capable assistant didn't joke. They didn't have that kind of relationship. Theirs was a well-oiled symbiosis that ran on a perfect synergy of efficiency, a mutual appreciation of hard work and the heady rewards and satisfaction of success.

At least it had.

Until that night when, drunk on success, their basest instincts had got the better of them. But they'd put that behind them. Saffie's work hadn't suffered. On the contrary, things had been better than ever. Granted, the first week after the Morocco incident he'd lived on tenterhooks, wondering if she would attempt to capitalise in some way on his error of judgement. Because giving in to uncontrolled hunger *had* been an error of judgement. Other men might approach lust with a cavalier attitude, but Joao Oliviera was singularly ruthless when it came to his bed partners. They were chosen strictly on a mutually agreed short-term basis from which he never strayed.

They weren't chosen based on an unexpected but breathtaking desert mirage come to life, a punch of unstoppable lust that had nearly felled him and deep, dark craving that had blinded him to common sense until it was too late.

The fact that it'd happened, that for the space of one night he'd been no better than the man he despised the most in his life, still had the power to sour his day.

Sure, he hadn't gone looking for it, and Saffron wasn't a hooker on a street corner, but the acute absence of control still left a bitter aftertaste in his mouth.

Fortunately, like him, she'd been only too happy to bury the incident in the past. And while the realisation had initially grated, he'd eventually welcomed that discretion.

So what if the experience had the unsavoury ability to replay in his memory when he least expected it? What if those memories left him aroused and aching at the most inappropriate times?

It had rightly stayed in the past where it belonged, never to be repeated.

Except for some reason, while he'd believed his world was back on an even keel, Saffie had been making other plans.

Plans that threatened to wreak havoc on the most crucial undertaking of his life.

Suppressing his fury, he searched her face. Read the fierce determination on it and realised she actually meant it.

She meant to leave him. To free herself so she could chase so-called dreams.

For a family.

A baby.

She inhaled sharply and he realised he'd spoken the words out loud. Spat out, like one of the few foreign languages he wasn't fluent in. Two terse words tossed out like the vile, bewildered curse he believed them to be because they had no place in his working day.

In his life.

Not since the day he'd wiped the word *family* from his soul.

Certainly not now when his goal was so close. When the chance to shatter his enemy once and for all was a mere handful of weeks away.

That off-kilter sensation deepened, that feeling of being flung unexpectedly into a turbulent ocean without a life jacket causing his gut to clench.

He had countless life jackets. Endless contingencies to ensure not a single thing in his life was irreplaceable. Yachts and planes and CEOs and leaders of the free world, all at his beck and call.

Except Saffron Everhart had carved out a unique place in his life, set herself up on a pedestal marked exactly that. *Irreplaceable.*

And now that he needed her most...

He whirled away from his desk, strode to the wide floor-to-ceiling windows where he usually took one of his many espressos as he juggled the demands of his empire. He breathed through the tension riding his frame, his brain already in counter-strategy mode.

'Let me get this straight. You're ditching your career, and the countless benefits that come with it, to what? Go on some journey of self-discovery?' he threw at her.

She took her time to answer. Time that grated along his nerves, fired up his already smouldering discontent.

It didn't help that he usually welcomed her thoughtful consideration when answering his questions. That she wasn't the type to blurt out the first thought in her head as some people did.

'Yes, Joao. If you want to drill it down to one oversimplified statement. I'm leaving for me but I'm not ditching my career. Far from it. You can pour scorn all you want on it but my mind is made up. I have eight weeks of accrued vacation. I can stay and help train your next assistant or—'

He whirled to face her, a savage urgency *to do something*

ripping through him. 'You're getting ahead of yourself. I haven't agreed that you can leave,' he bit out.

Her chin lifted. 'Then it's a good thing there are laws in this country preventing you from holding me in a job I don't want any more, isn't it?'

He smiled a smile he didn't feel. 'You wish to take me on in court?'

'If you drive me to it, absolutely.'

Again, the absolute certainty that she meant it ploughed a jagged path through him. Something about the way she was holding herself, boldly meeting his gaze where others would've backed down, fired up a much different sensation in him.

It…drew him.

Otherwise why did he find himself standing in front of her, his gaze tracing the delicate lines of her throat, when he was across the room moments ago?

He smashed the sensation down and drilled deeper into the subject at hand.

'When I said you were getting ahead of yourself, Saffie, I meant that we hadn't exhaustively discussed the subject you just dropped in my lap. What do you mean, you're not ditching your career? You're going to work for someone else?'

She blinked. Attempted to regroup. 'Well…yes, I am.'

'Who?' he fired back.

'It doesn't matter—'

'Of course, it matters. Who is it, Saffie?' At her hesitation, the churning in his gut intensified. 'Tell me now,' he breathed.

Her stubborn chin tilted higher, daring him in ways Joao wasn't sure he wanted to discover. 'It's William Ashby.'

As competitors went, this one wasn't a worthy one. Which absurdly infuriated him further. That she would

leave him for someone significantly inferior businesswise…
'I didn't think you foolish, Saffie.'

'Excuse me?'

'Do you really think I'll allow you to take a position
with my competitor, knowing what you know about my
company?'

Twin flickers of anger and hurt darted across her face.
'You think I'll break your confidence? After…' She stopped
herself but he already knew.

Wasn't this a subject *he'd* dwelt on for far too long in
the past few weeks?

'After what?' he taunted. 'After *Morocco*? Or are we finally getting to the heart of this little scene?'

She blinked, shook her head, drawing his attention to
the rich gloss of her hair. What it'd felt like tumbling freely
over him—

'No, we're not. I don't want to talk about it.'

'Well, I do. Tell me Morocco is not why you've dropped
this bombshell on my day and we can move on. And no,
we won't be moving onto this so-called dream of a family or child because we both know you don't even have a
boyfriend.'

Fire sparked in her eyes. 'What makes you think you
know everything about me?'

Her spirited reply drew him even closer. He rounded
his desk, closed the gap between them, felt tendrils of her
light floral perfume wrapping around him. 'You've been
in charge of organising my life for over four years. That
means I'm equally aware of yours and it isn't that much of
a secret, Saffie—'

'I beg to differ or you would've seen this coming,
wouldn't you?'

Joao took a breath. This wasn't working. For whatever
reason, his assistant seemed hell-bent on this path. This un-

satisfactory desire to leave him high and dry at this most crucial juncture of his life.

'You wish me to apologise for what happened in Morocco?'

Her eyes widened, the deep pools of blue pulling him in. 'What? No. I said—'

'I'm aware of what you said. Just as I'm aware what women tend to say often differs from what they truly mean.'

Her eyes flashed. 'Sorry to disabuse you of the notion but I'm not like your other women. I'm not hiding behind some nefarious ulterior motive. And while it may bruise your ego to hear the word no for the first time in your life—'

'Watch it, Saffie.'

She carried on regardless. 'That's exactly what I'm saying. I don't want to be your assistant any more. My life is my own. I can do whatever I want. You have my letter. I've been in touch with HR. As soon as you accept, they'll get my termination papers ready.'

She turned on her heel, presenting him with the rigid curve of her spine that again commanded his attention to the curve of her hips, the tempting swell of her bottom.

He cursed under his breath. 'Aren't you forgetting something?' The arctic snap in his voice froze her in place.

Giving him the time he needed to stride over to join her at the door.

They weren't done. Far from it. He needed her far too much to let her walk out of his office.

Perhaps it was their close proximity that made her pulse race in her throat as she stared at him. Perhaps it was because she sensed he was about to pull out the big guns, as he was wont to do when the occasion demanded it.

Whatever the reason, he watched her drag her inner lip between her teeth, felt the unwelcome sensation deep in his pelvis.

Meu Deus. He needed to put this thing to bed, pronto.

'What?' she blurted.

'There's a clause in your contract that states all future employers will be vetted and approved by me. Tell me, do you think I'll let you run off and work for Ashby?'

The demand was soft. So soft Saffie didn't feel the warm knife slide into her ribs until it was too late.

'Why are you doing this?'

'Because I wish to keep the best personal assistant I've ever had.'

There was a time when the flippant compliment would've lit up her day. Not any more. 'I'm sure the next will do just as well.'

His nostrils flared. 'You can have an extended vacation after we put the Archer deal to bed.'

'Joao—'

'I will get my pilot to fly you to any destination of your choosing. You have my word that I won't ask you to return until you're well rested and you've worked whatever... lingering discontentment you have out of your system. Whatever it takes to get my level-headed executive assistant back.'

Despite his more than generous offer, the words dropped like icy bullets from his lips, his body language broadcasting his extreme displeasure.

The intimacy of his proximity and the sheer headiness of his masculine scent sent heat blooming through her as he continued to stare her down, reminding her that she hadn't always been level-headed.

She'd slipped and fallen from grace in Morocco.

His gaze dropped to her mouth, stayed and for a second she knew he was recalling it, too.

Then she realised she was full-on gnawing at her lip.

Her renowned rock-solid composure was slipping and, for the life of her, she couldn't get herself under control.

'I told you. I can't stay here and get what I want.'

His eyes narrowed. 'This accusation interests me greatly. Tell me on what basis you arrived at it,' he invited silkily.

'I've worked with you for four years. You might be progressive with your other employees, but I know, for instance, that the subject of families and babies doesn't interest you.'

One eyebrow spiked. 'You know this for a fact when you and I have never discussed it?'

'We may not have, but I've been present when business acquaintances have brought up the subject. Your eyes glaze over and you change the topic as soon as possible.'

One thick shoulder rose and fell. 'Because the subject of other people's children bores me,' he stated coldly.

Saffie forced herself to breathe through the sharp pang of hurt. 'Well, if you'll be so kind as to step out of my way, I'll stop boring you.'

She went to move around him. His hand whipped out and captured her wrist. Heat blazed from the contact, raining sharp tingles and making her gasp, this time for a completely different reason.

At the very top of her list—and underscored in indelible ink—of ways to avoid her tightly reined composure slipping around Joao was to never come into direct physical contact with him.

She'd learned that lesson in one sizzling, unforgettable way.

The Montcrief Pipeline deal.

The months' long negotiations for the Brazilian-Canadian deal had left her with little sleep and living on the very edge of her nerves alongside Joao.

Her usually unflappable boss had been like a man possessed, his focus on securing the multibillion-dollar contract razor-sharp.

It was the first time the name Pueblo Oliviera had truly registered. The first time she'd witnessed something other than the fervent need to bag the best deal. It'd been clear Montcrief was personal for Joao.

It hadn't taken a genius to connect the dots and conclude that he wanted to win against Pueblo Oliviera.

His father.

Joao had not only bagged the Montcrief deal, he'd signed another multibillion-dollar deal that had granted him ownership of his third premier soccer team in Brazil.

The double-barrelled success against his father had triggered a euphoric celebration, Joao's breathtaking exclusive Marrakesh villa and its grounds the scene of one of the most sophisticated parties Saffie and the entire executive staff had ever attended.

It had been there, surrounded by flame throwers, jugglers and exotic belly dancers, that she'd given in to illicit temptation, one that she couldn't recall without her stomach flipping and her skin burning with remembered excitement.

She wished she could blame it on one too many glasses of the Krug Clos d'Ambonnay, two thousand dollars per bottle, which had been flowing at the party.

Or the singular thrill of attempting her first belly dance, dressed in the midriff-baring costume and exotic jewellery that had made her feel feminine and sexy.

No.

It had been the expression on Joao's face when she'd looked up and found him leaning against a stone pillar, staring at her, the euphoric glaze of success glinting in his eyes.

It had been the unfettered excitement at seeing the heat in his eyes flame brighter as she'd swayed towards him.

And it had been the absolute rapture at the thickly muttered Portuguese words and searing brand of his touch when he'd jerked her close, stared down at her for a charged minute before kissing her with a sizzling intensity she'd never experienced before.

The kiss, the fever it'd sparked in her bloodstream, and

the urge to taste danger, *just once*, had been too heady to deny. So when he'd swept her off her feet, she'd willingly twined her arms around his neck. When he'd walked away from the party, marched them up to his master suite and kicked the door shut, she'd almost wept with anticipation.

And when she'd finally known what it felt like to be the lust-drunk focus of Joao's attention, what it felt like to be completely possessed by him, she'd feared her life would never be the same.

She'd been right.

'You are not other people. You don't bore me, Saffie. Quite the contrary.' His growled words slammed her to the present.

To the reminder that the morning after that night in Morocco, Joao had greeted her with stinging indifference. As if what had happened was of little consequence to him.

Then and now.

Her pulse hammered against the fingers curled around her flesh. And she died a little knowing he could feel it, too. 'What's that supposed to mean?'

His gaze shifted to where he held her, to where his thumb was moving slowly, seductively across her skin. 'You are my right hand,' he said, his accent thickening ever so slightly. 'One of the most important cogs in my business wheel. I would be a fool to let such an asset walk away. But if you need to hear the words, I value you for your intellect. Which is far from boring.'

Cog. Business. Asset.

Cold labels that spelled out all she would ever be to Joao. From the beginning she'd known that. Somewhere along the line she'd finally accepted it. So why did the words douse her with such icy, isolating coldness?

Joao Oliviera was the biggest shark in an immense ocean. And as with all sharks there would come a day when she would become his prey. When he would chew her up and spit her out without so much as a blink of his whisky-gold eyes before moving on. She had enough sense to rescue herself before that happened. Especially when she had a goal much closer to her heart.

'You're really determined to do this? To walk out on your career?' he pressed.

She found the strength to reconnect with his gaze. 'To leave you, yes.'

He stared at her for a long, unblinking minute before eyes that were far too shrewd leisurely travelled over her body. They lingered at the frantic pulse beating at her throat, the agitated rise and fall of her chest she couldn't quite control, the dark purple silk of her blouse, right down to her legs and shoes before travelling back up again. This time they lingered on her hips, then her breasts, causing her flesh to tingle.

Reprieve came in the form of the phone on his desk ringing. Her inbuilt work ethic kicked in and she automatically glanced at it.

'Leave it,' he instructed gruffly. 'One of your assistants can get it.'

Very early on, she'd realised the sheer volume of work Joao produced meant she had to delegate less-sensitive work to others and she'd hired two assistants who answered to her.

He leaned closer, wrapped her tighter in his intoxicating scent. 'And nothing I can say can change your mind?' His tone had turned deadly silky, the kind that could weave spells around her.

She shook her head. Nowhere on their trajectory did their interests collide. It was why it'd taken her years to summon up the strength to walk away.

The breakneck lifestyle Joao led was no place to make long-term plans. Certainly not one that included her yearning for a family of her own. A baby.

How many times had she booked a ski trip to Aspen

only for him to ski one black run and decide he would much prefer the slopes in Switzerland, preferably that same day?

Hadn't he woken her up in the middle of the night only a month ago and ordered her to arrange a tour of the Chilean vineyard he'd just purchased on the spur of the moment for forty million dollars? She had still been rubbing the sleep from her eyes when his private jet had taken off from his Greek island fifty minutes later.

And this relentless, *sizzling* awareness of him surely couldn't be good for her health?

No, she couldn't put this off any longer.

'No. There's nothing you can say to make me change my—'

'I know this is about Morocco. Specifically *the sex* we had in Marrakesh, is it not?' he enquired with a low, terse rumble that resonated deep inside her.

Saffie sagged against the door, very much aware her mouth was agape. 'What?' she murmured with a voice that didn't sound like her own.

'You can put it out of your mind, Saffie. It was a mistake that shouldn't have happened. If you need it to satisfy you so you stay, then have my apologies,' he continued tersely, his body held in military rigidness that didn't in any way detract from the mouth-watering package.

'I… No,' she strained out.

Latin temper flared in his eyes. 'You don't accept my apology? Or is it the veracity of it you doubt?'

She almost laughed.

Joao was a great many things—ruthless, acerbic to the point of cruel sometimes, impossibly arrogant. Too damn good-looking for words. But in all his dealings, he had never spoken a word he didn't mean. His core of integrity was the reason less powerful men envied him almost as much as they feared him. It was the reason she loved her job even when he slave-drove her to the brink of sanity sometimes. There was a synergy in their dynamic, a thrill that came from working so close to a brilliant mind that she never got bored with.

'No, it's not that,' she stated.

She couldn't stay.

This man was so dangerously intoxicating every atom in her body shrieked at her that anything other than walking away would be a mistake.

The Archer deal would be done in three months, sooner if Joao's single-minded determination bore fruit.

But at what ultimate cost to her?

Her breath shuddered out.

Too high. The penalty would be too high.

He nudged her chin up with one finger, compelling her to meet his eyes once more. The dual thrill of touch and stare dragged her deeper into the cauldron of temptation.

'Three months, Saffie. That is all I ask. Stay. Finish the deal with me. Then leave if you insist,' he urged with a mesmerising drawl.

Three months. Not an eternity in the grand scheme of things, but, if she was having a hard time walking away now, how would it be in three months, knowing she'd once again put off pursuing the one thing that was so precious and close to her heart?

She couldn't.

She sucked in a breath, the action bringing her far too close to his solid heat and the earthy, evocative scent she knew didn't come from the grooming products his French *parfumier* specially designed for him and him alone. She knew it because one of her many, endless tasks was to pack for him and she'd given into a weak moment very early on and taken a long inhale of his aftershave. And then spent far too long after that attempting to decipher where that scent ended and his unique musk began.

She would probably never know.

Before the alarming weakness could totally take over her body, she turned blindly towards the door.

'Saffie.' Her name was a low growl. 'Where are you going?'

'Out for air. Or back to my desk. Either way my answer is still no.'

Her hand latched on the door but the heaviness of his silence stopped her from opening it. She fought a fierce battle against the need to turn, see his reaction to her response. But she was too scared. Silence meant that algorithm that passed for his brain was recalibrating, recalculating a way to get what he wanted.

Still, she wasn't prepared for the words that came next.

'I need you.'

Her lips parted in a stunned gasp. In four long years she'd never heard him utter those words. To her. To anyone. Joao wasn't a man who needed.

He wanted. He desired. He took.

She spun around, her stunned senses seeking an explanation on his enigmatic face. 'Are you manipulating me, Joao?'

Feet planted apart, hands on lean hips, his stare undaunted and unwavering, 'I want you to stay,' he stated with that brutal honesty that often disarmed and weakened an opponent before he went in for the kill. 'I'll do anything to achieve that. It also helps that you know me better than anyone else will in this lifetime.'

Swiftly she added that vital little extra needed to put the right spin on his words.

When it comes to business.

When it came to anticipating his needs and ensuring he had every last detail of a deal at his fingertips, she was second to none.

She was even exceptional at reading between the lines of his latest private liaisons and, more often than not, guessing when it was time to put together the staggeringly expensive it's-been-fun-but-now-it's-over package that soothed the most desolate of broken hearts.

But until recently she'd painstakingly safeguarded herself against the pitfalls of deeper emotional curiosity, had deliberately stopped herself from digging into the personal details that had seen Joao Oliviera dig himself out of a *favela* in Brazil to become one of the most powerful men in the world. Sure, the media had endless reports on his past and his page on the company website featured a three-paragraph bio, but besides a mother who'd reportedly died at a young age of thirty-five, there was very little else.

She had no idea what his favourite colour was, what had caused the deep, three-inch scar across his left palm, or where he went when he bade her a curt goodnight on Christmas Eve and disappeared for twenty-four hours. The holiday was the only day in the year when her phone didn't ring with endless demands from him.

All she knew was that Joao was driven by a rabid intensity that bordered on the obsessive. Self-preservation dictated that she take herself out of his orbit.

'I don't know you, Joao. Not really. And there's nothing wrong with wanting to take a different path to achieve my goals.'

A muscle rippled in his jaw. 'You thrive on the challenges I grant you, Saffie. You'll be bored rigid in the slow lane.'

She couldn't lie. In the past four years he'd shown her a lifestyle that most people tried to conjure in their wildest dreams and fell far short of. She'd seen the world many times over, had watched as he'd conquered it over and over again. Not to mention earning enough money and benefits to not need to work again for the rest of her life if she lived a quiet, uneventful existence.

She dismissed the dreary sensation that thought triggered, reminding herself that life would be far from dull with a baby in it.

'My mind is made up, Joao. I'll stretch out my four weeks' notice period to six if—'

The imperious slash of his hand chopped off her response. 'I don't want you here with one foot out the door. I need you here, fully committed to the Archer deal. To me.'

'What if this deal drags out longer than three months?'

'It won't. But be warned, Saffie. This is the last time I will ask.'

That final gauntlet snatched her breath from her lungs.

Saffie couldn't deny that the thought of waking up without the adrenaline buzz of plugging herself into Oliviera Enterprises and Joao's world had left her curiously empty, her horizon a grey landscape with only the glowing mirage of a baby to sustain her.

Granted, that glow had grown, the craving for a family she'd ignored for years suddenly rearing its head on her twenty-eighth birthday, reminding her that time was slipping through her fingers.

Her emotional well had been left depleted for the better part of half her life. She'd needed to put her emotions aside to nurse her foster mother through the long months of ill health and her eventual death. After that she'd shut herself off, unwilling to delve into her grief for fear she'd never find her way back out of the dark tunnel.

Ironically, it had been a terrifying incident on Joao's private jet and the emergency landing in Canada in the first year of her working for him that had forced her to confront her grief. Joao had given her a rare day off, believing it was the incident that had left her shaken and withdrawn.

She'd spent it mourning the foster parent who'd come into her life late and exited far too early. It'd also shone a very harsh, self-reflecting light on the emptiness in her life. One she hadn't wanted to face after that first, soul-destroying glimpse.

Luckily, having fallen in love with her new job, she'd

been able to bury the emptiness. It hadn't stayed buried. And with each passing year, the light had burned brighter until she couldn't ignore the ache any more.

But while she'd experienced a soul-shaking satisfaction to be finally moving forward with her dream, hadn't a part of her also felt a little shame that the dream she'd held onto for so long no longer felt enough? That a different yearning burned just as bright and it was all her fault for nurturing it?

She stared at Joao, caught the ferocious swell of determination in his eyes. They could part on acrimonious terms with a possibility of an employment tribunal in her future— depending on how difficult he chose to be. Or she could have twelve unforgettable, stimulating weeks with the most charismatic man she was likely to encounter in her whole lifetime, while guarding the deeper yearning in her heart.

'I want to hear it, Saffie,' Joao pressed again, spotting her weakening and going for the kill. 'Three months of your undivided attention on the Archer deal with no talk of leaving.'

She swallowed, attempted to think through the euphoric haze shrouding her common sense. 'Fine. I'll stay until the Archer deal is done.'

Joao didn't gloat.

What he did was stand to his full, imposing height, his gaze raking her frame, lingering on her hips, her breasts, before reconnecting with hers. Something shifted in his eyes, a calculating gleam that sent a spark of apprehension down her spine.

'And, Joao?'

'*Sim?*' he prompted, intent eyes fixed on her as a muscle ticced in his jaw. 'What is it?'

'I want your word that you won't stand in my way when the time comes.'

CHAPTER THREE

HE HAD WHAT he wanted.

She was staying. He'd bought himself the time to formulate a plan to rid himself of this issue of her leaving.

His agreement was all that was required.

And yet the *yes* that should've fallen from his lips stuck in Joao's throat, his satisfaction at heading off disaster laced with something he couldn't quite decipher.

Uncertainty, he finally decoded.

She had pulled the proverbial rug from beneath his feet and now he was uncertain where he stood.

Perhaps he was better off setting her free so she could go and play happy families with some faceless stranger...

The harsh rejection of that idea stopped him cold.

Absurd. The whole discussion from start to finish was absurd.

He shouldn't be aggravated this much by the whole thing. Not when, as Saffie had pointed out, he had zero interest in most of the reasons she'd stated for her desire to leave.

While he didn't want a child or, heaven forbid, a *family*, since he'd permanently erased that idea out of his life's mission very shortly after his tenth birthday and not once spent a second reconsidering it, he'd accommodated others' desire for it, if barely. The right gift baskets and monetary bonus found their way to each employee on the announcement of a child's birth.

So why did the thought of his executive assistant taking a similar path grate so much? Why did the thought that one day in his future Saffie might exercise her right to walk away permanently trigger nothing but cold dread?

The answer blazed through him a second later.

Because he wasn't ready to let her go.

Her value had multiplied over the years. And what was he if not a man who capitalised on the value of his assets?

He'd simply been caught off guard. He'd spent far too long putting out this fire when he should've been behind his desk, formulating better plans to add the Archer Group to his portfolio.

Just as he'd spent far too many years moulding Saffron Everhart into the perfect right hand to release her prematurely from her role.

Right or wrong, and while he knew that, ultimately, he couldn't stop her, she belonged to him—

'Do you agree?'

Her husky voice cut through his thoughts, retraining his focus on her.

The heat that lanced his groin was shockingly brazen and had grown in intensity ever since *that night*. The one he'd spent long weeks afterwards fighting to forget without success.

He'd ruthlessly disguised that hunger, enough to even take pride in his ability to watch her walk into his office without showing that he was losing his mind to that immediate groin-stirring arousal. And yes, it'd infuriated him to know his success in wrestling down his carnal demon had been fed by Saffie's own easy dismissal of the incident.

'Joao?'

He gritted his teeth, wishing he hadn't insisted she address him by his first name shortly after she'd started working for him. Of course, he hadn't divulged the fact that he detested his surname but had hung onto it purely to show Pueblo Oliviera that he wouldn't be dismissed as easily as it'd taken him to instruct his security to throw him out of his Sao Paolo mansion that fateful day two decades ago. Never mind that he'd hated his mother for saddling him with the name of a man who'd had zero interest in assuming the role of fatherhood.

'Are we going to discuss this or are you going to keep staring at me like I've grown an extra set of eyes?' Saffie questioned briskly.

He shook off the sticky vines of his past and focused on her eyes. Alternately blue or grey depending on her clothing or mood, the wide, almond shapes were clear and direct. Intelligent. *Alluring.* As arresting as her full Cupid's-bow lips currently pressed into a prim line beneath her pert nose. They hadn't been so prim when he'd tasted them. They'd been soft, supple, mind-alteringly delicious when she'd parted them beneath his, gasped her pleasure, screamed her climax—

He flicked that torrid recollection away before it wreaked havoc on his groin. 'You seem so certain of the future, Saffie. What makes you think you won't be begging me to let you stay in three months' time?'

Her breath caught, alerting him to the fact that his tone had been harsher than he'd intended.

At his continued stare, she bit her lip just as she had minutes ago, exhibiting an agitation unlike her.

Joao's attention was once again drawn to her perfect curve of slightly reddening mouth, to the small teeth dragging over her flesh. He clenched one fist over the other as more blood rushed south.

'I know what I want,' she insisted, once again triggering that unnerving sensation that had arrived when he'd read that damn resignation letter and felt the searing vacuum of her loss.

His teeth gritted but he saw no way to deny her. '*Bom.* Then you have my word. Now can we get back on track?'

Despite the telltale sign of her less than cool state, her eyes boldly met his as she nodded and quickly regrouped. It made him wonder how often his seemingly unflappable assistant had stumbled and corrected course without him noticing.

'I'll draw up the list you requested.'

'Good. Did you like the necklace I commissioned for you?' he asked as she opened her door.

Wary blue eyes met his. 'Yes, it's stunning—'

'Now that you're staying, I'd very much like for you to wear it when we attend the auction of the Shanzi orchid in Shanghai with Lavinia Archer. Unless you're going to argue with me over that, too?'

She exhaled calmly, not rising to his bait. He should've been glad his EA was back to her unflappable self. But he wasn't. Not completely.

'We've reached an agreement, Joao. Things will run as normal for the duration. I'll ensure your plate is clear and Lavinia is free to be in Shanghai so you can present her with the orchid, which will bloom, for the first time in eight years, two weeks from now. Was there anything else?'

Her question contained more than a spark left over from their encounter and Joao was almost tempted to stoke it.

But enough.

Now he'd put out this little fire of her intended desertion he needed to refocus on his father. Specifically ensuring Pueblo didn't come out the victor in their battle to win Lavinia Archer's business.

Dark anticipation twisted with bitterness in Joao's gut. These days the man who'd fathered him might still call himself a billionaire but Joao's was the Oliviera name people uttered in deference and awe. It was he world leaders turned to for business and geo-political counsel.

Joao knew it stuck in Pueblo's craw that the bastard son he'd cursed to damnation, the product of a drunken indulgence with a prostitute one wholly forgettable night, had become a man of untold power and means. It was a status his father was desperate to overturn.

In turn, Joao intended to devote his time and effort to maintaining his superior position. To do that he needed his sharpest players, including his right hand, in their rightful place.

So he reined himself in but not before he went to his desk, picked up her resignation letter and ripped it in two.

'You may take this with you.' He held it out to her, watched her retrace her steps to where he stood next to his desk.

The sway of her hips reminded him that he hadn't indulged himself for several weeks. Not since Morocco. Not since that night he'd celebrated his victory over his father with a tumble into temptation and awoken to learn of Pueblo's interest in the Archer Group.

And he wouldn't indulge himself for a while yet. Not if he didn't want to lose his way and lose this fight. He knew first-hand what chaos unbridled lust could create.

He had no intention of falling into that trap again.

With enviable composure, Saffie took the ripped page from him. 'If that's all, I'd like to go and get on with the day?'

'By all means,' he murmured.

He watched her walk briskly out of his office, feeling as if he'd freshly emerged from an industrial-sized centrifuge.

Sure, some of the spur-of-the-moment deals he'd capitalised on had been the best of his life…but had any of them left him reeling like this?

And all over his assistant wishing to jump ship?

Growing up in abject poverty, seeing the lengths to which people would go to step over one another for the sake of putting food in their belly or dragging themselves out of the gutter, had triggered a fierce opposition against fathering a child. That had been long before his double rejection from both parents. *That* had merely cemented what he already knew. *Família* was a foolish illusion people wrapped themselves up in until the going got tough, then they were all too quick to throw off its burdens and disavow themselves from their responsibilities. As for that other worthless notion of familial love—?

The ringing of his silver phone shattered his bitter thoughts, and, with more than a little relief, he strode to his desk and snatched it up.

'Joao Oliviera,' he announced himself with the power and authority that was second nature to him these days. Within minutes he'd returned to his natural habitat of proficient mogul with his eyes on the next challenging prize.

It was almost as if the last hour hadn't happened.

Except that it had.

Again, that noxious mix of imbalance and uncertainty welled inside him. It was an upsurge of memories of his past that was causing his disgruntlement, he concluded. And like every adversity, he'd conquer these, too.

With that firm assurance, he threw himself fully into his day.

When Saffie knocked and entered a few hours later, she too had returned to her rightful business mode. She was thoroughly up to speed with what his investigators had unearthed about Lavinia and put forward cogent ideas that perfectly augmented his own plans for the heiress.

By Wednesday morning the scene was set to step up the campaign to win over Lavinia Archer.

Joao had every intention of getting her to board the private jet he'd sent for her in South Africa. By midday he had his confirmation that she was on her way.

All it'd taken was a simple yet brilliant idea from Saffron to send her a gold-embossed envelope containing nothing but the name of the renowned auction house in Shanghai.

For a jaded heiress like Lavinia Archer, the bait had been too much to resist.

It was a coup worth celebrating. He would have if his mood had improved since Monday. It hadn't.

So it was also a good thing Saffie had been out of the office at his stylist readying herself for their extended trip to Shanghai. For the last thirty-six hours he hadn't been able to glance at her without the aggravating reminder that she'd intended to walk away.

As a reminder to her of just how much she loved this job she'd been so eager to throw away, he'd set her endless tasks, at which she'd excelled. And yes, along the line, he'd been filled with a deep desire to watch her bone-deep composure crack.

Now he'd caught a glimpse of the fire that burned beneath her serene façade, he wanted to see more. Wanted to know what made her tick. So he wouldn't be taken by surprise again, he assured himself.

But deep down he knew it was more than that. This particular fire had been blazing since Morocco. Since the singular experience that came close only to the milestone years of turning his life around. Of making his first million.

It was the circumstances, he assured himself. The Archer deal consumed his life day and night. It was logical that everyone involved in it should take up space in his thoughts, too.

Lavinia.

Pueblo.

Saffie.

He swung away from where he'd been staring at the view.

The latest file on Pueblo needed to be read.

About to click on it, his fingers froze when warm, husky laughter reached his ears.

Saffie was out, and very few people were granted access to her office.

Rising and crossing his office, Joao pulled his door open and froze.

It was Saffie, chatting to another member of staff.

Mild shock pummelled him as he listened. He'd never heard Saffron like that before. Light. Airy. Friendly. *Utterly captivating.*

Utterly surprising, just as she'd surprised and captivated him in Marrakesh.

In what other ways was she different away from his sphere?

The need to delve deeper, uncover her secrets, propelled him forward. 'Is this a private gathering or can I interrupt?'

She stiffened before swivelling around. The younger man looked equally startled. Joao took little satisfaction in his discomfort. He was still reeling over the latest facet of Saffie he'd just glimpsed.

'I got back a short while ago. My computer was frozen, so I got Andy from IT to take a look for me.'

'If he's done then perhaps normal service can resume?' he asked without taking his gaze from Saffie's flustered face.

Saffie barely nodded before Andy beat a hasty retreat.

'Did you have to do that?'

'Do what, exactly?'

'Talk to him that way. He was showing me pictures of his newborn niece.'

'He was wasting your time and therefore wasting mine. And I asked you to bring me the Hunter-Shrike file when you returned.'

'I put it on your desk two minutes after you asked for it. You were at your window staring at the view when I came in.'

Joao frowned. She'd been in his presence and he'd missed her? 'I was thinking.'

'About what?'

'About your little speech.'

She tensed, her eyes widening. 'What little speech?'

'Something along the lines of being a vampire who just takes and takes?'

Heat flowed into her cheeks. Joao rammed his hands in his pockets to resist the urge to trace the flow with his fingers. 'I didn't… I… Perhaps I could've phrased that better.'

'Only perhaps?'

Her lips pursed. 'So you were thinking about my speech…and?'

'You don't want a pay rise and you protest when I offer other incentives so I've decided to double the charitable donations I'll be making this year instead. We'll have a working dinner this evening and you can bring your list.'

'*My* list?'

He shrugged. 'You hurled the accusation, Saffie. You can help me become the better man.'

He returned to his office in a better mood.

Which lasted for a handful of hours, right until the moment his EA froze before the lift doors leading to his penthouse.

'Problem?' he asked, aware of the tension in his voice.

'Why are we having dinner in your…in the penthouse?'

'Because you left a notification in my diary that four of my ten departments are using every conference room and dining space for client mixers and would appreciate a ten-minute meet-and-greet if I had the chance? Did you forget, Saffie?'

She flushed. 'Oh… I… Yes, it slipped my mind.'

Joao held the lift door open as it went to close. 'Get in the lift, Saffie. I promise the only blood-red thing I'm after is the colour of my wine.'

She slanted an irritated glance at him. 'I'm not going to live that down, am I?'

A quiet satisfaction pulsed through him when she entered without protest. 'Likening your boss to a vampire? It's a subject I'm looking forward to discussing thoroughly at your next evaluation.'

She stared at him for several beats; blue eyes dark with apprehension and uncustomary uncertainty met his.

She sailed past him in heels that made her shapely legs seem endless. Her pinstriped dress tastefully followed her curves, with a zip that extended from her nape to the hem, and set his fingers tingling with torturous visions of him undressing her.

He took a sustaining breath as the lift doors glided shut.

Sim, they were swimming in uncharted waters. But it was a challenge he welcomed. Relished, even.

They exited into his penthouse and Saffie paused, her curious gaze flicking through the living room. It occurred to him that, despite their close working relationship, she'd only been up here a handful of times.

While work consumed a significant part of his life, he also relished the pleasures his lifestyle brought him. A helicopter on the roof of his building ensured he could be in any one of his four London or country residences within half an hour, entertaining clients or friends away from the office.

The setting sun slanted sultry light into the living room, directly onto the wide plush sofa, the orange glow uncomfortably reminiscent of a certain divan in Morocco.

Before he could halt it, memory returned full force, bombarding him with fiery blasts.

Gritting his teeth, he headed towards his dining room, relieved when his executive chef arrived minutes later and placed her dish of baby bok choy and noodle salad with shaved truffles in front of her, then returned with his chosen prime-cut Brazilian wagyu steak.

He picked up the bottle of red Chilean, a vintage from his personal vineyard, decanted and left to breathe by his chef, and frowned when Saffie shook her head.

'None for me, thanks. I have a headache.'

Like many things this week, that was a first. He redirected the crystal decanter to his own glass, aware he was frowning as he poured.

'Have you taken anything for it?'

She shrugged, although her gaze remained on her plate. 'I've been busy.'

He warmed his wine glass in his cupped hand. 'Too busy to take ten seconds out of your time to take care of yourself?'

She pushed a piece of bok choy around her plate before spearing it with a fork. 'Normally, it goes away by itself.'

He frowned. 'Normally?' he pressed, raising his glass to take a healthy mouthful. Something hot and heavy strummed inside him when her gaze fell to his mouth, then dropped to linger at his throat. She'd kissed him there that night in Morocco, he recalled a little too heatedly. Bit him, in fact.

'Why are you interested in my health issues, Joao?'

'This week you've accused me of working you to death or implied something just as unsavoury. So now I'm resolved to helping you get rid of your headache,' he countered, that dart of displeasure at drinking alone evaporating in the thrill of their banter.

'And you intend to do that by grilling me?'

'It's a good alternative to watching you push your dinner around your plate while you avoid my gaze.' Standing, he went to the sleek cabinet, took out the medical pouch stored there and brought back the tablets. 'Here.'

She set her silverware down in precise movements, lifted a pristine linen napkin to dab at her lips before accepting the mild headache pills.

Aggravatingly avoiding his gaze, she swallowed them. 'There, all sorted. Now shall we get off the subject?' she demanded in a tone far removed from her usual brisk delivery.

Joao settled back in his seat, forgoing the last bite of his excellent steak in favour of this discussion.

'Certainly,' he replied, his gaze clashing with eyes that were more grey than blue in the muted light of his private dining room. 'Did you bring your list? I'm aiming for you to think much better of me by week's end.'

She released her napkin with an abrupt toss, her face flaming. He curled his fingers tighter around his glass as the fierce desire to trace her cheek with his fingertips rammed deep.

'If you're trying to make me feel bad about what I said, don't bother,' she stated drolly.

He sipped and savoured another mouthful of wine. 'What if I mean it, Saffie? Will that make you…bend a little?'

Her eyes went wide. After a moment, she swallowed. 'I… I'm sure the charities in question will appreciate it.'

'I'm not talking about other charities. I'm asking about you.'

Her nostrils flared delicately as she took a long breath. The action expanded her ribcage, drawing his gaze to her full, heavy breasts. 'I guess that would be a start.'

'*Bem.* Let's do it.'

She eyed him a little warily, deepening his own questions about his motives. He already gave her far more than any other assistant. Was he really willing to go this far just to keep her?

Yes. Until his father was brought to heel, he would lasso the moon itself for her if required.

The little twinge that indicated his reasons weren't wholly altruistic, he chose to ignore, holding his hand out for the tablet.

He perused the list, noting that more than half were family and children-orientated. A different sort of twinge niggled him, one that forced him to consider whether she'd truly meant to leave him to chase flight dreams of babies and family.

Joao realised he was frowning when he handed the tablet back. 'Approved. You have my permission to gift each of them one hundred thousand pounds.'

Her lips parted in shock. 'That…that's too much.'

'I'm confident the organisations in question won't feel the same. Thank me and let's move on, Saffie.'

Her soft lips remained parted for another second, before her eyelashes swept down. 'Thank you, Joao,' she murmured huskily.

'*De nada.* What's next on the agenda?'

'Vincent Gingham is calling you in thirty minutes. Maybe we should—'

'Gingham can wait. You haven't had any dessert yet. I had Chef Bouillard prepare your favourite.' As if on cue, the Michelin-starred chef who travelled around the world with Joao and cooked almost every meal entered, holding aloft a silver platter. Joao nodded approvingly as he placed the dish in front of Saffron and retreated.

She eyed him suspiciously. 'What is it?'

He remained silent, watching her steadily. Her lips pursed again, then she lifted the cloche off the platter.

She inhaled sharply at the concoction before her. 'Joao, what are you doing?'

Not the response he'd been expecting. 'We are having a meal.'

She shook her head. 'Don't give me that. First that insanely expensive necklace. Now this?'

'It's dessert, Saffron. Let's not make a mountain and all that.'

'You said it was my favourite. A favourite thing is something you love and indulge in *occasionally*. This is a chocolate mousse topped with truffles and twenty-four-carat shaved edible gold. I've had it *once*, when you talked me into eating with you on New Year's Day.'

Joao shrugged. 'I thought you'd want to mark your continued employment with something you enjoyed. The necklace doesn't count. That's for the Archer deal, and was given before you enlightened me of your plans. Now eat up. Gingham is a bore when he's kept waiting inordinately.'

Saffron wouldn't exactly lower herself into glaring at him, but the look she sent him was close. Had he not still been caught up in alternate moments of surrealism and imbalance he would've smiled.

Instead he raised his glass, took another sip and watched Saffron dig her fork delicately into the gold and ochre creation, lift a mouthful to her lips, sneak a quick taste with the tip of her tongue before sliding it into her mouth.

He watched her suppress a moan and bit back one of his own as she gave a little shiver of pleasure.

Feeling the blood rush to his groin, he drained his glass and picked up his phone. He could've left her to it and returned to his office. But too many things had skidded off kilter this week. As absurd as it sounded, he wasn't in the mood to tempt fate by breaking this simple ritual of a working dinner.

Five long minutes later, he looked up at the delicate clatter of her fork on the plate.

'Thank you, Joao. That was amazing.'

He gave a brisk nod and stood, veering sharply away before her eyes dropped to the swell behind his fly. 'We'll have the meeting up here,' he said, heading for the door to his penthouse study. 'I want you on the Gingham video-conference. He behaves himself when you're present, and he definitely talks less bull.'

'You mean I reel him back when he goes off script?'

'Exactly.'

She nodded. 'I'll go and grab his file.'

Joao went to his desk, tugging off his tie and discarding it as he went. His casual attire would annoy the newspaper magnate from the Deep South but the great thing about the back-breaking climb to reach this pinnacle of success was that he was in an excellent position not to give a damn.

These days potential business partners needed him more than he needed them.

It hadn't always been the case, though...

He stilled, his fingers freezing against his shirt as memory crashed through him.

His mother screaming insults at him for deigning to be born.

Hunger the likes of which he wouldn't wish on his worst enemy.

A ruthless gang attempting to steal what little food he'd managed to scrounge from tourists.

The fight with one particularly vicious gang member that had nearly cost him a limb.

He unfurled his hand, stared at the scar that still tingled its reminder of that fateful night and the *favela* doctor who'd been his saviour.

'Joao? Is everything okay?'

He whirled around to face Saffron. Eyes that saw too much bore into him. '*Sim.* Everything's fine.' He freed his top button.

'Are you sure? Only you looked like—'

Her words strangled when he reached out, stroked his thumb over the corner of her upper lip. A delicate shiver raced through her, and her eyes darkened, right before she took a hasty step back.

'What are you doing?' she demanded huskily.

'Chocolate,' he stated abruptly, his own voice gruff and uneven. 'You have a tiny smear of chocolate on your lip. I don't think you want to take a video call wearing your dessert, do you?'

She exhaled. 'No. Uh…thanks.'

He brought his thumb to his lips, taking the time to lick and savour the delicacy and her taste.

Saffie made a tight, erotic little sound in her throat, one that punched through his resistance straight to the heart of forbidden desires.

Meu Deus.

He needed to move, turn away. Put some distance between them. But he couldn't. Worse still, he didn't want to.

Not when she was watching him with those wide blue eyes. Not when those lush lips called to him with siren-strong temptation.

She blinked, her nostrils quivering as she inhaled. 'Gingham…'

'We have ten minutes. More,' he rasped.

'I should…we should…'

Joao caught her to him, lust, hot and torrid and alarmingly strong, burning a blazing path through him.

What he was doing was terribly unwise. But he couldn't help himself.

He wrapped his arm tight around her slim waist and brought her flush against his body, his senses singing when she didn't resist.

Then, far too many weeks after that mild-altering first time, Joao fused his mouth to hers and tasted the woman who by all reason and logic should've remained untouchable.

CHAPTER FOUR

SAFFIE'S BODY WAS on fire, bypassing every shred of common sense to blaze in gloriously forbidden delight, even as her senses went to war with each other.

This wasn't supposed to happen.

Her every nerve ending shouldn't have awoken at that simple touch of his thumb on her mouth. Her breasts shouldn't have tingled in wild anticipation.

Joao wasn't supposed to drive her to the brink within seconds of kissing her. He wasn't supposed to use his hard, virile body to drive every thought from her head so easily... so masterfully.

And she...

Thoughts melted away as she strained against him, her mouth eagerly opening beneath his, craving more of the delirious pleasure that shouldn't have been flowing through her bloodstream.

A platonic three months.

No repeat of Morocco.

No loss of control.

And yet here she was, her every cell crying out in glee as Joao took complete and effortless control with just one touch. Every touch revving her senses into overdrive.

In her not too distant past, she'd been in a relationship that had lasted several months before it'd fizzled out and died a natural death.

Nothing she'd experienced then came close to what she'd felt with Joao in Marrakesh. Or the sensations he was evoking in her now.

Her breasts grew heavy and tingled as Joao pinned her

against the glass wall in his study, propped her up with one muscular thigh between hers.

A thick, helpless moan spilled out of her.

They kissed with wild abandon that bordered on rabid. When the need for oxygen drove them apart, Joao stared down at her, his eyes blazing with hunger as desire arced between them, snapping and sizzling like forked lightning.

It was the same look he'd levelled at her that night in Marrakesh. The one that made her heart leap with frenzied anticipation, her core desperately needy with a hunger she'd never known before.

But there was also a hint of apprehension.

Because from the first moment she'd set eyes on him, hadn't she sensed that he could wreak wicked sorcery on her senses? And hadn't that observation been conclusively proven two months ago?

Joao made a gruff sound under his breath, his hands sliding up her ribcage to boldly cup her breasts. Shamelessly, he moulded them as his kiss deepened, introducing an edge of hunger and possessiveness that robbed her of what little breath remained in her lungs.

When his fingers found the stiffened peaks of her nipples and mercilessly teased them, she shivered and strained into his touch with an eagerness bordering on abandon.

'Touch me, Saffie,' he grunted against her ear.

With a feverish little exhalation, she dragged her hands down his broad shoulders, over his chest to explore the hard planes of his stomach.

She barely felt the hem of her dress being lifted, the tops of her lace-stockinged thighs being exposed. But she certainly felt the heat of his fingers as they caressed her hip, revelled in the trail of fire as his fingers brushed the tops of her satin panties.

Joao's lips found hers again as his fingers delved beneath, seared her damp heat to stroke her core, began to explore her with expert skill that turned her knees liquid. That made her whimper.

He swallowed the sound, parted her, and—

Froze at the distinct tone of a videoconference summons ringing through the study.

Joao muttered something under his breath, the meaning lost between their lips as he plastered his masterful lips against hers once more.

The sound stopped for a moment before starting again.

Saffie blinked, barely managing to drag herself from the psychotropic effect of his kiss. 'Joao...'

'Ignore it, Saffie,' he growled.

But the icy brace of reality was sinking in deeper, reminding her where she was, what she was doing.

And with whom.

Dear God...

She pushed at his shoulders. 'No... Joao, stop.'

This time his curse was succinct, tossed out in sexy, pithy Portuguese. Against her belly, the thick evidence of his arousal pressed insistently, sharpening the hunger tearing through her.

He stepped back and whirled away, his fingers driving through his hair as he placed half the width of the room between them.

Saffie sucked in a desperate breath and frantically adjusted her dress as thick silence pounded through the room.

After a minute he glanced at her, one finger poised over the answer button. 'Are you ready?' he asked.

He was once again composed, master of all he surveyed, which was more or less the whole world, while she squirmed in the pit of unfulfilled desire.

But Saffie managed to nod, managed to drag herself into the chair next to Joao with her tablet poised before her as the screen flicked to life.

And when they were done and Joao had effortlessly

hammered another deal, she scrambled to her feet. 'I'm going back to the office. I have a million things to do before we fly tomorrow afternoon.'

She told herself she was thankful that he barely glanced up from the file. That when he replied, 'Very well. I'll be down in ten,' his tone was once again cool and indifferent.

It was what she needed to keep her from falling for temptation again.

So why did it bruise her heart so badly?

Exiting the penthouse, Saffie wrestled quaking fingers into functionality long enough to summon the lift and stumble into it, before her legs gave way and she sagged against the polished mirror, her breaths coming in frantic little pants.

Dear God…

The way he'd commanded her body. The way she'd thrilled to all of it.

She swallowed, feeling another fierce blush heat up her face as her hand went to her throat, caressing the skin as if it would soothe the rawness that echoed in her head from her loss of control.

She'd fallen into each caress, each kiss, like a sex-starved lover, eagerly welcoming her paramour, offering herself to him on a silver platter.

Her breath shook out.

She had no business experiencing the awe trawling through her. Not when she'd finally understood over the past two days just how much the Archer deal meant to him. Not when she now suspected the reason for the absence of a new lover in his life stemmed from his zeal to win the Archer deal.

So, she could've been any of the supermodels or socialites he usually dated, a way to slake his needs without the tedium of wining and dining a new paramour.

Just like that night in Marrakesh, she'd been there, available and willing. Simply a warm body gracing his bed until he worked her out of his system while ensuring she stayed put to play her part in his business deal.

The thought tossed a cold wave at her, restoring a little of her shattered equilibrium.

From the start, Joao had represented a heady but *temporary* thrill. She just needed to remind herself of that, perhaps a little more forcefully and constantly so this feeling of transcendence, this foolish quaking of her heart would cease.

Despite the admonition, heat rushed to her core in remembrance of how he'd touched her, her belly clenching with cloying hunger.

Desperately suppressing it, she threw herself into the last items on her to-do list.

By the time Joao came downstairs she was at her desk. She sensed him prowling his office, her awareness of him almost superhuman as her frayed senses refused to settle.

'You didn't tell me how the session with the stylist went.'

She jumped, unaware he'd been standing in the doorway.

Whisky-dark eyes surveyed her with deceptively lazy focus, the espresso cup held between long, tapered fingers.

The dark trousers and burgundy shirt he wore highlighted his superb musculature. A warm, tight body she'd explored less than an hour ago.

Saffie's pulse tripped and she scrambled to think straight. Then decided against pointing out that their conversation when she'd returned from her outing had been anything but affable. Or that he'd never shown an interest in her stylist sessions before today. 'It went fine. No hiccups,' she said briskly.

His jaw clenched for a taut moment before he nodded. *'Bom.'*

He remained in the doorway. And, unwitting fool that she was, Saffie's gaze flicked to his. She attempted to read his expression. Felt her stomach drop when she read nothing but neutral, professional interest.

As silently as he'd appeared, Joao retreated.

And then proceeded to make demand after impatient demand, as if determined to recoup every minute of the time they'd spent in that illicit embrace.

For the first time in her life, Saffie found herself clock-watching. And grabbing her bag the moment the clock struck nine.

He had the phone to his ear when she poked her head through the door, although those piercing eyes locked on her and narrowed as she indicated she was leaving. When he made to pause the conversation, Saffie waved him away.

And fled.

On a wild whim, she instructed the personal driver Joao had hired for her to take her home to Chiswick.

She'd bought her flat two years ago, mostly to invest her more than generous salary. Her frantically busy role as Joao's EA meant she got to stay in her flat once or twice a week if she was lucky. Half of the plants she kept defiantly buying because she expected her life to miraculously slow down survived only because her next-door neighbour took pity and watered them when he could.

The majority of what little down time she got was spent in one of the executive condos Oliviera Enterprises kept for its high-ranking employees. It was where she kept her work clothes, where she'd crashed in the early hours of yesterday morning after working with Joao for sixteen hours straight on the top ten deals he was juggling.

And now, as she walked around rooms that should've felt familiar but didn't, Saffie's mind was back in the penthouse. Back against that glass wall, her senses clamouring for everything Joao had to give.

How she wanted to be back there now, caution be damned.

With grim determination she pulled out her suitcase and gathered the few essentials she kept at the flat. It struck her that she could walk out of her flat and never return because everything she needed was taken care of at the company's executive suite.

The awareness that she had allowed herself to become fully dependent on Joao sent a pulse of apprehension through her. She shook free of it a moment later.

She'd pulled herself back from falling into total disgrace after vowing to keep away from her powerful, charismatic boss today. She was allowed a few wobbly moments.

Order would be restored tomorrow.

Except it wasn't.

Joao's bad mood arrived, and stayed, displaying a full spectrum of his Latin temper that sent her assistants cowering. Eventually, knowing Joao would be locked in meetings and conference calls in the hours before they flew to Shanghai, she gave them permission to leave mid-afternoon.

With the videoconference she'd set up for him about to commence, Saffie decided to make herself scarce, too.

She was eager to flee her thoughts, but more than that she was eager to shake off the addictive hunger that had taken root inside her and wouldn't shift.

Standing up from her desk, she started as the intercom buzzed to life.

With unsteady fingers, she answered. 'Yes?'

'Come into my office, please, Saffie,' Joao commanded.

She replaced the handset, feverishly making a list of what he could possibly want and abandoning it after a few seconds. Joao's needs were fluid and numerous.

Thoughts of needs immediately intensified her hunger, thickening the vein of desire he'd effortlessly triggered in her. Desire he'd more than fulfilled in Morocco only for it to return ten times stronger.

Her footsteps faltered outside his doors despite her traitorous senses yearning for the man within.

She slicked unusually clammy hands down her merino-wool-clad thighs. She worked for the man and knew it wasn't her overactive imagination broadcasting his impatience from behind the closed doors.

And when she opened those doors she wasn't fooled for a second by his seemingly relaxed pose behind his desk.

Fiercely intent eyes latched on her the moment she stepped inside and tracked her mercilessly across the plush carpet.

'What do you need?' she asked in a voice nowhere near her usual even tones.

He stared at her for a terse few seconds before he flicked a glance at his watch. 'The Silverton team weren't ready with their report. They're under orders to get themselves into shape and reconvene for the videoconference in half an hour.'

She frowned. 'I spoke to them this morning. We went through the bullet points and everything was in place. I wouldn't have arranged the meeting otherwise.' She'd learned to her advantage that triple-checking those with access to Joao was better for everyone concerned, including her.

He pushed back his chair and rose. 'They weren't ready to my satisfaction. So we have fifteen minutes. Correction, we *had* fifteen minutes. Since you wasted five minutes with your dawdling, now we have ten,' he drawled as he rounded his desk.

The swift spike of excitement robbed her of breath and immediately replaced it with a racing heart and shrieking warning that this…*anticipation* coursing through her was skating dangerously close to foolhardy. 'Ten minutes for what?'

He raised one mocking eyebrow. 'To discuss what happened yesterday. Specifically, if it's going to cause another episode like Monday's.'

Her heart flipped in her chest. 'Why should it?'

'You tell me. I would've had this conversation with you last night, but you made yourself rather...unavailable.'

She couldn't hide the blush that suffused her face. 'I went home. To my flat,' she added for emphasis she wasn't altogether sure was necessary. 'As for dissecting what happened...there's no need.'

His eyes narrowed as he rounded his desk to perch on the edge. Her pulse skipped erratically at the sight of his thighs bunching beneath his tailored trousers.

'Are you sure?'

'Absolutely. Let's chalk it under a lapse of judgement.'

His lips compressed and his nostrils thinned as he inhaled. 'How magnanimous of you,' he drawled.

Dragging her gaze from the enthralling sight, she cleared her throat. 'If there's nothing else, I have a meeting in three minutes.'

He scowled. 'What meeting?'

'The executive assistants' meeting. It's scheduled in sync with your call.'

'Cancel it,' he growled.

She shook her head. 'I've cancelled it three times already. As head of the executives I can't not turn up.'

For the longest time, he didn't answer, his eyes lingering on her. Then abruptly he stood and returned to his desk.

Saffie started to walk away but then paused.

'Joao?'

'Hmm?' His gaze was hooded as it lingered on her.

'Were the Silverton team really not ready?'

A look very much like chagrin flashed across his face. 'They spent too long trying to get the projector to start the presentation. I grew impatient.'

'By too long, you mean ten seconds, possibly less?'

He clawed his fingers through his dishevelled hair. The action was so sexy, she forced her gaze away before she made a fool of herself by drooling. 'Perhaps. The other reason I wanted you in here is because I want your input on Silverton. He's hiding something, I'm not exactly sure what. But, of course, if you need to attend your meeting...'

Slowly, Saffie retraced her steps. Leaning forward, she picked up his phone and dialled the familiar number. 'Hello, Mr Oliviera?'

'No, Justine, it's Saffie. Something's come up. I won't make the meeting. No, don't cancel it. You can take it for me. Send me the notes when you're done.'

'Oh. Okay. If you're sure?'

'I'm sure. Thanks.'

She hung up and met Joao's gaze. 'There. That's taken care of.'

Whisky-gold eyes stayed locked on hers for a long moment then an expression crossed his face. It was hard. Bitter. Enough to make her stomach tense. *'Obrigado.'*

'What exactly do you want me to watch out for?' she asked, desperate to stop her mind from searching for reasons behind that look.

'I'm not sure, but, whatever it is, I will get to the bottom of it.' The grit coating the words made her wonder if he referred to something other than the Silverton meeting.

As had been happening far too often lately, her mind began to stretch, yearning for knowledge she wasn't entitled to. A need to know the man beneath the outer dynamism and authority.

Why did she sometimes find him staring at the scar in his palm with a mixture of anguish and poignancy? Why did he always close his fist as if holding a precious memory close?

She glanced up and caught him staring at her, a puzzling expression on his face.

'What?'

'I think the Silverton team are ready for us now,' he said with a touch of brittle amusement.

Her startled gaze dropped to the ringing phone. Face flaming, she snatched it up. 'Oliviera Enterprises. Of course, Mr Silverton. I'll let him know you're ready for him.'

She hit the mute button. Without glancing at Joao, she pressed the button that lowered the videoconferencing screen.

When she chanced a glance at him again, the bitterness had receded, and he was once again the all-powerful billionaire.

While she was evolving into an unfocused mess.

She swallowed, vowing to restore her composure by hell or high water, as the screen flickered to life.

'You're better prepared now, I trust?' Joao drawled.

Rick Silverton nodded almost fawningly. 'Of course, sir. And apologies for the earlier glitch.'

Joao waved him away. 'I am confident you will ensure it doesn't happen again. Now, your report, please. Then the projections.'

Saffie wasn't sure what made her glance at Joao then. His eyes were firmly fixed on her. And the look in them sent a different kind of sensation down her spine. The one that warned she'd just skated closer to the edge of the volcano.

They took off from a private airport in South London four hours later. Any one of the four bedrooms in the converted A320 Airbus's vast, jaw-droppingly luxurious interior would've been a perfect place to regroup after a very charged seventy-two hours.

Except her boss had other ideas and none of them included giving Saffie a moment to herself.

Five minutes after take-off, Joao beckoned her to the sumptuous chocolate-leather-and-mahogany-themed conference room that also served as his study on board. On two large screens, several Oliviera Enterprise executives from New York and India were poised to give an update on several projects.

That ate up three hours.

The moment they were done, Joao swivelled in his armchair to face her. He didn't speak immediately, an unsettling tactic that had failed to rattle her until recently. Until she'd become intimately acquainted with her boss one night in Morocco and now couldn't look at any part of his body without recalling in vivid detail what it felt like to be up close against his warm, vibrant skin. To experience the unleashed power of his masculinity. To remember the feel of those sensual lips suckling her nipple, wreaking dark magic between her thighs.

Enough!

It was clear he intended to throw her off-balance, probably because of yesterday's rebellion of leaving the office while he was on the phone. Well, he could try all he wanted.

Saffie cleared her throat. 'Mrs Archer landed in Shanghai two hours ago. I have it on good authority, she's thrilled with her suite and the presents we arranged for her.'

'*You* arranged. Feel free to take credit where it's due.' The suggestion was delivered in a laconic rasp, his eyes leaving hers to trail lazily over her body, his eyes heating where they touched on her tasteful soft beige trousers and blush-pink off-the-shoulder cashmere top.

Too unnerved to look into those eyes just yet, she pulled her tablet closer.

'We'll have dinner with her at her favourite restaurant two hours after we land. Chef Bouillard has been given exclusive charge of the kitchen for one night and been apprised of her culinary preferences. But I've suggested he delight her with a few of his own signature dishes. Same old, same old won't impress her.'

'My sentiments exactly.'

She nodded. 'Two more bidders have joined the private auction for the Shanzi orchid. That brings the total to eleven. Sadly, the auctioneers couldn't be persuaded to keep it at nine.'

One eyebrow rose. 'Are you losing your touch, Saffie?' he mused.

'It's more like word has leaked that you're interested and that's attracted the usual upstarts who think they can beat you on any arena,' she replied, then realised how sycophantic she sounded.

A quick glance showed a wider, more arrogant smile that irritatingly made her stomach dip in excitement. He rose from his seat, ventured closer until his scent reached out and wrapped around her. Saffie kept her gaze trained on her tablet, cautioning herself not to do anything stupid, like look into those compelling eyes. Or trace the back of the large hand that landed on the table next to hers as he leaned down to peruse the list on her tablet.

'It is of no consequence. I intend to win at all costs,' he rasped low and deep.

She shivered, unsure whether he meant the auction specifically or the Archer deal.

Winning was everything to him. And yet, something in his demeanour blared alarm to her brain. One she couldn't decipher when he stood this close to her. When she felt as if he could hear her every heartbeat.

She really needed to get herself together.

She pulled up the next item on the agenda. 'The investigators sent the latest report on Pueblo Oliviera.'

The hand next to hers curled on the table and a different sort of tension seized his frame. This time, Saffie couldn't stop herself from looking up.

A hard, cynical mask stared back at her. But this close, within the depths of his eyes she saw something else. Ferocious, supremely intimate purpose. The kind birthed through whispered vows made in chilling darkness. The kind she'd made to herself when despair had held her in its tightest grip. When deepest yearnings had risen to the fore and threatened to consume her alive.

It was on one of those dark nights that she'd sworn she would never remain alone, that she would fulfil her promise to her foster mother and surround herself with a family, even if it was a family of two, and put the desolate solitude and heartache she'd suffered as a child behind her.

Pueblo Oliviera.

Even though she'd suspected, she'd never asked Joao for confirmation. From the naked flames leaping in his eyes, now wasn't a good time either.

And yet…a small voice called to her, urged her to probe.

'He's your father, isn't he?'

'A biological donor I had the dubious honour of being named after, *sim*,' he replied with a harsh rasp.

She'd done an Internet search early on in her role when she'd spotted the confidential memos on the man. Pueblo was rich and influential. Nowhere in his son's league, of course, but with enough clout in the business world to go after the same deals Joao did.

It hadn't taken long to recognise the brutal rivalry between the two men. Rivalry that went beyond mutual business interests.

'Do you two speak?'

He laughed bitterly. '*Sim*, we do. Through the profit-and-loss score board. Specifically, my profits, his losses.'

'Why?' She didn't need to elaborate.

His eyes hardened and she held her breath, afraid she'd overstepped. She was about to excuse herself when he straightened abruptly and strolled to the elaborate drinks bar set into the side of one sleek table. He poured himself a shot of Hardy L'Ete Lalique champagne cognac that Saffie knew cost more than most people's monthly salaries. In another glass, he poured mineral water and returned to the desk. She took the glass and set it down, too frazzled to drink.

He downed his in one go, and slid the glass onto the polished table.

'My birth was a mistake. One he wasn't prepared to acknowledge. So, let's just say I've made it my business to remain in his crosshairs.'

She gasped. 'He said that to you? That you were a mistake?'

Hooded eyes met hers before he shrugged. 'In certain circumstances, words aren't needed. A child is aware of how its parents feel about him without vocal expression. It's not a failing to admit you're not ready for fatherhood and take steps to prevent it. I know that for myself. It is a shame he didn't.'

A tight hollow pushed against her diaphragm, making it agonising to breathe. 'You don't want children?' she asked through numb lips, seeking clarification despite everything she'd learned about him pointing to this.

He didn't answer for the longest time. A stretch of time when something shrivelled inside her.

Eventually he shrugged. 'It's not a goal I've set for myself. Pueblo could've walked away from his mistake, instead he set out to make himself my enemy. It's been... infinitely amusing to lock horns with him.'

'You don't look particularly amused,' she replied, throwing herself back into the conversation so she wouldn't have to examine why her heart mourned.

'*Não*, not this time. Because he's got it into his head that he can steal the Archer deal from under my nose.'

'That's why you're so determined to win, isn't it? Because he's your main opposition?'

'You forget that I'm first and foremost a businessman. And this is the most lucrative deal to cross my desk in a few years.'

Despite the reminder, Saffie knew that wasn't all. Joao intended to beat his father at the highest level, once and for all.

Why? What exactly had happened between father and son?

Self-preservation rattled its warning again. She glanced at his set features and knew it was time to exercise discretion. To curb that growing need to dig beneath the wildly successful mogul to the man who...what?

Held the world in the palm of his hands with wizard-like ease that secretly fascinated her more and more with each passing day?

What good would come of knowing him?

They would never be in the same league.

For the next three months she would live on the edge with him. But after that—

She stepped away from the bleak picture stretching in her mind's eye. She'd been up for...goodness, she couldn't even remember. She needed to finish this task and head to bed. But before she could continue, he spoke.

'Do you think less of me, Saffie?' he asked abruptly.

'What?'

'Given the choice, would you not pay your own mother back for abandoning you? For leaving you to be cared for by strangers?'

Her breath shrivelled in her lungs. 'You know that I grew up in a care home?'

'*Sim.* You know enough about my life. Seems fair I knew about yours.'

She took a minute to absorb the news, to will calm into her racing heart. 'I have questions, of course I do. But until I hear her side of the story, I don't know what I would've done.'

'But you must have imagined a scenario of some sort?' he pressed, making her wonder if he'd done the same and been met with disappointment. Was that what had turned him bitter?

She shrugged. 'I've been through every emotion you can think of. But when it comes down to it, I simply don't know why she did what she did. And…somehow I've learned to live with it. To be thankful for the time I had with my foster mother.'

His lips pursed and his eyes probed as if he was attempting to see beneath her words.

Unwilling to unmask the depth of her loneliness, she shifted her attention back to business. 'Would you like me to read the report?' she asked.

He shrugged. 'Let's hear it.'

She clicked on the document, perused the list of Pueblo's activities in the past month. 'His business dealings in Qatar are up for renegotiation next month. There's a bid for six wineries in South Africa. An Italian cargo haulage firm has approached him about merging.'

'I want the names of the parties in the Qatar deal. The rest he can keep. What else?'

She swallowed, a tad apprehensive about mentioning the final item. 'Lavinia Archer has an appointment with him next Monday in San Francisco.'

His smile was chilling. 'She won't be taking that meeting.'

The sheer arrogance of that statement was thrilling and frightening. 'May I ask why you're so confident?'

He sauntered around the table, sure and agile, self-assured and, oh, so sexy. 'Because *we* will be making plans to take Lavinia to Brazil.'

'But… Brazil wasn't on the agenda.'

Joao tugged the tablet out of her nerveless hands, tossed it on the table before drawing her chair firmly back from the conference table. 'It wasn't five minutes ago. Now it is.'

With a neat little flick of his hand, he swivelled her to face him. The solid column of his body threatened to trip her senses. 'I… Okay. Would you like me to—?'

'I think I've slave-driven you enough for one day. I'm not inclined to give you another excuse for a repeat of Monday's performance.'

His fingers tightened over the leather and Saffie couldn't look away from his hands. It was almost as if he held her. Heat flooded through her system, concentrating between her legs with a vivid insistence that made her stomach clench. 'In that case, I think we should head to bed.'

His gaze grew hot and hooded, his hands sliding down the side of the chair, drawing inexorably closer to where her arms rested on the cushion. 'Or…at least, I should,' she clarified hastily.

'Ah, *sim*. Your fragile humanity is rearing its head again? I believe this is where my supposed immortality dictates I should press on?' he rasped in deep, sexy tones.

Saffie flushed, angled her body away from him and hopped to her feet. When she'd put a few much-needed feet between them, she cleared her throat. 'Are you incapable of letting anything go?'

A peculiar light intensified the gold in his eyes. 'Apparently not.'

'If you expect me to apologise—'

His lips parted, the hint of a rare smile lightening his features, throwing her insides into chaos. 'And miss the chance to hold it over your head for the foreseeable future? Why would I do that?'

Saffie shook her head, more to clear it than anything else. 'You should go to bed. We need to sync our body clocks with Shanghai time.'

Whisky-gold eyes narrowed. 'You're also uncharacteristically skittish. Would you care to explain why?'

'Perhaps because I'm exhausted?'

He moved towards her. When his hands descended on either side of her hips, and he leaned in, she stopped breathing. 'You thrive on the work I give you, Saffie. This is something else.'

A shower of shivers rained over her as his gaze pinned her in place. 'It's nothing but exhaustion. Now, if you don't mind?'

'I do mind. You're not planning on another skirmish, are you? Because I warn you, my patience isn't infinite.'

She barely stopped herself from snorting. 'Tell me about it,' she said under her breath. He heard it. And grasped her chin to tilt her gaze to his. When she met his eyes, there was a hard glint within, one that sent awareness racing down her spine. For the longest time, he stared, hard and deep, probing beneath her skin.

'It's too late for regrets, Saffie. I hope you're aware of this and don't intend to disappoint me by reneging.'

At this point she feared it would be as impossible as cutting off her arm. 'No, I'm not.'

A curious tension eased out of him and, for a flash of time, she wondered if he felt the same as her.

With a shake of her head, she dismissed the absurd notion. His ultimate goal was the Archer deal. Everything else, including her brief sojourn in his bed, was a pleasant extra.

'*Bom*, as long as we're on the same page.'

'Now that's settled, I'm going to bed. If you need me let me know.'

His gaze rushed over her face, settling on her mouth with a ferocity that made it tingle. When that tingle arrowed south, she knew it was time to go.

His lips firmed. 'I'm not a complete tyrant. I'm sure I'll manage without you for a few hours while you rest.'

'Okay…well, I'll set my alarm to wake up a couple of hours before we land.'

He nodded, abruptly dismissing her.

On legs that felt weirdly reluctant to carry her forward, she walked to the door.

'Saffie?'

She froze, held onto the door handle for dear life. 'Yes?'

'Sleep well.'

Her sleeveless red-sequinned gown followed the contours of her body before dropping dramatically to trail on the floor behind her. Saffie wasn't sure why she'd let the stylist talk her into this outfit. It was by far the most exquisite piece of couture she owned.

The only problem was she'd never worn anything so... *red* or so bold in her life. To pick now, with her senses in deep disarray—when every cell in her body felt as if it were going to turn itself inside out every time Joao got within touching distance—felt like one challenge too many.

She examined herself more closely and breathed a little easier that the faint shadows she'd woken up with just before they'd landed were hidden beneath expensive concealer. The gown projected the confidence she needed. The kind of sophistication Joao Oliviera exuded so effortlessly and expected those in his sphere to emulate, no matter how much they wanted to lock themselves in a hotel room and hide from their perplexing emotions.

Therefore, she was suitable for purpose. Especially tonight, when the first charm offensive to win over Lavinia Archer needed to go off without a hitch.

She stepped away from the mirror.

There was no hiding from this.

Accepting that she couldn't go back on the promise she'd made to stay had been easy. What had caused her to toss and turn on the sumptuous king-size bed on Joao's jet was how quickly the composure she'd been sure would hold for the next three months seemed to career out of control.

It was reassuring that whatever was ailing her emotions hadn't affected her professional performance.

The fact that her spirits remained flat despite that small comfort she chose to put down to jet lag. She was repeating that to herself when a hard rap shattered the silence in her suite.

The walk across the vast floor of the Sky Suite of the Shanghai Reign Hotel, the top half of the seven-star skyscraper hotel exclusively reserved for individuals with billionaire status, gave her time to take a few composure-restoring breaths.

Which proved pathetically useless when she opened the double doors and caught a glimpse of Joao.

She'd seen him in a tuxedo countless times.

But there was an indefinable, utterly mesmerising layer of magnificence that reached into her chest and squeezed the oxygen from her lungs. She couldn't fight the sly little voice that suggested it was that intimacy she feared that was creating havoc with her senses.

His hair gleamed under the soft lights of the private marble-floored foyer, his razor-sharp cheekbones shadowed as he leaned forward slightly and perused her from head to toe.

She held her breath, unsure whether she wanted him to comment on her appearance or remain aloofly impersonal. What she received was a slow stiffening of his body, a tightness to his jaw that sent a shiver down her spine.

'Something wrong?' she asked with a tremor in her voice that drew an inward grimace.

He didn't answer, merely conducted a return journey, slower this time until his glinting, blistering gaze clashed with hers.

'Voce parece sublime.' The words were growled out, as if they annoyed him.

'I only caught the last word.' And unless she was mistaken, it'd been a compliment, albeit a curt one. Her heart flipped, then began an insistent banging against her ribs.

'Then perhaps you should learn Portuguese, Saffie. With your brilliant abilities I'm surprised you haven't done so already.'

She was leaving in a few short months. What would be the point? The sharp prickle in her chest robbed her of her next breath but she powered through it. 'Since you speak impeccable English, I didn't see the need to prioritise it. Are you going to translate what you just said?'

Burnished gold eyes clashed with hers. 'That can be your first translation lesson.' Tension eased out of him, his powerful body assuming another, equally skin-tingling stance. The kind that heightened her awareness of his sheer animal masculinity. The kind that made her breath shorten even further and flung the sharpest arrows of lust to her sex.

'Did you…did you want something, Joao?' Why did his name have to leave her lips with such throaty emphasis?

His gaze dropped to her neck. 'I thought you might appreciate help with your necklace.'

The diamond and ruby necklace he'd given her on Monday. The day she'd announced she was going to leave him. The day he'd told her he needed her…

Had that been four short days ago?

'Oh. I was saving it for another occasion.' Like a summons to Buckingham Palace, which might hopefully never come.

His gaze lingered at her throat, then dropped down to her dress. 'Did you not pick this dress with the necklace in mind?'

He caught her slight grimace. 'What's the problem?'

'I still think it's a little too much.'

'I don't care what people think. You shouldn't either, Saffie. Either wear it or don't. Your choice.'

His lips firmed before he glanced pointedly at the one-of-a-kind Richard Mille watch on his wrist. The timepiece came with a staggering price of two million dollars, and had been a gift, an astute move that had seen the iconic Swiss watchmaker's profits soar after Joao had been seen wearing it. 'Either way, we're stretching the limits of being fashionably late.'

Now he was leaving the decision to her, she admitted reluctantly, the gown was the perfect foil for the breathtaking necklace.

She crossed the room, the feast of wealth and opulence all around her in the form of gold-leaf-embossed cabinetry, expensive suede sofas, Tiffany lamps and a fringed waterfall chandelier made of Swarovski crystals and flawless tanzanite, paling in comparison to Joao, who followed her to the thumb-printed safe set behind a French Impressionist painting.

She took out the necklace and held it out to him.

He looked from the necklace to her throat. 'Turn around,' he instructed a little gruffly.

Struggling to take one more breath, Saffie turned. He stepped close, enough for the suppressed power of his presence to engulf her like an expensive cloak. For her body to tremble when he brushed up against her back.

She squeezed her eyes shut, praying for better composure as the cool, heavy weight of priceless diamonds and rubies encircled her neck. She didn't need the mirror to know it would be dazzling, and Joao's satisfied nod when he caught her shoulders and spun her around to face him was sign enough that she'd passed his elegance test.

'Perfeita,' he murmured.

The warm glow the compliment sparked stayed with her long after they were ensconced in the back of a gleaming Rolls-Royce Phantom, the bodyguards Joao never travelled without in two SUVs in front and behind them as they travelled along the Bund towards their destination in Pudong.

He remained rigidly courteous as they alighted in front of the vaunted House of Pearls auction house twenty minutes later. The hosts of the event, dressed in sharp suits, fell over themselves to greet Joao, ushering them inside the hallowed red-carpeted room where the pre-auction champagne reception was being held.

Lavinia Archer was the first to spot Joao.

The septuagenarian, dressed in a stunning dove-grey gown and a haphazard combination of diamonds and pearls, smiled as they approached.

'You're a wicked one, Oliviera. Tempting me with that little puzzle you knew I wouldn't be able to resist.'

He took her hand, placed a charming kiss on the back of it, before smiling. 'I insist you call me Joao, and I'm glad my ruse worked but the credit must go to my executive assistant. You remember Saffron?'

Now she knew a little of his history, Saffie suspected her invitation to call him by his first name stemmed from not wanting anything in common with the man who'd sired him. What other demons lay beneath his smooth surface?

As if he'd caught her question, his sharp gaze flicked to her, and narrowed.

'Of course.' Lavinia turned to Saffie and gasped. 'Goodness, what a fabulous necklace! It looks simply divine on you. Whatever you did to earn that, my dear, take my advice and keep doing it.'

Saffie tensed, and, although Lavinia's tone was more generous awe than maliciously salacious, the blood froze in her veins.

Before Morocco comments like that would've bounced off her skin. After all, working for the richest man in the world came with the guarantee that the eyes of the world would be on her twenty-four-seven. So why were her insides churning now? Was she broadcasting her inability to think straight around the man?

Hysteria bubbled up her throat.

'What's wrong?' Joao asked from beside her.

Frantically, she shook her head. 'Nothing.'

His eyes narrowed, a disappointed gleam lighting the depths. 'You've always spoken your mind to me, Saffie. Don't start hiding now.'

But how could she tell him how exposed she felt? How one night with him had turned her emotions inside out so that she couldn't even recognise them any more?

She glanced away from him, relief seeping into her when they were led from the reception room to the auction room. She was further saved from examining her feelings as a familiar, smiling face approached.

William Ashby III. The man who'd tried to poach her countless times in the past until she'd finally hinted that she might be in the market for a job soon. As with all things Will, he'd responded to her email on Monday to say she wouldn't be accepting his job offer after all with cheerful charm.

Lanky, congenial and fair-headed with a work-less-play-harder ethic, he was as different from Joao as night from day. An English aristocrat with a few billion to his name, Will by his own admission did just enough to keep his company's balance sheets in the black and spent the rest of his time chasing material highs.

And attempting to headhunt Saffie whenever they met.

'I thought that was you,' he said with a wide, boyish smile.

'Hello, Will.'

His smile widened. 'Almost didn't recognise you over the sparkle of that bling,' he teased.

Self-consciously, her hand went to the necklace, excuses rising and then dying on her lips as she concluded that she didn't owe anyone an explanation for Joao's generos-

ity. Her chin rose and something in her expression made
Will's eyebrow spike.

'I thoroughly approve of that fierce look, Saffie. Enough
to make me throw caution to the wind and say I'll double
whatever Oliviera's paying you if you change your mind
and come work for me.'

Saffron smiled for the first time in a while. 'Just double? I'll have you know I received an offer just this week
to triple it. An offer I refused.'

'Ouch.' He clutched his chest and gave a booming laugh
that attracted interested gazes.

Including Joao's chilling look of disapproval, which
stayed on her for several heartbeats before it swung to Will.
There it intensified, a combative gleam filming his eyes.

'Oops, I think I've stepped right into your boss's crosshairs. Should I be terrified?' Will's tone was amused with
a trace of speculation.

'Maybe,' she teased. 'He knows about your job offer,'
she explained, dragging her gaze from Joao.

Will stared down at her, his eyes twinkling. 'Dear God,
did you feed me to the lion without as much a heads up?'

She bit her tongue, unwilling to divulge the circumstances surrounding why his name had come up.

Will was still staring at her when Joao approached them,
his prowl animalistic and irritatingly hypnotic.

'Ashby,' he greeted him with icy curtness.

'Oliviera, you caught me attempting to poach your assistant again,' Will said without a trace of apology.

'So I see. Perhaps it's time for me to stake my claim
once and for all,' Joao replied, his narrowed gaze holding a chilling challenge that slowly dimmed Will's smile.
Without giving the man a chance to respond, he turned
darkly gleaming whisky-gold eyes on her. 'Do you think
that would be necessary, Saffie?'

Her mouth dried because she knew they weren't talking

about work any more. They'd strayed into something brutally personal. Something spellbinding and exhilarating. Something that made her breasts tingle and swell, made her pulse heat up and her feminine core clench with unashamed need.

'That won't be necessary. Will knows where he stands,' she said a little too hurriedly.

Will's shrewd gaze swung between her and Joao. Then he smiled and nodded. 'Indeed I do. Enjoy the rest of the evening.'

He walked away with a brisker stride than she'd ever seem him adopt, leaving her with an intensely brooding Joao.

'If I didn't know better, I'd say you encourage him in his erroneous beliefs,' he slanted at her.

He was understandably disgruntled. Normally she would have circumnavigated it by tactfully changing the subject. And considering she'd spent her life tempering her emotions, squashing her hurt and sorrow in the hopes that her prayers would be answered, that she would be picked next time and her desolation and loneliness would end, she should've been able to mask it now.

But for some unfathomable reason, Saffie didn't want to. She wanted to stamp her feet and shout that this was supposed to be an enjoyable experience. A thrilling swansong to end all swansongs before she swapped the roller coaster for what her heart yearned for most.

Joao had never demanded that she temper herself. She'd chosen that path because it was what had served her well in the past.

So why now? Why the urge to flex her emotions, take a leaf from his Latin temperament book and *let go*, just this once?

Because that's how Morocco happened!

The bracing reminder made her clutch the glass of champagne she'd barely sipped tighter. 'Well, I don't. But I think we need to talk when…when we get back to the hotel.'

'No,' he replied succinctly.

'What? You don't even know—'

'Don't I? You've been squirming your way to this since yesterday.'

'I don't squirm.'

His smile was tight and taunting. 'You didn't before Monday. But the past few days have been enlightening for both of us, haven't they, Saffie?'

Her insides flipped. 'I…don't know what you mean.'

'No? Well, let me speak for myself, then. It's been eye-opening to see the woman beneath the cool exterior. To feel the passion beneath all that rigid efficiency.'

Her face flamed. That extremely masculine smile widened. 'It's too late to put the genie back in the bottle, Saffie. Whatever the outcome, I won't allow you to scurry back to prim placidity.'

She opened her mouth, but an usher was heading towards them, the front seats reserved for them ready and waiting.

Saffie was forced to swallow her response as the room hushed and they rejoined Lavinia.

Joao stayed firmly beside her as the auctioneer stepped up to the podium. 'As we all know, this isn't a run-of-the-mill auction. Occasions like these only come around once in a blue moon. Tonight, we're extremely honoured to have such an esteemed gathering here to witness the unveiling of the Shanzi orchid. This eight-year-old wonder is set to bloom in the next fourteen days for a precious six hours only…'

'Oh, my goodness!' Lavinia literally clutched her pearls, her eyes glittering with girlish excitement as she turned to Joao. 'Joao, you wicked man. You're aware that I must have it, aren't you?' she whispered as a trio of ushers wheeled out a glass pedestal within which a bronze, hand-painted plant pot held a single dark green stem with three, thick purple bulbs branching out at the end. Along the slender stem, several nodes circled the plant, all ready to burst forth with their sacred seed.

Momentarily, Saffie forget her angst as she stared at the rare, exquisite plant. Her research had revealed that the last Shanzi orchid bloomed fifteen years ago. She was in the presence of one of the true wonders of nature.

'What you wish for will be yours. You have my word.'

The words were directed at Lavinia, but when Saffie's gaze lifted, she found Joao staring straight at her.

For a tense few seconds, they traded gazes, and, even though his remained enigmatic, another shiver went through her.

The spell was broken when they were directed to take their seats.

Bidding started at an eye-watering quarter of a million dollars. Joao immediately countered with double the price, and from then encouraged Lavinia to go to town with her bidder's paddle. One by one, the stragglers fell away and he won the bid at three point seven million dollars.

Lavinia clapped with glee as she approached the pedestal to inspect her prize. 'It's simply marvellous.' She turned to Joao and Saffron. 'I'm cancelling all my plans and remaining in Shanghai until this spectacular thing blooms. You two must be there for the event. I insist.'

It was a neat segue for Joao. 'We'll be honoured to join you. And I too must insist you let me treat you to a special dinner to mark the occasion.'

For a hardened businesswoman, Lavinia proved no woman was above Joao Oliviera's charms when she blushed. 'I'd like that.'

'Sim. We will leave you to enjoy your gift.'

He caught Saffron's arm and they headed outside to the waiting limo.

Beside her, he lounged but she wasn't deceived by his casual stance. Restlessness prowled his frame, and, in direct effect, escalated her own nerves.

To counteract that, she slid open her tablet. 'I'll organise entertainment for Lavinia while she's in Shanghai and I'll get started on something to mark the blooming—'

'I don't wish to talk about Lavinia. There is such a thing as over-preparation. There comes a time when you need to leave things to play out naturally. Don't you think?'

Saffie frowned. She'd never known Joao not to fine-tune a deal or meeting despite knowing his stuff inside out. But her emotions were still dangerously close to the surface. She risked letting herself down if she didn't borrow a leaf from his book and go with the flow.

She cleared her throat. 'Okay, what would you like to discuss?'

He angled his body towards her, dousing her with that unique scent that made her head spin. When his gaze lingered on the bold red lipstick the stylist had insisted was the only colour to wear with the dress, her blood rushed faster through her veins.

'Your mid-year review is coming up.'

She opened her mouth but he stopped her with a slash of his hand.

'Regardless of whether you intend to leave in three months or not, a review is necessary.'

Apprehension skittered over her. Everything suddenly felt wrong. 'You want to do that now? In the fifteen minutes before we return to the hotel?'

He raised an eyebrow at her. 'You doubt my ability to be efficient?'

'I question your need to do it now, without a member of HR present, as per the company's guidelines.'

He shrugged. 'Call this an informal one, then.'

Before she could object, he carried on. 'One of your

tasks is to take inventory and assess the efficiency of my homes around the world, *sim*?'

'Of course. Did I miss something in my report?' He had twenty-seven residences, all in tip-top shape with a full complement of staff should he be struck with a sudden urge to take a rare vacation.

'According to the latest report, I haven't used my Amalfi Coast property in two years. I've instructed for it to be transferred into your name.'

She went cold, her jaw sagging for several mind-numbing seconds. 'My mid-year bonus is a nine-million-euro *mansion*?'

He scowled at her screechy response. 'No need for hysteria. A simple thank you will suffice. And considering your trying behaviour this week, you can add further thanks for my magnanimity.'

'There's been nothing wrong with my behaviour. I know you said you don't care about appearances but I'd thank you not to scream what happened in Morocco from the rooftops.'

His gaze grew cool. 'I wasn't aware I was doing any such thing.'

'A twenty-bedroom mansion doesn't scream discreet, Joao. It screams *pay-off for services rendered*,' she hissed under her breath, aware of the driver's presence.

Joao hit the partition button, ensuring she was even more alone with him than her excitable senses suggested was wise. 'Don't make it a bigger deal than it is, Saffie. I'm simply rewarding you for your hard work. You will do well to remember that and be grateful.'

'This isn't ingratitude, Joao. This is…way over the top. And if this is in reaction to Will, it's not necessary.'

His tension spiked and she berated herself for mentioning Will. It was clear the other man irritated Joao. Had she done it deliberately, to get a rise out of him?

To what end? To see if he felt something?

'Nevertheless, it is done. My lawyers are in the process of drawing up the papers.'

He said the words with a finality that sent a heavy dose of apprehension skittering over her nerves. 'Joao—'

He wrapped his hands on her upper arms, a dark intimacy trapping them as he brought her flush against his body. 'You're right, it vexes me that Ashby keeps attempting to steal what's mine. But he's not worthy of my attention and you won't go to him because he'll never challenge you the way I do. Now, I'm completely weary of this new argumentative side to you, Saffie. So do me a favour, and stop, hmm?'

Affronted, she opened her mouth to do the opposite. He countered with a simple, devastating act of sealing her mouth with his, stealing her protest and every thought in her head as blazing sensation flared wild and wide through her body.

He made a gruff noise and she realised she'd parted her lips to let him in, her ready invitation crackling the flames higher, straining her body closer to absorb more of the heady sensation.

Where was her circumspection? Her willpower?

Non-existent when it came to him, she was quickly realising.

She needed to get herself under control…and fast.

Because existing in this wild and unfettered state of sensual addiction was dangerous to every single goal she held dear.

CHAPTER FIVE

HE HAD TAKEN clean leave of his senses, allowing that burr of imbalance and dissatisfaction that had taken hold of him recently to inform his actions in a way he hadn't acted since his *favela* days when rash decisions had regularly landed him in trouble.

But this was trouble of the most delicious kind. Trouble he wanted to dive headlong into and feast on, regardless of the consequences.

Sim…the kind that could alter his short-and long-term plans, pave way for his father to get the better of their battle of wills, if he wasn't careful.

He shuddered as Saffie's fingers spiked into his hair, gripping it with a silent demand and breathless enthusiasm that fired his blood and dragged a groan from his throat.

The sound froze them both, their tongues halting that control-shredding dance he yearned to continue. But knew he couldn't.

He needed a little clarity.

Jeopardising this final defining battle with his father was out of the question.

Already he was on edge over his inability to stop thinking about bedding Saffie. That little incident in his study and her calling a halt to it had grated, but uninhibited fumbling in the back of his limo only attested to how badly she affected his control.

With superhuman effort, he eased her away.

Her lips were swollen, beautifully bruised, slick and ripe for another tasting. He hardened painfully, his manhood demanding satisfaction of the most carnal kind with an insistence he hadn't experienced in a long while.

He wanted to have her, to give and receive pleasure, to hear her cry out in that husky voice that set his body aflame.

And the fever of it bewildered him in the extreme.

At his continued perusal, a blush suffused her face. The force with which he wanted to trace that heightened colour with his tongue had him setting her back in her seat.

Meu Deus. Where was the care he'd vowed to take? Where was the reminder that this kind of dangerous blind lust was how *he* himself had come into being? That, like his father, one time hadn't been enough. That Pueblo had given into his baser urges repeatedly until Joao had been created? And then and only then had the man who sired him selfishly slithered away from his responsibilities?

Não, he wouldn't slip down the same path.

For the rest of the journey, he directed his gaze out of the window, stared blindly at the water taxis and boats sailing the Huangpu River as he fought to bring his body back under control.

He exhaled in relief when the driver pulled up to the hotel entrance a few minutes later. He alighted, helped her out and strode quickly for the private lift that serviced his suite.

She didn't speak on their way up.

And he, Joao Oliviera, the man who'd talked himself out of more tricky situations in his precarious youth than he could count, was inarticulate in the grip of unrelenting lust.

He laughed grimly to himself, then even that amusement evaporated when he found he couldn't take his gaze off the racing pulse at her throat. Or her very delectable backside and swaying hips as she exited the lift, the train of her dress caught up in one hand.

Pelo amor de Deus...

He dismissed the hovering butler when they entered the suite, and turned to her, but Saffie got there first.

'This needs to stop,' she announced, her chin raised.

'We have to find a way to be civil without this…*thing* between us.'

He clenched his jaw. 'I agree.'

'You do?'

He should've been pleased at her quickly disguised disappointment. But the need to reverse his own statement almost as soon as he'd uttered it pulled him up short.

He'd fought for her to stay his right hand so he could show Pueblo once and for all that he was more than worthy of the name he'd wished to deprive him off. That he was miles better than any Oliviera. That if he chose to change his name tomorrow, the world would bow to whoever he reinvented himself as.

That if he ever had a child of his own he would—

The alien thought, springing from nowhere, froze him in place.

Doce paraíso!

Why? And why *now* when even abstract thoughts of children had been dismissed with chilling rejection in the past?

Was it Saffie? Had the thought of his assistant flouncing off to create a family at some point in the future crept insidiously into his own subconscious, pushing him to question his own mortality and legacy?

Impossível.

'Joao? Are you all right?'

He throttled back his scowl. 'I don't want any distractions to jeopardise the Archer deal. Lavinia might have been bowled over by the event tonight but we need to capitalise on the advantage, especially in Brazil.'

She dropped the train of her dress, eyes that were more green than blue tonight assessing. 'Because your father will be there?' she probed.

'Because he'll know by morning that I've stepped up the pressure and he will be doing likewise.'

'And you want to win, at all costs?'

The question was soft, curious, unlike any tone she'd used on him before. Absurdly that eroded some of his anger. Not enough, of course, to make him forget that she was sticking her nose where it didn't belong. 'That is none of your business.'

Her chin went up, a taunting little act that made him want to breach the space between them, taste her defiance for himself, then make her yield with soft moans.

'Isn't it? Didn't you all but beg me to stay just so you could achieve this...whatever vendetta you have against your father?'

'Watch it, Saffie.'

A shadow crossed her eyes and he felt the sting of regret briefly before he stemmed it.

'It may be none of my business but I think you know I care enough about yours to know I won't betray your confidence. Or use anything you tell me in any way other than to help you achieve your goals.'

'Even if you won't approve of them?'

'Would it matter to you?'

Sim, *it would.* The grim realisation disconcerted him, enough for him to jam his hands into his pockets. Beyond the window, Shanghai's spectacular night-time view was a feast for the senses. His gaze skittered over the Bund, Pudong's distinct skyline and the beautifully illuminated outline of City God Temple.

But he wanted a different feast entirely, one that started and ended with gorging on Saffron's body, slaking this hunger overtaking his body and threatening to take over his mind.

His manhood throbbed behind his fly, eagerly offering its consent on the very subject he was fighting. In the window's reflection, he saw her hand rise to her chignon, stroke it nervously. It was a mannerism he realised he'd spotted before but not clocked. What else hadn't he clocked about his assistant?

And why this need to appease her by way of personal divulgences? He had nothing to prove to her.

Conversely, he had nothing to lose by giving her a little insight into his motivations. After all, if it helped her better serve him, where was the harm?

'My father informed me when I was ten that I would amount to nothing.' The words rubbed his throat raw but he smothered the pain. Just as he'd ignored the burrs scraping the wounds of his past. It was baggage he'd had to leave behind lest it dragged him down.

Behind him, Saffie gasped. 'Why would he do that?'

He laughed, a grating sound etched in bitterness he couldn't stem. 'Most likely because of who else helped to sire me? Or perhaps it was because my conception wasn't part of the dirty little tryst he had going on with my mother, if you could even call it that. Except I came along and ruined his perfect life and he decided he'd never fail to remind me where I came from.'

He turned around in time to see her tongue sweep across her lower lip, a distracting action as she grappled with what he'd divulged. 'So he and your mother…had an affair?'

He laughed again. 'An affair? That's a little too civilised a term. My mother was a prostitute, Saffie. They met on a seedy street corner, where she traded her wares near the *favela* where I was born, purely to fuel her drug habit.'

Understanding dawned on her face. 'And your father didn't want to know?'

Bitter tunnelled deeper. 'Of course not. I was the physical manifestation of his recurring weakness. The no-hoper whose geographic circumstances meant I had two choices. Become a drug addict or become a drug dealer.'

'You chose neither option, obviously.'

He started to laugh again but the scar in his palm tingled with a force he hadn't felt since his teenage days. He pulled out his hand and stared down at the jagged white line. The mark that had changed his life. 'No. But it was a very close call.'

'How did you get out of it?'

She'd ventured closer, enough for him to inhale that stimulating scent that seemed programmed to attack his defences.

Voce parece sublime...

She was beyond sublime and he didn't want to further stain her with his past, especially not with secrets he'd guarded with fervent zeal so far. Secrets he would prefer to take to his grave.

'Through the magnanimity of a stranger. That's all you need to know.'

He read the hurt in her eyes and steeled himself against it.

'But your father...what he said...'

He shrugged. 'I decided to prove him wrong. He didn't take the lesson very well. I intend to repeat it until he accepts—'

'You? That's what you want, isn't it? For him to accept you?' she asked softly.

Something fierce tightened in his midriff. Try as he might, Joao couldn't dismiss it.

'Pueblo Oliviera would find that as difficult as swallowing the moon, so no. That's not my aim. But I want him to accept that he will lose every time he pits himself against me. That by the time I'm done we will both know who is the victor.'

A sort of bewildered understanding widened in her eyes, tinged with sadness. Again, he dismissed it.

He didn't need her understanding. Or whatever misplaced sympathy she wanted to bestow on him.

He repeated those words to himself as he approached

her. At her nervous glance, he nodded at her necklace. 'Turn around, let me help you with that. Unless you intend to sleep with this on?' Immediately images flashed in his mind of her wearing nothing but the necklace that highlighted her beauty.

When she complied and presented her back to him, it took every control-gathering technique he could summon not to bend his head and trail his lips over her delicate nape. Not to bury his nose in the curve of her neck and inhale deeply, infuse her in his senses.

He completed his task, handed the necklace over and stepped back.

She faced him again, and seemed as if she would push the conversation.

But her eyes widened suddenly, her hand going to her mouth.

He frowned. 'What's wrong?'

Her hand dropped and she shook her head abruptly. 'Nothing. I think something I ate disagreed with me.'

He watched her take a breath, then two. He started to reach for her but she danced out of his way. His jaw clenched. 'Would you like me to summon the doctor?'

'No. I'm fine. It'll pass, I'm sure.' With an abrupt goodnight, she left him standing in the middle of the living room.

Alone, Joao willed his turbulent senses and heightened libido to settle. But ten minutes of pacing later, he was nowhere near calm.

Work.

That always produced welcome challenges. He could look into Ashby's business, for instance. Embroil the other man in a tussle that would teach him a lesson not to sniff around what didn't belong to him.

He grimaced when not even that spiked an ounce of interest. Everything pressing had been taken care of by

Saffie leaving him with a rare freedom he should take advantage of.

But whatever peace he'd hoped for by retreating to his suite, he was woefully denied as night tumbled into dawn.

As he found himself outside Saffie's door, knocking softly before cracking the door open to find her sleeping peacefully.

As he returned to his suite, unable to shake the grim truth from his mind.

Saffie Everhart was well and truly under his skin.

The nausea that had threatened last night in the living room propelled Saffie out of bed moments after she'd opened her eyes. It was strong, immediate and shocking enough to leave her weak and clinging to the porcelain by the time she was done retching.

God…no.

She moaned quietly, unwilling to be overheard despite the vast bathroom that could easily swallow up her whole flat back in Chiswick. She couldn't be ill. Not now when she needed every weapon in her arsenal.

Her night had been disturbed by vivid, lurid dreams of Joao that had left her hot and needy, her sheets twisted with restless yearnings.

She couldn't afford to have her days disrupted by illness, too.

Her temperature wasn't high and her stomach didn't ache. With weak relief, she ruled out food poisoning. She'd sampled a few of Chef Bouillard's delightful concoctions but overall her appetite had been low. Whatever was messing with her system would remedy itself sooner rather than later.

She staggered to her feet, exhaling thankfully when she felt a little better. By the time she'd showered and dressed, only faint shadows remained beneath her eyes to remind her of her restless night and the bathroom mishap.

Her ivory-coloured designer power suit and three-inch heels lifted her spirits and lent much needed confidence as she headed for the dining room.

Joao was sitting at the head of the table, perusing the *Financial Times*. For one stolen second, she froze, their conversation last night unfolding through her mind.

She knew rejection, had felt it deep in her soul each time she'd been passed over at the orphanage. But she couldn't imagine what Joao must've felt when his father had said those horrible, cruel things to him.

It was clear that, like her, he'd used it as fuel to achieve his goals but it was also clear now that it'd left an indelible mark. One he possibly carried inside as well as outside in the form of that scar across his palm. One that made her yearn, impossibly and foolishly, to soothe.

What other damage had it done? Was that why he couldn't accommodate the idea of children? Bewilderingly, her heart lurched at the thought. What did it matter how he felt about children? This journey she intended to take when she was free of him was hers and hers alone.

So why did that idea suddenly further dampen her spirits—?

'Are you going to stand there all morning, Saffie, or would you like to join me so we can start the day?' he drawled in a deep, skin-tingling voice from behind his newspaper.

Saffie jumped, grimacing at the heat that rushed into her cheeks. She approached, momentarily wondering why the superb coffee she usually loved suddenly smelled so strong and pungent, enough to cause her stomach to roil.

Joao lowered his paper and her stomach calmed as if he controlled even *that* somehow.

Dear heaven, he really had no business looking *this* effortlessly magnificent. His Milan-designed grey shirt and matching tie both held a dulled gloss that drew attention to the streamlined torso beneath. Coupled with the hand-stitched pinstriped suit that made his broad shoulders even broader and more powerful, they made Saffie's palms grow clammy with need as Joao's every powerful sensual asset hit her like a sledgehammer.

She grabbed the back of the dining chair for support, the whole effect weakening her knees so she sank into it with less than her customary poise.

If Joao noticed, he chose not to comment. Nevertheless, his gaze scrutinised her face with sizzling thoroughness, and his face clamped into a frown seconds later.

'What's wrong?'

'Excuse me?'

He tossed his newspaper away. 'Are you still unwell?' he asked, angling his mouth-watering body towards her. 'You were sleeping well enough when I checked on you.'

Surprise lit her up. 'You checked on me during the night?'

For the first time in her life, Joao looked anything but supremely arrogant. Even his shrug was a little off. 'Of course. I'm a vampire, you will recall.'

She wasn't fooled by his flippancy. She was more alarmed by the warm softening inside her. The thought that he'd been concerned with her well-being.

Realising he was still scrutinising her face, she hastily answered. 'I'm fine,' she replied, swallowing the disturbing amount of moisture that filled her mouth.

One eyebrow lifted. 'If that's a pat little statement to throw me off the scent, think again. I have eyes, Saffie.'

She reached for her napkin, busied herself with opening it so she wouldn't have to look at him. 'If you ever need another challenge, don't take up the medical profession. Your bedside manner is atrocious.'

'My current position in life satisfies me greatly. And don't change the subject,' he replied. 'If your stomach still ails you I will call the—'

'I said I'm—' She stopped as the dining-room door opened and the resident tail-coated butler entered, holding aloft a silver platter.

She knew what would be on offer.

Eggs Benedict. Her favourite breakfast. Ordered for her by Joao and prepared by Chef Bouillard.

Saffie felt the ripples in her belly intensify as the butler set the dish down in front of her. Lifted the sterling-silver cloche with a discreet flourish.

'Good morning, ma'am. I hope you will enjoy—'

She lurched away from the table, praying her legs would hold her and her stomach wouldn't disgrace her as she raced for the guest bathroom. She made it just in time to hurl the almost non-existent contents of her stomach. To continue to dry heave as she heard a perfunctory knock before Joao entered.

She squeezed her eyes shut for a few shameful seconds before opening them to glare at Joao, who was pacing the bathroom, his phone glued to his ear, his features grim.

'What are you doing?' she demanded weakly.

'Doing what I should've done last night and summoning the doctor,' he said tensely.

About to tell him not to bother, she was hit with another bout. The hair that had loosened from its knot during her panicked flight from the table unravelled. Before she could reach up, strong hands gathered the tresses, holding them back from her face as her stomach lurched.

Drowning in humiliation, she barely heard Joao hang up. But she felt his fingers brush her temple in soothing strokes as she moaned weakly and attempted to stand.

Strong arms wrapped around her waist and lifted her onto the vanity. She accepted the glass of water he handed her, unable to look at him as she rinsed out her mouth, but when a cool towel dabbed at her forehead, providing merciful relief, she couldn't help but glance into his eyes.

He didn't speak but his gaze was narrowed, teeming with turbulent questions as he administered to her. She chose to face the primary question head-on, her heart suddenly hammering wildly against her ribs.

'It's just a stomach upset.'

His eyebrow spiked again. 'Is it?' he stated coolly.

'What else could it be?'

His lips compressed, and his lashes swept down as he stepped away to run the hand towel under the tap. She watched his fingers curl around the towel, tried hard not to imagine them on her body as he returned to stroke her brow.

'The doctor will provide the answers we need, I'm sure.'

'But I feel fine.'

'Then you won't mind humouring me. Do you feel well enough to move?' he asked, his tone almost gruff.

Frowning at the peculiar throb in his tone, and the building tension in his body, she nodded.

He tossed the towel away. About to hop down, she gasped when he gathered her in his arms, hoisting her high against his chest as he strode out of the bathroom.

'I'm perfectly capable of walking, Joao,' she objected, only for a new weakness to assail her, this time from the warmth of his body and the virile, masculine scent of him, which, unlike the unfortunate breakfast choice, she wanted to inhale in greedy, fervent gulps.

'You're trembling and for the first time since I've known you, you're less than one hundred per cent put together,' he said, his eyes flicking up to her unbound hair, which now trailed over his arm in unfettered waves. 'That tells its own unique story.'

'I'm sorry to disappoint you,' she said a little tartly, then bit her lip.

He laid her down on the large sofa in the living room and flicked open the single button that held her jacket closed. 'It's not an accusation, Saffie.' Again, his voice pulsed with a unique timbre that sent waves of bewildering need to her belly.

Before she could distance herself enough to decipher it, a knock came on the door. The butler answered it and in walked a bespectacled man, introduced as Dr Chang.

Joao rose, shook hands with him before proceeding to take command of the situation.

Quietly astonished, Saffie listened to him list everything she'd eaten and drunk in the past twenty-four hours. Only when the questions got personal did Dr Chang turn to her. 'If you wish privacy, I can—'

She shook her head. 'It's okay, we can speak…' She paused. Somehow, divulging that she and her boss were intimate didn't emerge easily. She cleared her throat. 'But as I told Jo—Mr Oliviera, I'm fine. I'm sure whatever this is will pass soon.'

'Saffie.' His tone was tense, wrapped with that surprising concern again. 'Answer his questions, *por favor.*'

She realised she was fiddling with the hem of her jacket and immediately linked her fingers in her lap.

She concentrated on the doctor's cool touch on her wrist as he took her pulse, counting back to answer the question about her last period.

Quick calculation done, she opened her mouth to relay it, then froze as a bolt of shock went through her.

No, that wasn't right. It couldn't be.

But the deafening clang of her heart dropping like a stone told her it was.

Times and dates that flared like neon signs in her mind.

'Miss Everhart?' the doctor prompted.

Her gaze flew to Joao. He was watching her with brooding, lethal intensity, his body coiled taut as he awaited her answer. 'I… It's been almost nine weeks since I had my period.'

Joao froze completely, his eyes glistening with a stunned light that made her shiver even as a layer of colour receded from his sharp cheekbones.

He jerked forward. 'Nine weeks?' The question was barely a whisper but no less sharp. 'Morocco?'

Her lips tightened. 'Can we talk about this later?'

'This requires a simple yes or no, Saffie.' Again, his voice was hushed. Soft, even. But she wasn't fooled.

She swallowed. '*If* I'm pregnant, then yes.'

His nostrils flared in a long inhalation, his jaw tightening as a cascade of emotions flitted across his face.

'So it is fair to assess that you could be pregnant?' Dr Chang asked.

She swallowed, her senses tumbling into free fall as the ramifications brutally hit home. As the possibility of the fragile and precious life growing inside her drew an awed breath. But how could that be when…? 'I…don't think so… We used protection.'

But even as she said it, something inside her clicked into place, a deep, visceral certainty she couldn't escape.

A fierce joy spiralled through her shock, blooming in her heart even as she felt the centre of her gravity shifting, altering her reality into something that was at once everything she'd ever wanted from the moment she'd understood what family meant, but also something *other* than she'd planned for herself.

Perhaps it was the slow, tectonic change going through Joao that transmitted to her? It was almost imperceptible and he hadn't moved from where he stood but Saffron could feel its immense power, knew that the repercussions of it were yet to fully manifest themselves. But it was coming. Inexorably. Like lava, slow but lethal, flowing down the side of a majestic mountain.

'No contraception is foolproof. Is your cycle regular, Miss Everhart?' Dr Chang asked.

Like clockwork. 'Yes.'

'Then a pregnancy is most likely the answer to your nausea,' he said gently but firmly. 'But a simple test should give you the answers you need.'

She glanced at Joao. He didn't speak but the gleam in his eyes broadcast his thoughts.

Thoughts that matched hers. If she was pregnant…she had to know. 'Do all the tests you need to,' she whispered.

The doctor nodded. 'Of course, miss.'

Joao prowled closer, his gaze skating over her to settle on her belly for one ferocious moment before he refocused on the doctor. 'How long will it take to know for certain?' he demanded in a low, vibrating tone.

'A matter of hours.'

She cleared her throat, drawing the attention of both men. 'Will a blood test tell me how…how far along I am?'

Dr Chang shook his head. 'For that you'll need an ultrasound.'

She glanced at Joao but his gaze was fixed on the doctor, his body bristling with electric purpose. 'Such a machine is portable, yes?'

Even before he'd opened his mouth Saffie knew the answer was going to be yes. Nothing was beyond the reach of the richest man in the world. 'Yes, the hotel provides a full private medical service to guests.'

Joao's eyes locked on hers, his gaze compelling. 'Is that satisfactory, Saffie?'

Her heart thudded, then expanded to further absorb the news. 'Yes.'

Dr Chang nodded. 'I will make the arrangements.'

'Bom.' Joao gave a satisfied nod without removing his gaze from hers.

Unable to withstand the raw blaze in his eyes, she fixed

hers on the doctor. 'Could there be another explanation for the nausea?'

He gave a benign smile. 'Most likely not. According to Mr Oliviera you barely ate anything last night. I'm almost positive this is morning sickness. If you're worried, it goes away after a few weeks. In the meantime, you can combat it with dry crackers and small, frequent meals.'

Joao frowned. 'Crackers?' His suddenly pronounced accent turned even that word sexy.

'They're biscuits, Joao,' she muttered, then forgot that she was using his given name in company. 'I can get them from the shop later.'

'The only place you'll be going is back to bed. Give me the name of the product you need and I'll provide it for you.'

The idea of Joao browsing the shops for crackers almost made her chuckle. But the doctor was opening his bag, readying to take a blood sample. When he was done, he packed up his bag and rose.

Reality hit home harder.

She was pregnant.

A wave of dizziness rushed over her. She swayed in the chair, causing Joao to curse and leap for her. 'Is there something you can give her?' he demanded tersely.

The doctor hesitated. 'I'm reluctant to prescribe anything if she's pregnant. I recommend weak tea, and rest. No matter how strong you are, the news of a child is a little overwhelming.' He gave a small smile. 'I'll be back with definitive news in a few hours.'

Joao walked him out and as she drew a shaky hand over her forehead, Saffie heard them talking in low murmurs. Five minutes later he was back.

'Should I ask what you were talking about?'

Hawk-like eyes watched her as he shrugged out of his jacket and draped it over a silk-covered chair. 'This is new territory for us. I was merely arming myself with the relevant information.'

'I don't see why. This has nothing to do with you. Besides, I'm aware of what to expect so you don't need to trouble yourself.' She started to rise.

His face, already tightening from her words, stiffened further as he came towards her. 'Sit back down, *por favor*, and explain to me why you think this has nothing to do with me?'

'I can't. Your meeting with the Shanghai team is in forty-five minutes.'

'I cancelled it two minutes ago.'

'Why?'

'Because we have a more pressing situation to deal with, don't you think?'

There it was again, that peculiar note that made alarm tingle at the back of her head.

'You heard the doctor. We… I won't have confirmation for three or four hours. Besides, even if I am, being pregnant isn't a debilitating condition.'

'It is when you barely ate last night and reported that you've thrown up twice this morning. I've instructed the butler to bring you some tea. In the meantime, you will explain what you meant.'

His dark, implacable tone caused a small quake inside her. 'You don't want children, Joao. It doesn't feature in your grand plan, remember. *But I do.*' Her hand crept over her stomach in silent wonder, even while her heart thundered at Joao's continued fierce expression.

He didn't answer for a long minute. 'There's a vast difference between imagination and reality, *querida*,' he breathed softly. 'For instance, I imagined that my own circumstances with my father would be different than they are today. Equally, I imagined that this…*fever* in my blood where you're concerned would have abated by now.'

While she sucked in a stunned breath, he continued. 'But while I'm willing to let go of the one thing, I fully intend to claim the other. Do you understand me?'

She shook her head, almost too afraid to grasp his meaning. 'No. I don't.'

'Let me be clear. I may not have wanted a child but, confronted with the reality of it, you can rest assured that there is no way I will relinquish my claim on my blood.'

As she sat there, grappling with it, he rose, staring down at her with a fierce light gleaming in his eyes she thought would singe her if she looked at him too long. 'We'll discuss this more when you're feeling a little more yourself.'

She wanted to laugh, but sudden rising hysteria advised her to curb the urge. If she was truly pregnant—and the subtle changes in her body she'd put down to her agitated state suddenly pointed to that status—then her life was changed for ever.

Dr Chang returned just before midday.

Saffie, having managed to keep down a piece of dry toast and two cups of tea, stood in the middle of the living room. Aware of Joao's imposing presence beside her, she linked her fingers in front of her as Dr Chang entered. The two technicians who followed, wheeling in a large ultrasound machine, couldn't have spelled out her condition louder if it'd been written in fifty-foot letters in the sky.

The room spun around her but Saffie wasn't aware she'd moved until Joao's arm wrapped firmly around her waist.

'This is our new reality, Saffie,' he rasped softly, almost soothingly, in her ear. His voice was gruff, but there was a layer of intent as he watched her that drew goosebumps across her flesh.

Dr Chang approached, leaving the butler and technicians at a discreet distance as he gave a shallow bow. 'Miss Everhart, I have the results of your blood test.' He cast a quick look behind him. 'You can probably guess what it is. Congratulations.'

Her nod was shaky, her heart hammering against her ribs so hard she feared she would pass out. 'Thank you,' she murmured.

'Would you still like me to perform the ultrasound?'

Beside her Joao stiffened, a coiled tension seizing his frame.

'Yes, thanks.'

Joao relaxed a touch, his arm temporarily drifting over her hip before claiming her waist once more.

Within minutes, she was lying on her bed, Joao's overwhelming presence beside her as Dr Chang rolled the wand over the cold gel on her abdomen.

When the coloured 3D image appeared on the screen, Saffie's heart leapt into her throat. A moment later, a rapid heartbeat joined the picture. A breath of wonder shuddered out of her, her eyes prickling as she watched the wriggling bean on the screen.

Her baby. Her family. Every hope and aspiration within reach. But as she watched the dancing blob, Saffie's breath caught for another reason. For as long as she'd yearned for this dream, she'd pictured just herself and her baby. Two against the world.

In all the years of hoping and dreaming, all she'd wanted was a mother. Someone to hold her close, tell her she mattered. Perhaps because she knew it was her mother who'd left her behind, she'd been the parental figure Saffie had wanted the most. A father had been an even more impossible dream. One totally out of her reach.

But now she was faced with an even more impossible scenario.

The shadowy shape of the stranger who would one day father her child had now taken the form of the most formidable man she'd ever met. The richest man in the world, with endless power and influence, who would remain way out of her league for ever. A man who intended to claim her baby, but not her.

That bruising reminder that all she was good for was the Archer deal made her heart lurch, clouding her joy.

Dr Chang made a sound under his breath, his brow furrowing slightly as he stared at the screen.

'What is it?' Joao demanded fiercely.

'Well, first of all I can confirm that you're indeed approximately nine weeks pregnant.' He moved the wand a short distance, paused, and then smiled. 'And I can also confirm that there isn't just one foetus but two.'

Joao's nostrils pinched as he inhaled sharply. *'O que voce disse?'*

'What?' They both demanded at the same time.

'Miss Everhart is carrying twins,' the doctor said, his even voice confirming the thunderbolt he'd just delivered.

Fresh shock powered through Saffie, her hand flying to her mouth. 'Oh, my God!'

'It's too early to determine the sex but you can do that in a few weeks if you wish.'

She made the mistake—or perhaps it was a fortunate occurrence—of looking at Joao then as his gaze moved from the screen to her stomach. And stayed.

There is no way I will relinquish my claim on my blood.

Her heart hammered.

If his words hadn't driven his intention home before, it certainly did now.

'Joao...'

'Not now, Saffie.' His lashes swept down as if shielding his thoughts from her. She wanted to believe he was shaken by the news but she couldn't be certain. Not with that fierce light she'd glimpsed in his eyes.

After the machine was wheeled out, Dr Chang delivered

a short lecture on pre-natal care, left her with the appropriate vitamins, then made himself scarce.

Joao, who'd planted himself at the window of her bedroom, finally turned around when they were alone.

For the longest moment he said nothing.

Nerves ate at her as she slid out of bed. 'We need to talk.'

'Were you on the Pill in Morocco?'

She inhaled sharply, sagging back into bed. 'I hope you're not suggesting this was a deliberate act on my part?'

He frowned. 'That did not occur to me. I'm merely trying to work out the evolution of our current situation.'

Our situation. Two words that drove home in no uncertain terms that he'd placed himself firmly in the middle of her future. 'Oh, Okay. Well, thank you. No, my old Pill wasn't agreeing with me so I was between prescriptions. I didn't say anything that night because you used protection when we…'

His eyes glinted darkly. 'When we had sex. It's not a dirty word, Saffie.'

She flushed. 'I know it's not.'

'Protection which failed, obviously.'

Her breath shuddered out and she couldn't stop her hand from stealing over her stomach.

Twins. Conceived on the night when she'd gone insane and thrown caution to the wind. A night that was about to come back to haunt her?

She flicked a glance at Joao's face but, with the sunlight at his back, his expression was unreadable.

'Obviously this changes things,' he intoned.

A vice tightened around her chest, making her light-headed. 'In what way?'

He sent her a droll, mocking look. 'In every way you can think of, I imagine.' He strolled towards the door. 'But at your insistence, I rescheduled my meeting with the Shanghai team, so we'll have to dig further into this later.'

She rose, straightening her clothes as she followed him out. 'I'll tell the driver to meet us downstairs in five minutes.'

He stopped with a hand on the front door. 'I'm going alone, Saffie.'

The vice around her chest tightened. 'Why? Have I suddenly turned invalid?'

'No, you haven't. But you *are* carrying twins. And whether you wish to admit it or not, news like that takes getting used to. I'm simply giving you the time to accustom yourself to it. And I would prefer it if you did that in bed.'

'So why does that sound uncannily like an order?'

He released the door and retraced his steps back to her. Without warning he spiked his fingers into her loosely bound hair, and one thumb grazed over her lower lip. 'I don't doubt your ability to shoulder this news and do your job. But I think you need time to absorb the news properly, do you not?'

Her chin lifted. 'Are you calling me emotional, Joao?'

'*Sim*, I am,' he stated boldly.

And to her eternal shame, she confirmed it with a great big lip wobble, one overwhelming feeling after another chasing through her.

He caressed her again with his thumb, before he stepped back and started to walk away.

'"I need you." "I want you to stay." "I'll do anything to achieve that." Any of those words ring a bell, Joao?'

He froze, then whipped around to face her. 'No. I haven't forgotten.' His gaze dropped to her stomach, an inferno of possessiveness in his eyes. 'But I also protect what's mine, Saffron.'

Before she could find adequate words to counter that, he was gone. And traitorously her weakened legs necessitated her do exactly as he'd said.

She crawled back into bed.

* * *

Joao realised his hands were shaking as he sat back in the leather seat of his limo, exhaling as it pulled away from beneath the hotel's portico.

Deus, his whole body was shaking.

Twins.

His first absurd thought when the doctor had delivered the news was that he'd willed them into existence with thoughts of heirs and legacies last night.

His second was...*why twins?*

But then the searing reminder that he had no real clue as to his family tree hit home. Everything he'd bothered to find out about Pueblo Oliviera revolved around the man's business interests, with a brief investigation into any possible adverse genetic traits he might have inherited. He had dozens of files on the former and just enough to satisfy himself on the latter.

But what moved him next, what continued to prowl relentlessly through him now, was the complete and utter *need* to claim what was rightfully his. The need to protect the investment he hadn't even known he was making when he'd succumbed to his desires that night in Morocco.

He grimly admitted to himself that he'd left Saffie behind partly because *he* needed time to come to terms with the emotions rampaging through him. And, yes, to strategise in light of this new development.

She was bearing his child. His children. His...*heirs*.

A cold wave of shock was followed by the hot grip of determination.

No way was she leaving him now.

For a man who'd never thought in such terms, the realisation was profound and bracing enough to drive his fingers through his hair.

But, adversely, accepting his new reality wasn't as testing as he'd imagined. Perhaps it was even divine intervention, giving him another chance to best his father.

Sim.

He relaxed against the seat as his limo whisked him into the financial heart of Shanghai, acknowledging the savage intent twining with a peculiar elation swelling inside him.

He hadn't planned for this, but, as he'd said to Saffie, reality brought its own specifications.

And this demanded complete and utter lock down of both his children and the woman who carried them.

He would stamp his legacy on his heirs, make the worthless Oliviera name mean something.

Finally.

CHAPTER SIX

SAFFIE ROSE AN hour later, dressed and summoned her car.

She didn't need to consult her electronic diary to know Joao's next meeting would be starting in twenty-five minutes.

Blessed with light traffic, she arrived just as his staff were taking their seats around the large conference table.

Joao's eyes widened, then narrowed fiercely on her face as she took up her position next to him and fired up her tablet.

'Saffie,' he breathed. 'What are you doing here?'

'My job, Joao. And, yes, before you ask, my power nap did wonders for me. Your people are waiting. Would you like to start?'

His jaw clenched but while his thunderous gaze suggested he was considering throwing everyone out, after a charged minute he swivelled his chair away and addressed his COO.

The meeting finished two hours later. Knowing he was going straight into another videoconference and would be tied up for most of the afternoon, she typed up the meeting notes, then caught up her bag.

Outside, she dismissed her driver, hoping that a walk would provide enlightenment about what carrying Joao's babies meant now he'd vowed to claim them.

She crossed over from Pudong to Old City Shanghai, trailed her way through the stunning temples in Yu Garden and arrived at her destination with one clear thought.

She wouldn't give up her desire to form a unit with her babies. Not for Joao. Or anyone.

The members-only Xinqu Tea House was situated in

a tastefully converted temple, complete with stunning Chinese screens and miniature tinkling waterfall over smooth stones.

Every aspect of the tea house was designed to soothe the senses.

Joao's arrival barely five minutes after her exquisite tea was served put paid to her desire for calm.

The sight of him striding towards her minus his tie, with the top buttons of his shirt undone, sparked naked flames of lust through her.

Without invitation, he seated himself across from her, his eyes pinning her in place.

'You left without telling me. Or telling your driver where you were going.'

'Which begs the question, how did you find me?'

His jaw rippled. 'What exactly are you trying to prove, Saffie?'

'I just wanted to clear my head. And have some tea.'

'Clear your head of what?'

She pressed her lips together. She couldn't tell him what she hadn't worked out for herself. And even if she did, what were the chances he would accommodate her wish to keep her children? Exclusively?

'Saffie?' His voice throbbed with warning. 'I hope the fact that your current circumstance doesn't strictly fall in with your original plans doesn't mean you intend to do anything foolish.'

She frowned. 'Foolish? Like what?'

His eyes darkened and he pursed his lips as if he didn't want to voice the words.

Several seconds ticked by before Saffie grasped his meaning. She gasped, her hand flying to her stomach. 'You think… I would never!'

Tension eased out of him. The fisted hand on the table

loosened. *'Bom.'* The single word throbbed with feeling. 'As long as we're on the same page.'

But her senses were flailing at the very thought of even considering what he'd thinly accused her of.

'Of course we are. This is all I've...' She stopped and took a breath. 'I intend to cherish my children, Joao. Make no mistake about that,' she vowed with a voice that trembled with the depth of her emotion.

Something shifted in his eyes and he stared at her long and hard before he nodded. 'Your point is well made, Saffie. As is the other point you made in my boardroom.'

'Good, then I too am glad we're on the same page.'

They weren't. Not completely. She didn't know exactly what he intended to do with regard to the babies she carried.

But Saffie had had enough emotional shocks for one day. Tomorrow was soon enough to slay the next dragon.

The knock came on the door just after seven the next morning.

Saffie, attempting to remain completely still in a bid to quiet her roiling stomach, called out a weak, 'Come in,' expecting the butler or another member of the suite staff.

Joao strode in with a large sterling-silver tray in hand.

She gasped, sat up a little too hurriedly and triggered a strong protest in her stomach. Her fingers flew to her mouth, and she sent a fervent prayer to not disgrace herself.

Halfway across the floor, he froze. 'Are you all right?'

She took several deep breaths. 'Sudden movements aren't conducive to holding morning sickness at bay, I'm finding.'

He nodded. 'I'm told it's to be expected.'

She eyed him as he strolled forward, brimming with mouth-watering vitality while she felt like several paler versions of herself. 'What are you doing here?' she asked when he simply looked down at her.

He deposited the tray across her lap. 'It's recommended that you have something to eat before you get out of bed, is it not?'

Glancing down, she saw the tray contained a pot of tea, a few condiments and a brand of crackers she'd only ever seen in one place. 'These crackers are sold exclusively at Winthrop's in New York.' She knew because she'd purchased them as part of Oliviera's senior executives' Christmas hamper last year.

'*Sim*, they are. I contacted your assistants and they informed me these were the best. I had them flown in overnight.'

Her mouth dropped open. 'You had a box of crackers flown in?'

'Several boxes to see you through this phase of your pregnancy. You need them to combat your condition. It's no big deal, Saffie.'

Not to him, obviously. The richest man in the world only needed to click his fingers for his every whim to be fulfilled.

And you're carrying his children.

If she was honest with herself, that hooded, claiming look in his eyes had kept her tossing and turning last night. Because if there was one thing she knew well, it was how relentless Joao could be when he pursued a business deal.

And this was way more than a business deal.

She'd given herself a night's grace. She couldn't afford to bury her head in the sand any longer.

Her hand moved towards the teapot as she contemplated how to tackle the subject. But it froze when she realised Joao was staring at her. Specifically, at her hair.

'Something wrong?' she asked a little tartly because she knew she didn't look her best.

His gaze stayed on her hair for another second before

meeting hers. 'I've never seen you with your hair down,' he said, a low throb in his voice.

Her fingers flew up, self-consciously curling around a long strand of hair. 'Oh.'

The atmosphere thickened, enveloping them in a heavy, sensual bubble as he freed the strand and wrapped it around his own fingers. *'E lindo,'* he murmured.

She knew what that meant. *Beautiful*.

Against the brush of her satin and lace nightie, her breasts, suddenly ultra-sensitive, grew heavy, their peaks hardening in reaction to his voice, his scent, his caress.

Joao's gaze dropped to the visible signs of her arousal, his Adam's apple moving in a thick swallow as he deepened the caress, his fingers gently threading through her hair in a hypnotic caress.

The tray in her lap forgotten, Saffie leaned into his touch, cravings heightened and firing between her thighs. But when a moan surged up her throat, she realised what she was doing, how easily she was falling under his spell.

She pulled herself back, one hand dragging up the sheet to cover her chest.

His gaze remained on the tendril caught between his fingers. Then he tucked it behind her ear and met her gaze. The fiery hunger in his eyes nearly undid her. She grasped the handle of the delicate teapot a little desperately, and concentrated on pouring a cup.

When he hitched one thigh up and sat down on the side of the bed, Saffie struggled not to be affected by his potent proximity.

She took a sip of tea and scrambled to think beyond her all-consuming arousal. 'Did everything go smoothly with the Macau team? You hadn't returned by the time I went to bed.' They'd returned to the office after their stop at the tea house but she'd left him to return to the hotel after setting up his last meeting.

One eyebrow spiked. 'Were you waiting up for me, Saffie?'

She felt a blush creep up her neck. She'd waited up for him until sudden weariness had descended on her at an unconscionable nine p.m. 'Only because we needed to talk.'

His face hardened slightly. '*Sim*, we do. But perhaps not yet.'

Her pulse tripped. 'What do you mean?'

His response was to pick up the small platter of crackers and hold it out to her. 'Eat,' he urged firmly.

She took one tiny bite into the dry but exquisite wheat cracker and washed it down with another sip of tea. Realising he wasn't going to engage in their discussion until she'd eaten, Saffie ate a few more, relieved when her stomach showed no signs of rebelling against the meal.

With a decisive click, she set the cup down and cleared her throat. 'I've eaten. Let's talk.'

His gaze moved slowly over her face, lingering on her tingling mouth for several seconds before he abruptly rose and padded over to the window. She couldn't help but follow the pure animal grace of his movement.

'Now that one of your primary reasons for wanting to leave me is…taken care of, is it fair to say that you'll be staying?' he asked without turning around.

She frowned. She wanted to say yes, but the vivid warning that she was wandering further into dangerous territory emotionally stayed her tongue. But wasn't it already too late? By falling pregnant with his children, hadn't she ensured a permanent link with him? 'I… I don't know.'

He swivelled on his heel, his gaze hooded. 'When will you know?'

'Why?'

'Because my next decision depends on it.'

'What decision?'

His lips pressed flat in a formidable line. 'Nothing that

cannot wait until we've dealt with Lavinia. But going forward, you should know I've instructed HR to hire two more assistants for you. And from now on, there'll be a personal doctor with us when we travel.'

Her frown intensified. 'Are you trying to make me feel like some…exotic animal on exhibit in a zoo?'

'*Que?* What are you talking about?'

'Hiring more assistants? What is that if not sending a message that I'm either overworked or something else is up with me? And a doctor? Why don't you shine a spotlight on me while you're at it? Announce to the world that your executive assistant is pregnant and you happen to be the father!'

His jaw clenched. 'Saffie—'

'No. I want this to be a normal pregnancy—'

'Well, it is not!'

The quiet thunder of his response froze her into stillness, her vocal cords ceasing to work as she watched him prowl back to her bedside.

'Once the customary twelve weeks have passed, we will revisit the subject of whether you're staying or leaving. I trust you'll have arrived at a decision by then?'

She opened her mouth to argue, then closed it again. She knew the statistics, knew that the first trimester was the most precarious, with the risks higher with multiple babies. Her hand smoothed over her belly, her heart squeezing at the thought of the worst happening. It wouldn't.

It just…*couldn't*.

As for the Archer deal, they'd worked hard for it and she wanted to see him win it. She ignored the *why* that pulsed hard and insistent at the back of her mind. Smothered the voice suggesting that, after his revelations about his father, her emotions were entangled with the deal that should've been purely professional. 'Yes,' she answered him.

Satisfaction lit his eyes. 'Good. Join me when you're

ready. I've put together a counter-proposal for the takeover of that Qatar company Pueblo was dealing with.'

She didn't remind him that it was Sunday.

In fact, Saffie was secretly thrilled that, while this new part of her life seemed poised on some unknown precipice, her work life was mostly stable.

She joined him in the suite's study thirty minutes later, and, besides the heated scrutiny he gave her form-fitting lilac dress, Joao easily slotted into billionaire magnate mode.

It set the tone for the next week.

And when Lavinia announced that her prized orchid looked set to bloom within forty-eight hours, Saffie sent out the invitations for Lavinia's party.

After the stops she'd pulled out to ensure an unforgettable event at short notice, it was satisfying to see the RSVPs flood in almost immediately, the event bold and unique enough to become the talk of the business world within hours.

Even Joao cracked a smile when he saw her plans.

'You've outdone yourself, Saffie,' he drawled, then leaned forward to trace her cheek with his fingers. 'I knew you wouldn't let me down.'

The words burrowed deep, wrapping warmly around her heart in a way she knew was unwise but she couldn't have stopped if her life depended on it. To combat the sensation, she replied briskly, 'Don't thank me just yet. It's costing you an eye-watering bundle.' Seven million dollars, to be precise, a sum that still made her feel a little sick when she thought of it. But then he'd given her a twenty-million slush fund to play with and since Lavinia had kept to her word and stayed in Shanghai, impressing her felt essential.

Joao shrugged. 'The return will be worth it, I'm confident.'

His deep confidence in her abilities further lightened

her heart until Saffie felt as if she were floating on a cloud of happiness.

By Sunday evening, though, nerves were eating at her. She stood in front of a long gilt-edged mirror in her dressing room, her gaze flitting over her cream floor-length gown.

Even though she knew it was too early to be showing, the dress that had felt comfortable just a week and a half ago suddenly felt a little too snug at the bust and waist, the hint of cleavage suddenly too...ripe.

The asymmetrical bodice was studded with multi-hued Swarovski crystals, their brilliance throwing into relief skin turned a light golden from the sun and the luxury cosmetics she'd pampered herself with during her hour-long bath. She bit her lip, unsure about leaving her hair down.

The hairdresser that came with stylist team exclusively serving the suite had gushed about her hair, exclaimed it was a sin to keep it bound and so had styled it into thick, wavy curls over one shoulder, lending her an elegant look.

Thankfully, tonight her jewellery was a little more modest. The heart-shaped diamond hanging from its white platinum chain didn't compete with the crystals in her gown.

With a decisive nod she swivelled from the mirror.

Traversing long marble-floored corridors lined with stunning, priceless works of art, she stepped into the living room and found Joao at the window, his gaze on the view.

Excitement kicked into her throat when he swivelled to face her. The hand lifting the crystal tumbler of cognac to his lips froze halfway, his body stilling as he stared at her.

He muttered something she didn't understand.

She made a moue of annoyance, even while her skin tingled giddily at his intense scrutiny. 'If that's a compliment, I really wish you would say it in English so I understand. Unless I'm mistaken and you're making a joke at my expense?'

The barest hint of a smile accompanied the quirk of his

brow. Both expressions fizzled away as he approached, every step rendering her breathless. 'It's a compliment but one that loses its power in translation so you'll just have to step up your efforts to learn my language.'

Saffie chose not to tell him that she'd begun listening to Portuguese language tapes in bed at night, both for that purpose and because over the last week it'd dawned on her that her children would be half Brazilian. And going on the promise she'd made to herself, she wouldn't fail them in any aspect of their heritage, the way she'd been failed.

She plastered on a cool smile. 'In that case, thanks.'

'De nada.' His gaze roved over her, lingering on her hair.

Bracing herself for another comment, she watched his lids sweep down to veil his expression before he tossed back his drink.

'Shall we?'

She nodded. 'Guess so.'

He eyed her. 'You don't sound very confident, Saffie.'

'It was a feat to pull this off. I'm just worried about last-minute glitches.'

He flicked a hand in arrogant dismissal. 'There won't be any. I won't permit it.'

She almost laughed. But then he held out his arm to her in a smooth, gallant gesture that caused her throat to dry up.

Her fingers slid over his tuxedoed forearm, her heart flipping over as she encountered his tensile strength. It took a study in composure not to stumble over her own feet as they walked to the lift.

Downstairs, he helped her into the plush seat of the Rolls, buckled her in before seeing to his own.

The evening was clear, the temperate weather set to hold for the duration of the party. But nerves continued to attack her for the twenty-five-minute drive to the Lupu Bridge.

Right up until Saffie witnessed for herself the fruits of her labour.

She knew her request for the bridge to be shut for a private event hosted by the richest man in the world had been granted in theory. But seeing it first-hand, with electric-blue spotlights illuminating the bridge, the red carpet stretching from one end of the visually stunning bridge to the other, and ten same-colour-themed tables elaborately decorated for their guests, made her heart swell, her sense of accomplishment extremely satisfying.

They alighted and were escorted by white-gloved liveried footmen to the sound of a string quartet serenading guests as they mingled and enjoyed cocktails.

As a pre-birthday event for the woman whose business Joao intended to acquire, it was second to none, and when the guest of honour arrived, Saffie held her breath as Lavinia alighted from her limo.

The look on her face as she stared up at the thousands of lights strung up around the single, wide arc of the bridge was awestruck.

'I told you that you had nothing to worry about,' Joao drawled from beside her.

She turned to him, and the effect of the devastatingly stunning smile he sent her hit her squarely in the solar plexus. She was still recovering from it as he walked her down the long red carpet to the middle of the bridge and the centre table laid out with pristine silverware and a breathtaking centrepiece flower arrangement, and candelabras that had cost ten thousand dollars each.

Lavinia beamed, holding out both hands to Joao as she reached the table.

'I didn't think you could outdo yourself, Joao, but you've proved me wrong.'

'You're not the first to underestimate my determination, Lavinia. Or my considerable skills.' The words were warm but the undertone of steel was unmissable.

Several guests at the table, mostly Lavinia's executives

and family, greeted Joao with reverence as he held out Saffie's chair, then folded his impressive frame into the seat between hers and Lavinia's.

'But again, the person who is responsible for all this is Saffron.'

Lavinia's gaze flicked to her, and she blinked. 'I'm beginning to see she's a priceless asset. Take care you don't lose her.'

Whisky-gold eyes caught and locked on hers. 'I have no intention of doing so.'

Saffie's heart flipped again, and, even though she told herself it was foolish, her emotions chose to remain feverishly buoyant all through the pre-dinner cocktails and canapés service. And if anyone noticed she was drinking sparkling water instead of vintage Dom Perignon, they chose not to comment on it.

Conversation flowed, many guests including high-ranking political figures, heirs and heiresses, and A-list stars approaching to schmooze Joao while attempting to bask in his unique limelight. Saffie watched him mingle, exuding effortless charm, and she wondered how a boy who'd grown up in the slums of Brazil had risen to this. What had he sacrificed? Did that sacrifice still weigh on him?

She was pondering that when he stopped mid-conversation with another guest and speared her with fierce eyes. 'Something wrong?'

Saffie blushed, a little embarrassed at being caught gawking. 'No, nothing at all.'

He continued to watch her for another long spell, then, without warning, wrapped his hand around her waist, pulled her close and carried on with his conversation.

Saffie was too stunned to react so she stayed put, and when the head waiter came and whispered in her ear that the next segment of the evening was ready, she berated herself for the hollow that assailed her when she moved from Joao's side.

The six-course dinner went off without a hitch, with each course drawing stunned murmurs from the guests.

But the pièce de résistance came during the dessert course, when a spotlight at the highest point of the bridge's arch illuminated a single figure dressed in a white three-piece suit. Guests hushed as the first sweet strains from a violin filled the air. For a breathtaking minute, the violinist played from a stationary position, then was slowly lowered by a tensile cable.

The sound swelled, beautiful and enchanting, until he landed smoothly on his feet beside Lavinia, then knelt on one knee to finish off the exquisite piece.

Then, while the last echoes of the violin faded, the excited usher tasked with caring for the Shanzi orchid approached.

With one hundred honoured guests gathered around the pedestal that held the rare plant, they watched the first bud slowly part to reveal the black, cream and purple striped orchid. For a soul-stirring fifteen minutes each bud flowered, gifting them with its beauty and sweet scent.

As the last bud burst open, thunderous applause echoed on the bridge.

Lavinia dabbed discreetly at her eyes as she went to the pedestal and picked up the newly flowered plant. 'My goodness, now the plans I have for my own birthday celebrations look mediocre compared to this.'

'Hopefully you'll have a great reason to make it special,' Joao said as he escorted her back to their table.

'Perhaps I will,' she said cryptically.

An hour later, when Joao leaned close to Saffie and murmured, 'You pulled it off. Bravo,' she couldn't help the relieved smile that broke over her face.

His breath audibly caught.

'Something wrong?' she asked, her own voice trembling.

His molten gaze raked her face. Then, 'Everyone is singing your praises. I think I need to redouble my efforts to ensure you stay.'

Saffie opened her mouth but whatever answer her brain was scrambling to come up with was halted when Lavinia cleared her throat delicately.

'I had lunch with your father a few days ago.'

Joao stiffened, an arctic chill sweeping over his features. 'Did you?' he replied silkily.

Lavinia gave an enigmatic smile. 'Hmm. I heard his vision for my company. It's interesting to say the least.'

He smiled grimly. 'By interesting you mean you know he intends to break up your company in little pieces and sell every last scrap for profit even while assuring you it's the best solution for your legacy?'

A wave of sadness passed over Lavinia's face. 'He wasn't as plain-speaking as that.'

'No. I bet he wasn't. But in case you're doubting your instincts, that's exactly what he'll do given the chance.'

She sipped her champagne before setting the glass down. 'It's difficult to imagine one's life work headed for the scrapheap.'

'Then why are you resisting me?' he enquired smoothly.

She toyed with the stem of her wine glass, her shrewd eyes meeting Joao's. 'Because I'm not completely convinced you're not your father's son.'

Saffie felt the silent fury vibrating off Joao. But Lavinia put her hand over his. 'I'm sorry if that sounds harsh but you wanted to know my reservations? There they are.'

After nerve-shredding silence, Joao nodded. 'I appreciate that. Perhaps you'll give me a chance to prove you wrong.'

Lavinia sat back, her eyes gleaming at the prospect of another adventure. 'How on earth can you top this?' She indicated the spectacular setting.

'Easily. Come to Brazil.'

'I've already been. Many times.'

His smile was steeped in self-assurance. '*Sim*, but not *my* Brazil.'

She lifted her glass and took another long sip. 'After what you've shown me tonight, I'm excited to see what else you have up your sleeve.'

Joao nodded before his gaze hardened. 'I do, however, have one condition. Before you leave Brazil you will give me an answer. I'm a busy man with other interests to pursue.' His eyes flicked to Saffie and she felt her insides dip. 'Interests I do not wish to put off much longer. Are we agreed?' His gaze remained on her for several seconds before returning to spear Lavinia's.

The older woman's gaze shifted to Saffie and without a doubt Saffie knew she was reading between lines and coming up with her own conclusions.

'We're agreed. And now I must leave. Sadly, as much as I wish otherwise, I need a minimum of eight hours' sleep to function.' She rose and held her hand out to Joao, who took it and brushed a gallant kiss across the back of it.

The last of the guests departed shortly thereafter, leaving behind a charged, electric silence. The quartet still played softly in the background, and the look in the eyes that rested on her made every cell in her body tingle.

'Joao—'

'Dance with me,' he demanded abruptly.

'I… What?'

He pushed his chair back, rose and held out his hand. 'We have this place to ourselves till midnight. It'll be a shame to let it go to waste, no?'

Saffie swallowed the lump in her throat. The force of the need driving through her made her limbs weak, her heart hammer with giddy exhilaration at the thought of being held within those strong arms, enveloped in that stunning magnificence that was Joao Oliviera.

'I'm waiting, Saffie,' he murmured, supremely seductive.

She took a breath. And gave into the weakness.

It was for one magical night, a moment in time.

She slid her hand into his, let him tug her up, draw her to his powerful body.

One large hand splayed on her back, the other catching her hand in his and laying their entwined fingers against his broad shoulder.

As if conjured up by the same magic swirling around them, the violinist reappeared and started a slow, seductive tune, one that required only a simple swaying of bodies across red-carpeted asphalt.

The enthralling scent of him.

The seductive warmth of his body.

The intoxicating power he exuded so effortlessly.

The combination was almost too much to bear.

So when, after they'd swayed in a full circle, his lips brushed over her temples, Saffie closed her eyes, sighed, and surrendered to the hypnosis. And when he gathered her closer, until her breasts tingled and her nipples peaked against his chest, all she could do was give a low moan and tuck her face into the crook of his shoulder, and dream for a moment that she belonged.

That she wasn't alone in the world with only the promise of the babies growing inside her to give her hope.

She wasn't sure how long they danced, only that she never wanted the moment to end. Never wanted to face the reality that included admitting that she was experiencing more than a surge of pregnancy hormones. That she was straying, or probably had already strayed, into the dangerous territory of unprofessional, unacceptable feelings for Joao Oliviera.

Her boss.

A warning tingle of self-preservation attempted to rise.

Another brush of Joao's mouth down the side of her neck dissolved it.

'I want you, Saffie.' The statement was raw, pulsing with savage hunger that drew a decadent shudder through her and drained every last ounce of resistance she'd thought to summon. 'Just for tonight, I want you to be mine.'

One night only.

Dared she do it?

Yes, came her heart's fierce response.

Still she hesitated, waiting for a sign that never came, while the desperate clamouring in her heart built and built, until she could do nothing but raise her head, meet his heated gaze full on.

'Then have me,' she said simply.

His eyes turned almost black, only a tiny dark gold around his iris blazing down at her.

Without speaking he gripped her hand in his and walked her down the carpet to where the Rolls waited. The driver, spotting them approach, opened and held the back door.

Saffie got in, followed quickly by Joao, and between one breath and the next the lilting strains of the violin were cut off and nothing but their urgent breathing filled the private enclosed space.

They leapt towards each other at the same time, rabid hunger dictating their movements. Joao spiked his fingers into her hair to angle her face for the hard pressure of his mouth.

She moaned as his tongue breached her lips to boldly taste her. She strained into his touch, eager for every kiss and caress now that she'd permitted herself to take this night for herself.

Joao delivered, savouring her like fine wine. And like fine wine he went straight to her veins, rousing her senses to life.

The partition was up so when he captured her waist and repositioned her in his lap, brushing away the folds of her gown until her centre was boldly imprinted on his groin, she didn't hold back her moan.

With one hand, he tugged her away from the kiss, then with deliberate, wicked movement, he dragged her hips over his engorged length.

'Oh, God,' she gasped as fire blazed through her bloodstream.

He smiled, a wicked and thrilling smile that made her heart lurch, then thunder wildly. She fell into another kiss, welcoming the hand that cupped her breast.

They stayed like that for the short drive back, and she was thankful when Joao gruffly instructed his driver to deliver them to the VIP entrance.

Within minutes they were stumbling into the living room. He swept her off her feet and strode confidently into the master suite.

Her dress came off in seconds and Saffie stood naked before Joao.

He took his time looking at her as he disrobed. 'This is the first time I've seen you truly naked.'

For some reason that struck a vein of apprehension in her heart. She dammed the feeling, telling herself she had nothing to fear.

This was only for tonight.

'And?' she asked, a whisper of cheekiness striking her.

'And you're even more beautiful than I imagined you to be,' he returned thickly.

She swayed beneath the power of his words. He caught her easily, laying her out on the bed, and finished undressing.

Then his hard, beautiful body was covering hers, his mouth tasting every inch of skin he located until he reached her breasts, and slowed his pace.

He moulded the heavy globes, blew a wicked little

breeze across the stiff peaks and sent several shudders racing through her.

'Too sensitive?'

Blushing, she nodded.

Lowering his head, he kissed around the areola for endless minutes, before, his eyes tracking her every involuntary reaction, he sucked her flesh into his mouth.

'Joao,' she groaned, clutching the back of his head as sensation pummelled her.

'You were beautifully responsive before, but now you're simply…breathtaking.'

Another helpless moan left her lips as his expert fingers slid between her legs, caressed her, then mercilessly teased the sensitive nub at the apex of her thighs.

She cried out, her fingers clutching blindly at him. 'I need… I need…'

'Tell me what you need, *querida*, and it will be yours,' he commanded.

'I need you…inside me. Please.'

His nostrils flared and she felt a fine tremor shake his body before he levered himself over her. Fingers sliding into her hair, Joao angled his lean hips between her thighs. His gaze fused to hers, he entered her with one powerful thrust and settled himself deep inside her.

He fell on the moan that ejected from her throat, devouring it as if it belonged to him. Then he angled her head up.

'Look at me, Saffie.'

She dragged half-closed eyes open, met his fiery ones.

'Wrap your legs tighter around me,' he ordered gruffly.

When she did, he shuddered, grunted in satisfaction, then began to move with sure, heady strokes, drawing whimpers of need with each thrust.

High colour scoured his cheeks and a harshly beautiful face etched in fierce arousal filled her vision as she began to climb towards that spellbinding crest. Before enchantment completely consumed her, Saffie caressed and kissed every-where she could reach, greedily tucking away sensation for later, when she could relive this experience from memory.

Shaky fingers traced his cheekbones, the mouth that could wreak such sweet chaos, and when he turned his head and kissed her palm, she felt her eyes prickle with tears.

It was too much.

He was too much.

Yet she couldn't stop it. Had no intention of doing any-thing but surrendering to this unique feeling.

When she finally crested the peak, when there was no-where to go but over that blissful edge, Saffie wrapped her arms tight around him, the only solid thing in her free-falling universe.

Beyond the wild rush of her climax, she heard him mut-ter in terse Portuguese before his movements grew uncoor-dinated, the force of his own climax drawing harsh grunts from his throat.

For several minutes only the frenzied sounds of their breathing echoed in the vast bedroom.

Then Joao rolled over, taking her with him and sprawling her over his large body. Long fingers combed through her hair, smoothing it back from her sweat-dampened forehead.

Saffie kept her eyes closed, the hypnotic pounding of his heartbeat lulling her into post-coital drowsiness. But it wasn't enough to fall asleep. Nor did she want to. She didn't want to miss a second of this out-of-time experience.

When his hand made another pass over her face, she caught a glimpse of his scar and her heart lurched. Aware she was treading on dangerous territory but unable to stop herself, she caught his hand in hers, traced her finger along the long white mark, then braved his gaze.

'How did you get this scar?'

CHAPTER SEVEN

JOAO TENSED AT the question, everything inside him freezing at the subject he didn't want to broach. He didn't want to be pitied. Nor did he want to leave himself vulnerable to exposition. Or gossip.

Hadn't many of his lovers asked the same question, their eyes brimming with curiosity, while their carefully crafted concerns hid more salacious intentions of what they could do with post-sex pillow talk?

Not once had he given them the satisfaction.

But Saffie was different. In the past four years, not once had she broken his confidence.

Except...this was *personal*.

And what they'd just done? His seed currently growing in her belly? Did it get any more personal than that?

He caught her wandering finger, stared down at her when she gave a soft gasp, but saw nothing but open, unsullied curiosity.

That need to unburden struck him hard again.

Deus, what was happening to him?

Her eyes began to dim, her expression growing wary at his silence.

He exhaled. 'You remember when I told you my mother was a drug addict?' he said, noting his strained tone.

She nodded.

'Well, if there was anything left over after she was done shooting up, she considered buying food for her son. If there wasn't...' He shrugged. 'Let's just say that the moment I learned to talk and reason for myself I was left to my own devices.'

Her eyes softened with sympathy. 'Joao.'

He swallowed a curious lump in his throat and fought the need to bury his face in her throat, inhale her very essence.

'Did you see much of her before she died?'

'No. She severed the umbilical permanently when I turned ten years old.'

Saffie raised her head, pain patent in her eyes. 'She left when you were that young?'

He pressed his lips together. '*Sim*. Much like you were,' he murmured, finding it strangely comforting that they had that in common.

Her lovely eyes shadowed. 'But you knew your parents. I…never knew mine.'

'Consider yourself lucky, then.'

'Well, I don't,' she said sharply, then took a deep breath. 'Maybe knowing and enduring what you did feels like the worst torture—'

Joao couldn't help his derisive snort.

She pressed on regardless. 'But not knowing where you came from or why you were abandoned on a park bench with a note that said you were better off without your mother is also a hell of its own, trust me.'

Trust me. A dart of discomfort pierced him.

As a rule he didn't trust anyone. That had served him well. Not trusting meant no one could let him down.

'Did you ever attempt to locate your mother?'

Her eyes grew darker and something twisted inside Joao. He wanted to take her pain away, he realised with a stark, sharp kind of clarity.

'I spent the better part of a year's salary chasing leads that went nowhere,' she said. 'But then I realised she never tried to find me either, so perhaps I needed to honour her wishes and stay away.'

'And you're satisfied with not knowing? With honouring the wishes of a woman who made the choices she made?'

He was aware his tone was harsh but she shrugged. 'I

have to be. It hurt for a long time but I can't blame her when I don't know the whole story.'

'How very magnanimous of you,' he said dryly.

'Maybe it was, maybe it wasn't. I just knew I had to find a way to be okay with it for my sanity's sake. Besides, I promised my foster mother I would look forwards instead of in the past.'

He had no answer to that, nor could he fault her for it. After all, he'd had to find his own way to contain the bitterness and pain, to rise above it in order to move forward. But he was aware it was very much a part of him, that most times it fuelled his ambition. For a moment he envied Saffie her simple circumspection. Her acceptance. Her willingness to create something...unique from her experiences.

Joao realised his hand had wandered over her belly, was stroking the smooth skin beneath which his seed grew. That pulse of ownership returned, stronger than ever.

'But that doesn't explain how you got this, though.' She brushed her fingers across his palm once again.

He shuddered, partly from her seductive touch, partly from memories he couldn't avoid any longer.

'I spent the better part of my youth running away from gangs. In the *favela* you were either with a gang or against them all. When things got desperate I joined one for a few weeks but I always drew the line when they tried to get me to sell drugs or rob tourists.' He stopped, his heart thudding as he stared at the scar. 'One particular gang leader didn't take kindly to me joining up just to get something to eat and then disappearing. He found me and decided to teach me a lesson.'

Saffie gasped in horror. 'By cutting your hand?'

He smiled grimly. 'His intention was to cut off a few fingers. He didn't get the chance to finish the job.'

'How... Who stopped him?'

'*Um anjo negro*, if you believe in that sort of thing.'

'A dark…angel?' she translated hesitantly.

Joao smiled, a curious pulse of satisfaction hitting him in the chest. 'Your Portuguese is improving, *querida.*'

She gave a shy smile. 'Who was he?'

'I discovered later that he was a doctor attached to an international charity, which was fortunate because after he saved me, I ran away without thanking him. But when I developed an infection, I went to find him. He made a deal with me. I would clean his house and tend his garden and in return he would give me an education, free of charge.'

'And that's how…?'

Joao nodded. 'He started me off with the basics and when he saw how quickly I picked up the subjects, he hired a tutor for me. I was able to take the requisite exams to get myself into university in record time. When I graduated he gave me the capital I needed to invest in my first business.'

Her eyes widened. 'My God, Joao, that's amazing.'

He wanted to bask in her joy. God, he wanted to do more than that, and that forceful swell of need was what froze everything inside him.

He couldn't *need* like that again.

It came too close to the fervent prayers of a lost little boy who'd sent up hundreds of pleas to the cosmos only to be answered with stony silence. He'd learned to rely on no one but himself. And he'd succeeded.

There could be no turning back, no opening himself up to vulnerabilities. So he crafted a passable smile and shrugged. 'Like with everything else, I paid the price by earning my keep and turning failure into success. The good doctor has been repaid a hundred times over for his generosity. That's all there really is to it.'

The light in her eyes dimmed. 'Surely you don't really believe that?'

'What else is there?'

'That he saw something special in you, that you were more than just a simple project to him? Maybe he was trying to give you what your own father didn't?'

Ernesto Blanco had been a slave-driver, true. But there'd also been times when he'd just wanted to...talk. Find out Joao's hopes and dreams. Joao had ensured he'd curtailed those occurrences.

Because...where was the sense in opening himself up only to be disappointed? To be discarded and made to feel worthless and inconsequential?

Now an arrow of guilt lanced him, unfreezing him enough to make him glance down at Saffie.

'That was a long time ago. It doesn't matter now.' Just as he hadn't done with Ernesto, he saw no point in delving into his *feelings* with Saffie.

This way would ensure they didn't stray from their synergy.

But as she slowly laid her head on his chest, her fist curled in a ball against his skin, Joao wondered why that reaction didn't please him.

Why there was suddenly a hollow space where supreme satisfaction had reigned so majestically before.

The only answer that came to him, he totally rejected.

Because Joao Oliviera didn't *need* anyone. And he most certainly didn't yearn for feelings that were as ephemeral as snow in summer.

Saffron awoke with the sinking feeling that deepened in the minutes she wasted staring up at the high, crown-moulded ceilings in Joao's master suite.

She'd felt him leave the bed an hour ago and had pretended to be asleep. The predominantly cowardly part of her hadn't wanted to face him, see the regret she'd heard in his voice at the tail end of their conversation last night, transmitted to what had happened in bed. She already knew he regretted opening up his past to her. She'd seen it in his eyes before sleep had pulled her under.

The irony wasn't lost on her that she'd told herself this was a one-night-only thing, only to find she didn't want it to be for Joao.

She'd intended to indulge in the physical, only to end up feeling closer to the man he'd unveiled last night, the strength of character needed to overcome his adversities striking at her emotions, forcing her to admit what her heart already knew. He was special. And she wanted more from him.

Her hand cradled her belly, her heart tumbling over as she accepted the truth.

She wanted more than the children he'd made with her.

This not so secret yearning was the reason she'd talked herself out of leaving his employment all these years. It was the reason she'd agreed to another three months with him when she should've walked away.

Panic momentarily engulfed her at the admission.

But now that she knew the danger she was facing, could she halt her feelings? Accept that Joao would never feel that way towards her and carry on with her life without stepping into the pitfalls?

Even as she pondered it, she knew she was grasping at straws. Being around him, witnessing his intellectual brilliance and dangerous charm was what had led to her sleeping with him in Morocco.

But even knowing and fearing for her emotional well-being, was she prepared to walk away?

And what about his vow to lay claim on the babies she carried?

A knock came at the door, thankfully giving her the excuse to put aside her churning thoughts. She answered, her spirits dropping further because Joao wouldn't knock at his own door.

The butler entered, bearing a tray. Accepting it, Saffie asked, 'Is Mr Oliviera here?'

'He asked me to inform you that he was attending an early-morning meeting. That he'll see you at the office at lunchtime. You were to take your time this morning,' he delivered with a smile.

He wasn't sidelining her, she knew that. He often gave her part of the morning off after a big event, especially if there were meetings he could attend solo.

Still, her heart dropped.

He couldn't have sent a clearer message than to leave her alone in his bed the morning after their night together. She'd pried into his private life, he'd given her the answers she wanted. And was now distancing himself.

That distance bled into their second week in Shanghai.

They remained in complete synergy workwise and, in every other way, he treated her with cool professionalism.

Out of the office was a different matter. At events where she was required to accompany him—an occurrence which seemed to have suddenly tripled—Joao took every opportunity to make physical contact. He pulled her close when her attention wandered, took her hand when they happened to be at whatever red-carpet event, and he was required to interact with the media, and danced with her at every gala or fundraiser.

All without engaging her in anything more than perfunctory conversation beyond complimenting her on how she looked, asking about the state of her morning sickness.

All while making contact with some part of her body.

Her hand. Her face. Her hair. Her hip.

Saffie was completely tortured by it.

By the time they arrived in Sao Paolo a gruelling seven days later, after a brief stopover in London, Saffie was thoroughly sick of it.

So it was with gritted teeth that she stepped off the plane

the next Saturday. The SUV that would drive them a short distance to the helicopter taking them to Joao's estate idled a few yards away. As she dashed for it, her right wedge heel twisted.

'Atento!' Joao grasped her arm and steadied her. *'Deus,* if I didn't know better, I would think you were trying to get away from me.'

'And you would be right!'

He slid in beside her, his gaze coolly speculative as he slammed the door and reached for her seat belt.

'Care to tell me what's bothering you?'

She grabbed the belt from him and secured it herself, then immediately wished she'd worn her hair in its customary bun instead of brushed out and loose, when it got in her way. She reached up to flick the offending strand away but he beat her to it, his fingers slowly threading through her hair before tucking it behind her ear.

Her heart flip-flopped in an erratic rhythm when his fingers lingered on her neck before drawing away. 'What exactly are you playing at, Joao?' she asked abruptly. A little desperately.

'Be concise with your questions, *por favor,'* he rasped as the vehicle rolled for half a mile to stop next to another gleaming aircraft.

'When we're in the office you barely speak to me except to issue orders. And yet when we're in company you won't stop…*touching* me. You treat me like I'm some attention-seeking pet. And frankly I'm sick of it.'

She stopped, realised her breathing was as fitful as her heartbeat and her face was burning with what must be high colour.

Beside her, Joao stiffened. 'I wasn't aware my touch was so offensive.'

It isn't.

Saffie was fiercely glad her pursed lips stopped the

words from spilling free. But the task of holding them in caused another tremor to course through her body.

He saw her reaction, and his face grew tauter. 'Perhaps, for the sake of avoiding hyperventilation, we should discuss this when we reach our destination?' he quipped coolly with one spiked eyebrow.

'I'm quite capable of having a civilised conversation.'

'I beg to differ. You seem quite worked up about...whatever is on your mind.'

She opened her mouth to contradict him but he was alighting, holding his hand out to her while his gaze dared her to refuse. She knew it wasn't beyond him to transfer her bodily from SUV to helicopter, so she let him assist her.

Minutes later, they were airborne. And since this particular chopper provided no privacy, Saffie had to hold her tongue as they flew over stunning skyscrapers in the heart of Sao Paolo, then tightly packed and precariously stacked concrete housing that constituted the dirt-poor *favelas*.

Momentarily, Saffie curbed her own angst in the face of such deprivation, and when her gaze flicked to Joao, he was staring down, too, his face frozen tight.

Did you grow up here? she wanted to ask. But she didn't want to invade his privacy just to satisfy her curiosity. Perhaps he caught the question in her eyes when his head swivelled towards her because he shook his head.

'One *favela* looks pretty much like another but the place of my birth is a little further away, nearer Rio.'

The bleakness in his voice made her want to throw her arms around him, but if these past three weeks had taught her anything, it was that she liked bodily contact with Joao a little too much.

Which was why she was fighting his careless caresses. It was that or go mad or, worse, beg him to never stop.

The *favelas* gave way to a lusher landscape, stretching for miles in every direction. She'd been to Joao's estate in

Rio but not to this one. Unable to stem her anticipation, she leaned forward.

The giant shape of a white stallion etched into the side of a hill was breathtaking. It was Joao's personal crest and was stamped on every piece of stationery and property he owned.

They soared over rambling stables and open fields where stallions raced across the grass. Over giant gazebos and *churrascaria* pits smoking prime meats. Over cattle grazing on endless pampas to one side, and tennis courts, and not one but four separate summerhouses attached to Olympic-sized swimming pools on the other.

Then, past stylishly tiered, beautiful landscaped lawns, they soared over a sprawling red-roofed villa with several interconnecting wings that looked as if several properties had been artistically fused into one.

Her lips were still parted in awe when they landed on a designated helipad.

Saffie stepped out to a soft breeze that ruffled her hair.

Joao glanced over when she reached up to secure it, his lips pursed.

By the time they made the short trip up the steps to one of many entrances to the house, two dozen staff were lined up, all wearing pristine uniforms with a discreet stallion logo pressed into their nameplates.

Joao greeted them in his native tongue, then glanced at Saffie. 'These are the core staff you'll need to work with to prepare for Lavinia's arrival. You know how many staff work here, so if you need more just consult with the head housekeeper.'

At the last count, she knew they numbered seventy-five, just to take care of the villa and the grounds. 'Do all the staff live on the estate?' she asked as he stepped into a *salon* that looked as if it belonged in the pages of a glossy magazine.

'Like with the executive condos, I provide extensive housing to all my top staff. I believe it's easier that way.'

And as perks went, they were second to none. Saffie knew it was why Joao remained the number one desired boss to work for. But she was beginning to think it was more than that. 'Easier or because you want to make a bigger difference in their lives?' she asked before she could stop herself.

He froze in the middle of one of the many hallways that branched off into the villa.

'Are you attempting to romanticise my actions, Saffie?' he queried with a quiet, softly dangerous tone that filled every pore of her skin as surely as his body filled her vision.

Behind him a painting she very much suspected was an original Mondrian failed to hold her attention because the man staring at her was a masterpiece head and shoulders above all others.

He was even more to her, and to so many. Did he see that? Or was he blind to it all? 'You said you wanted to teach your... Pueblo that he was wrong to make himself your enemy. But you're so much more than one man's opinion of you, Joao. I've seen people react to shallow, selfish rich folks who throw their money around. That's not what I see with those who work for you. I've also seen the company poll. Do you know how many people said they would work for you even if you cut their salary in half?'

For the briefest moment, he looked mildly shocked, shaken even. Then his mouth tightened. 'I'm not exactly sure where you're going with this but let me assure you of one thing. I'm no one's knight in shining armour,' he answered tersely.

The slight quake in her body sent her fingers to her hair only to recall it wasn't in a bun. 'Just because you don't want the prize doesn't mean it doesn't belong to you,' she muttered.

Joao's gaze dropped from where he'd been watching her toy with her hair. For several seconds, he didn't breathe, only watched her with something akin to bewilderment. Then abruptly, he stepped back. 'I have a few calls to make. Since you seem to have a bee in your bonnet about my presence, I'm sure you'll welcome the chance to rest and explore on your own.'

He started to walk away.

'No, I won't,' she said firmly.

Joao knew he should walk away. That the simmering emotions that had left him far from calm since their night in Shanghai were in serious danger of erupting.

'Excuse me?' The question was just to buy himself time, straighten thoughts that lately scattered in her presence.

But nothing seemed to be working. She'd burrowed deep inside him to a point where his thoughts started and ended with Saffie. As for that hard-core masochism he'd developed where the need to touch her felt as vital as breathing? He silently shook his head.

Like an addict, he'd known he was courting trouble. But again, he'd found justification for it. More public appearances with Saffie…just so he had an excuse to touch her without falling foul of their agreement in Shanghai. Just so he could allay his dread at the thought of her leaving. As if touching her, making sure she was by his side, was all he needed at any given time.

He still desired her. And even before their night together was over, he knew it would never be enough. That he should've negotiated for more.

But they'd agreed. And he'd left his bed the next morning knowing he'd rather she stayed by his side, as his assistant, than left because he wanted her in his bed with a fever that consumed him.

Saffie shrugged. 'Thanks to your actions, the world

seems to think we're either about to or already are sleeping together. I don't want to *rest* and I don't want to *explore* or do anything until you explain to me why you've been acting as if I belong to you when we're in public.'

Since that was exactly what he'd been doing, Joao experienced a pang of guilt. One which he immediately justified. 'You mean beyond sending out a clear message that I won't welcome my assistant being poached?'

Anger and a touch of disappointment flitted across her face. 'Don't take me for a fool, Joao. That message could've been relayed with a few words from you like you did with Will Ashby in Shanghai.'

He padded back to where she stood, fighting the temptation to touch her. When the warmth of her body called temptingly to his.

But even as he tried to talk himself down, his hand rose, hovered over skin so smooth and alluring he felt his heart flip over. Only by flattening it against the wall beside her head, and gritting his teeth, did he stop the urge.

Saffie tilted her head, boldly met his eyes, demanding an answer without the faintest knowledge that she set his emotions aflame with a simple look. Or did she know? She'd made herself indispensable in one area of his life. Was she making herself indispensable in that part of his life he'd never let anyone else?

She licked her bottom lip, a nervous action that left him far too weak and far too vulnerable for his liking.

Again, he knew he should walk away. And yet he found himself answering.

'You wish to know why?' he asked after several, pulse-destroying seconds had passed. 'I'm trying to understand you, Saffie. I'm trying to see beneath the insane need to the *why*.'

Her delicate nostrils pinched. 'Why what?'

'Why I expose things to you that no one else knows.

Why lately I tolerate your mild insubordination and you delving into matters that don't concern you when I would've fired others on the spot. Why I can't stop you from getting under my skin,' he breathed.

Her eyes darkened and a slight tremor went through her. He yearned to explore that reaction but he knew he was already skating on the edge. From that moment he'd confessed he needed her, his world had tilted on its axis. That visceral confession seemed to be one he couldn't take back no matter how hard he tried.

'It still doesn't explain why you touch me, Joao.'

The breath expelled from his lungs; he watched it ruffle the soft hair at her temple and once again fought the desire to touch her. 'Do I need to spell it out? I still desire you. But we agreed on one night, and I don't want to give you an excuse to walk away.' He gave a short, self-deprecating laugh. 'But you needn't worry. I may have let myself get carried away but I don't intend to act on it.'

She licked her lips, and the simmer turned into a torrent. 'Do I want to know the reasons behind that conclusion?'

A sliver of ice cut through the heat, scalpel-sharp and re-opening wounds he believed long decayed. 'Because blind lust jeopardises everything. My father had a wife and children of his own at home, and yet he repeatedly gave into weakness, which led to my unwanted birth. And then he spent a significant amount of time attempting to diminish my existence. *We* gave into blind lust, too, didn't we? Look where we are.'

Sharp lacerations bloodied her heart and for a moment Saffie couldn't breathe through the pain to tell him he was wrong. That he was a far better man than his father could ever hope to be. That Shanghai wasn't a mistake for her.

He placed one long finger over her lips before she could respond. 'No need for more protest. I know where I stand.

And you were right when you said this needed to stop.' He dropped his hand and stepped back. 'You won't need to suffer my touch any longer.'

With that, he strode away.

She was still there, her heart thudding dully in her chest, when Rubinho, the head butler, found her.

'Would madam like some refreshments in the salon or in her suite?' the young man asked.

She tried to focus beyond her deafening despair. 'I... My suite would be fine.'

He nodded briskly. 'Allow me to escort you to the south wing, *por favor*.'

She followed on wooden feet through several more stunning hallways and sweeping staircases.

Villa Sábia was magnificent in a way that awed and lifted the most depleted spirit. And Saffie was no less immune to the magic of the sprawling estate as she took in the authentic Brazilian architecture, the ethnic woodwork and international objets d'art that had gone into making the property one of the most stunning in the world.

By the time they approached the hallway that led to the south wing, she understood why she'd fended off numerous requests from top magazines to photograph Joao's home.

Style, luxury, elegance, comfort. There wasn't one piece of furniture or art that didn't seamlessly elevate the true beauty of the villa. Not a surface she didn't want to caress or just stand and admire in awe.

Her suite was no exception. And she wasn't surprised when her love of Joao's villa directly fused with her dangerously emotional sentiments for the man himself.

She knew it might be a futile attempt but she tried to counteract it by immersing herself in her own work. An hour after arrival she'd forced herself to eat a light tapas meal, after which she'd met with the senior household staff to discuss menus, wine and the guest list for the reception dinner planned in Lavinia's honour the next night.

Afterwards, she was going through her diary when a reminder pinged that made her breath catch.

She'd officially reached the end of her first trimester yesterday. Her morning sickness had passed but Joao still insisted on the doctor accompanying them on their trips.

The same doctor would be conducting another health check tomorrow morning, including the ultrasound. Her heart skipped a beat, swelling with a love almost impossible to contain.

Everything she'd wanted was nestled in her womb.

Almost everything...

And she would have to be content with that because Joao had made his stance clear. He might desire her, but the emotional risk wasn't worth taking for him. Perhaps he even secretly couldn't wait to see the back of her once she'd fulfilled her usefulness on the Archer deal?

The stark agony that accompanied that realisation made her set her tablet aside. Shakily, she walked to the edge of the large terrace she'd chosen for her meeting. Beyond three tiers of landscaped garden and off the right of a trellised gazebo she saw the largest of the four swimming pools, sparkling in the late-afternoon sun.

She had two free hours before dinner and, eager to occupy herself with something other than her anguishing thoughts, she hurried to her suite and changed into a swimsuit.

The bra cups of her bikini felt a little snug and she avoided looking at herself in the mirror as she secured the ties. She hadn't had time to buy new ones, so they'd just have to do.

Throwing on a silk beach robe, she fished out her sunglasses and sun cream and headed downstairs.

At the poolside, Saffie discarded her robe and stood on

the edge of the pool, her face lifted up to the warm sun, wishing she could blank her mind of the anxiety for just a minute. Or, failing that, wishing she had a crystal ball to see into a future where she was fully content with just her and her babies.

Where the absence of Joao didn't cut her like a knife.

Shaking her head free of fairy tales, Saffie lowered herself into the pool. She swam lazy laps, the joy of the cool water washing over her soothing her senses, until thirst drove her out. After drinking half a glass of her lime-based punch, delivered while she'd been in the water, she returned to sit on the wide shallow steps of the pool, her feet in the water.

Then, as so often happened in her quiet moments, her mind went to the babies growing within her.

Her breath caught softly.

Twins.

Double the love. Double the joy. Her hand glided over her stomach as her eyes drifted shut and momentary sadness overwhelmed her. She would've given anything for her foster mother to have been alive, to share her happiness.

The letter from her foster mother, written in the last weeks of her life, the one Saffie kept between the pages of her childhood diary but knew every word of, flipped through her mind.

Don't dwell on the past.
Find your own happiness.
Never settle for loneliness.

I'm almost there, she said softly under her breath. But I think I need more, Mum, her heart defiantly added.

As if he were configured by her imagination, her skin began to tingle with hyperawareness that only came with Joao's presence.

The shape of that *more*.

'Saffie.' Her name was a warm, deep throb.

Breath snagged in her throat, she opened her eyes to find him a few feet away. His gaze was riveted on the hand on her stomach; a depth of emotion she'd never seen before blazing in his eyes.

Her fingers spread, an instinctive awareness of her womanhood that came out of nowhere. 'Joao. Did you want something?'

'*Sim*, I do.' His gaze didn't rise from her belly but he continued to speak. 'The Brazilian sun isn't one you want to underestimate. Did you put any sunscreen on when you came out here?'

She swallowed, not because of the question but because in all their time together she'd never seen Joao clad in all white. The effect of the white linen trousers that sat low on his hips and the unbuttoned white linen shirt threw his vibrant olive complexion into stunning relief. When that was topped with his slightly dishevelled hair, whisky-gold eyes and the faint stubble caressing his jaw, Saffie was in danger of being completely overwhelmed by his presence. 'I was going to swim again before—'

He made an impatient sound under his breath before striding over to grab the sunscreen bottle she'd left on the table between two loungers.

Without care for his clothes, Joao returned and brazenly waded into the pool. One step up from where she sat, he took up position behind her and flipped open the lid of the bottle.

'What are you doing?' she asked breathlessly.

'Helping you avoid sunburn. Lift your hair out of the way, Saffie,' he ordered, his tone a husky rasp that wrecked havoc with her equilibrium.

Caught under a spell she couldn't, and secretly didn't want to, extricate herself from, she sat up straighter, one hand on her belly while the other twisted her hair in a rope and held it up.

Beyond her peripheral vision a bee buzzed, and the earthy, smoky scent of *churrascaria* fire teased the air. Samba music played faintly in the background. But all Saffie could concentrate on was the powerful frame bracketing hers, the smooth exhalations teasing the wispy hairs at her nape.

The combination of the cool cream and warm fingers made her bite back a gasp, then fight harder to suppress a moan as his hand glided in firm strokes across her shoulders. Between one breath and the next, the atmosphere around them thickened, the only sound their arrhythmic breathing and the gentle susurration of the sparkling pool.

Saffie swallowed when both hands moved over her upper back. Back and forth in a seductive dance that made her thighs clench, made her squeeze her eyes shut as need clamoured dizzyingly through her.

Joao encountered the string at her back and gave an impatient grunt. 'I'm going to untie this,' he said in a low, deep voice, his breath brushing her earlobe and sending a fresh shiver through her. 'The staff are discreet. You won't be seen. Okay?'

The sound she made under her breath was pathetically weak but he took it for the assent it was and tugged the strings free.

The wicked combination of damp, loosened material and his expert touch instantaneously stiffened her sensitive nipples into hard, needy peaks.

Behind her, Joao exhaled harshly as his hands moved down her waist to the small of her back, then around to brush her hand away before gliding over her midriff and belly.

The doctor had warned her that with twins she would start to show very soon, and over the last few days a definite bump had appeared, and with it the wondrous ability to take her breath away simply by looking down at her belly.

'*Você é tão bonita,*' he whispered under his breath, almost to himself as he caressed the taut skin of her belly.

But she heard. And understood.

You are so beautiful.

She started to turn towards him. 'Joao...' The sudden urge to cover his hand with hers blossomed but before she could give into the insanity, his fingers moved up to the lower curve of her heavy breasts.

This time she couldn't smother her moan or stop her head from lolling back against his shoulder.

Joao exhaled heavily, then his hands moved behind her to secure the ties again. '*Cristo, isso é loucura,*' he muttered tersely under his breath.

No, he wasn't the only one going insane.

'I trust you can take care of the rest?' he growled in her ear.

She gave a jerky little nod but his hand lingered for a pulse-thumping five seconds before he stood up abruptly, his feet splashing lightly as he stepped out of the pool.

'Don't stay out here too long. I've asked for dinner to be served at seven.'

Saffie nodded again, then forced herself to remain still, knowing that if she turned and faced him, if she so much as caught a glint of hunger in his eyes she would do the unthinkable and beg him to sweep her off her feet, carry her to his bed and make love to her.

Several minutes after he'd left, she remained in the throes of sensation, her oversensitive body unwilling to release her from Joao's all-powerful thrall.

But it was more than that. Saffie knew the problem was her heart and the unstoppable yearning growing with each second.

Just as she knew she had to find a solution soon…before she reached the dreaded point of no return.

The dress she chose for dinner was a stylish one-shouldered below-the-knee design that clung to her breasts and hips. The soft cotton accentuated her slight bump and she caught Joao's gaze on her belly when she arrived in the living room.

He waved the butler away and pulled out her chair, his gaze lingering over her throat and bare arms as he retook his seat. 'No signs of a burn?'

'None at all,' she replied with a forced lightness.

By silent mutual agreement, they made light, business conversation, choosing not to discuss the sensually charged scene at the pool.

'You think Lavinia will enjoy the soccer match?'

His lips compressed before he swallowed a mouthful of the exclusive Oliviera red burgundy he enjoyed with his steaks. 'My teams aren't at the top of the national and international leagues for nothing,' he stated with the casual arrogance of man who knew the kind of power and influence he wielded.

After purchasing his first Brasileirãoclub, Clube de Magdalena Santina, he'd spent millions seducing top players from around the world to his team. They'd immediately started winning trophies, the most prized of which currently sitting on a mantel in Joao's Rio de Janeiro villa.

'And the team they're playing against tomorrow?'

'Below us in the championship. Where they belong,' he added with a hardened edge of satisfaction.

The curious answer triggered a memory. 'That's your father's team, isn't it?'

'*Sim,*' he confirmed with a grim smile.

'Is he going to be there tomorrow?'

He rolled the stem of his glass between long fingers. 'I should think so.'

Enlightenment widened her eyes. 'You knew he was, that's why you wanted Lavinia to be there.'

Joao shrugged. 'I thought it was time to stop dancing around her decision and make her face us once and for all. Everything is in place, I trust?'

'Of course.'

He picked up his glass in a silent toast. '*Bom*. Here's to all our hard work paying off.'

CHAPTER EIGHT

SUNDAY DAWNED BRIGHT and glorious.

Having taken advantage of the king-size bed on Joao's private jet, Saffie found the effects of jet lag were minimal, which helped a little with her frame of mind as she took a long, luxurious shower and dressed for breakfast.

The flared white halter-neck dress swung soothingly around her knees as she left her suite.

Carlotta, Joao's deputy housekeeper, met her at the bottom of the stairs and smilingly led her through another series of hallways to a vast courtyard overlooking the second largest swimming pool on the estate.

Joao was already seated, lazily flicking through a Portuguese newspaper. He lowered it as she approached, his gaze hooded as it rested on her face.

'*Bom dia*. Did you sleep well?'

'*Sim, obrigado.*'

One corner of his mouth lifted, unmistakeable satisfaction framing his smile. 'You're making good strides with your Portuguese. Soon you'll be more fluent than I am.'

'You're much too competitive to hand me that advantage.'

A shadow passed over his face but he didn't comment, instead offering her the fruit platter, and nodding at the butler, who stepped forward to fill her cup with aromatic tea.

Calmly, he went back to his paper, leaving her to wonder what she'd said to garner that reaction.

She was almost done with breakfast when Carlotta stepped onto the terrace. '*Senhor*, the doctor is here. We have set him up in the Redondo Suite, as instructed,' she said in slightly accented English.

He thanked her and rose. 'Shall we?'

She remained seated. 'Has something happened? You seem to be…in a mood.'

His lips twisted. 'Do I?'

She pressed her lips together, then decided to forge ahead with the elephant in the room. 'If it's about what happened by the pool yesterday—'

'That was a mistake,' he interrupted with calm precision. 'But perhaps it's precipitated the need for a few changes.'

Her heart plummeted. 'What kind of changes?' she asked with a voice that tasted ashen.

Joao hesitated. 'Necessary changes we'll discuss after the Archer deal is put to bed. One that might mean I remain here in Brazil.'

He was planning to stay in Brazil without her?

She felt the colour drain from her face, her windpipe squeezing alarmingly. 'What…exactly are you saying?'

'The doctor's waiting, Saffie. Let's not get drawn into protracted conversations.'

She wanted to remind him that he was Joao Oliviera. That he called shots in his sleep and grown men jumped. But he was already stepping behind her chair, pointedly urging her into movement.

The Redondo Suite was exactly as described, a circular guest suite with spectacular views and breathtaking murals etched into its domelike ceiling. The Brazilian doctor who'd travelled with them from London greeted them and efficiently set up the machine.

Within minutes, the sound of twin heartbeats filled the room.

Between Shanghai and London, Joao had ordered the most sophisticated ultrasound machine and Saffie's breath caught as the 3D image of her still-forming babies loomed large.

'Their growth chart is excellent. Well within the expected parameters,' the doctor said. 'Your babies are doing fine.'

She chanced a glance at where Joao sat at the end of her bed, his thigh brushing her knee. He was staring transfixed at the screen, his throat working. A moment later, his gaze shifted to her stomach, and when it flicked up to meet hers, his expression was awed.

He isn't unaffected, her brain screeched loudly. *This isn't just a blind asset-claiming for him.*

Her heart started to hammer for a completely different, breathtaking reason. Did she dare hope for more? Should she risk telling him she was considering staying beyond three months?

'While it's still a little early, I can hazard a guess as to the sex of the babies if either of you wish to know?'

'They are healthy. That's all that matters,' Joao said.

But Saffie shook her head. 'I want to know, please. I can't stand the suspense.'

The doctor smiled. 'There's a strong likelihood that you're expecting twin boys.'

Joao inhaled sharply, his face tightening with raw, unfettered emotion before the mask slid back into place. His hand rose to hover beside her. After a moment he swallowed and dropped it back down.

And just like that, wild hope turned to dust.

She kept her gaze firmly fixed on the doctor for the remainder of the examination, and breathed with strained relief when it was over.

As Joao escorted him out, the sound of rotor blades filled the air.

Lavinia's arrival forestalled any private interaction with Joao, a fact Saffie wasn't sure whether to be pleased or further agonised about.

The older woman, bright-eyed and raring to go, promptly demanded an extensive tour of the estate.

In the custom-made air-conditioned buggy, Saffie caught Lavinia's subtle questions, probing Joao's values and intentions.

As she listened to him field them with a dextrous mix of charm and intellect, Saffie also realised one thing.

While Joao might be locked in battle with his father and was bitter about his upbringing, it hadn't diminished the part of him that selflessly provided for those in need or gave back to people who served him. He could have easily become selfish and close-minded over his start in life. But he'd done the opposite. He'd provided jobs to a staggering amount of Brazilians, invested in organic, self-sustaining ventures that were the envy of most organisations, and there was the unabashed pride in his heritage that throbbed in his voice when he spoke of his country.

She'd known he was a man of integrity from her first professional interaction with him.

And as their helicopter came in to land in the middle of the football stadium that held one hundred and twenty thousand screaming soccer fans chanting Joao's name, Saffie knew there was no point talking herself out of the inevitable because it'd already happened.

She was in love with Joao Oliviera.

The earth-shaking admission both terrified and thrilled her. She placed a balled fist against her heart, as if it would stop its reckless pounding.

'What's wrong?' The question was sharp.

Startled, she realised that even while he'd greeted his players, introduced them to a goggle-eyed Lavinia, and acknowledged the crowd, he'd kept an eye on her.

She hurriedly composed her features. 'Nothing. The crowd's a little overwhelming, that's all.'

He nodded tersely. 'Then we will retire to somewhere more private. Come.'

He held out his arm to her, his gaze enigmatic as he

watched her. She was reminded of their conversation and his promise that he wouldn't touch her, and her heart skipped a beat. But the moment she took his arm, he held out the other to Lavinia, disavowing her of the notion that it was anything other than simple courtesy, and led them off the red carpet laid out especially for him on the field.

The immense owner's box granting unfettered access to the field was decked with twenty-five sumptuous luxury leather seats, while on the tables vintage champagne, oysters, caviar and other glorious canapés teased every appetite.

After introductions were made to the mayor and several dignitaries, Saffie left Joao to further dazzle Lavinia and took a seat as the countdown to kick-off began.

But even removed from the power gathering, she couldn't stop her gaze from devouring Joao's stunning male beauty, from wondering when it'd happened.

At what exact moment had her heart decided to risk everything by falling in love with her boss?

What did it matter?

It was done. Her heart belonged to him.

The only problem was, did he want it? Now or ever? Or was that promise of distance just the beginning of a chasm she might not be able to breach?

Her heart dropped, her fingers clenching painfully at the searing truth that she might have to. That the cardinal sin of falling in love with an unattainable man might be her undoing.

A throat cleared beside her. Again, Saffron startled, heat rushing to her face when she realised she'd been staring at Joao like a lovelorn fool, probably projecting her feelings to the world.

The middle-aged man staring at her had hard features born of harsh living, but surprisingly kind, shrewd eyes.

'I don't believe we were introduced, probably because I arrived late. I'm Ernesto Blanco.'

Memory fell into place, and her breath caught. 'You're Joao's mentor.'

His brown eyes widened fractionally as he held out his hand. 'I'm not sure whether to be surprised you know about me or astonished that Joao used that term for our relationship.'

She thought it best not to mention that Joao hadn't. 'I'm Saffron Everhart.'

'*Sim*, the assistant worth her weight in gold.'

'Now it's my turn to be surprised.'

'Because you don't think you are?'

She shrugged. 'Because you're aware of my existence but I didn't know about yours until…recently.'

Ernest tilted his beer bottle in Joao's direction. 'Ah, but isn't that very much like the man we both know? A grandmaster at compartmentalising?'

As if pulled by powerful magnets, her gaze swung to Joao. He was staring at her with an electric gaze that rooted her to the spot for several seconds before swinging to Ernesto.

'Perhaps not for much longer,' Ernesto murmured.

She dragged her gaze back to him. 'I don't know what you mean.'

'You will, soon enough,' he said with a cryptic smile.

Saffie knew Joao was approaching from the way every cell zinged to life.

Ernesto stood and the two men clasped hands in that sombre way men who knew each other's gravest experiences did.

But within the older man's eyes, she spotted quiet pride and affection, the kind Saffron had only felt for a brief, blessed period before she'd lost the only parent she'd ever known.

Her heart plummeted further.

If Joao hadn't accepted the love of the father figure who'd pulled him out of a dismal future, what hope did she have that he'd accept hers?

The two men engaged in a low-murmured conversation before Ernesto moved away and Joao's hypnotic eyes slid to her. He didn't speak, but his gaze slid over the loose, stylish knot she'd heaped her hair into, then lower to the diamond studs in her ears and the simple diamond chains at her throat and wrists, over the sky-blue flared sundress and matching platform shoes.

Every second that passed with his eyes on her made her feel *alive*. Vital.

So unbearably needy for an emotional connection.

In that moment she didn't want to contemplate a time when she would be deprived of even the sight of him. But just as she'd had to accept the diagnosis of her mother's illness, she had to make room for the fact that the love foolishly swelling inside with every breath she took might not find its rightful home.

The very thought threatened to shatter her into a thousand useless pieces.

Joao's hands suddenly gripped hers. 'You're pale, Saffie. Are you unwell?' he rasped with fierce urgency.

She hurriedly shook her head and tugged her hands from his. 'No, I'm fine. But…we need to have that talk. I'd prefer it to be sooner rather than later.'

A shot of apprehension clouded his narrowed eyes. 'Any reason for the sudden urgency?'

Yes, my heart is on the line.

'Call me overoptimistic but I think the Archer deal is yours so, really, I've fulfilled my end of the bargain, don't you agree?'

An undecipherable look crossed his face. '*Sim*. If that is what you prefer, we will talk later.'

Saffie forced a nod. 'Thank you.'

Joao led her to the front row. Beyond the panoramic windows, the band struck the first notes of the national anthem.

From the moment of kick-off, Joao's team displayed breathtaking skill. With Ernesto taking up the self-appointed mantle of explaining the intricacies of soccer to Lavinia, Joao was freed to fully immerse himself in the sport he loved, a fact that didn't seem to please the man in the adjacent owner's box.

When Saffie caught his gaze for a third time, she forced herself to examine him. A second later, she knew she was staring at Pueblo Oliviera.

Her gaze flew to Joao. He was staring at her, a grim little smile on lips.

'That's your father, isn't it?' she asked a little redundantly.

When Joao's gaze shifted to the man, it was as if he'd been hewn from ice. 'If you mean the man whose sperm sired me, then yes,' he rasped grimly. 'But he doesn't deserve the title you bestow on him and he never will.'

The final whistle was a sharp trill, breaking the tense atmosphere.

Lavinia turned to Joao, a wide smile on her face. 'That was incredible. Now I get the whole buzz around this game.'

Joao inclined his head, made the appropriate responses as celebratory champagne was served, but Saffie could cut the tension cloaking him with a scalpel.

It thickened unbearably when Pueblo Oliviera strolled uninvited into their box.

Conversation trailed off but Pueblo, a man in his late fifties with salt-and-pepper hair, and face and frame that unmistakeably resembled Joao's, was undaunted. He exchanged greetings with guests, then sauntered over to where Joao stood with Lavinia.

For several minutes, he ignored his son, while ingratiat-

ing himself with Lavinia. But even while the older woman
smiled and remained gracious, her attention repeatedly
strayed to Joao, seeking his input on the match, the wine
in the region, his plans for Archer Cruise Liners, rumoured
to be the investment she'd established her name on.

'I intend to keep it,' Joao answered. 'It's not a secret that
I have Greek shipbuilders on contract for my own liners.
But I am prepared to rename it the Archer Oliviera Cruise
Line, if you're amenable.'

The older woman gasped. 'You would do that?'

Joao nodded. 'You have my word. Which is more than
I can say for some.'

Pueblo snorted. 'I suggest you wait until it's written in
indelible ink before you believe him, Mrs Archer.'

'One thing your son has a reputation for, Mr Oliviera,
is never breaking his word,' Saffron blurted before she
could stop herself.

Beside her, Joao stiffened, but when she glanced at him,
his face was woodenly neutral, his fixed stare on his father.

Pueblo's eyebrows slowly went up as he slid a scathing
glance over Saffron. 'I see you have another eager woman
racing to your defence,' he said, addressing his son for the
first time. 'I thought I'd seen the last of that with your pa-
thetic mother.'

Saffie's breath caught but Joao responded evenly. 'We
both know she was doing that simply to score money for
drugs. The question here is who is more deplorable for ex-
ploiting a drug addict in return for sex?'

Pueblo went red in the face, fury steaming from him as
he took a menacing step towards his son. His mouth worked
but no words emerged.

'What precisely do you want to say to me?' Joao taunted
icily. 'That I'm worthless? That I'll amount to nothing? Or
that you've been proven wrong on your every prediction but
still believe you hold the upper hand in the game?'

His father gave a scoffing laugh. 'You truly think you're better than me?'

Joao spread his arms wide and smirked. 'My achievements speak volumes for themselves.'

Either Pueblo Oliviera was too dense to see he was nowhere in his son's league or too proud to admit when he was beaten. Saffie suspected it was the latter.

'I was winning long before you were born,' he growled.

'And still you haven't learned your lesson, that all it takes is a little nurturing to make the difference between long-term success and instant gratification. I see what I want, I claim it and I *keep* it, while you grab then toss without seeing the value in anything.'

The flash of uncertainty briefly blunted Pueblo's fury. But a moment later, the older man's gaze flicked around the room, saw the audience he'd garnered.

Without a word, he turned on his heel and left, his small entourage trailing him.

The tight expression on Joao's face eased, enough for her to catch a glimpse of his agony. Unable to stop the visceral need to comfort him, she placed her hand on his arm.

Joao started, his gaze flicking to Saffie as sharp blades continued to lash at his insides. Confrontation with Pueblo had always been on the cards but he'd underestimated the older man's power to unsettle him even further. Or perhaps he was feeling it even more since he hadn't quite managed to return to an even keel since Saffie had announced she was leaving.

Or perhaps the answer lay in the features he'd looked into that had seemed so much like his own he'd spent an alarmed moment wondering what else he'd inherited from the man who'd sired him.

Was he deluding himself that he was the better man? Was his DNA programmed to repeat history and damn his relationship with his unborn children even before it'd begun?

He swallowed, a quiet terror rumbling within him he couldn't stop.

You're so much more than one man's opinion of you.

He wanted to cling to Saffie's words. But was he?

He'd shown that he could make money and wield his fortune with admirable expertise. But beyond that where else had he been tested? Certainly not on the emotional battlefield. He'd never let anyone close enough to test his mettle in that arena.

But you have a chance now.

Did he? His gaze fell to her slightly rounded belly, and the twin sons growing within her. He stifled the sharp yearning cloying through him. He still didn't know whether Saffie intended to take that chance from him.

But he could take steps to alter that. He could ensure he at least got a fighting chance.

He gritted his teeth, the determination to make that happen settling deeper into him.

Saffie watched as an expression shifted over his features, a betraying yearning, before he snuffed that out, too.

But that glimpse had rebirthed her wild hope.

Yesterday, he'd admitted he wanted her.

Could they not build on that? With a little time, couldn't she show him that, while their foundation had been based on the physical, there could be more? *They* could be more?

He turned to Lavinia. 'My apologies for the interruption,' he said.

The older woman shook her head, her gaze introspective. 'No need, Joao. There's a reason my own sons aren't by my side during this transition. Family is complicated.'

As if a switch had been flicked, the atmosphere lightened. Conversation flowed until Lavinia, having spent another fifteen minutes talking to Ernesto, suddenly turned to Joao. 'I understand there's another project of yours I need to see.'

Joao frowned, spoke sharply to Ernesto in Portuguese. The older man gave a sad little smile and responded. After another heated exchange, Ernesto shrugged.

Joao's lips firmed, displeasure clouding his face.

'What's going on?' Saffie asked.

'Ernesto insists on poking his nose where it doesn't belong.'

But Lavinia, sensing a rare weakening in her host, pressed her advantage. 'Forget another dinner party in my honour or whatever other wonders of your beautiful country you have in store for me. Show me this project and you will have my answer by morning.'

His lips firmed. 'This has nothing to do with our negotiations.'

'But it's everything to do with who you are,' Ernesto pressed with quiet, steely insistence that gave a glimpse of the willpower it'd taken to nurture an overwhelming personality like Joao's through the formative years of his life.

Joao didn't immediately respond and for the first time, Saffie spotted a sliver of vulnerability in the eyes that zeroed in on her and stayed. 'Joao? What are you talking about?' she probed.

His gaze shifted away, and she was left with the peculiar sensation that he was hiding himself from her, protecting himself from exposure.

'It seems I must rise to one final challenge,' he said tersely.

They left the stadium as they'd arrived, in Joao's helicopter. But with one further guest in the form of Ernesto, and a pregnant silence nobody seemed in the mood to break.

Flying north, they headed for the outskirts of Sao Paolo, where there were more wide open spaces than *favelas* and neat little houses that spoke to a middle-class neighbourhood. More untouched land spread beneath them for another few miles before the chopper started to descend.

The setting sun bathed the brand-new housing development in golden colour as they landed in a large, beautifully landscaped park.

Saffie knew all of Joao's business concerns off the top of her head. This housing project wasn't one of them.

'Where are we?' she asked after he helped her out.

Ernesto smiled. 'Joao Cidade.'

Saffie's eyes widened. 'Joao City?' she translated.

'No one calls it that,' Joao interjected briskly.

'Except everyone who lives in it,' Ernesto parried.

She'd counted thirty blocks, set at architecturally pleasing angles from each other. About a quarter of a mile away, cranes and diggers were busy constructing another development.

The grounds were paved and landscaped, the apartments the kind that would command several hundreds of thousands in London.

Even before the chopper's rotors had quietened, a large group had formed in the park, families calling out to Joao in deferential greeting. He acknowledged the greetings with nods but he remained tense, his gaze darting repeatedly to Saffie's as they toured the nearest block.

They passed a small garden where someone had carved *Joao Cidade* into a bench with hearts on either side.

Saffie stopped. 'Joao City…you built this, didn't you?' she whispered.

'He not only built and is still building five hundred homes per quarter, he gives them away free of charge to families from *favelas* all over Brazil every December,' Ernesto expanded with unmistakeable pride.

Saffie's jaw dropped. 'You do?'

'Extraordinary,' Lavinia agreed. 'Simply extraordinary.'

Joao said nothing, and when they entered an apartment large enough to comfortably house a mid-sized family, she watched him stride over to one window to look out onto a courtyard where a fountain splashed water onto cobbled stones.

'How long has this been going on?'

He tensed at Saffie's question and flicked her another neutral glance. 'I started the process eight years ago. Bureaucratic red tape meant it took another two years to get off the ground. The first phase finished eighteen months after that.'

'So you've been rehousing families for four years?' Mild shock coloured her voice. For a man who didn't want children and didn't believe in families, it was staggering. And the hope that kept wanting to push through surged again. Enough to draw shaky breath into her lungs.

Perhaps something of what she was experiencing showed on her face. He took a step towards her.

'Saffie—'

They were interrupted by a small commotion at the front door. Turning, she saw a pregnant mother with two toddlers clutching at her skirts hesitantly address Joao.

When he gave a curt nod, she entered, and Saffie saw that she clutched a bouquet of flowers. Tears spilled from her eyes as she spoke in rapid Portuguese.

Saffie didn't need a translator to know she was thanking Joao for changing her life. He withstood her effusive gratitude with a staid demeanour, only cracking a smile when one child came forward at her mother's urging to utter a solemn, *'Obrigado, Senhor Oliviera.'*

Saffie felt tears prick her own eyes. She quickly blinked them back, aware that Joao hadn't moved from the pillar of stone he'd turned into. For whatever reason, he'd wanted to keep this special deed under wraps.

Why, she didn't completely understand. But she could guess.

Deep down, Joao was attempting to rewrite his own history. Giving back where he'd been cruelly denied.

She wanted to shake him, tell him it wasn't a weakness. One look at his stiff profile warned her against tackling it here. Now.

Ernesto and Lavinia rejoined them and they left.

They were halfway to the helicopter when she noticed he'd left the flowers behind.

Lavinia left within an hour of returning to Villa Sábia, but not before announcing her intention to sell her empire to Joao.

Joao's response was triumphant but curiously solemn.

The formal announcement was scheduled for Monday morning, Brazilian time. Saffie had already sent an approved press release to London and New York to be circulated concurrently.

Now, two hours later, she strolled onto the edge of the first-floor wraparound terrace of the north wing, her heart once again hammering with panic and wild hope. The sun had long set, cicadas wide awake and chirping in the gardens below.

Behind her, one of the two dozen bottles of Krug champagne she'd had placed in the wine cellar for this very celebration chilled in a silver ice bucket. The silk wrap she'd brought out in case the breeze turned cool trailed from her fingers as she strolled from one end of the terrace to the other.

This was more than a celebration for her.

This was the biggest undertaking of her life.

It wasn't every day you confessed your overwhelming feelings to your boss. To an extraordinary man like Joao—

'You've helped me win the biggest deal in my life, yet you pace like the world is on fire.'

She whirled, saw him lounging in the doorway, his eyes brooding, tension still vibrating off him. She wanted to ask why *he* wasn't celebrating.

But she wouldn't be veered off course, a feat he managed all too easily. To focus herself she dropped the wrap on a lounger and went to the ice bucket.

Small platters of Oscietra caviar on crackers, wagyu beef strips and grilled prime lobster bites were laid out on the table.

'I ordered these in case you were hungry.'

'How thoughtful of you.'

She slid a furtive glance at him. His smile as he sauntered forward didn't reach his eyes and she watched as he reached out to pluck the bottle from her nerveless hands with one hand while setting down a large, flat velvet box.

'What's that?'

'We'll get to that in a minute. You can't drink so what's the purpose of the champagne?'

'As you said, you've just closed a deal of a lifetime. I thought one of us should celebrate.'

His lips firmed, and he worked the cork until it popped. Weirdly, it was a flat sound that barely registered in the evening air. Saffie wondered if it was an omen. He poured out two glasses, set the bottle back and made no move to pick up his glass.

Instead, he reached for the velvet box. 'This is for you.' He held it out.

Saffie didn't take it. 'I sort of guessed it might be. I don't want it, Joao.'

His eyes narrowed. 'You don't know what it is.'

'It's another priceless trinket, offered with some sort of unnecessary ulterior motive for simply doing my job.'

Ignoring her, he pried the lid open. Despite herself, her gaze dropped. Along with her heart and her jaw.

Because, by far, this was the most stunning present he'd ever given her. The yellow diamonds were too many to count. He'd probably cleaned out Harry Winston's entire supply for this necklace, never mind the matching teardrop earrings, cuff bracelet and what looked suspiciously like an anklet.

'Why do you do this?' she whispered brokenly.

'I like to reward a job well done.'

'You don't need to buy me, Joao. I'm already—' She stopped herself at the last moment, self-preservation prompting her on a different path. 'Why did you keep the housing project a secret from me?'

The box snapped shut and he tossed it on the table as if it were worth nothing. 'Because it's no one's business but mine.'

The punch of hurt shouldn't have felt so disproportionately agonising, but it did. Because her feelings for him were larger than life.

'There's nothing extraordinary about providing decent homes for those who need them,' he continued with suppressed tension in his voice. 'It's a simple case of supply and demand.'

'Don't belittle your achievements, Joao, especially not one that clearly means so much to you,' she said softly. 'This is where you disappear to on Christmas Day, isn't it?'

Again he smiled an empty smile. 'Watch it. Next you'll be accusing me of playing Santa.'

'I wouldn't stoop so low. But I will say that while you may not think yourself a knight in shining armour, you're certainly theirs.'

'There you go, romanticising again. I'm not the man you take me for, Saffie.'

'There's nothing wrong with admitting that you wished

someone else had done the same for your mother, that if you'd had somewhere to go maybe your childhood would've been less…'

'Less dire? Less horrific? What's the point of wishing? The past cannot be changed.'

'I know. But you're changing the present and the future. I just don't get why you feel it's something to hide.'

'There's a difference between keeping something private and hiding.'

'But why—?'

'Why would I not shout to the world that I'm the son of a prostitute? That my own father didn't want me?' he slanted at her, his voice a bleak desert.

'Joao—'

'Enough, Saffie. Do you still intend to leave me?' The question was raw, charged.

The urge to say *no* flew to her lips. She stopped herself at the last moment. 'That depends.'

A tic throbbed at his temple. 'I'm not good with ultimatums.'

She sucked in a sustaining breath, her palms growing clammy with the realisation that she had to navigate carefully. 'It's not an ultimatum. It's… I just want to know where I stand.'

His jaw rippled. 'You stand where you've always stood. At my right hand.'

Her heart dropped but she forced herself to go on. 'I don't mean with your work, Joao. I mean with this…thing between us. With our babies.' *With my heart.* 'I know you want to claim these babies as yours too but…' she licked dry lips, her heart hammering wildly '…will you do it with me in the picture, too?'

His eyes narrowed. 'What exactly are you asking me, Saffie?'

'You know what I'm asking. A proper commitment.'

He turned to stone. 'One bound in hearts and roses, perhaps?' he added bitingly. 'I'm sorry to disappoint you but that will never be on the table.'

'Why?' The question cried out from her fractured heart.

'Because I don't wish either of us to delude ourselves with frivolous emotions. Now I ask you again, are you going to stay?'

Her heart splintered into sharper pieces that made it harder to breathe. Harder to think. But he was waiting. And as much as she wanted to crumble, she had to stand her ground this one last time.

'No. The Archer deal is done. And so am I.'

He stared at her for several frozen moments. Then from his back pocket he produced a document. 'I had my lawyers draft an agreement.'

Her heart lurched. 'Why?'

'Because I have new interests to protect.' He set it down next to the jewellery box and turned away, abruptly. 'Read it. Then come to my study.'

He left the terrace without a backward glance, his untouched champagne turning as flat as her heart.

CHAPTER NINE

'IS THIS SUPPOSED to be a joke?' Saffie's voice shook like a leaf in a hurricane.

Joao didn't turn from where he stood gazing out of the window. Not for several pounding heartbeats when she walked closer, searching his towering frame for signs of humour.

There were none.

The gritty set of his jaw told her he'd heard her question. The intense gleam in the narrow-eyed gaze he'd finally directed at her when he'd deigned to face her told her everything she'd read in the agreement was exactly as he'd wished it.

'It's a legal document. What do you think?' he taunted, giving her all the confirmation she needed.

Her hand shook as she raised the document. 'It has to be,' she argued. 'Because it says that you're...' She stopped, swallowed disbelieving words she wanted to speak out loud. 'You're seeking custody of my babies!'

'They're my children, too, Saffie,' he corrected with icy patience.

'And...the date on this thing...it's the day after we found out...after the first ultrasound.'

'When have you known me to waste time on something I want?'

'So...your questions just now...you were testing me?'

His gaze clashed with hers, raw power blazing so fiercely, terror tap-danced down her spine. With deceptively casual steps, he approached, reached out and captured her chin, his grip gentle but firm. 'You're carrying my heirs, Saffie, and I'm claiming what's mine.'

The tap-dancing sped up. 'Stop saying that. They're not yours! If anything they're *ours*.'

He shook his head. 'Not if you plan on racing off into the sunset with them.'

She tried to speak but no words emerged. Not for several heart-pounding seconds. 'Please explain to me what's going on, Joao. Make me understand why, a few weeks ago, you ridiculed my intention to have these babies and now you're doing this!'

Again he said nothing for the longest time. Then his hand dropped. 'I told you, reality lends a different perspective.'

'I presented you with two shiny new toys and now you can't help but take them away from me?' she demanded scathingly.

He stared at her for a moment before he sighed. 'I'd rather it not come to that.'

'But it will. Why?' That last word came out in a cringing, bewildered wail.

'I'm simply safeguarding my position. You will never have my agreement to take my children from me, Saffie.'

The document slid from her nerveless fingers, her whole body wracked in tremors. 'My God. To think I defended you to your father.'

'You shouldn't have. Perhaps I may be more his son than you bargained for. I see what I want and I go after it, consequences be damned. Doesn't that sound familiar to you?'

The question was harsh but she caught the barest glimpse of doubt in his eyes, as if he truly believed that about himself.

'We both know that's not true. And it's a little too late to hide behind his shadow. You've been your own man for a very long time, Joao.'

'Perhaps, but DNA speaks for itself,' he said. There was no remorse in his voice. Only true purpose.

'Is that what you intend to teach your sons? To accept that the apple doesn't fall far from the tree so they should accept whatever fate their grandfather and father's DNA hands them?'

His jaw clenched so tight, she thought it'd crack. 'They will never hear Pueblo's name from my lips.'

'That gives me my answer. I don't know if you're reacting to the meeting with your father—' She stopped, feverishly trying to read his face. Something bleak flitted across his face but again he wrestled it under control. 'You're letting him get in your head, Joao. But…even if I'm wrong, I won't sign this document. You know that, don't you?'

His face turned rigid. 'Then you'll be hearing from my lawyers.'

Bewilderment whipped through her. 'Why are you doing this? Was that what Shanghai was about? What these past few weeks have been about?'

His brows clamped together. *Do que voce esta falando?*

'Don't give me that. You know exactly what I'm talking about. The sex…the public displays of affection. Were you softening me up for this…this hostile takeover?'

He strolled to his desk and sat, no, he *lounged*, owner and master of all he surveyed. But he didn't own her. Or her children.

Another tiny earthquake shook through her at the reminder that she was responsible for precious twin lives.

Lives he wanted to control.

'It won't be a takeover if we discuss it sensibly,' he said, confirming her fears.

'You want sensibly? Then tear up this document!'

He frowned. 'Calm yourself, Saffie.'

'Don't you dare use that tone with me. Not when you've been planning this for weeks. Take it back, Joao.'

'Will you stay?'

'No.'

A momentary flash in his eyes was all the answer she needed that he wouldn't shift from his stance. 'Then we have nothing else to discuss.'

She felt the colour drain from her face. But she took the tiniest satisfaction in ripping the agreement to shreds and tossing the pieces on his desk, even while she prayed the hot tears prickling her eyes wouldn't fall. 'Have a nice life, Joao!'

It was the party to end all parties.

Or so everyone insisted on gushing the moment he came within hearing distance.

His mansion tucked into the exclusive peninsular of Saint-Jean Cap-Ferrat was awash with dazzling lights, laughter and music that bounced off the still water. A quarter of a mile away, his superyacht was outlined by more dazzling lights, guests who wanted to see another area of his life partying on the decks of his vessel. Between the two venues, every imaginable whim was catered for by the expert hands of an executive assistant no longer in his employ.

Joao experienced a flash of acute, blazing irritation, which immediately snuffed itself out beneath the agony tightening his sternum and the heavy weight of his morose mood. But in its wake he felt searing loss the likes of which he'd never experienced before but had lately become a constant companion.

Three long weeks she'd been gone. But everywhere he looked, she lingered. Taunting him. Defying him with her absent perfection.

He stared down into the dregs of the cognac Saffie had convinced a French distiller to produce solely for him. Hell, he couldn't even drink now, or eat, or sleep in his own bed without being reminded of her every accomplishment. Her absolute perfection.

Behind him, world dignitaries and celebrities drank and danced on his dime as if there were no tomorrow.

While he suffered a thousand cuts of loss because the ache inside decimated him in ever-expanding agony.

He dragged a hand through his hair, absently noting its tremor, and the spine-cracking tension it took to hold himself together.

The greatest professional achievement of his life had arrived with a side serving of a pile of ashes in his mouth.

How he'd managed to conduct a sane conversation with Lavinia at the formal press conference yesterday, he would never know.

He'd made the right noises and confirmed he would safeguard her legacy.

And all the while, the colossal mistake he'd made regarding his own legacy mocked him mercilessly.

All the while, the woman who it turned out knew him more than he knew himself had taken herself out of his life with such ruthless efficiency, he almost admired it.

A remote private Caribbean island accessible only by invitation and not a single dime of her existence came via him. She'd rejected the Amalfi villa, returned all his jewellery and refused every single one of his calls.

His only glimpse of her so far was via a grainy picture of her on the beach, her hand cradling the sweet curve of her stomach where his children continued to blossom.

His children.

The ones his last encounter with his father had driven him to claim on a visceral but totally misguided level. His toxic encounter with Pueblo had fuelled a savage need for history not to repeat itself. Except he'd come at it from totally the wrong angle.

A deep shudder racked his frame, infusing every fibre of his being with the misery he hadn't been able to shake since Saffie's departure. Did he even have the right to call them his after what he'd done?

After brazenly believing he could fight this fate worse

than death and plough on as if nothing had happened, only to compound his woes?

His staff cowered when he approached. The new assistant he'd hired irritated him with the simple, fatal flaw that he wasn't Saffie.

When midnight rolled around and the silence of whichever office he happened to be in oppressed him, none of his residences felt remotely like home.

Not without Saffie.

His fists balled, the anguish that even thinking of her name brought ravaging his insides.

She'd opened her heart to him, laid bare her most precious wish. A wish that ran parallel to one he'd been unwilling to admit to.

To be better versions of the lives imprinted on them.

Instead he'd taken it and soiled it.

Now it was too late.

He heard footsteps approach but didn't turn around. 'Monsieur Oliviera? Your guests are waiting for you on the terrace so the fireworks can begin.'

His fist tightened so hard he felt a bite of pain. But this pain would never come close to the one in his heart. And he couldn't live with it. Not any more. 'Tell them I have better things to do. They can all entertain themselves.'

'Monsieur?'

'Call my pilot. Tell him to get my plane ready.'

It might be too late but he needed to hear her say it to his face.

The richest man in the world had, with the Archer acquisition, solidified his position once and for all, leaving his nearest competition in the dust.

Saffie set aside the newspaper screaming Joao's success, his sheer brilliance and a dozen more superlatives.

She shouldn't have opened the paper. Shouldn't have given into the temptation for just one more glimpse of him.

Even thousands of miles away, the man could so very easily devastate her.

She struggled to calm the agonised roaring within, then realised the rush of sound wasn't in her head.

It was coming from outside, and growing louder by the second.

Standing, she went to the French doors to the villa she'd rented for the month, the beauty of the space not registering.

It would've been easier to return to her Chiswick flat, attempt to make the space she'd never truly lived in a loving home for when her children were born.

Except it'd been far too close to where she'd given four years of her life to Joao. She wasn't ready yet to share a metropolis with him. She might not be for a long time.

The sound grew louder. Deafening. Opening the doors, she stepped out. 'What's going on?'

One of the caretakers turned to her. 'There's a helicopter approaching.'

She frowned at the looming speck. Watched it whip up the sand on the beach and then simply…hover. 'What's it doing?'

'Attempting to land, miss.'

Her heart dipped for reasons she couldn't explain. 'But… there's no helipad. Doesn't he know how dangerous it is?'

The caretaker glanced from her to the aircraft and back again. 'I don't think he particularly cares, miss.'

She frowned. Then her heart began to hammer. Only one person would attempt the kind of magnificent recklessness the pilot was exhibiting. Only one person would brazenly come here uninvited like this.

She was sorely tempted to instruct her housekeeper to call the authorities. But if she knew nothing else, she knew Joao wouldn't give up. His silence in the past weeks had merely been the lull before the storm.

And the storm had arrived.

Her hand slid protectively over her stomach, the quiet astonishment and awe at how rapidly her babies were growing filling her heart before searing anguish emptied it.

'Miss? Shall we call the police?'

She refocused on the chopper, watched it slowly pivot until the pilot was in clear view.

Hovering fifty feet off the ground, Joao stared at her from behind the controls.

Swallowing thickly, she shook her head. 'No. Let him land.'

As if he'd heard her, the aircraft descended immediately, sending the tops of the palm trees swaying wildly as the blades whipped the air and the chopper settled on the lawn.

Unable to stay and watch him, let him see how desperately she'd missed him, how the sight of him both thrilled and frightened her, she turned and fled indoors.

Joao found her in the living room, the sight of her close up, the curve of her stomach beautifully visible, glowing with health even while her eyes flashed hurt and fury at him, stopping his breath for an age.

'*Você é linda*, Saffie,' he whispered reverently before he could stop himself.

'Brava on your spectacular entrance. But know that I've instructed the housekeeper to alert the authorities if you're not off this island in the next thirty minutes, so don't waste your time telling me I look beautiful.'

He raked a hand through his hair. 'I will risk jail if you would hear me out.'

He watched her debate for an eternity before waving him to the seat farthest from her.

'Saffie...the things I said...the things I did in Sao Paolo...'

'Deplorable things I will probably never forgive you for.'

He held tightly to the *probably*.

'I was a boy who came from nothing and had nothing for more than half my life. I didn't want children because deep down I didn't think I would be in any way a fit enough father. And frankly, the thought of giving something so vital of myself terrified me. But…when we found out in Shanghai that you were pregnant, things changed. I wanted them, but admittedly not for altruistic reasons, initially. Even then, Pueblo fuelled my reasoning. Because what better triumph than to show the old man everything he'd done wrong with the bastard son he'd sired, then callously rejected, than to be the better father than he could possibly be and rub his face in yet another failure? Succeed where both he and my mother had both failed so abysmally?'

Understanding flitted across her face. But there was also pain. Disappointment.

He swallowed. He held out his hands, pleading without words for her understanding. 'I've never made a deal when I walked away with nothing. You threatening to walk away, first from being my right hand, and then with my child—'

'Our children.'

'*Sim*. Two of the most precious things I've ever helped create… I just reacted the only way I knew how. Then coming face to face with Pueblo after so many years in Brazil…'

She frowned. 'When was the last time you saw him before the match?'

'The first time I bested him in a deal I was twenty-four. I insisted on him being there to sign the company I'd just bought from under him. Sao Paolo was the next time. After almost a decade, I'd fooled myself into thinking I'd be able to handle it. But you were right. I let him get to me. And believe me, I heard what you attempted to tell me that night in Sao Paolo. You were exposing every part of myself I've striven to hide and, well… I'm learning to accept some of it. Because to trust so completely...was another new phenomenon I couldn't contemplate.'

'But you trust me. At least in part.'

'I trust you wholly. It was simply easier to delude myself that the professional front was the only one that mattered. Confessing after that I wanted to do things differently, learn to love where I wasn't loved, was far too exposing. The agreement was the perfect way to attempt to leave my emotions out of it.'

'But you couldn't.'

He gave a low, self-deprecating laugh. 'Did I not manipulate you to ensure I would have a hand in your life even if you left me?'

Her stunning eyes swept away from his, her hands cupping her shoulders in self-protection that made him feel like the lowest of the low. 'I hear all of this. But how do I trust you now? After everything that's happened?'

Pain slashed his insides as he slowly approached her. 'By giving me a chance to prove myself. I stood the lawyers down the day you left. The precious children you carry will bear whatever name you wish them to bear. All I ask is that you give me a role in their lives. That you give me a chance to be their father by not owning them, but by loving and cherishing them the way every child deserves. But... if you don't want me to have anything to do with them—'

Her fingers on his lips stopped his words. 'I would never do that. Not after what we've both been through. That was what I'd planned on telling you that night on the terrace. That I wanted us to co-parent our babies. That even if you didn't have...feelings towards me you would at least love *them*. I needed that commitment from you for them, Joao. Because anything less than that won't do.'

A deep shudder shook him to his toes and he squeezed his eyes shut. 'The most valuable deal of my life and I messed it up spectacularly.'

Soft hands found his jaw and he pried his eyes open. 'It's not too late. If you meant what you just said. If you're willing—'

He caught her hand in his, infusing his vows through touch. And then through words. '*Meu Deus*, yes. I'm willing, Saffie. More than.'

Her eyes dimmed. 'So this is just a co-parenting role you want?'

'What right do I have to ask for more?'

'Has that ever stopped you?'

'*Meu amor*, I may not be bright when it comes to…certain things but I'm a quick learner. I will stop if—'

'You're brazen. You're cunningly clever and you're scarily ruthless when you need to be. Don't let me down now, Joao,' she urged huskily.

He heard the plea in her voice and his heart began to hammer against his ribs. 'Saffie…are you…?' He swallowed, for the first time in his life unable to voice his need.

'Ask me, Joao,' she insisted.

He sucked in a breath, and laid it all on the line. 'I want to be more than the father to our children. I want your heart. I want your trust. I want the right to call you mine and to love you as you deserve to be loved. With adoration. Completely. For as long as I draw breath.'

He held his breath as she stared back at him. As her eyes filled with tears. As a sob broke free and she threw herself into his arms.

As he caught her and held her and experienced the first, true taste of homecoming.

'So, how was the party?'

Joao nuzzled his face deeper into the sweet curve of her throat, the need he'd thought sated after four hours in bed with Saffie astonishingly rising again.

'I don't know. I left half an hour after it started.'

She gasped, moved back to look into his face. 'You didn't.'

Now, well into her second trimester, she glowed with the health and beauty attributed to a lucky few pregnant women. But he liked to think there was an extra-special something that made the woman of his heart a vision in his eyes.

'Without you it wasn't a celebration. And I don't care about anyone else there as much as I care about you. Only you. I love you, Saffie.'

Tears she'd blushingly attributed to hormones filled her eyes again. 'I love you, Joao,' she sighed against his lips. They kissed for an eternity before he raised his head.

'Besides, I have a feeling I've been a little…scary lately. People flinch when I approach. I need you to come back and…soften my edges.'

She laughed. And it was the best sound in the universe. A sound he wanted to roll in. Replicate until it played in an endless loop in his soul.

'You've proved conclusively that you have what it takes to remain the richest man in the world. People are bound to be intimidated whether I'm around or not.'

'I don't care about being the richest man in the world. I care about being the best husband to you.' His hand glided over her stomach and his breath strangled all over again. 'The best father to these two and however many we have in the future.' He looked up, deep into her eyes. 'Marry me, Saffie. Make me the happiest man in the world?'

Again her tears spilled. But she nodded through it, her husky, *'Sim. Para sempre sim,'* making his own eyes prickle.

They made love again, and just as she was about to drift off he reached for her hand and performed one last task.

Saffie's eyes opened, then widened as she saw the large, exquisite diamond ring on her finger. 'Now this piece of jewellery I love. Just as I love you.'

Her eyes met his and she gave him a smile that woke his soul and promised him eternity.

EPILOGUE

Four years later

'JOAO? WHAT ARE YOU—?'

Saffie's steps slowed as her husband raised a finger to his lips in a *hush* gesture. She paused, studying his expression.

Half amused, completely besotted, he flicked his attention away from her after a second. She smiled, knowing what was absorbing his attention as she tiptoed down the hall in bare feet towards where he was leaning on the wall next to the door that led into their twin sons' bedroom.

His gaze flicked back to her, lingered on her full breasts, her hips, down to where her peach-coloured night slip ended mid-thigh. When he raised his gaze again, his eyes were filled with the fierce carnal heat that hadn't dissipated an iota since that first time they'd made love on his divan in Morocco.

It was their first night back in their estate on the outskirts of Sao Paolo. It was good to be back home but she was exhausted and had been waiting for her husband to join her in bed. His continued absence had sent her in search of him.

A noise drew his attention back to their sons' room. Joao held out his arm and silently motioned for her to join him.

Smiling, Saffie tiptoed past the doorway, and melted into her husband's side. After he'd dropped a quick kiss on her lips, they peeped together into the room where identical twins, Carlos and Antonio, stood face to face.

'Watch,' Joao murmured.

They were engaged in a heated argument, three-year-old Carlos holding aloft his favourite toy, a blue whale he never travelled without. In his hand, Antonio held his second favourite toy. As he blabbered in toddler Portuguese, Antonio started to reach for the whale. A frantic argument broke out.

Saffie started to disengage but Joao held her back. 'No, *meu querida*. Watch,' he insisted under his breath.

The two boys babbled for another few minutes. Then Carlos haltingly held out his blue whale. After a few seconds, Antonio walked off and returned with his red toy truck. They exchanged toys, then the grinning boys fell into each other's arms, laughing in triumph.

'A month ago, they would've fought like wild horses. They're learning negotiation skills,' Joao said, pride stamped in his voice and on his face as he drew Saffie fully into his arms.

She wound her arms around his neck. 'I don't think they're quite ready for the boardroom yet, Joao.'

He brushed his lips over hers, eliciting a thrilling shiver that drew a smug smile to his lips. 'Perhaps not, but they're learning to fight for what they want and not walk away until they're satisfied.'

'A bit like what you did with their *mama*?'

He slanted his mouth over hers and kissed her for a long, wickedly thrilling minute before raising his head. *'Exatamente.'*

With a suave move that left her breathless, he swung her into his arms, paused to check that the nanny was overseeing their sons, before carrying her down the hall to their bedroom.

He laid her out on the bed, then shrugged out of his polo shirt and cargo pants in two smooth moves. Naked, he prowled over to join her. Elbows braced on either side of her head, his eyes burning bright, he stared down at her. 'Tell me you're satisfied, *meu coração*. Tell me I've made you happy?'

It still stunned her that a man as powerful and charismatic as Joao sought reassurance from her. That her happiness meant so much to him. But somehow it did.

'Words cannot truly express the joy you bring me, Joao. But perhaps I can find a few for what I need to tell you.'

His eyes feverishly probed hers. 'What is it?'

She caught up one hand, brought it to her lips and kissed his scarred palm. Intertwining their fingers, she drew them down to rest on her stomach.

His breath audibly caught. 'Saffie?'

Tears prickling her eyes, she leaned up and kissed him. 'I went to see Dr Demarco today. I'm ten weeks along.'

Whisky-gold eyes caressed her face, then dropped to her stomach. '*Meu Deus.* I thought I knew what happiness was. You've just shown me a whole new dimension.'

They shared a slow, languorous kiss, during which Joao managed to divest her of her negligee. She welcomed him home, waited until he was deeply seated inside her and they were frantically catching their breaths before she delivered the final news.

'There wasn't just one heartbeat, Joao. There were two. We're having another set of twins.'

His whole body visibly shook and Saffie caught a glint of tears in his eyes as his mouth dropped reverently over hers. 'Saffie. My Saffie. With you my cup has truly run over. *Eu te amo muito.*'

'I love you, too.'

* * * * *

CLAIMING HIS ONE-NIGHT CHILD

JACKIE ASHENDEN

To my dad.

He'll probably never read this book,
but just in case he does…

Hi, Dad.

CHAPTER ONE

As one of Europe's most notorious playboys, Dante Cardinali was used to waking up in strange beds. He was also used to beautiful women standing beside said beds and looking down at him. There had even been a couple of instances where he'd woken up with his wrists and ankles still cuffed, the way they clearly were now.

What was unfamiliar was the barrel of the gun pointed at his head.

Dante had never been a man who cared over much about anything, but one thing he *did* care about was himself. And his life. And the fact that the beautiful woman standing over him was holding a gun in a very competent grip.

The same beautiful woman who'd been in the VIP area of his favourite Monte Carlo club and with whom he'd spent some time…talking…because he hadn't been in the mood for seduction—something that had been happening to him more often than not of late. It was a worrying trend if he thought about it too deeply, which he didn't. Because he didn't think about anything too deeply.

Whatever. He couldn't remember how long he'd spent talking to her, because he couldn't remember full-stop. In fact, he couldn't remember much at all about the evening and, given his current situation, it probably meant he'd blacked out at some point.

What he did remember was the beautiful woman's piercingly blue eyes, fractured through with silver like a shattered sky.

Those eyes were looking at him now with curious intentness, as if she was trying to decide whether or not to shoot him.

Well, considering his wrists and ankles were cuffed and he wasn't dead already, it meant there was some doubt. And if there was some doubt, he could probably induce her to give in to it.

He could pretty much convince anyone to give in to anything if he put his mind to it.

'Darling,' he drawled, his mouth dry and his voice a little thick. 'A gun is slightly overkill, don't you think? If you want to sleep with me, just take your clothes off and come here. You don't need to tie me to the bed.' He frowned, his head suspiciously muzzy but beginning to clear. 'Or put something in my drink, for that matter.'

The woman's cool gaze—she had told him her name but he couldn't remember it—didn't waver. 'I don't want to sleep with you, Dante Cardinali,' she said, her icy tone a slap of cold water on his hot skin. 'What I would like very much is to kill you.'

So. She *was* trying to kill him and she *was* very serious.

He should probably be a little more concerned about that gun and the intent in her fascinating eyes, and he definitely was. But, strangely, his most prevalent emotion wasn't fear. No, it was excitement.

It had been a long time since he'd felt anything like excitement.

It had been a long time since he'd felt anything at all.

He stared at her, conscious of a certain tightening of his muscles and a slight elevation in his heartbeat. 'That seems extreme.'

'It is extreme. Then again, the punishment fits the crime.'

The barrel of the gun didn't waver an inch and yet she hadn't pulled the trigger. Interesting. Why not?

He let his gaze rove over her, interest tugging at him.

She was very small, built petite and delicate like a china doll, with hair the colour of newly minted gold coins, falling in a straight and gleaming waterfall over her shoulders. Her precise features were as lovely as her figure—a determined chin, finely carved cheekbones and a perfect little bow of a mouth.

She wore a satin cocktail dress the same kind of silvery blue as her eyes and it looked like silky fluid poured over her body, outlining the delicious curves of her breasts and hips, skimming gently rounded thighs.

A lovely little china shepherdess of a woman. Just his type.

Apart from the gun in his face, of course.

'What crime?' Dante asked with interest. 'Are you Sicilian by any chance? Is this a vendetta situation?' It was a question purely designed to keep her talking, as he knew already that she wasn't Sicilian. Her Italian held a cadence from a different part of the country and one he was quite familiar with.

The sound of the island nation from where he'd been exiled along with the rest of the royal family years and years ago.

The island nation of which he'd once been a prince.

Monte Santa Maria.

'No.' Her tone was flat and very definite. 'But you know that already, don't you?'

Dante met her gaze. He was good at reading people—it was part of the reason he was so successful in the billion-dollar property-investment company he owned with his brother—and although this woman's cool exterior seemed completely flawless he could see something flickering in the depths of her eyes. Uncertainty or indecision, he couldn't tell which. Interesting. For all that she seemed competent and in charge, she still hadn't pulled that trigger. And if she hadn't done it now, she probably wouldn't.

He'd seen killers before and this woman wasn't one. In fact, he'd bet the entirety of Cardinal Developments on it.

'Yes,' he said, discreetly testing the cuffs on his ankles and wrists. They were firm. If he wanted to get out of them, she was going to have to unlock them. 'Good catch. I love an intelligent woman.'

She took a step closer to the bed, the gun still unerringly pointed at his head. 'You know what I love? A stupid man.'

Her nearness prompted a heady, blatantly sexual fragrance to flood over him, along with bits and pieces of his memory.

Ah, yes, it was all coming back to him now—sitting in his club in Monte Carlo, this pretty little thing catching his eye and smiling shyly. She'd been innocent and artless, a touch nervous and, despite her strongly sexual perfume, when she'd said it was her first time in a club he'd believed her.

He hadn't been in the mood for small talk but, as he hadn't been in the mood for seduction, and there had been something endearing about her nervousness, he'd sat beside her and chatted. He couldn't remember a single thing about that conversation other than the fact that he hadn't been as bored as he'd expected to be, as he so often was these days.

He was not bored now, though. Not in any way, shape or form.

She was looking at him coolly, like a scientist ready to dissect an insect, no trace of that shy, nervous woman he'd talked to in the club. Which must mean that it had been an act. An act he hadn't spotted.

Oh, she was good. She was very good.

His heart rate sped up even further, the tug of interest becoming something stronger, hotter.

Are you insane? She wants to kill you and you want to bed her?

Was that any surprise? It had been too long since he'd had any kind of excitement in his life, too long since he'd had anything like a challenge. The closest he'd come to interesting had been when his older brother Enzo had married a lovely English woman and Dante had been tasked with making sure Enzo's son behaved himself. A shockingly difficult task, given the boy had already decided that Dante was less uncle than partner in crime.

Dante had had to spend at least a week afterwards in the company of various lovely ladies simply to recover.

Marriage and children were *not* the kind of excitement he was after. They were too restrictive and far too…domestic for his sophisticated tastes.

Though, given the state of his groin, if a lovely woman could get him hard simply by waving a gun at him maybe his tastes had grown a little too sophisticated even for him.

Then again, it didn't look as though he was going to be able to escape any time soon, unless he charmed his way out. It wouldn't be the first time that he'd used his considerable physical appeal to manipulate a situation and this was a situation that definitely required some degree of manipulation.

And besides. It might be fun.

'Stupid, hmm? Maybe I am.' He allowed himself to relax, looking up at her from underneath his lashes. 'Or maybe I knew who you were all along and simply wanted to see what you wanted from me.'

Her lovely mouth curved in a faint, cool smile. 'I see. In that case, care to enlighten me on why you're here?'

Dante raised a brow. 'Isn't that your job? I'm still waiting for your villain monologue.'

'Oh, no, you apparently know all about it already, so don't let me stop you.' She cocked her head, the light gleaming on her golden hair. 'I'd like to hear it so, please, go on.'

Adrenaline flooded through him in a hot burst. This was getting more and more interesting by the second. And so was she, playing him at his own game. Little witch.

He allowed his gaze to roam over her, giving himself some time to collect his thoughts. If she wanted him to give her the run down on what he thought was going on so far, then he was happy to oblige her. Especially as he was starting to get some idea.

If she was from Monte Santa Maria—and that seemed certain—then the most obvious explanation for his current predicament was an issue with his family. The Cardinalis had once been rulers of Monte Santa Maria, at least until Dante's father had mismanaged the country so badly that the government had removed him from his throne and exiled their entire family.

Luca Cardinali hadn't earned them any friends during his troubled reign.

So, did that mean she was from a family whom Luca had wronged? She looked young—younger than he was—and he'd only been eleven when their family had had to leave, so she was likely to be someone's daughter.

He didn't remember much of his Monte Santa Marian history—he'd tried his best to forget about his country entirely—but he seemed to recall an aristocratic family who'd been famous for their beauty, and most especially their golden hair.

'Well, if you insist,' he said. 'Your accent is familiar—from Monte Santa Maria, if I'm not much mistaken—and, given your general antipathy towards me, it's likely you're someone my father wronged at some point.' He watched her lovely face intently. 'But you're young, so I don't imagine Luca wronged you personally, but your family. And, given your accent again, I would say you're from one of the aristocratic families. Probably...' His brain finally settled on the name it had been looking for. 'Montefiore.'

Something in her shattered sky eyes flared. Shock.

So. He'd been right. How satisfying.

'Guess work,' she said dismissively, her chin lifting, her hold on the gun tightening. 'You know nothing.'

'And you are very good at pretending.' He smiled. 'If you're going to pull the trigger, darling, you'd better do it now. Or do you want the suspense to kill me before you do?'

'You think this is a joke?'

'With that gun in my face? Obviously not. But, if you imagine this is the first time I've woken up tied to a bed, you'd be wrong.'

'This isn't some sex game, Cardinali.'

'Clearly. If it was, you'd be naked and so would I, and you'd be calling me Dante. Or screaming it, rather.'

A whisper of colour stained her pale cheekbones and he didn't miss the way her gaze flicked down his body and then back up again, as if she couldn't help herself.

Excellent. It would appear she wasn't immune to him after all.

His satisfaction with the whole situation deepened, not to mention his excitement. This was indeed going to be a lot more fun than he'd initially envisaged.

Her jaw had tightened. 'You seem very casual for a man who's about to die.'

Apparently she didn't like his attitude. Well, not many people did.

'And if I was really about to die, I would be dead already. But, no, you put something in my drink, dealt with my bodyguards, somehow managed to transport me to…' he took a brief glance around the room which looked like a standard five-star hotel room '…wherever this is. Cuffed me to the bed. Waited until I woke up, then started talking to me instead of pulling that trigger.' He allowed his voice to deepen and become lazier, more sensual. 'And, darling, considering that little look you gave me just now, it's not killing that you want to do to me. It's something else entirely.' He let his smile become hot, the smile that had charmed women the world over and had never failed him yet. 'In which case, be my guest. You've already got me all tied up. I'm completely at your mercy.'

Stella Montefiore had never thought killing Dante Cardinali would be easy. He was rich, important and more or less constantly surrounded by people, which made getting an opportunity to take him down very, very difficult.

But since she'd taken on the mission she'd spent at least six months planning how to get access to him and, now she had, her family was counting on her to go through with it. Especially her father.

It was a just revenge for his son's death and a chance to reclaim the lost honour of the Montefiores. It was also her chance at redemption for her brother's death, a death for which her parents still hadn't forgiven her, and she did *not* want to make any mistakes. There was no room for error.

In fact, everything had gone completely to plan, and here he was, at her mercy, just as he'd said.

So why couldn't she pull that trigger?

He was lying on the bed in the hotel room she'd managed to get him into with the help of the hotel staff, having told them he was drunk, and he was cuffed hand and foot. He shouldn't be dangerous in the slightest.

And yet...

There was something about the way he took up space on the bed, all long and lean and muscular, the fabric of his expensive black trousers and plain white shirt pulling across his powerful chest and thighs. Not to mention the lazy way he looked at her from underneath his long, thick, black lashes, the glints of gold in his dark eyes like coins on the bottom of a lake-bed. Completely unfazed. As if he dealt with guns in his face every day and it didn't bother him in the slightest.

And it didn't help that he was so ridiculously beautiful in an intensely masculine way. All aristocratic cheekbones, a hard jawline, straight nose and the most perfectly carved mouth she'd ever seen. A fallen angel's face with a warrior's body, and the kind of fierce sexual magnetism that drew people to him, whatever their gender.

She hadn't anticipated that, though she should have, given she'd put a lot of work into researching him.

In fact, there was quite a lot about Dante Cardinali that she hadn't anticipated, including her own response to him.

Her heartbeat was strangely fast, though that was probably due to the sheer adrenaline of the moment and the unexpected success of her mission, nothing at all to do with the seductive glint in Cardinali's dark eyes.

Not that she should be thinking about how seductive he was when she was busy trying to work up the courage to pull that trigger.

'In which case,' she said, trying to maintain her cool, 'Perhaps you should be begging for your life instead of making casual comments about me sleeping with you. Which, I may add, I would rather die than do.'

He laughed, a rich sound that rolled over her like velvet, all warm and soft with just a hint of roughness. 'Oh, I'm sure you wouldn't.' That fascinating hint of gold gleamed from underneath his lashes. 'In fact, give me five minutes and you'll be the one who's begging. And it won't be for your life... Stella Montefiore.'

Shock trickled like ice water down her back, smothering the heat his sexy laugh somehow had built inside her, and distracting her totally from his outrageous statement.

He knew her name.

Kill him. Kill him now.

Her palm was sweaty, the metal of the gun cool against her skin. She'd practised this, shooting at tin cans in the makeshift gun range her father had set up in the barren hills behind the rundown house they'd had to move into after her brother had been arrested, working on her aim in between shifts as a waitress at a local restaurant—the only employment she could get, as no one wanted to hire a Montefiore. Not when they were such a political liability.

But shooting a can was very different from shooting an actual man. A man who would have his life snuffed out. By her.

She swallowed, her mouth dry.

Don't think of him as a person. This is revenge. For Matteo. For yourself.

Yes, all she needed to do was pull that trigger. A muscle twitch, really, nothing more. And then all of this would be over—her father's quest for blood done, Matteo's death avenged and her role in it redeemed.

You asked for this, remember?

Her father had wanted to hire someone and she'd told him, no, that it was better for one of the family to undertake the mission, to minimise discovery, and that the person who did it should be her. He'd told her she was too weak for the job, too soft-hearted, but she'd insisted she wasn't. That she could do it.

And she could. It should be easy.

But still her finger didn't move.

'You're wrong,' she said, not quite sure why she was arguing with him when a single movement would solve all her problems. 'That's not my name.'

'Is it not?' His eyes glinted, the curve of his beautiful mouth almost hypnotising in its perfection. 'My mistake.' His voice was as deep and rich as his laugh and the sound of it did things to her that she didn't want.

The same things it had done to her all evening from the moment she'd seen him in the flesh and not as an image in a photo or an online video. She'd spent months studying him, reading up on his history, his lifestyle, his business practices and personality. Basically everything she could find on him, building up a picture of a dissolute yet charming playboy who seemed to spend more time in his string of clubs than he did in the offices of Cardinal Developments, the huge multi-national that he owned with his brother Enzo. He ruled the gossip columns and the beds of beautiful women everywhere, apparently.

'The world won't miss him,' her father, Santo Montefiore, had said viciously. 'He's selfish, just like Luca was. Another useless piece of Cardinali trash.'

Yet when she'd stepped into that club in Monte Carlo, sick with nerves—unable to adopt the veneer of icy sophistication she'd perfected to get past the VIP bouncer—and Cardinali had appeared out of nowhere telling the bouncer that it was fine and she could come in, it wasn't trash she'd been thinking of. Not when he'd smiled at her. Because it hadn't been a practised seducer's smile. It had been kind—reassuring, almost—and inexplicably comforting. In fact, he'd been kind all evening. He'd taken her under his wing, sitting her down in a quiet end of the club and getting her a drink. Then he'd sat opposite and talked easily to her about everything and absolutely nothing at all.

She'd been expecting predatory and cynical and he hadn't been either of those things. To make matters worse, she'd found him so utterly beautiful, so magnetic, so charming, that she'd almost forgotten what she'd come to do. He'd overwhelmed her.

The attention he'd given her had made her feel like she was the centre of the world and, for a girl who'd come second best most of her life, it had been an intoxicating feeling.

Until he'd looked at his expensive, heavy gold watch that highlighted the bones of his strong wrist and said that he was going to have to leave soon. And she'd re-alised that if she wanted to make a move she was going to have to do it then. One more drink, she'd said. Just one more. And he'd agreed, not noticing when she'd slipped the drug into it.

Cardinali was watching her now and the smile turning his mouth wasn't kind this time. No, there was something else there. A hint of the predatory seducer she'd been ex-pecting, along with a certain calculating gleam. Almost as if he now saw her as an equal and not the nervous, inexpe-rienced woman she'd been in the club, or the soft-hearted, weak girl her parents had always thought her.

It made her heart thump hard in her chest, an inexpli-cable excitement flickering through her.

'My name is Carlotta,' she said. 'I told you that in the club.'

'Ah, then you'll have to forgive me my poor memory. Someone must have spiked my drink.' He shifted on the bed, as if he was getting himself more comfortable, a lazy movement that drew attention to his powerful body. 'So, are you going to stand there all night talking at me or are you going to murder me in cold blood? If it's the former, I hope you don't mind if I go to sleep. All this excitement is exhausting.' He shifted again and she caught a hint of his aftershave, warm and exotic, like sandalwood. It was delicious.

She took a steadying breath, trying to ignore the scent. 'Don't you care at all which one it is?'

'Since you're not going to kill me, not particularly.'

Her finger on the trigger itched. 'You don't know that.'

'Please, darling. Like I've already told you, if you'd really wanted to kill me you would have done it by now.'

He's right. You would have.

Except she hadn't. She'd told herself she couldn't shoot an unarmed and unconscious man. Plus, he needed to know why he had to die, otherwise what would be the point? But now he was awake and she wasn't telling him why he had to die. She was lying and pretending to be someone else instead.

What was she doing?

You don't want to kill him.

A shiver passed through her. She had to kill him. This was the job she'd undertaken months ago, for her father and for the sake of her brother's memory. For the honour of the Montefiores.

An eye for an eye. Blood for blood.

One of Luca Cardinali's sons had to die and, as his older brother Enzo was untouchable, that left only Dante.

Except…

His eyes were inky in the dim light of the room and they seemed to see right into her soul. There was no sharpness in them, only a velvet darkness that wrapped her up and held her tight.

'Lower the gun, sweetheart,' he said quietly. 'No matter what I've done, nothing is worth that stain on your soul.'

No, she shouldn't lower the gun. She needed to keep everything her father had told her about blood, honour and revenge in the forefront of her mind. She needed to be strong and, most important of all, hard. There could be no emotional weakness now.

And yet...her hand was shaking and she didn't understand why he should be so concerned with her soul when she herself didn't care about what happened to her after this was over.

'My soul is none of your business.' She tried to keep her voice firm and sure.

'If you're preparing to risk it to kill me, then it most certainly is my business.' His dark gaze held hers and there was no fear in it at all, only an honesty that wound around her heart and didn't let go. 'I'm not worth it, believe me.'

How curious. He made it sound as if her soul was actually worth something.

She should have shot him right then and there, but instead she found her hand lowering, exactly as he'd told her to.

He didn't glance at the gun, his dark eyes steady on her instead.

The weapon was heavy in her hand and she didn't understand why she hadn't pulled that trigger when she'd had the chance. Because now that chance had gone. The moment when she could have fired was lost.

You failed.

Shame rushed through her like the tide. How had he done it? How had he got under her guard? And, more importantly, why had she let him?

She'd worked hard ever since Matteo's death to excise all the soft, weak emotions inside her, the ones her parents had despised, and there shouldn't have been any room at all for mercy. But it seemed as if there was some small part of her that was still weak. Still flawed.

Anger glowed in her gut, hot and bright, overwhelming the shame, and before she realised what she was doing she'd put the gun on the bedside table and was bending down over him, putting one hand on the pillow on either side of his head. His hair was inky black on the pillows, his eyes almost the same colour as they stared challengingly back at her.

He smelled so good, the heat rising off him making her want to get close, to warm herself against him.

'What is it, kitten?' Dante murmured, staring straight up at her, gold glinting deep in the darkness of his gaze. 'Is it time to show me your claws?'

Again, there wasn't an ounce of fear or doubt in him, just as there hadn't been right from the start. He'd seen through her. He'd seen through her completely.

Her anger flared hotter, a bonfire of rage. How dared he find that weakness inside her? How dared he exploit it? And what was wrong with her that she had allowed him to do it?

Her perfectly executed plan was now in ruins and all because she hadn't had the guts to do what needed to be done.

Because, somehow, she'd let this man undermine her.

Well, if he wanted to see her claws, then she'd show them to him. And she knew exactly what to do to in order to cause maximum damage.

Her experience with men was non-existent, but she'd studied Dante Cardinali and she'd studied him well. Including what she could find on his sexual predilections. He was a man who liked being in control and who always, *always,* got what he wanted.

And it was clear that he wanted her.

Which gave her the perfect leverage over him.

'Not my claws,' Stella murmured, staring right back into his eyes. 'You can feel my teeth instead.'

Then she lowered her head and bit him.

CHAPTER TWO

THE LOVELY WOMAN who was probably Stella Montefiore, but definitely wasn't Carlotta, closed her teeth delicately around Dante's lower lip and every nerve-ending he had lit up with sweet, delicious pain.

He was hard instantly, his whole body tight, his wrists and ankles instinctively pulling against the cuffs with the urge to grab her, hold her.

He hadn't been expecting this particular move, though really the glittering flare of anger he'd seen in her eyes just before she'd bent her head should have warned him.

She wasn't as cool as she seemed, which was a delightful surprise.

In fact, the whole of her bending over him with that rich heady scent, her silky golden hair falling over one shoulder, her pale skin glowing against the fluid fabric of her blue dress, was a delightful surprise.

He'd been hoping for some fight and he'd certainly got it.

If only his hands were free.

Instead, he opened his mouth and touched his tongue to the softness of lower lip, a gentle coax.

She went still, her teeth releasing him, her lips a breath away from his.

So he bit her back, but not hard. A light nip to see what she'd do.

Her head jerked back and she looked down at him, her blue eyes glowing with anger, her cheeks pink. 'Damn you,' she whispered.

'Why?' His own voice had roughened. 'Because I stopped you from doing what you didn't want to do anyway? Because you're not a killer?'

She didn't reply, merely bent her head again, and this time her mouth was on his in a hard, furious kiss.

That she was inexperienced was immediately obvious, but she also tasted of anger and of passion, and his interest, already piqued, deepened even further.

He'd had inexperienced before, though he tended to steer clear of women who didn't know what they were dealing with when it came to him. He'd had plenty of anger before too, not to mention passion. But not all three at once, and not when the woman dealing them out had been on the point of shooting him in the head.

It made him even harder than he was already.

Still, that inexperience was a warning sign that this woman, no matter how cool and strong she seemed, no matter that she'd had him at gunpoint, had her vulnerabilities. And it was interesting that the mention of her soul had been the thing that had made her lower the gun.

But what had been even more interesting to him was the definite shame that had flared in her eyes after she'd put the gun down, only to be swiftly overtaken by rage. She hadn't liked failing her mission, that was for sure. And yet, instead of shooting him anyway, she'd kissed him.

Yes, that was very, *very* interesting.

Not only was she a woman with vulnerabilities, she also seemed to be a woman of strong passions. Which made for an intoxicating combination.

'Kitten,' he murmured against her mouth. 'Are you sure you know what you're doing?'

In response she bit him again, harder this time, the tips of her breasts brushing against his chest as she leaned in closer. Holy God, her nipples were tight and hard. He could feel them through the cotton of his shirt.

Lust uncurled in his gut, thick and hot, making him catch his breath.

It had been a long time since a woman had made him feel like this, he had to admit. And he wasn't a man who denied himself anything he wanted. Self-control was all very well in certain situations, but when it came to sex he would freely admit to being a glutton.

Then again, she'd had the gall to drug him then tie him to a bed, so why should he give her everything she wanted right now?

He moved his head on the pillow, pulling his mouth away from her. 'Sweetheart, if you want that, you're going to have to ask for it.'

She made an angry sound and tried to kiss him again but he closed his mouth against hers.

The breath went out of her and she lifted her head. Her eyes were electric with anger, her cheeks pink. She said nothing, merely looked at him for a long moment. Then she straightened and took a step back from the bed.

But he didn't think she was going to move away. No, he'd seen something shift in that furious blue gaze of hers. She'd made a decision.

Anticipation coiled inside him, his breath catching yet again.

This woman was proving to be more and more intriguing with every second that passed and he couldn't wait to see what she was going to do next, how she would answer this particular challenge.

He didn't have anywhere to be or anything much to do beyond the usual round of PR work that he undertook on behalf of Enzo's and his company, plus the running of the more pleasurable side of the business, the resorts and clubs he owned all over the globe.

Anyway, he was bound to a bed. He couldn't go anywhere even if he wanted to. Luckily he didn't want to.

His lovely captor stood there a moment, her breathing fast in the silence of the room. Then she lifted her hands and pushed the straps of her silky blue dress off her shoulders, allowing the fabric to slide slowly down her body before pooling at her feet.

She was naked underneath it apart from the scrap of white lace between her thighs.

Okay, *that* was a move he hadn't anticipated her making. Not that he was complaining. Not in the slightest.

He'd seen a lot of beautiful women in his lifetime—more than he could count. But it wasn't this woman's physical beauty that felt like a punch to the gut, though she was indeed lovely: small, delicate and pale, her breasts the sweetest curves, her nipples pink and pretty.

No, it was the way she stood there with her chin lifted and her back straight, proud as a queen, her gaze full of challenge. As if she was daring him to break his bonds and come to her. Kneel at her feet. Worship her the way she was obviously used to being worshipped.

His pulse accelerated, the ache in his groin becoming acute. He almost jerked against the damn cuffs again, but managed to control himself at the last minute.

'Is this a request?' His voice was uneven even though he tried to mask it. 'Because, if so, it's a very persuasive one.'

She said nothing. Her hands went to her hips and very slowly she eased down the lacy underwear she wore then stepped out of it.

Dio, she was golden between her thighs too.

His mouth watered, his heartbeat hammering in his head.

What is it with you? It's not like you to let yourself get all hot under the collar for a woman.

It really wasn't. He didn't care about much of anything these days, but he found he cared about this. He wanted her hands on him. He wanted her skin against his. He wanted to be inside her. Preferably right now.

It was concerning. He didn't want to want anything at all.

He gritted his teeth, for the first time in a long while considering denying himself. Because he shouldn't care if she didn't touch him or kiss him, or get that delicious body on his. It shouldn't matter to him in the slightest.

If it doesn't matter, why are you even thinking of refusing her?

Dante had no answer to that.

He smiled, though for the first time in years it felt forced, more like a grimace than a smile. And he tried to make himself sound nonchalant. 'Well, don't just stand there, kitten. Come closer and let me see you.'

And perhaps she heard the strained note in his voice, because an expression that looked an awful lot like satisfaction flickered over her lovely face. Then she moved back over to the bed, clearly in no hurry at all, and looked at him very deliberately, the same way he'd looked at her. She was flushed now, the pink extending down her throat and over the pale curves of her breasts, and it deepened as her gaze dropped to where he was hard and ready and aching.

And stayed there.

Electricity crackled the length of his body.

What the hell was she doing to him? He didn't let himself get like this, not with anyone.

'I can get hard for any woman,' he murmured lazily, trying to keep the hoarse note out of the words. 'But it'll take more than you being naked to get me off.'

She gave him a brief, scorching glance. 'Who says I want to get you off? Maybe I just want to play with you.'

Sneaky kitten. So this was a power play, was it? She'd seen the general state he was in and thought she could take advantage, clearly.

Well, she could try. He might be finding it a tad more difficult to be his usual cool self, but when it came to bedroom power games he was the master. Even cuffed to the bed.

'Obviously I'm not going to object to that.' He let his voice get lower, become seductive. 'But, if you want to play, you'd better know what you're doing.'

'Who's to say that I don't?' She reached out and stroked lightly over the hard ridge just behind his fly.

More electricity crackled along his nerve-endings, the light brush of her fingertips maddening. Dante ignored the sensation. Instead, he gazed at her from beneath his lashes, letting the look in his eyes burn hot.

She was inexperienced—that kiss she'd given him had proved it well enough—and even though it wasn't something he'd normally use to his advantage, given the circumstances, beggars couldn't be choosers.

'That kiss for a start.' He let his gaze roam over her, blatantly sexual. 'Best to know what you're getting into, darling. I'm a lot for a little kitten to handle.'

A deep-blue spark glittered in her eyes as she stroked him yet again. 'You're very arrogant for a man tied to a bed.'

'And you're very confident for a virgin.'

The deep pink flush staining her skin became scarlet, gilt lashes sweeping down, veiling her gaze and hiding her expression. And he was conscious of a very particular kind of satisfaction spreading through him. Firstly, for guessing right and, secondly, for the fact that he was perhaps the first man she'd ever touched like this. The first man with whom she'd ever been naked.

He normally steered clear of virgins, as he wasn't a man an innocent should get entangled with, but he couldn't deny that for some reason he liked the thought of this particular woman being a virgin. He liked it very much.

A virgin with a gun. How…intriguing.

'Don't be embarrassed, darling,' he said, watching her intently. 'Even I was a virgin once.' Though, thinking back, he honestly couldn't remember how or when he'd lost it.

She didn't say anything for a long moment. Then suddenly she lifted her head and moved to the bed, climbing on top of it and straddling him. The weight of her was slight, but the heat of her bare skin seeping through his clothes was astonishing.

His breath caught as the blatant sweetness of her perfume surrounded him, but underneath that was something light and fresh, combined with the musk of feminine arousal.

Pretty, pretty kitten.

She rose above him, the pressure of her body against his groin an agony, the sway of her lovely breasts making his mouth go dry. Her skin was glowing, a sheen of perspiration at her throat, the look in her eyes all fire and challenge.

There was not a hint of shyness in her, or at least none that she let him see.

'I'm not embarrassed.' She reached for the top button of his shirt. 'Why would I be?'

Her naked heat had sharpened his hunger while her refusal to back down ignited something far hotter. Something he'd thought he'd killed long ago.

His determination to win.

He smiled, allowing some of his sexual hunger to show. 'No reason at all. But if you want to play with me then I do suggest learning the rules of the game first.' He paused. 'You don't want to lose on your first try, do you?'

For the merest second an uncertain expression flickered over her face. Then it was gone.

'But I'm not going to lose,' she said coolly, pulling open the buttons on his shirt one by one then spreading open the white cotton, baring his chest. 'I might be a virgin, but I'm not stupid. And a man is only a man.' She pressed her palms to his skin, the heat of her touch like a brand, her blue eyes burning into his. 'Like you said, Mr Cardinali. You're at my mercy. And there's nothing you can do about it.'

Dante laughed that intensely sexy laugh of his, the sound heating everything inside her to boiling point, making her skin feel hot and tight, as though she wanted to claw it off and step out of it.

He was giving her the most blatantly sexual look from underneath his lashes, all liquid darkness and heat, and the feel of his muscular, powerful body made her lose all her breath.

It wasn't supposed to be this way. Biting him, taking off her dress, touching him, was supposed to tease him, taunt him with what he couldn't have. Prove her strength to him and also punish him for making her lose her nerve so badly.

And yet the only one feeling as if all of this was a punishment was her.

She hadn't expected that bite to ignite something inside her. She hadn't expected his mouth to be quite so soft or for him to taste quite so delicious, like dark chocolate, fine whisky and all the seven sins rolled up into one.

She hadn't expected the way he'd looked at her naked body to make her feel as if she was going to burn to ash where she stood. Or that touching the hard length that pressed against the wool of his trousers would feel so astonishingly good.

She hadn't expected the intense throb between her thighs to be quite so demanding either.

Damn him. This was supposed to be a strong moment for her, not one where she felt as though she were standing naked in the path of an oncoming storm with nothing to protect her.

You've only got yourself to blame.

It was true. Sadly. She'd been the one who'd decided to bite him, to kiss him, to get naked and touch him. And now here she was, sitting on top of him, completely at the mercy of the desire inside her that had gripped her by the throat and wouldn't let go.

That wasn't supposed to happen. Sexual desire was supposed to be another of the weaknesses she'd cut out of her life. And yet his bronze skin beneath her palms was so smooth, the muscle under that so very, very hard, and all she wanted to do was press harder, test his strength, spread her fingers out and soak in all his heat.

But the hidden glints of gold in his dark eyes held her completely hypnotised and she couldn't look away.

'Poor kitten.' His voice was rough and deep, the rich amusement in it like a caress against her skin. 'You don't understand, do you? I'm not at your mercy. You're at mine.'

It seemed a ridiculously arrogant thing to say, when he was the one on his back and cuffed to the bed. Yet...

He was fluid and powerful underneath her, and hard, like granite carved direct from a mountain. She could see that power beneath her hands, feel it in the tight coil of his muscles and in the heat running through his body. It was there in his eyes too, an arrogant certainty of his power that made her want to tremble.

She felt that certainty within herself, in the desire that

wound through her, exposing her. In the way her breath came short and fast, and in the relentless throb of heat between her thighs. In the tightness of her skin and the acute awareness of every part of her that touched him and every part of her that didn't. In the delicious, warm scent of him that made her mouth water and her heart beat faster.

You're weak. You've always been weak.

Stella shoved the thought from her head. There was only one answer to that and that was simply to be stronger. She had to be if she was to overcome the insidious dragging need to surrender to him and the relentless pressure of her desire.

Dante Cardinali had seemed to be a simple man. A man driven by the single-minded pursuit of pleasure, a slave to any pretty face that came his way.

But it wasn't him who was the slave. It was her.

'No,' she whispered, both to him and to herself. 'I'm not at anyone's mercy.'

'Prove it, then.' Deep in the velvet darkness of his eyes, golden fire burned. 'Get off me and walk away. Put on your dress and leave this room.' His hips lifted as he said the words, the hard length behind the wool of his trousers brushing up against the soft, sensitive tissues of her sex.

Pleasure bolted like lightning straight through her and she couldn't stop the soft gasp that escaped.

'Do it.' His voice was rough with heat. 'If you think you can.'

She could. Of course she could.

Except he was moving subtly against her and the rhythmic pressure against that aching place between her thighs was making her shiver with delight. She'd denied herself many things in the quest to become better and stronger than the girl who'd betrayed her own brother into prison, and that included physical pleasure. She hadn't thought she'd missed out on anything, but...

Get off him. Walk out. Deny him. That's what you were going to do, wasn't it?

Of course it was. And, yes, she would get off him. Right now.

Except...the heat of him, and the power of his body beneath her, and the gentle rocking of his hips were all mesmerizing and she didn't want it to stop.

You have to do something.

He wasn't expecting her to get off him. That was obvious. He was expecting her to stay, to be at his mercy, exactly as he'd said. And her body simply wasn't going to let her leave. Which meant she was going to have to do something else to prove her strength.

She shifted back on him, shivering at the brush of the fabric of his trousers against her. Then, with shaking hands, she pulled at the buttons of his fly.

He stilled, his big, rangy body tensing beneath her. 'Oh, kitten,' he breathed. 'I'm not sure that's a good idea.'

She ignored him, tugging down his zip and reaching inside his boxers. Her fingers closed around him and she blinked, her breath sticking in her throat at the feel of him in her hand. So long and hard and hot.

She pulled the fabric away from him, staring at the length she held in her hand, completely fascinated.

'Stella.' Her name this time, in a rough and hungry growl. 'I wouldn't do that if I were you.'

But it was too late. Backing down was an impossibility. It would make this entire evening an even bigger disaster, not to mention reveal the depths of her weakness, and she'd already revealed more of that than she wanted to when she'd put down her gun.

She lifted her gaze to his, the molten heat in his dark

eyes making lightning crackle in her blood. 'What did you want me to prove again?' It was another challenge and she didn't wait for him to answer. Instead she lifted her hips and fitted that hard shaft of his against the entrance to her body. Then she lowered herself down on him.

The feel of him pushing inside her was exquisite. There was no pain, only a wonderful stretching sensation and a pressure that tore a groan from her throat.

His smile vanished, his mouth twisting into a snarl, a rough, masculine sound breaking from him as she slid down on him even further.

Then she had to move and she was helpless to stop herself, the urge overwhelming. Rising and falling on him, at first hesitant and uncertain, then finding a rhythm. He'd gone silent, his hips lifting with hers, the fierce hunger on his beautiful face holding her captive.

They stared at each other as pleasure began to unwind in a shining cord, wrapping around both of them and pulling tight. Getting tighter. Then tighter still.

Stella braced herself with her hands on his chest, the world narrowing down to the rock-hard body under hers and the astonishingly good push-pull of him inside her... to the coil of pleasure that was tightening and tightening and tightening.

Her skin felt raw and over-sensitive, the desperation inside her growing teeth. She hadn't thought sex would be like this, that she'd be so feverish and hungry. That she'd be so desperate.

The room was cool and yet she'd broken out into a sweat, her palms damp on his chest. A moan escaped her, because somehow he was dictating the pace now, the movement of his hips faster, her body trying to catch up, chasing some kind of glory she didn't understand and which agonisingly kept moving out of reach.

'Touch yourself,' he murmured, his rich voice rough with dark heat, no trace of the polished playboy in it now. 'Do it now.'

And she found herself obeying him without hesitation, driven by her own hunger, moving her hand between her thighs and touching her own slick flesh. And as she did so he lifted his hips, thrusting up hard into her.

Pleasure suddenly detonated like a bomb, and she cried out, throwing back her head, feeling herself come apart in the most incredible blaze of light.

Dimly she felt his body tense, another roughened growl escaping him, but she couldn't seem to focus on that, not when her whole body was busy being flooded with such sharp, intense ecstasy.

As it faded, she fell forward onto his hard chest and for a second or two simply relaxed there, her cheek against his hot skin, breathing in the delicious scent of sandalwood, salt and musk. It was like lying on a rock in the sun and she wanted to close her eyes and drift, listening to the strong, steady beat of his heart beneath her ear. The sound was reassuring in some way, as powerful and enduring as the sea…

'Kitten,' Dante Cardinali said, his deep voice echoing through her.

The delicious warmth was fading, the feeling of reassurance going out like the tide, leaving her cold and shaking, and not in a good way.

Her arms trembled as she pushed herself up and met the darkness of his gaze staring back.

What have you done? You were supposed to kill him, not get into power games. And you definitely weren't supposed to have sex with him.

Shame flooded through her, crushing her. This was a mistake. A terrible, terrible mistake.

'Stella,' Dante said.

But she couldn't stand being in this room a second longer, surrounded by the ruins of her mission and the evidence of her weakness.

She slid off him, pulling on her dress and underwear with shaking hands, pausing only to grab the little clutch she'd brought with her. Then she moved quickly to the door on legs that felt as if they might give way at any moment.

'Stella,' Dante repeated, more forcefully this time.

But she didn't turn. She couldn't bear to look at him.

She opened the door and fled, the sound of him roaring her name one last time ringing in her ears.

CHAPTER THREE

'WHAT DO YOU THINK, Dante?' Enzo asked. 'Do we want to go with Tokyo on this one or stick with the New York office's plans?'

Dante wasn't listening, too busy restlessly pacing around in front of the windows of the boardroom in Cardinal Developments' London office. Rain pelted against the glass, obscuring the view of the city below but, just as he wasn't listening to his brother, he wasn't paying much attention to the view either.

He was in England with Enzo to work out some of the details of a new project in the City, which had been hijacked by some disagreement between their people in New York and Tokyo, and quite frankly he didn't have the patience for either thing right now.

Not when his head was full of Stella Montefiore.

It had been over a month since she'd left him cuffed to a bed in that hotel room in Monte Carlo, running out on him mere minutes after the most unexpectedly intense sexual experience of his life, and to say he was annoyed about it would be to understate things massively.

He wasn't simply annoyed. He was furious.

And he wasn't furious that she'd not only drugged him and cuffed him but then tried to kill him. No, he was furious firstly because she'd run out without even a thank you, and secondly because, try as he might, he simply could *not* stop thinking about her.

That brief moment of excitement and pleasure should have been more than enough for him. After all, there were a great many other lovely women in the world, so he shouldn't be fixating or caring about one particular woman.

But for some reason he hadn't been able to stop.

For weeks all he'd thought about was the feel of her tight, wet heat around him and the scent of her arousal, the unbelievable pleasure that had licked up his spine the moment she'd lowered herself down on him.

Of the challenging look in her beautiful eyes as her fingers had closed around him, upping the ante on their little game in a way he hadn't expected. Or the way that look had turned to wonder as she'd lowered herself down on him and the heat and the pleasure between them had taken hold.

He'd never seen that look on a woman's face in bed before and he'd been riveted. Caught too by the knowledge that she was experiencing this for the first time and he was the one who was giving it to her.

Maybe it was simply because she'd been trying to kill him that had heightened everything, including the pleasure.

Whatever it was, one thing had become very, very clear to him: given that she had in fact been trying to kill him, and that he had no guarantee she wouldn't try again, he couldn't simply leave her to run around on the loose.

So for the past month he'd spent most of his efforts on investigating her and, more importantly, finding her. Efforts that had all ended up with frustrating dead ends.

Until now.

'Dante, for God's sake,' Enzo said curtly. 'You're giving me a damn headache.'

Dante blinked then turned around, shoving his hands into the pockets of his suit trousers. Enzo was leaning against the long, sleek black table that dominated the boardroom, his arms folded, his golden eyes disturbingly sharp.

'Are you going to tell me what the matter is?' he asked. 'Or are you going to continue to pace around, pretending to be me?'

His brother wasn't wrong. Pacing was definitely Enzo's speciality, not Dante's.

With an effort, Dante tried to relax. He didn't want Enzo to know about Stella, not yet. His brother was happy for the first time in his life and Dante didn't want anything to worry him, such as attempts on Dante's life from enemies back in the old country.

Besides, Enzo would no doubt start taking charge of the operation if Dante did tell him, and there was no way Dante wanted him to do that. This was his problem and he was going to handle it his way.

Nothing at all to do with wanting Stella Montefiore in your bed again, naturally.

Naturally. He'd had her once. He didn't need to have her again, no matter how beautiful she was or exciting he'd found her. He just wanted her found, any threat she presented negated.

'There's nothing the matter.' Dante consciously tried to relax his tense muscles. 'Why would you say that?'

'Because you haven't listened to a word I've said and you're pacing around like Simon does when he's restless and wants to go outside and play.'

'Though presumably with fewer tantrums,' Dante muttered. He loved his nephew but, as Simon was only four, Dante didn't much appreciate the comparison.

One of Enzo's black brows rose. 'Is that a comment on my son's behaviour? Because if so—'

'Of course not,' Dante snapped, unaccountably irritable.

There was an uncomfortable silence as Enzo stared at him.

'What?' He stared back. 'There's no problem.'

'And our father is alive and well and ruling peacefully at home,' Enzo commented dryly. 'Tell me. And it had better be work related. Simon starts school in a couple of months and the last thing he needs is one of his uncle's scandals all through the media.'

Since Enzo had married Matilda six months ago, he'd got very protective of his little family. Annoyingly so, in Dante's opinion. His brother had never minded his affairs before, but in the past few months he'd turned into a damn prude. It was irritating.

Dante had managed successfully to build a life that consisted entirely of seeing to his own comfort and he was more than happy with the present arrangement. He did *not* want anything to change it.

'It's nothing that need concern Cardinal Developments,' he said, trying to find his usual casual smile. 'Or Simon. It's merely a distracting entanglement.'

Enzo frowned. 'That doesn't sound promising. She's not married, is she?'

'Brother, please. A married woman? It's like you don't know me at all.' There, that sounded more like his usual self, didn't it?

Enzo's gaze narrowed, studying Dante in that sharp way he had. 'You're lying.'

'I'm not,' Dante said with perfect truth.

'She must be very distracting to get you tied up in knots like this.'

Enzo didn't know the half of it, but Dante wasn't going to enlighten him.

It had indeed been Stella Montefiore who'd drugged him and cuffed him. As soon as he'd got out of the hotel room, he'd called his personal assistant and asked her to find out everything she could about the Montefiore family. She'd given him a complete dossier the next day and he'd spent most of the day going through said dossier, trying to work out why on earth Stella had targeted him.

Not that it was all that difficult to find out once he knew her family history.

The Montefiores had been one of the leading aristocratic families on Monte Santa Maria until Dante's father, the king, had been exiled.

After that, because the Montefiores had supported the old regime, they'd suffered a terrible fall from grace that had led to Stefano Montefiore sinking everything he owned into Luca Cardinali's plans to retake his throne. The family had been beggared and then, to add insult to injury, the authorities somehow had found out about Stefano's machinations. While Stefano had escaped being implicated, his oldest son Matteo had not. Matteo had been imprisoned, along with various other of Luca's supporters, and then, years later, had died while still incarcerated.

It didn't take a genius to work out why Stella Montefiore had been trying to kill him: she and her father wanted Dante's blood in return for the death of a brother and son.

It was a vendetta worthy of a Sicilian.

Except she hadn't gone through with it.

'You know how it is,' Dante said aloud. 'The right woman can be...lethal in certain circumstances.' Though not so much in his case, except for the lethal blow she'd dealt to his self-control.

Enzo lifted a brow. 'Is that a fact? Care to talk about this particular woman?'

Dante looked back blandly. 'Not really.'

'In that case, can I please have your attention concerning this—?'

Dante's phone buzzed in his pocket and he forgot about his brother entirely, pulling it out and turning round to look down at the screen.

It was a text from one of the private investigators he'd hired to locate Stella, giving him an address in Rome.

He smiled, an intense feeling he couldn't quite name filling him. It was mainly satisfaction, but there was something else there too. An undeniable, feral kind of excitement.

It had been frustrating not being able to find her, that she'd somehow managed to escape all the people he'd sent out looking for her.

But now, *now,* he had her.

She wasn't going to escape him again.

Seems like you do care about something after all.

Of course he cared when it was about his own life. Though what he was going to do with her once he'd found her, he hadn't quite decided. Probably, if he was feeling particularly merciful, he'd give her a warning that if she made another attempt on his life he'd report her to the police. And, if he wasn't feeling merciful, he might just call the police then and there.

That's not what you want to do to her...

Well, no, of course it wasn't. He wanted to punish her a little too, for how she'd taken up so much space in his head and for the sensual memories that had tormented him for the past month. The memories that she'd given him.

It wouldn't be a painful punishment, naturally, but she'd definitely scream. With pleasure.

'You're looking pleased with yourself,' Enzo murmured. 'Does this mean you're going to listen now or are you going to interrupt me yet again?'

'It means,' Dante said, putting his phone back in his pocket, 'that something's come up. Looks like I have to head back to Italy.'

'I see,' Enzo said dryly. 'Nothing at all to do with a woman, I suppose?'

He gave his brother a brilliant smile. 'Not in the slightest. You won't need the jet? Good. I'm flying out ASAP.'

Enzo snorted. 'What about Tokyo?'

But Dante was already heading to the door. 'You know what to do about Tokyo,' he said over his shoulder. 'Don't wait up, brother mine.'

It only took a few hours for him to land in Rome, but he was impatient as he went straight from the jet to the car his assistant had organised for him.

Dante had never bothered with his own car, or even his own home for that matter, preferring the number of hotel suites in various different cities that he kept for his private use. He didn't like to stay in one place for too long, as he didn't like getting too attached to anything, so hotels suited his impermanent lifestyle.

He gave his driver the address the investigator had sent to him and told the man to get there ASAP. The traffic as per usual was hideous, and Dante tried to curb his impatience but, as the driver turned down increasingly narrower sets of streets lined with rundown-looking apartment buildings, his impatience turned into uneasiness.

The area reminded him of the dirty tenements in Naples where he and his mother had ended up after she'd dragged him away from his father and Enzo back in Milan. She'd told him they'd be going somewhere exciting where they'd begin a new life. A better life far away from Luca's petty rages and selfishness. And wouldn't that be nice? No, he wouldn't have his brother, but he'd have her and wasn't that important? Didn't he love her?

Naturally, he'd loved her, so he hadn't argued. Not that he'd minded leaving his frightening father, but he'd been upset at leaving his big brother behind. He'd hidden his distress, though, as it had upset his mother and he hadn't liked upsetting her. Especially when it had made her drinking worse.

The driver pulled up onto the narrow footpath and gave a dubious look out of the window at the graffiti on the walls of the nearest apartment block and the garbage in the gutter. 'You want me to get your bodyguard, Mr Cardinali?' he asked, glancing at Dante in the rear-view mirror.

Dante snorted. 'Please, Giorgio. I was raised in the gutters of Naples. I think I can handle a few tenements in Rome.'

He pulled open the door and stepped outside, giving the area a quick scan, his unease deepening still further.

The Montefiores had little money these days, but as far as he was aware they were still on Monte Santa Maria. So why was Stella living here? Presumably because it was easier to hide in a slum, but still. Not a good place for the small, delicate, lovely looking woman he remembered from back in Monte Carlo. Then again, she'd seemed very capable with a gun, so maybe she was perfectly able to fight off all manner of thugs.

He approached the address the investigator had given him—a large and rundown apartment block—ignoring the group of surly youths standing around outside the door. One of them said something to him as he went past, but all he did was pin the boy with a look. He still remembered the street-fighting skills he'd learned back when he'd been thirteen and he'd been beaten up for the fifth time while his mother had done nothing, passed out from another of her drunken binges. He'd decided that night that he was sick of being the neighbourhood punching bag and so had gone out to find someone to teach him how to defend himself. That was the last time anyone had laid a punch on him.

The teenagers, making the right choice in deciding they didn't want to take him on, didn't say anything else, leaving him to enter the building.

It was dark and dingy inside, the lift out of order, half the lights in the lobby out.

He ended up walking all the way to the fifteenth floor, grimacing at the dirty floors, stained walls and huddled shapes of people in the doorways and clustered in the stairwells. It was all too familiar to him. It was the 'new life' his mother had promised him when she'd taken him away. Only it had ended up with her dead a few years later, and him alone to fend for himself at sixteen.

An old anger twisted inside him, but he ignored it, as he'd been ignoring it for years.

There was nothing to be angry about, not now. Things had turned out well despite that. Enzo had come for him four years later, and together they'd eventually claimed that new life for both of them. His mother would have been proud.

On the fifteenth floor Dante scanned the hallway for the number the investigator had given him and eventually found it right down the end. He paused outside the door, aware that there was some kind of complicated emotion burning in his veins. However, since he didn't care to examine his more complicated emotions, he ignored it, lifting his hand to knock hard on the door instead.

There was silence.

'I know you're in there, Stella Montefiore,' he said without raising his voice. 'So you'd better open up, darling. Or, if you prefer, I can get the police involved. I'm sure your father would love that.'

There was another brief moment of silence and Dante found his heart rate accelerating for no good reason that he could see.

He had his hand in his pocket ready to pull out his phone and call the police when the door suddenly opened, a small, fragile-looking woman in jeans and a faded red T-shirt standing in the doorway. Her golden hair was in a messy ponytail, loose strands hanging around her lovely, if rather pale, face. Familiar cool blue eyes fractured through with silver met his.

And desire hit him in the gut like a freight train.

'There's no need for that,' Stella Montefiore said calmly, looking for all the world like she'd been waiting all day for him to show up at her door unannounced. 'Though, if you're afraid to be in a room alone with me, then by all means call the police.'

Stella's heart was racing, fear coiling tightly in her gut. The hard edges of the door handle were digging into her palm, but she didn't want to let go. Given the weak state of her knees, she'd probably collapse onto the floor without support, and there was no way in hell she was doing that. And definitely not right in front of him.

He'd found her. Somehow, he'd damn well found her.

Dante Cardinali stood in the doorway of her grotty apartment, blazing like an angel sent straight from God, the reality of his physical presence hitting her like a blow.

In the past five weeks, when she'd gone over that night in her memory—and she went over it a lot—she'd told herself that what had happened between them was an aberration. A momentary weakness on her part, brought on by inexperience and a failure to prepare herself properly for what she'd had to do. She'd also told herself that she'd overestimated the intensity of his personal magnetism. But all it took was one look to know that, if anything, she'd underestimated it.

He was so tall and broad, lounging on her doorstep as though he was at one of his exclusive parties and not in a rundown tenement in the middle of the worst part of Rome. He wore one of those phenomenally expensive custom-made suits he seemed to favour, with a black shirt and a silk tie the same inky blue as the Pacific Ocean. Somehow, the colour made the deep brown of his eyes more intense and highlighted the smooth bronze skin of his throat.

She'd touched that skin. She'd stared into those eyes as he'd been deep inside her...

Her breath caught.

No, she wasn't going to think of that. She *couldn't* think of that.

You have to. Considering that *got you into the situation you're now in.*

The fear she'd been battling the past few weeks returned with a vengeance, wrapping long fingers around her throat.

How had he found her? She'd thought she'd been thorough in her efforts to disappear. Initially, after the panic of her failure to complete her mission had worn off and she'd had some time to think about her next move, she'd briefly debated the merits of returning to Monte Santa Maria. But had then dismissed it.

She hadn't been able to bear the thought of going home and confessing her failure, of having to deal with the weight of her father's disappointment in her. Of having to tell him that, yes, he'd been right to doubt her. That she hadn't been strong enough to go through with it after all. That he should have got someone else to do what she couldn't.

No, she hadn't been able to accept that. Matteo's death would go unavenged and, as it had been her and her stupid soft heart that had got him imprisoned in the first place, she couldn't give up after just one failure.

It was true that another attempt on Dante Cardinali's life would be that much harder, considering he'd be on his guard, but what other choice did she have? Failure was not an option, not again.

So she'd regrouped, texted her father that it was taking more time than anticipated but would all proceed as planned and started considering her next move. She'd shifted from place to place to hide her tracks in case Cardinali tried to find her, using nothing but cash in an effort to keep her digital trail to a minimum.

Eventually she'd settled on Rome as a place to lay low for a little while—the apartment she'd found pretty much as low as she could get—to give her time to figure out another way of getting close to him.

But first her cash had run out, then so had her luck, and now he was here because apparently she hadn't been as careful as she'd thought at hiding her tracks.

Yet another failure to add to the list.

The weakness in her legs threatened to move through the rest of her, making her tremble, blackness tingeing the edges of her vision.

Oh, God, please don't let her faint in front of him. She wouldn't be able to bear the humiliation.

'Ah, there you are.' His voice was as deep and as rich as she remembered and his smile was just as beautiful. But there was nothing friendly in it or in his dark eyes. 'You're a difficult woman to find.'

Stella clutched the door handle, blackness creeping further along the edges of her vision like a piece of paper held over a flame and slowly burning. She fought to stay upright, but the nausea she'd been battling the past two days—that wasn't the stomach bug she'd desperately hoped it was—shifted and she had to swallow hard against the urge to be sick.

His gaze sharpened, the smile turning his mouth vanishing. 'What's wrong?'

Damn. He'd noticed.

'Nothing,' she said thickly.

And then her legs gave out.

Dante moved, lightning-fast, and strong arms were suddenly around her, catching her before she hit the floor. Then she was being lifted as the man she was supposed to have killed gathered her tight against his hard, warm chest and kicked shut the door behind him.

Humiliation caught at her and she struggled, but he only murmured, 'Hush.' And, strangely, the will to protest faded, her energy dwindling away to nothing.

As if her body had simply been waiting for him to arrive and take charge.

Shame grabbed her by the throat, but the past few days had been a nightmare of exhaustion, illness and shock, and she just didn't have any strength left with which to fight.

Instead, she found herself relaxing against him and shutting her eyes, conscious of nothing but the warmth of him seeping into her and the iron strength of his body. For some reason there was something reassuring about it which should have concerned her if she'd had the energy for it.

What are you doing? What do you think is going to happen when he finds out?

Ice penetrated the warmth of his hold.

She couldn't handle this right now. It had only been two days since she'd finally forced herself to spend the last of her cash on a pregnancy test, and she hadn't had time to come to terms with the result herself.

She'd been halfway to figuring out a new plan but now that plan was in ruins as the consequences of her failure that night in the hotel room returned to haunt her.

It hadn't been a simple failure. It had been a failure of catastrophic proportions and she still hadn't figured out what she was doing to do.

But now you'll have to.

Yes, she would.

Dante put her down on the ratty couch in one corner of the living area and she found herself almost reaching out to hold onto him as the warmth of his body withdrew. God, she must be even weaker than she'd first thought.

Managing to stop herself at the last minute, Stella gripped her forearms instead as he stepped back, looming over her like a building, his arms folded over his broad chest, his gaze narrowed.

There was a moment's dense, heavy silence.

She steeled herself, ignoring the frantic beating of her heart and the nausea sitting in her gut, lifting her chin and arching a brow at him. She couldn't afford to show him any further weakness. She wouldn't. Her pride wouldn't allow it.

'What just happened?' he asked finally.

'Nothing.' She was pleased her voice was so steady.

'Nothing,' he echoed, disbelief dripping from his tone. 'Darling, you collapsed right in front of me.'

Stella gripped her forearms tighter. 'I'm tired. And I'm not your darling.'

'You look more than tired.' He studied her, his gaze uncomfortably sharp. 'You look exhausted.'

She decided to ignore that. 'So, are the police coming? Isn't that why you're here? To arrest me?'

There was another heavy silence.

'No,' he said slowly. 'I think not. I'll handle you myself.'

And despite her exhaustion and sickness a small, traitorous thrill shot through her, memories tugging at her again of his rock-hard body beneath hers and the length of him inside her, the intense, rhythmic thrust of his hips and how good that had felt...

What would it feel like if he actually had his hands free to 'handle' her properly?

Her mouth dried, her pulse accelerating.

Stop thinking about that. Focus.

Stella gritted her teeth, forcing away the memory, ignoring the throb between her legs that, given how sick she was feeling, shouldn't be there.

'How wonderful for me.' She tried for cool and managed to hit it. Mostly. 'And how did you find me?'

'Money. And a lot of people looking for you.'

He must have paid them a *lot* of money then, because she'd been very careful.

He really wanted to find you.

Of course he had. She'd tried to kill him.

'I see. In that case, congratulations, you've found me.' She gripped her forearms tighter. 'What exactly does the "handling" involve?'

Gold glimmered briefly in his eyes, a glimpse of the heat she remembered the night she'd tried and failed to kill him. 'You know, I hadn't really thought about it. But I'm sure we can work something out.' One corner of his mouth turned up in a smile that held a whole world of sensual promise. 'Can't we, kitten?'

Something inside her glowed hot in response, another helpless surge of desire.

No. She couldn't allow herself to feel this. She'd already made one catastrophic mistake. She wasn't going to make another.

Pressing her nails hard into her skin, she used the slight

pain to chase away the heat lingering in her veins. 'I'll leave you my number then. Once you've decided how you want to "work that out" you can contact me. Until then…' she tried an icy smile '…perhaps you might want to leave?'

'Darling,' Dante purred. 'You really think that I'm going to simply leave now I've found you? After you tried to kill me? Who's to say you're not going to try it again?'

Stella swallowed, her mouth dry, the nausea roiling yet again. She should have eaten something that morning but she hadn't been able to face it. And now hunger was making the nausea worse. Her own stupid fault.

The fainting spell was bad enough, but throwing up in front of him would be ten thousand times worse.

'How about if I promise I won't do it again? Will that do?' She let go the grip she had on her arms, and tried to push herself to her feet, desperate for him to leave. But her legs were still wobbly and she swayed on her feet, dizzy.

Dante's sensual smile vanished and he reached out, putting his hands under her elbows to steady her, looking down into her face, his dark gaze sharp. 'You're not well. Kitten, what's wrong?'

She gritted her teeth against the sick feeling and the strange urge the concern in his voice had prompted, the urge to tell him everything, to let him deal with it. Because now it was his problem too.

But she couldn't. She had her plans and, though they might be in ruins now, there was a chance she could still salvage something from them. And if he knew that she was pregnant he might… Well, she had no idea what he'd do. She only knew that she couldn't risk him finding out.

'It's nothing.'

'It's not nothing. You can barely stand.'

His palms were warm against her skin and there was a part of her that wanted simply to stand there and rest, let him hold her up. A part of her she'd very purposefully excised from her soul years ago.

How ridiculous. What was he doing to her?

Forcing down the urge, she tried to pull away, only to have his fingers tighten, keeping her where she stood. Probably a good thing, now she thought about it, because she had a horrible feeling she wouldn't be able to stand upright if he didn't.

The physical weakness made a hot, sharp anger wind through her. At herself for being so weak, and perversely at him, for being stronger than she was and making her so aware of that fact.

She knew she looked fragile, but she'd worked hard to overcome that by being emotionally strong. And the way he was holding her, with his palms resting under her elbows in support, made that strength feel brittle somehow. As if taking that support away from her would shatter her.

She hated the feeling.

'I'm fine.' She tried to gather enough strength to pull away from him. 'And I don't know why you're so concerned with my health. Don't forget I tried to kill you a month ago.' Might as well name it, as it wasn't likely he'd forgotten that particular aspect of their night together.

If he found that uncomfortable, he didn't show it, his gaze narrowing as he searched her face. Then his hold tightened and he eased her back down so she was sitting once more on the couch. 'Stay there,' he ordered.

Stella wanted to protest, but the sheer relief of not having to hold herself upright took all her energy, so she simply sat there as he turned and strode through the doorway that led to the tiny kitchen area.

Damn him. The last thing she needed was for him to be nice to her.

She leaned back against the couch and let her eyes close,

exhaustion overwhelming her for a second. Part of her wanted to curl up and go to sleep, pretend the last couple of days had never happened. Pretend she hadn't slept with the man she was supposed to kill and wasn't now pregnant with his child.

Pretend he hadn't found her and that her plans weren't in ruins.

But that would be futile. All those things had happened—no point trying to convince herself otherwise.

The back of her neck prickled.

Her eyes snapped open.

Dante was standing in the kitchen doorway, staring at her. He was holding a glass of water in one hand and there was a curiously intense expression on his face.

A premonition gripped her.

He knows.

No, that was ridiculous. There was no way he could, not if she hadn't told him.

'What is it now?' She tried to keep her voice level.

Deep in his dark eyes, golden fire leapt, his jaw tight, his beautiful mouth gone hard. 'So were you going to tell me? Or were you simply going to get rid of it?'

All the air vanished from her lungs as shock washed over her.

'And in case you were wondering…' Dante raised his other hand, a piece of paper in it. 'You left this on the counter.'

It was one of the pregnancy pamphlets she'd collected from the pharmacy where she'd bought the test.

Ice collected in her gut, making her feel even sicker, and for the briefest second she debated pretending not to understand what he was talking about. Telling him that those pamphlets weren't hers, but a friend's. Because if he knew the child was his…

It might not be the disaster you're anticipating. This could be the perfect moment to get close to him.

Stella held herself very still, examining the idea. Another attempt on his life was impossible now, because, as much as she hated to admit it to herself, if she hadn't been able to pull the trigger while he'd been lying there bound and helpless she wasn't going to be able to pull it at all.

But there might be another way to salvage her mission. A way to save herself from the failures of the past month and avenge Matteo's death. Redeem herself in her father's eyes, too.

Revenge. Make him hurt somehow, take away something he loved so he could feel the same pain as her family had at the loss of Matteo. It wasn't what her father wanted, but it was still something.

In fact, in many ways, having him remain alive yet broken could be even more satisfying than his death.

However, for that to work she would need to get close to him in order to find out who or what he cared most about.

So…perhaps she shouldn't deny she was pregnant after all.

Perhaps she needed to admit it.

And what about the child?

No, she couldn't think about the child just yet. Not making another mistake was the most important thing for her right now. She would think about the implications of her pregnancy later, when she'd completed her mission.

Stella forced herself to hold his furious gaze. 'I…hadn't decided.' She tried to keep her voice level. 'I only found out a couple of days ago.'

He said nothing for a long moment, but then he didn't have to. There was no trace of the charming smile she remembered. Or the warmth. Or the kindness. There was only anger burning in his eyes.

He's right to be angry with you. It's your fault, after all.

And it was. Her failure. She'd been the one who'd so given herself over to physical pleasure and wanting to prove something to him that she hadn't even thought about a condom. In fact, it hadn't been until she'd realised how late her period was that she'd even remembered she hadn't used one.

Despite her new resolution to finish what she'd started, heat rose in her cheeks, shame returning under the pressure of his black-velvet gaze.

He didn't say anything, moving over to the couch and stopping in front of her, holding out the water glass. 'Drink it,' he ordered flatly.

His tone made her hackles rise and instantly she wanted to argue. But there was no point risking antagonising him right now. He might actually decide to leave and then she'd have to start all over again with a new plan, the opportunity she had now lost.

In fact, given how angry he was, that might still happen. He was, after all, a notorious playboy and an unexpected child wasn't exactly conducive to the kind of life he led.

No, she needed to be careful here.

Stella took the glass and sipped, the water cool in her dry mouth easing the nagging sickness in her gut.

He watched her, the look in his eyes burning. 'Well?' he demanded, the current of his anger running underneath the rich timbre of his voice like lava. 'Were you going to tell me you're pregnant? Answer me.'

'Yes, of course I was going to tell you,' she said coolly. 'Once the danger period was over.'

'So you're not planning on getting rid of it?'

The question set off a little shock inside her and she answered instinctively before she'd even had a chance to think. 'No. Of course not. Obviously I'm going to have it.'

'Obviously, you are.' The words were flat, the look on his face starkly uncompromising. 'Since that baby is mine.'

That little shock reverberated, stronger this time, reacting to something in his voice. He sounded...possessive, almost. As if he actually wanted the baby.

A hollow feeling opened up inside her, a kind of longing. But it didn't make any sense to her so she ignored it. 'How do you know the baby is yours?' she asked. 'It might not be.'

He snorted. 'Darling, you were a virgin. And, unless you went straight to another man's bed after our little interlude, it's pretty much guaranteed that the child is mine.' Intention blazed suddenly in his eyes. 'But of course, if you require a paternity test, then by all means let's take one.'

The way he looked at her made her tremble, though she didn't understand why, and she had to glance away to cover the momentary weakness.

What on earth was wrong with her? So it seemed as though he wanted the baby. So what? It wasn't going to make any difference. He was still a mistake she had to correct and she would. As soon as she'd figured him out.

'No,' she said. 'That won't be necessary.'

'Of course it won't,' he echoed, something hard and certain in his voice. 'Then again, it'll probably be one of the things I'll have to organise once we get back to my hotel, anyway.'

Stella frowned. 'What? What do you mean "when we get back to my hotel"?'

Dante's dark gaze was steely and utterly sure. 'I mean that I'm leaving in five minutes and I'm taking you and my child with me.'

CHAPTER FOUR

SHOCK WAS WRITTEN all over Stella Montefiore's lovely face, but Dante didn't care. He wasn't staying here longer than five minutes, not given the pallor of her skin or the dark circles under her eyes.

She needed rest and she needed it somewhere safe and that wasn't here.

She was carrying his child.

His child.

The reality of the fact was still echoing inside him like a bell being struck.

He'd seen the pamphlets on the kitchen counter as he'd got her a glass of water. Pamphlets with information on pregnancy.

And he'd felt something yawn wide inside him.

They'd only had sex once that night but... *Dio.* They hadn't used a condom. How was that even possible? He was fanatical about always using protection, but that night... He'd been drugged, had woken to find himself handcuffed to a bed with a gun in his face, only to be blindsided by desire for the very woman who'd threatened him. And she'd been so hot and he'd wanted her so very badly that it hadn't even entered his head to tell her that he had condoms in his wallet.

You fool.

She'd been a virgin. The onus had been on him and he hadn't even thought about it. And now look what had happened.

He hadn't been able to move for long moments, staring at those pamphlets, the realisation that she was pregnant and that the child was his slowly settling down inside him.

After the disaster that was his own childhood, he'd never wanted children for himself. Everything in life was transitory and painful so why not take as much pleasure as you could while you could get it? He couldn't do that with children and a family. In fact, the only family he'd allowed himself was Enzo—mainly because his brother refused to let Dante distance him—but that was it.

He didn't want anything else. He didn't need it.

So where the intense possessiveness came from that wrapped its fingers around his throat, almost choking the life out of him, he had no idea. But it was there, the need to grab Stella and take her away, keep her and his baby safe, impossible to deny.

It made sense in a way, since the woman had tried to kill him, which meant he couldn't trust her, let alone trust her with his child. Taking her somewhere where he could keep an eye on her seemed logical.

He was aware that he was trying to rationalise it, but right now he didn't care. There was an unexpected bio-logical imperative he was responding to and he simply couldn't stop himself.

Except it was clear that Stella had other ideas.

Her stubborn little chin had lifted and, despite her pallor, anger glinted in her silvery blue eyes. 'Go with you?' she asked flatly. 'I think not. But by all means, if you want to—'

'There will be no argument,' Dante interrupted, in no

mood for protests. 'You're not staying in this hellhole and risking the life of my child.'

She gave him a look he couldn't interpret. 'Really? And since when does a notorious playboy give a damn about the life of his child?'

A memory shifted inside him, of that ghastly apartment in Naples—very similar to this one in Rome, now he thought about it—and his mother passed out on the couch, the sounds of someone shouting in the hallway outside. And he'd been terrified—*terrified*—that the person who'd been shouting would somehow break down their door and come in. And there would be no one to protect him...

A dull anger that had been sitting inside him for years, that he'd made sure to drown under alcohol and women and too many parties to name, flared to life, bringing with it a latent protectiveness.

His mother hadn't given a damn about *his* life. No matter how many times she'd slurred that she loved him, that she'd take care of him, she hadn't. She'd been drunk when he'd needed her, preferring the oblivion of the bottle to caring for him.

Do you want to end up being like her?

No. No, he did not.

Dante met her guarded blue gaze. 'Strangely enough,' he said, acid edging his tone, 'I find that I do give a damn. Unfortunately for you.'

Her expression turned contemptuous. 'Oh, please, don't tell me that the most infamous man-whore in Europe has had a sudden change of heart. Do the gossip columns know?'

He decided to ignore that, folding his arms and staring at her. 'Kitten, pay attention. Because I'm only going to say this once. You have five minutes to get your things and then we're leaving. And, if I have to pick you up and throw you over my shoulder, then believe me I will do it.'

There was a moment of silence, the tension between them gathering tight. Her eyes glowed, her beauty in no way dimmed by her obvious exhaustion. Neither, apparently, was her anger.

He didn't care. She wasn't staying here, not when she was pregnant with his child and he didn't trust her one single inch.

Nothing to do with how exhausted and sick she's looking.

Dante dismissed that thought. Yes, she wasn't looking well, but taking her away didn't have anything to do with *her*. He was protecting the baby. Plus, he really needed to deal with the question of her attempt on his life and whether she might have another go.

Stella's expression was still mutinous, and it was obvious to him that she was trying to contain herself, but the silvery glow in her eyes gave her away.

Again, he didn't care. Let her be angry. This wasn't about her and this time it wasn't about him either. This was about their child.

Abruptly, she glanced away. 'Fine. I have nothing I want to take except my handbag on the table.'

Expecting more of a fight, Dante stared at her.

There was a set look on her face and she was holding her forearms tightly. Too tightly. Her nails were digging into her skin. And she'd gone white again, the circles beneath her lovely eyes like bruises. The strands of golden hair hanging around her face looked lank, as if she hadn't washed it in a while, and the jeans and T-shirt she wore were rumpled and stained, as if she hadn't washed those either.

A far cry from the perfect china shepherdess, in her blue satin cocktail dress and her perfect shining hair.

She'd been on the run, from the looks of things, hiding from him. Which meant that finding out she was pregnant must have come as a shock. Certainly enough of a shock that she hadn't been taking care of herself.

Something else shifted in his chest, that protectiveness again. But he didn't want to examine that feeling, so he didn't.

Instead, impatient all of a sudden, and suspecting that the reason she'd made no move to get up was because she couldn't, Dante bent and scooped her up in his arms once again.

'Stop,' she murmured, pushing ineffectually at him, while at the same time her body relaxed, as if his arms were the bed it had been searching for all this time.

That shouldn't have made him as satisfied as it did so he ignored that feeling too.

'Can you walk?' he asked instead, glancing down at her face.

She'd gone pink, which was a damn sight better than the pallor that had been there before. 'Of course I can walk.'

'Then do you really want me to put you down?'

Her mouth firmed and she glanced away again, staying silent.

Satisfied, Dante moved over to the table to allow her to grab her handbag, then turned to the door and carried her out of the apartment.

People stared at them as they passed, but he ignored the stares, just as he tried to ignore the slight, fragile weight of her in his arms. She was all softness and heat, and her scent was warm with a hint of feminine musk, no trace of the overwhelmingly sexual perfume she'd worn in Monte Carlo.

Which was good. Because his body, the traitor, was hardening at her physical proximity and he didn't need that on top of everything else.

In fact, he decided that, given how complicated this particular situation was, it would probably be best if he didn't further complicate it with sex. Denying himself didn't come easy to him, it was true, but there was a time and place for such things, and now was not the time and this was definitely not the place. Even his hotel was not the place.

Because she was not the woman he should be doing any of those things with, and certainly not after he'd already made the catastrophic mistake of having sex with her in the first place.

Ignoring the demands of his body, Dante carried her out of the building, conscious of the dealers and junkies in the hallways and the youths out on the pavement by the front. Giorgio had his wits about him enough to get quickly out of the car and pull open the rear door so Dante could put her inside.

'To the hotel,' Dante ordered shortly once Giorgio was back behind the wheel. And, as they pulled away from the kerb, an odd sense of satisfaction collected inside him. As if for once in his selfish, useless life he'd done something right.

Stella said nothing the entire trip, but he let her have her silence. She looked exhausted and for once he could think of nothing to say.

The hotel wasn't far from the Spanish Steps and the hotel staff, whom Dante all knew by name, were waiting to usher him to his usual penthouse suite.

He had a moment as he helped Stella from the car where he realised that there might be some curiosity about her, given she wasn't exactly dressed like his usual type of woman, and that wouldn't exactly be a good thing.

The Montefiores had fallen a long way since Dante's father had been exiled, but people might be curious enough about Stella to investigate who she was and why she'd suddenly turned up at Dante's side.

It wasn't a comfortable thought. He'd never cared about gossip—usually he openly courted it—but things were different now. He didn't want people drawing conclusions about her and he definitely didn't want anyone finding out about the baby. Not yet, at least. Not until he had some time to decide how best to proceed.

Ignoring half-formed ideas of getting someone to attend Stella, he decided to do it himself, pausing only to give the butler responsible for his suite instructions to bring up some food, while making sure the hotel staff knew to be discreet about Stella's presence, before dismissing everyone and shutting the door firmly.

Then he went into the luxurious living area where he'd left her sitting on the edge of one of the white linen-covered couches, gazing out over the fantastic views of Rome's ancient roof tops.

She wasn't sitting now, though. Clearly exhaustion had overtaken her because she was curled up, fast asleep, her head on one of the white linen cushions, her gilt lashes lying still on her pale cheeks.

Silently he went over to where she lay and looked down at her.

She seemed so small. A tiny, delicate china-doll of a woman with her big blue eyes and her corn-gold hair. A woman who'd first tried to kill him then given him one of the most intense sexual experiences of his life.

A woman who was now carrying his child.

The protectiveness that had washed over him at the

apartment washed over him again, a rampant surge of emotion that he hadn't asked for, didn't want and yet couldn't seem to do anything about. It swamped him and he found himself grabbing the pale-grey cashmere throw that had been slung over the arm of the couch and tucking it securely around her so she didn't get cold.

For the baby's sake, naturally. He didn't much care about the woman who'd pointed a gun at his head five weeks ago.

So you do, in fact, care about the baby.

A certain tension settled in his jaw and in his shoulders.

He'd gone through life very happily not caring much about anything, so it came as something of a shock to realise that very much against his will he cared about this.

His child.

Back at that awful apartment where he'd found Stella, he'd thought it was simply about keeping that child safe. But, now Stella and the baby she carried were here in his territory, he was conscious that it went deeper than mere safety.

There was something else inside him, something he was pretty sure was that biological imperative operating again but, whatever it was, the fact remained that the baby mattered to him.

Of course it matters to you. Why else did you insist she have it?

The thought was sharp and deeply uncomfortable.

There had been a time once before when he'd walked away from a problem he hadn't wanted to deal with and he'd had to live with the consequences ever since. Consequences that even now he tried very hard not to think about.

So these days, whenever a situation looked like it might get complicated, he avoided it like the plague. Yet this was the very definition of complicated and for some reason he simply could not bring himself to walk away. Not this time.

The child hadn't asked to be born to a selfish playboy and a potential murderer. The child was innocent. And, if anyone knew what it was to be an innocent caught up in adult problems, it was him.

That baby needed someone to be there for it and, even though Dante knew he was possibly the worst man on earth to be a father, he nevertheless wanted that someone to be him.

Whether Stella Montefiore liked it or not.

Stella didn't want to wake up, but there was something delicious-smelling in the room. And for once she didn't feel sick. In fact, she almost felt hungry.

Except eating would involve having to open her eyes and she didn't want to do that quite yet.

She was lying on something ridiculously soft, and there was something equally as soft tucked around her, and she was warm, and moving felt like an impossibility.

Someone was talking nearby. A man, his voice rich and dark and somehow soothing. He was speaking English and he must be on the phone since she couldn't hear any responses. Something about a child…

Reality hit her like a bucket of ice water dumped straight on top of her head.

The pregnancy test. Dante Cardinali coming to the door. Dante Cardinali finding out that she was carrying his child…

Every muscle in her body stiffened as that deep, beautiful voice rolled over her like a caress.

Him.

She'd been surprised when he'd insisted on her coming back to his hotel suite with him—she hadn't expected him to take responsibility for the baby quite so quickly, not a selfish, dissolute man like him. But it was all going to work very nicely for her plan, so she'd only put up a fight enough that he wouldn't suspect her motives. She'd even let him carry her to the car, nothing at all to do with the fact that she'd been too dizzy to stand.

Without moving, she lifted her lashes slightly so she could see where she was and what was happening.

It looked to be early evening, the pink light making the white walls of the room look as if they were blushing. The large glass doors of the living area were standing open to the terrace outside and there was Dante, standing with his back to her, one hand in his pocket, the other holding his phone to his ear.

She tried to muster some rage at him for the arrogant way he'd brought her here, as if he owned her, but her anger kept slipping out of her grip every time she tried to reach for it.

She was too warm and too sleepy, which was an issue when what she needed to be was cold, on her guard and wide awake.

He turned suddenly and his dark eyes found hers. And, just as it had back in that awful apartment when she'd opened the door to find him standing in the doorway, the impact of his gaze drove all the breath from her lungs.

He was smiling, but it wasn't for her, because as soon as he finished up the call and put his phone in his pocket the smile vanished.

A chill crept over her. It felt as though the sun had gone down even though rays of light were still filling the room.

'You're awake,' Dante said and it wasn't a question.

Since there was no point in pretending she was still asleep she sat up, pushing a lock of hair back behind her ear and drawing the soft wool of the throw around her. 'Yes. So it would seem.'

There was something in his eyes she couldn't read, something that made her uneasy. As if he'd made a decision about something. Had he changed his mind about the baby and called the police after all, perhaps?

No less than what you deserve.

Stella swallowed, fighting not to let any sign of her unease show.

'I had some food delivered.' He nodded towards the small stone table on the terrace, a couple of cushioned stone benches flanking it. The table had been set and there were plates of food on it, tea lights in small glass holders casting a golden glow. 'You should eat.'

It looked warm and inviting, and the smell of the food made her stomach rumble.

She gritted her teeth, instinctively wanting to refuse him yet managing to stop herself at the last minute. Letting him get to her would be a mistake and she couldn't afford any more of those. No, if she was going to figure out a new revenge plan then she had to lull him into a false sense of security, get him to see her as no threat. Which meant not fighting with him.

And you're hungry.

Yes, well, since the nausea had faded it appeared that she was indeed quite hungry.

Stella got up from the couch slowly, pleased to discover that her legs weren't as wobbly as they had been before and that she could at least stand up by herself.

Dante's gaze was completely and utterly focused on her, and she had the impression that if she fainted again he would probably know before she did and would catch her the very second that she fell.

She found the thought intensely irritating.

'I'm fine now,' she said shortly. 'You don't have to stare at me like I'm going to keel over any second.'

His gaze didn't waver. 'You said you were fine before and look what happened.'

'Again, you're very concerned about my health. Why is that?'

'You're carrying my child, kitten.' His expression remained impassive, though there was an acid bite to his tone. 'If you hadn't noticed.'

Stella decided to ignore that for now, taking a couple of tentative steps. No dizziness threatened, so she took a couple more, moving through the doors and stepping out onto the terrace.

Dusk was settling over the city and, even though it wasn't particularly cold, she kept the throw wrapped around her. The air was full of the scents of the food on the table and the ancient city spread out below the terrace, plus the slightest hint of something warm and exotic. Sandalwood. Dante's aftershave.

He hadn't moved, yet somehow she'd got close to him. Which she hadn't meant to do at all. His gaze was very dark in the fading light, the sunset picking up the strange gold lights in his eyes and the odd golden glint in his thick, nearly black hair. That same golden light gilded his skin too, making him look like the angel he'd appeared to be back in that apartment.

A whisper of electricity crackled in the air between them, making her very aware of his height and the powerful body underneath all that cotton and wool.

You remember that body. You remember what it can do.

Oh, yes, she remembered. She remembered acutely. And she wished she didn't. In fact, that had been the one thing she'd wished many times the past five weeks. That she could forget what she'd done and most especially forget what he'd done to her.

You can't forget now. You'll have a reminder for ever.

Her hand had almost crept to her stomach before she stopped herself, though quite why she'd done it she had no idea. She couldn't think of the baby, not yet. Not when she still had a job to do.

Annoyed with herself and her physical awareness of him, she quickly stepped past his tall figure, moving to the table and sitting down on one of the cushioned benches. The food arrayed on small silver platters was simple but looked delicious: cheeses, olives, bowls of salad, hummus and some fresh crusty bread. There were cold meats too, but she couldn't eat that, or at least not according to the pamphlets.

A glass of wine had been poured for Dante, while orange juice in a tall glass stood waiting for her, condensation beading the sides.

She was desperately thirsty all of a sudden.

As she picked up the juice and took a sip, Dante moved to sit opposite, still watching her with that strangely focused look.

'How are you feeling?' he asked, picking up his wine glass and holding it loosely between his fingers.

'Fine. How long was I asleep?'

'A few hours.' His thumb stroked up and down the stem of his glass in an absent movement. 'You should eat. If you've been feeling sick, food will help.'

'I'm well aware of that, thank you.' She knew she should be good and fill her plate, not cause a fuss. But for some reason she felt stubborn and not inclined to do what he said.

Before Monte Carlo, she hadn't thought of him as anything but a target. And then, when she'd finally come face

to face with the man, she'd had to think of him as a caricature rather than an actual person in order to do what
had to be done.

But since the apartment, when he'd unexpectedly been
protective of his child, she had the sense that perhaps he
wasn't the caricature of the selfish playboy she'd turned
him into. That perhaps there was more to him than she'd
thought.

A mistake to think that, though. She could not afford
to see him as a person. Once she started identifying with
him, revenge would be beyond her, which meant it would
be best not to feel anything at all for him. However, if that
wasn't possible, then anger was her best bet.

He didn't appear to notice her being stubborn, putting
his wine glass down, reaching for a plate and beginning
to heap food on it. 'I know you can't have the ham, but
you can eat all the rest.'

'So you're an expert on pregnancy now? Tell me, how
many other children have you fathered?'

'Believe it or not, I have none,' he said calmly. 'And,
as far as being an expert on pregnancy, my sister-in-law
just gave me a quick rundown.' He sent her a quick, burning glance, the corner of his mouth turning up slightly.
'Don't worry, kitten. If I'm not an expert now, I will be
by morning.'

She frowned, distracted from her anger for a moment.
Dante Cardinali was famous for his determination not to
settle down, no matter how many women had tried to make
him change his mind over the years. At least that was what
her research had indicated.

So why was he suddenly now interested in her pregnancy? And why had he been so quick to take responsibility for the baby back at the apartment?

She'd asked him about it back then, but he hadn't responded and she hadn't pushed, remembering that she wasn't supposed to rock the boat. But now…curiosity grabbed at her and she couldn't help herself.

'What does that mean?' She took another sip of her orange juice, the ice-cold liquid tart and delicious on her tongue. 'You can't tell me you actually want to be involved in being a father, or be desperate to settle down? And especially not with the woman who tried to kill you.'

Something glittered in his eyes and she couldn't tell what it was, though his voice when he spoke was mild. 'I don't know. Are you likely to try and kill me again?'

'I might.' She tried to echo his mild tone. 'I would advise sleeping with one eye open.'

He didn't say anything for a long moment and she found she was holding her breath, the hand holding her glass on the point of trembling. Then the sharp, glittering thing in his eyes faded, though the wicked glint that replaced it wasn't any better. 'Or I could just sleep with you and keep you thinking of…other things,' he murmured.

Unexpected heat rose in her cheeks, a gentle ache between her thighs, and try as she might she couldn't make either sensation go away.

'You're not going to try again, though,' he went on before she could speak. 'You weren't able to do it five weeks ago and I think it's highly unlikely that you'll manage this time round.'

He was right, but still she hated his arrogant assumption.

'How would you know?' she snapped before she could think better of it. 'You know nothing about me.'

'*Au contraire*, darling.' He put the plate he'd been filling with food down in front of her. 'I know quite a bit about you. In fact, in the five weeks I've spent hunting you down, I compiled quite the dossier.'

Sitting back, he picked up his wine glass again, the movement of his thumb on the stem oddly hypnotising. 'Stella Montefiore, youngest child of Stefano Montefiore. An avid supporter of my father's, even after our family was exiled. But then the Monte Santa Marian government found out about all the money your father tried to send mine, and all the plans they'd made to try and get his throne back. Yet for some reason they couldn't find your father. They could only find his son, Matteo. Who was the one who ended up in jail.' Dante's gaze was unwavering. 'And who died there.'

Old pain twisted in her gut, the guilt she'd thought she'd long put aside welling up and threatening to swallow her whole.

It was still there, that memory. Of the police coming to their house and demanding to know the whereabouts of Stefano and Matteo Montefiore. Her mother had wept incoherently, not able to tell them anything, which had only made them angry. And Stella had been terrified. She'd thought they were going to hurt her fragile, lovely mother, so she'd told the police what they'd wanted to know. That she'd seen her brother and father going down to the old caves by the beach near their house.

She knew that she shouldn't have told them anything, that she should have let her mother get hurt. That she should have let herself get hurt too, because the good of the family mattered more than any one person. Certainly more than herself.

But she'd only been ten and she'd always had a soft heart. She hated to see another creature in pain and it had been more than she could bear to hear her mother crying. So she'd told them.

And, while her father had managed to get away, her

brother hadn't been so lucky. He'd been captured and had gone to prison, only to die there five years later.

It was her fault. All her fault.

She tried to hold Dante's gaze, to be hard and cold, the way her father had tried to drum into her to be. 'Yes,' she said steadily. 'He did. Your point?'

'My point, darling, is that I know why you tried to kill me. Your father wants an eye for an eye.' Dante swirled the wine in his glass. 'Or, rather, a son for a son.'

Of course. He wasn't a stupid man by any stretch.

Stella took another measured sip of her orange juice, using the movement to cover the harsh bite of guilt and anger. 'You seem to have all the answers.'

'But I'm right, aren't I?' He glanced at the plate she hadn't touched yet. 'Eat, kitten. Or I might be forced to make you.'

Oh, she would love not to. Or simply to push the plate away. But she wasn't supposed to be fighting him, and besides, she did need something to eat or else she was only going to feel more sick later.

Picking up an olive, she pointedly held his gaze, then put the olive in her mouth, the sharp, salty taste suddenly making her aware of how ravenous she was. Damn. She swallowed and picked up another. 'My dead brother is no concern of yours,' she said, trying to stay cool, if only to prove to herself she had no issue with talking about it. 'Or, if we're digging up dead family members, perhaps we can talk about yours instead?'

The research she'd done on him had delivered a few truths of its own. Such as the father who'd died in penury in Milan. And the mother who'd abandoned her husband and her other son, taking Dante with her when he'd been only twelve. She'd died too, or so the records suggested, of a head injury in a hospital in Naples.

Dante's gaze flickered at that, which meant she'd scored a point. Good. And then he said, 'You want to talk about my parents? Fine. My father was a power-hungry, selfish man who loved his throne more than his family and who spent the rest of his miserable life trying to get it back. My mother was a drunk who took me away when I was twelve in search of a new life. And we certainly found it in the slums of Naples. She died when I was sixteen, leaving me to find my own way as a gutter rat. Which I did quite well until my brother Enzo found me.' At last, he lifted his glass and took a sip of the wine, watching her from over the rim. 'Any more questions?'

None of that came as a surprise to her—she'd known the facts. But he'd said everything so casually, as if none of it had touched him in any way.

She gazed back at him, curiosity tugging at her again. No, he'd sounded casual, but he wasn't. She could see the faint gleam of gold deep in his dark eyes. Was it anger? Pain? Or something else?

You're not supposed to be curious. He's not supposed to become a person to you.

He wasn't. And asking him questions about his past was a dangerous road to take.

Stella reached for a piece of the bread he'd cut for her, slathering some olive pesto onto it instead. 'No more questions. I have all that information already.' She took a bite of the bread, the sharp taste of the olive exactly what she'd been craving, then chewed and swallowed it. 'You're not the only one with a dossier.'

He lifted one shoulder in an elegant movement. 'In that case, why talk about the past? That's not what's important here. The important thing we have to discuss is what's going to happen with my baby.'

'*Our* baby,' she corrected before she could stop herself,

a tiny shock going through her. Since when had she decided that the baby was 'theirs'?

Dante's eyes gleamed. 'Oh, so is that how it's going to be?'

'How is what going to be?' Tension coiled inside her.

'We've already decided that you're going to keep the child. But what happens now? Are you laying claim to it, kitten?'

Her hand had slipped to her stomach, as if she could somehow touch the baby inside her. The baby she'd tried very hard not to think about.

You will be a mother. How can you not think of that?

But how could she think of it? When she still had an important task in front of her?

Taking petty revenge while you have a life growing inside you.

Her throat tightened unexpectedly. It wasn't petty. Matteo had *died*. And he'd died because of her, as her father had never stopped telling her. It was up to her to make up for that death. To make it mean something.

She'd been the one to take on the assassination of Dante Cardinali and she'd failed. Which meant she had to be the one to try and salvage something from that failure. No matter what happened.

She would think about her baby afterwards. When she had the time and the space to concentrate. When Matteo's death had been avenged.

Until then she needed to give Dante what he wanted. Play nice, be meek, mild and biddable. And definitely don't argue with him.

Except that wasn't what happened.

'What if I did lay claim to it?' The words came out despite herself, torn from somewhere deep inside, the tiny part of herself that had remained the soft-hearted ten-year-old she'd once been. 'What if I did want my baby?'

Dante's gaze intensified. 'That, kitten, is a whole other conversation.'

CHAPTER FIVE

SHE LOOKED so cool and untouchable sitting there staring at him, challenge in her eyes. Completely unruffled by his attempts to disturb her by talking about her family. Coolly telling him she'd probably try and make another attempt on his life. And then challenging his claim on their child.

As if she hadn't been the one to point a gun to his head the month before.

As if she hadn't been the one to take off her clothes and slide down on him, riding them both into the kind of ecstasy he'd only ever dreamt of.

Dio, it turned him on.

And it shouldn't, it really shouldn't. He'd already decided that he wasn't going to sleep with her, that it would make an already complicated situation infinitely worse, and yet...

She was so small and lovely, with the cashmere throw he'd tucked around her while she was asleep now snugly wrapped around her narrow shoulders. She had a bit more colour to her face, the shadows beneath her eyes less like bruises.

But the cool determination in her silver-blue eyes hadn't changed one iota.

Had what he'd said meant nothing to her? Not even the mention of her brother? He thought he'd detected a faint tightening of her mouth when he'd mentioned Matteo, and had experienced a fleeting sense of regret that he'd hurt her. Then again, she'd tried to kill him. And he'd wanted confirmation that she'd targeted him because of the blood debt incurred due to her brother's death.

She hadn't specifically answered that, but her change of subject had told him everything he needed to know.

Yes, he'd been right. Her brother had died, Stefano obviously held Dante's father responsible and he now demanded a price: Dante's life in recompense for the loss of his son's.

It was all very old school, and he might have found it amusing if the predicament he now found himself in hadn't totally been his fault.

But it was.

As much as he mightn't like it, Stella Montefiore was carrying his child. And he needed to make a decision about what to do.

He'd already decided that keeping her near was in his best interests, especially when he couldn't be sure she wouldn't make another attempt on his life, and he'd always been a fan of the 'keep your friends close and your enemies closer' approach.

But it wasn't just his life he was concerned about. It was the life of their baby too. He didn't trust her, which meant she wasn't going anywhere until the danger period of the pregnancy had passed. That would involve keeping her here, as he didn't want the media catching wind of it, plus he could ensure that she had the best medical care and treatment on hand should it be required.

Once the danger period was past, well…that was another discussion they would have to have. He certainly wasn't going to let her go free while she was still a danger to him and he hadn't seen any evidence that she wasn't.

It was either that or he called the police and he didn't want to do that.

They would find out who she was and then the proverbial would really hit the fan.

Since when have you cared what anyone would think?

Well, he didn't. It was his child that he cared about and he didn't like the thought of his son or daughter being born in jail.

Dio, he'd always thought that Enzo had gone slightly mad when he'd discovered he was a father, but now… Now Dante understood his brother in a way he hadn't before.

'And what conversation would that be?' Stella asked coolly. 'Is this the one we're going to have about what happens to our child when he or she is born?'

He stared back at her, just as cool. 'It's the one we're going to have where I tell you that when our child is born he or she will be staying with me.'

Oh, really? Since when did you decide that?

Apparently since right this instant.

Something flared in her eyes, anger probably. Good, let her be angry. She had to know where his line was and this was it right here. He'd lost both his parents—his father to his obsession with the throne, his mother to her obsession with the bottle—and that had been a painful lesson. And, even though he wasn't any better than either of them, he at least had the opportunity to do better, not to cause his own child that pain.

It was a surprise to him that he was considering someone other than himself for a change, but he didn't take the words back. He only met her gaze, letting her see the certainty in his own.

'You?' The word was layered with utter disdain. 'A reckless playboy who cares for nothing but himself? You seriously want your child with you?'

Her tone made his hackles rise, but he knew what she was doing. She was pushing him, just like she'd pushed him the night they'd met, which meant that he'd got under that cool veneer of hers in some way.

He smiled, relaxing against the stone of the terrace parapet at his back. 'You have to admit, it's better than having a murderer for a mother.'

She flushed, the anger in her eyes flaring hotter, and he could feel himself harden.

Dio, why did knowing he got to her affect him that way? Desire had got them into the situation they were in now and giving into it again would only make it worse.

'I know, kitten,' he purred, studying her face. 'You're not actually a murderer yet, but note that you did tell me to sleep with one eye open. And you have pointed a gun in my face and declared that you wanted me to die. The intention was there, no matter that you didn't do it.'

Her jaw had gone tight, her whole body stiff. Which was interesting. What didn't she like? Him pointing out what they both already knew? A sudden distaste about that particular word?

'What do you want me to say?' she asked tightly. 'That I'm not going to make another attempt on your life? Would you even believe me if I said it?'

Dante absently stroked the stem of his wine glass, noting the anger burning in her eyes despite her cool and contained veneer.

You don't believe she'd kill you.

Of course he didn't.

He knew sex. It was as close to a real connection with another person as he'd allow himself. Women showed their true faces to him in bed. When they were under him, transported with ecstasy, they allowed their souls to shine through and Stella had been no different.

He'd seen her soul that night in Monte Carlo and it was made of passion, joy and a wonder that had extended to include him.

It was not the soul of a killer.

He'd known it when she'd had the chance to pull that trigger and hadn't. And he'd known it the moment he'd watched pleasure overwhelm her.

But maybe she didn't.

'Put it this way,' he said slowly. 'I'd believe you. But I'm not sure you'd believe yourself.'

Shock flared in her eyes, a burst of bright silver as that cool veneer of hers cracked a little. 'What do you mean by that?'

'I mean, I don't think you're a murderer, kitten. I never have.' He studied her, fascinated by the gleam of emotion in her eyes that she couldn't quite hide. 'But you didn't like it when I pointed that out in Monte Carlo and I think you don't like it now. So you tell me. Are you happy to be called a killer, Stella Montefiore?'

An expression he couldn't name rippled briefly over her lovely face before she turned away, draining what was left of her orange juice. Her hand shook as she raised the glass—just a small tremble, but he noted it all the same.

Interesting. Did she really think she was a killer? Perhaps she'd had to tell herself that in order to go through with that first attempt on his life, and perhaps she had to keep telling herself that in order to finish the job.

Curiosity pulled tight inside him in a way he normally didn't allow.

How could this small, lovely woman, who seemed so delicate and vulnerable, who'd been nothing but softness and heat on top of him, think she was capable of taking a life?

Yes, she had a hard shell that she was clinging to for

all she was worth, the veneer of the stone-cold killer. But that was breaking—even he could see that.

Was it he who was making it shatter? Or was it the baby?

An ache he didn't want to acknowledge tightened inside him, which he ignored.

'And I suppose you're fine with being called a selfish playboy?' she said eventually, putting her glass down on the table with a click.

'That's not an answer.'

'Why should I give you one?'

'You don't have to.' He held her gaze. 'But I've seen your soul, kitten. You showed it to me that night you climbed on top of me and rode us both to heaven. And there's nothing dark in it.'

Why should it matter to you what she thinks about herself?

He wasn't quite sure. Maybe self-interest? After all, he didn't want her entertaining any further designs on his life. Then again, if he was so sure she wouldn't go through with it anyway, then what did it matter?

Perhaps this time it's not self-interest. Perhaps you care about her feelings.

Ridiculous. He barely even knew her let alone cared about her feelings.

Stella's cheeks had gone a deep pink, making the blue of her eyes more intense. And this time she didn't look away. 'If you think I'm not going to kill you then why am I still here?'

'You know why. The baby.'

'Strange that a selfish playboy famous for not settling down would suddenly be more than happy with an unexpected baby.'

There was a hot current of anger running through her voice, though she was clearly trying to keep it cool.

Yes, there was passion in her. Anger, stubborn will and fire enough to crack apart the fragile armour she was trying to hide behind.

What would it take to make it shatter entirely? And what would happen if it did?

The unwelcome pulse of desire that hadn't gone away no matter how hard he tried to ignore it beat harder, faster. Along with the tight coil of anticipation.

He shouldn't be thinking such things and he knew it. Temptation was something he'd never been very good at resisting, but he should be resisting it now.

Yet somehow he couldn't stop himself from baiting her.

'And I'm sure a killer such as yourself isn't best pleased to find herself pregnant either,' he commented. 'Surely it doesn't matter to you whether I claim my baby or not? After all, that'll leave you with more time to get on with killing and such.'

Silver flashed in her eyes, her jaw tight, tension in the line of her narrow shoulders.

It's wrong to push her and you know it.

Maybe he did. And maybe baiting her like this was a mistake. Then again, he'd made so many mistakes already, what was one more? Temptation had always been his downfall.

No, hunger for what you know you cannot have has always been your downfall.

The thought didn't make any sense to him so he ignored it.

'I will be a mother regardless of whether I'm happy about it or not,' Stella said fiercely. 'And, since I am, I will not shirk my responsibilities.' Her chin lifted slightly. 'This is my fault, after all.'

She looked so proud and serious and there was a certain kind of dignity to her. Like a queen nobly taking responsibility for the war she'd just started.

Ridiculous kitten.

This wasn't a war. This was a child.

'Really?' He swirled his wine in his glass, tilting his head and staring at her. 'So, in between drugging me and handcuffing me and pointing a gun at my head, then taking off your clothes and seducing me—while a virgin, I may add—you somehow should also have remembered to get a condom?'

The flush in her cheeks deepened even further. 'I'm not a child. I know about birth control.'

'Not, apparently, that night.'

Her eyes glittered. She was fragile and lovely sitting there wrapped in the soft cashmere throw, yet he could almost taste the sharpness of her fury. It poured through the cracks in her veneer like lava through the cracks in a volcano.

'Why are you pushing me like this?' she demanded. 'What's the point? You say you want our baby, but what does that mean? That you'll take it away from me the minute it's born?'

Dio, he wanted to see that veneer break apart completely, watch the fire he could see burning inside her leap high, the way it had done that night in Monte Carlo.

A mistake. Don't do it.

Except he couldn't seem to stop.

'And shouldn't I?' he shot back, putting his wine glass back down with a click. 'Don't you think that would be the best thing for the child?'

'No,' she snapped. 'I don't.'

'Then give me one good reason, Stella Montefiore.' He put his palms down on the table and half-rose to his feet.

Then, very deliberately, he leaned across the space between them, getting closer to all that heat, to the fire that burned inside her. 'Give me one good reason why I should trust you with my baby.'

Stella had no idea why she was letting Dante Cardinali get under her skin so badly. It was only that the way he sat there, all lazy arrogance, secure in the power of his own charisma, needled her.

He seemed so certain of everything about her, firstly with his repeated references to her being a killer, and secondly by mentioning the fact that somehow, because they'd had sex once, he'd seen her soul. And then, to cap it all off, implying that she couldn't be trusted with their child…

She shouldn't let it matter to her, but it did. He might know about her family from what he could find on the web, but he didn't know *her*. And did he seriously believe she couldn't be trusted with a baby? Yes, she might have been prepared to kill him, but she would *never* hurt a child.

Why does his opinion matter to you?

She couldn't answer that question and right now she didn't want to. She was too furious.

And it didn't help that she was *very* aware that he was the most phenomenally attractive man she'd ever seen.

He leaned across the table, the setting sun catching sparks of gold in the dark silk of his hair and outlining the strong lines of his handsome face. Close enough for her to see those very same golden sparks glowing in the darkness of his eyes.

Heat burned there, anger and a kind of demand that made something deep inside her clench tight with anticipation.

'Well?' he demanded, when she didn't say anything immediately. 'Do you have any answer to that at all?'

Of course she had an answer, but she didn't want to give it to him. She shouldn't have to.

Are you sure he hasn't got reason not to trust you?

Stella ignored that thought. The discussion was pointless anyway because, whatever he might say about the fact that she wasn't a killer, she still had a job to do. A mistake to correct. Matteo's death to avenge.

And everything had to wait until that had been accomplished.

So why are you arguing with him? You're not supposed to, remember?

Stella gripped the soft material of the throw draped around her shoulders, staring straight into the hot gaze of the man leaning across the table.

No, she shouldn't be arguing with him. She should be cool, calm and collected, ignoring him as if he didn't matter and nothing he said meant anything.

Because it didn't. He wasn't a person to her. He was barely even a man.

Except that was the problem, wasn't it?

Looking into his hot, dark eyes, feeling the spice of his aftershave and the warmth of his own personal scent wrapping around her, she couldn't think of him as anything but a man.

An overwhelmingly attractive man.

Her mouth dried and she knew she should look away, but she simply couldn't tear her gaze from his.

The atmosphere between them changed. Became electric, volatile.

All it would take was a single spark and the air between them would catch fire.

Stand up. Walk away. He's already got to you once. Are you really going to let him get to you again?

She couldn't. Yet her heartbeat was loud in her ears and

her skin felt tight, prickling all over with the awareness of how close he was.

'Oh, kitten,' Dante said, a rough thread of heat running through his beautiful voice. 'You really need to stop me.'

She should. She wanted to. And yet…his mouth was very close, the shape of his bottom lip the perfect curve. She'd taken a bite out of it in that hotel room in Monte Carlo, testing the softness of it between her teeth. The taste of him had been delicious, a dark, rich flavour that she'd wanted more of. God, she could still remember it even now.

Her own mouth watered. All she'd have to do was lean forward and she could taste him again…

'Kitten.' He sounded even rougher now. 'You're playing with fire—you understand that, don't you?'

It took effort to drag her attention from his mouth, to meet the molten gold gleaming in his eyes, evidence of a desire he didn't bother to hide.

A desire that was just as strong as it had been five weeks ago and just as hot. And against which he was just as helpless as she was.

You could use that.

A hot burst of reaction shuddered down her spine.

And why couldn't she use it? She had no power here, no weapons of her own. She needed something. She hated the feeling of being powerless and weak. It made her feel like she was ten again, after she'd betrayed her brother to the police and she'd had to watch him be dragged away to prison. Powerless to stop it. Knowing she was the one to blame. Her and her soft heart.

She wouldn't be that weak. Not ever again.

Playing with fire? Dante Cardinali didn't know the half of it.

Stella didn't answer. Instead she leaned forward and pressed her mouth to his. She didn't know how to kiss, but that wasn't really the point. This was a power move, a rattle of the sabre. A declaration of war.

Her heartbeat thundered, his lips against hers soft and hot. She could almost taste him and it made her tremble, because there was a hunger inside her and it wasn't enough. She wanted more.

But he didn't move.

Wanting a reaction, she touched her tongue to his bottom lip, tracing the shape of it, exploring gently, hesitantly.

Still, he didn't move.

Frustrated, Stella pulled back. Perhaps she'd been mistaken? Perhaps he didn't want her after all?

But, no, there was fire blazing in his eyes and it nearly burned her to the ground.

'I told you that you shouldn't have done that,' he said.

Then abruptly he pushed himself away from the table top and straightened, moving around the side of the table with all the fluid, athletic grace of one of the great cats.

Excitement gripped her, the thump of her out-of-control heartbeat the only thing she could hear.

This time she was the one who didn't move, watching him come for her, his searing gaze holding hers. And there were no smiles now, no lazy, arrogant charm. The veneer of the playboy had been stripped away to reveal the predator underneath.

Perhaps she should have been scared, because he was very big and very strong, and she was far smaller than he was. But she wasn't scared. No, the opposite. She felt powerful. Because this was her doing. She'd been the one to strip that veneer from him, no one else. Just her. And with only a kiss.

It was intoxicating. She'd never felt so strong.

Dante stood in front of her for a second then, very slowly, he leaned down, putting his hands on the table on either side of her, surrounding her with the power of his muscular body and his heat, the heady spice of his scent.

'What,' he murmured softly, a dark threat in his voice, 'do you think you're doing?'

Stella lifted her chin, wild excitement careening around inside her, every part of her alive and aware of him and how close he was. 'What do you think I'm doing?'

His eyes glittered and for a second she saw the extent of his hunger stark in the inky depths, wide and deep and endless. It stole her breath. 'Don't you dare play with me,' he growled low in warning.

She shouldn't challenge him, not when it was obvious to her that he was close to some kind of edge. But she couldn't help herself. There was a hot tide of exhilaration washing through her and she couldn't shut herself up. 'Why shouldn't I play with you? Or can't you handle it when the boot's on the other foot?'

A muscle flicked in the side of his jaw. 'I can handle it.' The roughness in his voice was pronounced, a velvet caress that made her shiver. 'But you can't.'

She smiled, half-drunk on her own power over him. 'Oh, really?' she challenged, deliberating trying to incite him. 'Try me.'

The look in his eyes seared her. 'Be sure, kitten. Be very sure you know what you're doing.'

'Oh, I know. But I don't think you do…'

But she never got to finish, his lips coming down on hers in a hard kiss that stole the words right out of her mouth and the rest of her breath from her lungs.

It was hot and desperate, his tongue pushing into her mouth, demanding. Taking. But she didn't pull away. She lifted her hands and shoved her fingers into the thick silk of his hair, half-rising from the seat to kiss him back, just as demanding, just as hard.

Then he reached for her, lifting her, and plates were smashing, the sounds of glasses shattering as he shoved the remains of their meal off the table to clear a space. He placed her on the table in front of him, his hips pushing between her thighs, his hands sliding up her back. One hand tangled in her hair, tugging her head back, while the other shoved down the back of her jeans, his hot palm sliding over her bare skin and drawing her right to the edge of the table, pressing the damp heat between her thighs to the hard ridge beneath the wool of his trousers. And then he took control of the kiss and of her, utterly.

It was as if she'd unleashed a hurricane and she was standing right in the middle of the howling wind and driving rain, letting the fury of it buffet her. There was no fear, only an intense excitement and exhilaration, knowing she was the one who'd called this raging storm into being, that it was here because of her.

And she didn't know why that was so damn thrilling, but it was.

She curled her fingers into his hair, trembling as he took what he wanted, and she let him, her mouth opening beneath his, the heat and fire of his kiss igniting her. Turning her to flame so she was burning too, just as bright, just as hot. And she kissed him back, revelling in the rich taste of him, the wine he'd been drinking a subtle flavour that had her desperate for more.

He made a harsh sound, a kind of growl, the hand in her hair pulling harder so her head was drawn back, her throat exposed. Then he tore his mouth from hers, moving down to her jaw, raining kisses over her sensitive skin, nipping at the delicate cords of her neck, licking the pulse at the base of her throat that beat hard and fast for him.

Stella shivered all over, arching back to give him more access, his hot kisses a shower of sparks on her skin. It made her feel tight and hungry all over, desperate and hollow for something to fill her up.

Him.

But he was way ahead of her. He lifted his hands and gripped the thin, cheap material of her T-shirt and, without any effort, ripped the whole thing down the front, exposing her hot skin to the cool air. She gasped, shivering as his palms stroked over her stomach and then up, his fingers gripping the delicate lace of her bra and ripping that apart too.

'Dante.' His name slipped out on a sigh and then, as he shoved the remains of her clothing off her shoulders and his palms found her bare breasts, *'Dante...'*

He said nothing, his mouth at her throat, his hands stroking and cupping her, squeezing gently, his thumbs finding the hard buds of her acutely sensitive nipples and teasing them.

Stella shuddered, her mind going blank as his hot mouth moved further down, finding one nipple and closing around it, sucking hard. Pleasure exploded brightly in her mind, a column of fire lighting her up from the inside, burning away her resistance, burning away all thoughts of power and who had it, who was weak and who wasn't. Of the revenge she had to take and the baby she was carrying.

There was only this fire, this intensity, and the pleasure that was burning them both alive.

It had been so long since she'd touched another person, since she'd been touched herself, and her hands found their way to his suit jacket before she knew what she was doing, shoving it from his shoulders and then scrabbling at the buttons of his business shirt, pulling them apart. Threads ripped, a button or two pinging on the floor of the stone terrace, and then his skin was beneath her fingers, smooth, hot and hard with muscle. His head lifted from her breasts, his mouth on hers again, the hunger in him demanding, and she met it, pushing her tongue into his mouth, exploring him with the same raw demand with which he was exploring her. She shoved at the cotton of his shirt, pushing that off his shoulders too, wanting nothing between her palms and his hot skin. And, *God*, he felt so good. So smooth and hard, with just the right amount of hair prickling against her palms, his muscles tightening as she stroked him.

She felt if she'd been drinking some incredibly delicious champagne that delivered only pleasure, and now she was completely and utterly drunk, and it was wonderful. There were no boundaries, no limitations. There was only this beautiful, *beautiful* man and his hands on her skin, his mouth on hers.

The man you were supposed to kill.

But she couldn't think of that, not now. There was an exquisite pressure building inside her and she was panting, his hands at the fastenings of her jeans, pulling them open. She wanted him to touch her so desperately that she thought she might cry if he didn't. And she never cried. Not since Matteo had been dragged away to prison.

Dante jerked her jeans off, taking her underwear with them, leaving her naked on the stone table, the remains of their meal surrounding them. The harsh sounds of his breathing filled the night and the dark fire in his eyes, the sharp, predatory look on his face, was all she could see.

He stood there shirtless, the setting sun gilding the hard, cut muscles of his chest and abdomen, and she couldn't stop from reaching out to touch him, her hands running lovingly over the width of his powerful shoulders and sculpted chest, his skin a perfect golden bronze.

He wasn't the charming playboy now. No, now he was pure predator, and he was starving for her.

She panted, reaching for the buttons on his trousers, wanting him, but he growled, knocking her hands away. 'No.' The word was bitten off and rough, and he took her wrists, guiding them behind her back and holding them there with powerful fingers. 'I'm in charge now, kitten. Not you.'

She struggled a little, purely for show's sake, because the feeling of being bound and held by him was like an electric shock straight between her thighs, increasing the already acute pleasure.

And he must have seen it, because he smiled fiercely, hungrily, an unholy light glittering in his eyes. 'You like that, don't you?' he murmured, running his free hand down her shuddering body, his fingers brushing through the slick folds between her thighs.

She groaned, wanting to deny it. Because of course she didn't like it when he was in charge. She wanted to be. Didn't she? And yet she couldn't the deny the electric pleasure of his touch and how it thrilled her that she couldn't move her hands to touch him back, at how she was at his mercy.

A shiver went through her and she gasped as his fingers stroked her wet flesh, finding the throbbing centre between her legs and gently stroking over and around, making her jerk and shiver in his arms.

'Please,' she gasped, pulling against his hold. 'Oh, please...'

There was a savage glint in his eye, a snarl twisting his mouth as he looked down at her. 'How does it feel to be held down, kitten? How do *you* like the boot being on the other foot?'

A thread of anger wound through the heat in his voice and the gleam of gold in his eyes, and she knew it was about the chemistry burning between them and how help-less he was against it.

But that only thrilled her, made her even more aware of her own power, and she arched up against his hand, pressing herself into his touch. 'Yes,' she moaned softly. 'More. Touch me more.'

He made a rough sound deep in his throat and muttered something vicious under his breath. But she was hardly listening, because then he was pulling open his trousers and pushing them down his hips, taking his underwear with it, and drawing himself out. Then he was urging her to the edge of the table, the furnace of his body pressed right to her bare skin. She groaned at the brush of his skin on hers, at the heat that felt as though it was burning her alive. And she was desperate to touch him, but his grip was too strong. Then he was fitting himself to the entrance of her sex and guiding himself inside, and she could feel the delicious, agonisingly pleasurable stretch of him as he began to push, her body giving way before his, adjusting to accommodate him.

She moaned, the harsh sound of his breathing filling the space between them.

He let her go for a moment, gripping her hips instead, angling her the way he wanted before drawing himself back and thrusting in again. Hard. Deep.

Stella gasped, reaching for his shoulders, her finger-nails digging into his skin, revelling in the feel of the tense muscle beneath it.

He made a growling, masculine sound and thrust again, deeper, harder. The pleasure was irresistible, unstoppable, a force of nature she couldn't withstand or hold out against. So she didn't. She wound her legs around his waist and clung on to him, pressing her mouth to his throat, want-ing to taste him, to get as much of him as she could any way she could get it. Because she was hungry for something she didn't understand, and the salt and musk of his skin was delicious.

She licked him, kissed him, nipped him, tasted him with every hard, deep thrust. Until his breathing became faster, harsher, and she found herself pushed down onto her back on the table top while he leaned over her, his hands gripping onto the opposite side of the table to give himself more leverage. The rhythm of his hips was hard and sure, his thrusts impossibly deep.

She'd never been to heaven before but she was pretty sure it was like this, on her back on a table, with Dante Cardinali's hard, muscled body inside her, over her, surrounding her in every way possible. His heat overwhelmed her, the subtle spice of his scent cut through with male arousal, and the evidence of his desire for her was in every line of his perfectly handsome face.

He looked like an angel in the process of falling, his features taut and hungry and desperate, a feral light glinting in his eyes.

And she was the one who'd driven him to this point. She was the one who'd made him fall.

She couldn't remember why she was doing this or what point she had to prove any more. There was only him and the sharp intensity of the pleasure slowly ripping her apart.

The orgasm came like a bolt of white lightning, electrifying her, lighting her up from the inside, and she screamed with the pleasure of it. But he didn't stop, he kept on going, forcing her higher, making everything inside her tighten once again before another impossible release.

She called his name, shuddering against him as it detonated inside her a second time, turning her hot face into his neck as the aftershocks rocked through her, feeling him move even faster, a wild rhythm that she couldn't match this time. So she let him go, let him take what he wanted until he groaned, hoarsely muttering something in her ear as his big body shook with the force of the pleasure that was turning them both inside out.

Afterwards there was a long period of silence, the sound of the city below the terrace going about its business as if nothing had changed. As if she hadn't been given a taste of the power that lay in her own femininity. A power she'd never understood even existed until this moment.

Then Dante moved, his hands coming to rest on the table on either side of her head as he pushed himself up a little, staring down at her.

Heat glowed in his eyes, the aftermath of pleasure and something else.

Fury.

'What are you doing to me, Stella Montefiore?' Dante demanded, as though all of this was her fault. 'What *the hell* are you doing to me?'

CHAPTER SIX

DANTE'S HEART WAS beating so fast it felt as if it was going to come out of his chest, the remains of one of the most intense orgasms he'd ever had making his head ring like a bell. He'd never had a response like this to a woman before and he couldn't work out what the hell was going on.

He'd told himself he wasn't going to make an already complicated situation worse by having sex, that he'd simply ignore the desire he felt for this impossible, lovely woman. But apparently he'd severely underestimated his own need to shatter that cool exterior of hers, get a taste of the passion that flamed beneath it. Slake the sudden, overwhelming hunger that had risen inside him the moment she'd laid her mouth on his.

Dio, he'd lost control, and he never lost control. Not like this.

Beneath him, Stella's gaze was wide, the flush that ran the entire length of her beautiful body making the blue of her eyes seem electric. She was looking at him as though she'd never seen anything like him in her entire life, and despite himself it made satisfaction clench tight inside him.

Because there was no trace of the cool, hard woman who'd sat opposite him just before, ignoring the cracks in the ill-fitting suit of armour she wore. No, there was only this woman instead, soft and passionate and hungry, with wonder glowing in her eyes.

Then the wonder faded, her gaze flickering. 'I'm not doing anything to you,' she said thickly.

Disappointment caught at him, though he had no idea why. Because since when had he wanted a woman to look at him the way Stella had just now? He'd never wanted it. He'd never wanted anything from a woman at all and he shouldn't be wanting anything now.

'Liar.' The word came out in a growl, his anger deepening for no good reason. 'You've been pushing me since the moment you got here.'

'And don't tell me you don't like it,' she shot back, silver-blue glimmering up at him from beneath her silky golden lashes.

Oh, yes, definitely her armour was firmly back in place. Little witch.

He was still inside her and her body was soft underneath his. He could feel her inner muscles clenching around him, and that and the heat of her bare satiny skin along with the scent of sex was making him hard again.

But, despite the challenging look she'd just given him, the shadows beneath her eyes had got more pronounced and there was a certain vulnerability to the curve of her bottom lip.

She was not only inexperienced but also pregnant and physically fragile and he'd just taken her roughly on the table. And, even though they were high up and probably no one would have seen, they were still outside and visible.

What were you thinking?

A certain tightness gathered in his chest. Since his mother's death he'd avoided taking responsibility for anyone else's wellbeing but his own, and it had never bothered him before. But, as it had back in her apartment, the urge to make sure Stella was okay tugged at him in a way he couldn't ignore.

'Did I hurt you?' he asked, searching her face for any signs of discomfort or pain.

She blinked and glanced away. 'No. I'm fine.'

He didn't think she was, though, because there was still a vulnerable look to her mouth and she wouldn't meet his eye. Reaching out, he took her chin in his fingers and turned her face back to his so he could see her expression. 'Kitten, you need to tell me if I hurt you,' he insisted. 'Because, believe it or not, that's the last thing I want to do.'

Her throat moved and he could feel the tension in her jaw, as if she wanted to pull out of his hold but was resisting it. 'I said I'm fine,' she repeated, glaring at him. 'And, no, you didn't hurt me. Okay?'

Which should have relieved him but didn't, because there was an undercurrent of anger in her voice that he didn't quite understand.

But now was not the time to push, so he said nothing, carefully pulling out of her. Then, amid the ruins of their dinner, he followed the instinct that had gripped him since the moment he'd met her, gathering her up in his arms and protectively holding her small, warm body against him.

She didn't protest, merely turned her cheek against his chest and relaxed into his hold as if she trusted him. Which of course she shouldn't. Because he was only taking care of her for his child's sake, naturally, not for any other reason.

And certainly not because he cared in any way about her.

Why would he? When he barely knew her?

Yet still the way she nestled in his arms made something in him want to growl with a possessive, primitive sort of satisfaction, a feeling he'd never had before and didn't particularly like.

Deciding it was probably another biological reaction, Dante ignored it, heading through the living area and into the bathroom.

Once there, he got rid of the remains of their clothing and turned on the shower, drawing Stella into the huge, white-tiled shower stall. There were about five different shower heads and he turned them all on, holding her as the hot water streamed over them.

She kept her head against his chest, her cheek pressed to his bare skin, her body relaxed against his. Her eyes stayed closed, her lashes spangled with drops of water, and the way she rested against him—as if she was safe—made the possessive feeling inside him deepen still further.

A mistake.

He didn't want to possess her. He didn't want to possess anyone. He didn't want, full-stop. It was safer, less painful and far, far less complicated not to want anything at all.

He'd learned that lesson the day his mother had dragged him away from the brother he'd loved to a lonely, dangerous existence in the gutters of Naples. Where she'd ignored all his childish pleas to stop drinking, seeming to prefer the bottle and the company of the violent boyfriend she'd hooked up with.

Dante had tried to protect her when he'd finally got old enough to give that bastard a taste of his own medicine, only to have his mother scream at him for hurting poor Roberto and then threaten to report him to the police.

Anger that he thought he'd extinguished a long time ago flared into life, glowing sullenly in his gut.

In fact, he'd tried to protect her for years and she'd thrown it back in his face every single time. And then, when she'd got hurt, as she inevitably had, she'd ended up blaming him for it. The way she'd blamed him the night she'd died.

She was right, though. That was *your fault.*

He ignored the thought entirely, getting some shower gel from a bottle on the shelf and stroking it over Stella's skin, washing her gently. She relaxed totally against him, not saying anything, her breathing deep and slow. Almost as if she'd fallen asleep standing up.

No, he didn't want to think about his mother, not here, not now. In fact, what he wanted was to push Stella up against the tiled wall and forget his doubts by exploring her lovely body and making her scream his name again. But he wasn't going to. She was clearly exhausted and needed sleep more than anything else.

Dante finished washing her body then began to wash her hair, as it was clear that hadn't been done in a while. She didn't protest and didn't move, only giving a sensual little sigh as he massaged the shampoo through her scalp. The sound didn't help his aching groin, but he ignored that too, making her hair smooth and shiny with the conditioner before helping her out of the shower and drying her off.

'Why are you being so nice to me?' she murmured as he picked her up again, gathering her close as he carried her out of the bathroom.

'Because you're pregnant and you're tired and you need looking after.' He moved down the hallway and into the massive bedroom with its view out over the rooftops of Rome. Facing the view, pushed up against the opposite wall, was the huge bed piled high with soft bedding and white pillows—he liked to be comfortable.

'No, I don't,' Stella muttered sleepily as he pulled back the duvet and laid her down onto the bed.

'For the sake of the baby you do.' He pulled the covers around her, making sure she was comfortable, ignoring the urge to climb in beside her and hold her soft, naked body against his, protect her while she slept.

She was safe here, and anyway lying beside her would only make him hard, and he definitely didn't need any more temptation where she was concerned. He'd given in to it out there on the terrace, but he wouldn't again, not with the possessiveness he was already feeling.

Best not to make it any worse.

Dante turned away, only to have her reach out unexpectedly, her slender fingers wrapping around his and holding on.

He stilled and looked down at her. 'What is it?'

Her hair was spread like damp, golden silk all over the pillows, her eyes wide and dark. 'Where will you sleep?'

'The couch probably.' He hadn't thought about it, not that he was tired.

A strange expression crossed her face and then her fingers tightened around his. 'Don't…don't go.'

Surprise caught at him. 'Why?'

'I just…' She stopped, glancing away. But she didn't let go of his hand. 'I'm…cold.'

He didn't think she was and it made something pull tight in his chest, something he didn't want to examine too closely.

He should refuse. Turn around and walk out of the room. Yet he didn't.

Instead he gently tugged his hand free then pulled back the covers and climbed into bed beside her. She settled against him as he arranged her so her spine was to his chest, the soft curve of her bottom fitting against his groin.

He wasn't used to dismissing his body's physical wants, yet he found himself doing so now, ignoring how hard he was and how he ached, biting back a groan as she snuggled back against him, nudging the ridge of his erection.

Then she sighed and relaxed and he found he'd unconsciously spread his palm out on her bare stomach in a protective, possessive movement.

Because of the baby. Of course for the baby.

And yet it wasn't the baby he was thinking of as her breathing deepened and became more regular, her body soft, warm and yielding against him.

It was the feel of her fingers gripping his hand.

As if she was afraid to let him go.

Stella woke to find sunlight streaming across her face. She was lying tangled in a white sheet in the middle of a massive bed, and she was completely and utterly naked.

She was also alone.

Which was a mercy, given the memories of the night before streaming through her mind in glorious Technicolour. Dante taking her passionately on the table on the terrace. Dante staring down at her with fury in his eyes, demanding to know what she'd done to him. Dante gathering her up in his arms and taking her into the shower, washing her gently before putting her to bed.

Dante looking down at her with surprise as she'd grabbed his hand and begged him to stay...

A wave of humiliation swept through her and she rolled over, burying her face against the cool white cotton of the pillow.

She couldn't think what on earth had possessed her. That she'd let him wash her and put her to bed like a child was bad enough, but then to ask him to stay with her... Why had she done that?

It was true that after the two orgasms he'd given her she'd felt utterly exhausted, what little strength she'd had long gone. And when he'd gathered her up in his arms and held her against his hard, muscular chest she'd felt... safe and cared for.

It had been a strange, intoxicating feeling.

No one had taken care of her when she'd been young. Not her mother, who had been too busy running around after her brother, and not her father, who hadn't wanted to concern himself with a mere girl. Since her brother, as the heir, had always been more important, she hadn't questioned her parents' priorities. And, if she'd occasionally ached for someone to put their arms around her and tell her she was loved, well, that sensation soon passed if she ignored it.

Except she hadn't ignored it the way she should, had she? Because it had been that need for love that had been her weakness. Her flaw. It had got her brother captured, had broken her mother's heart and had turned her father even colder and harder than he had been already.

She thought she'd overcome that part of herself years ago and she didn't understand what had made her surrender to Dante so completely the night before. What had made her relax against the heat and strength of his muscular body as he'd held her in his arms.

Perhaps it was the chemistry between them that had been the catalyst, blazing so brightly she'd been overwhelmed. Or maybe it was the discovery of her own power over him and the way she'd been able to strip that lazy playboy veneer away from him, exposing all the wild heat and hunger that lay beneath it.

Whatever it was, it couldn't happen again.

Stella closed her eyes, trying not to think about his fingers on her bare skin or how he'd felt inside her, moving hard and hot, holding her hands behind her back as he'd taken what he wanted from her...

No, most certainly it could not happen again.

'You're awake?'

She went still at the deep, rich sound of Dante's voice

then rolled over and sat up, clutching the sheet around her, even though she knew it was pointless, considering he'd touched every inch of her when he'd washed her in the shower the night before.

He was leaning against the doorframe watching her, his hands pushed casually into the pockets of his expertly tailored dark-charcoal suit trousers, the look on his beautiful face guarded, leaving her with no idea what he was thinking.

'Yes,' she said coolly, drawing the sheet around her in a more decorous fashion. 'Obviously I'm awake.'

A fleeting ripple of amusement crossed his features. 'You don't fool me with that "ice queen" act, kitten. Not after last night.'

Heat rose in her face. 'Is there anything in particular that you want? I need to get dressed.'

They would not be having any discussions about last night, not if she could help it.

Dante's smile faded as quickly as it had come, the look in his eyes becoming oddly intent, and she was conscious of the tension crawling through her.

Whatever it was he was going to say it was obvious he was deadly serious about it.

'I've been thinking,' he said. 'About what to do.'

The tension began to wind like a clock spring, tighter and tighter. She swallowed. 'What to do about what?'

'I told you not to play games with me.' Gold glinted in his eyes. 'You know what I'm talking about.'

Stella tightened her grip on the sheet. 'The baby, you mean?'

'Yes, the baby.' He shifted against the door frame. Today he wore a dark-blue business shirt, open at the throat, exposing smooth, tanned skin and drawing her gaze to the strong, regular beat of his pulse.

Her mouth dried, her skin prickling all over with heat as she remembered what it had felt like to touch him, and how hot his chest had been when she'd laid her head against it listening to the beat of his heart.

'When our family was exiled from Monte Santa Maria,' he went on, as if he hadn't noticed her staring fixedly at his throat, 'we settled in Milan. However, as you know, my mother wasn't happy with our change in circumstances and, after a year or so, she decided to leave to find something better.' Dante's dark eyes gave nothing away. 'She took me with her, dragging me away from my home, away from what I knew and into a life where there was no stability and no protection. She was more interested in wine and violent men than in looking after me.' His tone was expressionless—too expressionless.

Very much against her will, Stella felt that same stir of curiosity that she'd felt the night before, when he'd related the facts of his life with the same dispassion as he did now. Which was wrong. Facts were fine—she knew them already anyway—but she didn't want to know anything beyond them.

He couldn't afford to become a person to her, not in any way.

'That sounds…appalling.' She wasn't sure what else to say. 'But how does this relate to the baby?'

Dante's gaze darkened, an odd intensity creeping into it. 'I've never done the right thing in my life. I've always avoided responsibility. But I cannot avoid it now. And I will not allow my child to be dragged into the sort of life I had.'

She blinked. 'You think that I would?'

'I don't know. Would you?'

Of course. He didn't trust her. As she already knew.

'No,' she said flatly, forcing away the sudden, hot lick

of defensive anger, though why she should care what he thought of her one way or another she had no idea. 'I would not.'

'But I have no guarantee of that.' His voice was hard as iron, his gaze uncompromising. 'You have nowhere to go but that gutter I pulled you from yesterday or back to your parents in Monte Santa Maria. And, make no mistake, you will not be returning to either of those places.'

'I can—' she began hotly.

'Which leaves me with only one option.'

A formless, inexplicable dread began to creep through her. She hadn't thought about where she would go after her task was completed, because she hadn't allowed herself to think about it. And she didn't want to think about it now.

'And no doubt you're going to tell me what that is,' she snapped, angry that he was forcing this on her.

'Our child needs somewhere safe and stable to grow up,' he said steadily. 'And two parents to protect him or her.'

The dread pulled tighter. 'So what does that mean?'

'It means that you, kitten, will be staying here with me.' He paused, his gaze becoming even more intense. 'As my wife.'

Shock punched her hard in the gut and her brain blanked. 'Your wife?' she forced out, her voice hoarse. 'You cannot be serious.'

'I have never been more serious in my life.' There was nothing but darkness in his eyes now, every line of his handsome face set and hard. 'We will need to get married and then I intend to buy a family home where we will live together with our child.'

'But I—'

'It will be a marriage in name only,' he went on, ignoring her. 'I won't require anything from you physically. I'll find another outlet for my own needs.'

Stella fell silent, too shocked to speak, her brain struggling to catch up with what he was saying.

A marriage in name only. With the man she was supposed to revenge herself on. Creating a family with him and their child...

Her heart missed a beat, thundering loudly in her head, and for a second something hungry opened up inside her, a void she hadn't realised was there. Then she shoved the hunger away, before it settled too deeply, as another idea took its place.

This could be the opportunity she was looking for, a way to break him, to take the revenge that she needed for Matteo's sake.

He was famous for caring about nothing, except he cared about the baby. And he cared about giving that baby a home, a family. She couldn't bring herself to use their child to hurt him but...she could use herself, couldn't she?

Last night, on the terrace, she'd got a taste of her own power over him, the feminine power that was all hers. And she'd used it. So why couldn't she use it again? Why couldn't she use that to make him care about her the way he cared about the baby? Obviously, he had the ability to feel something, so there was the potential to make him feel something for her.

Make him fall for her, even.

Why would you think he'd fall for the woman who tried to murder him?

He might not. There were no guarantees. But this passion between them was too potent a weapon to ignore, and besides, what other option was there?

She had to try, at least. For Matteo's sake.

'You don't like that idea?' His voice came unexpectedly, almost making her jump.

Looking up, she found him watching her intently from the doorway.

'Wh-what idea?' she asked, struggling to remember what the conversation was about.

'A marriage in name only.'

'Oh, that.' She was pleased her voice sounded so level. 'That seems…fair.'

His gaze narrowed. 'Fair? I thought you might have more to say about it, quite frankly.'

Of course, he'd be expecting her to argue. And not to do so at least a little would seem suspicious.

You did so well with that last night.

Stella ignored the thought. Last night was last night. She could start by being conciliatory now. And, even though a marriage in name only obviously wasn't going to work, coming on too strong too soon would again arouse his suspicions.

'Is there any point saying anything?' she asked after a moment. 'You've obviously made up your mind. I would think I wouldn't get a say, correct?'

Dante's gaze sharpened. 'Do you want a say?'

'I suppose if a wedding is going to happen then I might want some input, plus I would like to help decide where we're going to live.'

He'd gone very still, watching her.

It made her nervous. Made her want to fuss around with the sheet to cover it.

'You're taking this very well,' he commented at last.

'Did you really expect me to fight?' She made herself meet his gaze, to show him she had nothing to hide. 'I don't have anywhere else to go, it's true, which means that staying here with you makes sense for the baby's sake. The marriage part of it seems extreme, however.' If she was going to put up a fight about anything to allay his suspicions, it needed to be that.

'It makes things easier from a legal standpoint and will also give the child some protection from your family.'

A little shock jolted her. 'My family?'

'They sent you to kill me, kitten,' he reminded her gently. 'Which means I do not want them anywhere near my child.'

She blinked. Of course. What was wrong with her? Her parents would no doubt have a reaction to her pregnancy and she knew already that it wouldn't be good. Her father would be appalled. He'd see it as an example of her weakness, her terrible flaw.

'I see,' she said blankly. She should probably protest that their child had nothing to fear from the Montefiores, but she couldn't say for certain that it didn't. Her father would do anything if he thought it would better their family.

'I'm sure you do.' Dante eyed her a second longer, then pushed himself away from the doorframe and straightened. 'You'll no doubt have some questions at some point. In the meantime, I'll be arranging a doctor's appointment for you.'

A doctor's appointment. A family home. Marriage…

The hungry black void inside her ached, sending a current of longing spiralling through her bloodstream. But she dismissed it.

All those things weren't going to happen. Because she was going to make Dante Cardinali fall for her. Care for her. And maybe let him think that she cared for him too. Then she would take all that away.

Perhaps starting that slowly was a mistake. Perhaps she should start making him fall for her sooner rather than later. Use the chemistry between them while it was still strong. Say…tonight, for example.

Dante's dark eyes scanned her face. 'You have something to say?'

'No.' Stella met his gaze, cold and hard and certain. 'Nothing.'

Yes, tonight. She'd start tonight.

CHAPTER SEVEN

Dante sat back on the big, white linen-covered couch and frowned at the laptop on the coffee table in front of him. He'd called one of his assistants that morning to send through a list of possible family properties, and he'd spent most of the day going through that list, viewing each one online to see whether any were worth visiting. There were a couple of likely looking candidates and he'd already got his assistant to make the arrangements for a viewing time.

He probably should have got Stella's thoughts on them but, now he'd decided what he wanted to do about the situation he'd found himself in, he wanted to move fast. With no half-measures either.

If he was going to claim his child and create the family he'd never had, then he was going to go all the way. He would marry Stella and buy a house where they would all live together as a family.

After all, it had worked for Enzo, so why wouldn't it work for him?

That way he could make sure his child had the best start in life, unlike himself.

He had thought Stella would baulk at the idea but, as he wasn't going to be moved on the decision, he'd decided to make it more palatable and less complicated by making it a marriage in name only. They didn't love each other and, besides, sex wasn't something he needed from her specifically; he could find physical satisfaction elsewhere.

She seemed in agreement, which in retrospect was odd, as challenging him appeared to be what she liked to do best. But he decided not to allow himself to think too deeply about it. Her agreement was all he required and she'd given it to him.

Of course, it had been a bit difficult to think about anything while she'd been sitting there draped in nothing but a sheet, looking all warm, sleepy and sexy.

Dante scowled at the laptop screen as his groin hardened, memories of the night before making him catch his breath.

Marriage in name only? Are you sure?

He forced the desire away. Of course he was sure. He could get sex anywhere. It didn't have to be with her. And certainly not, given how intense the sex had been between them. Because for this arrangement to work the focus had to be on the child, not each other. He didn't want...complications.

And if she wanted to get sex from somewhere else?

Then she could. As long as she was discreet, what did it matter to him?

Yet the thought made his jaw harden and tension coil inside him, the possessiveness he'd felt about her the night before returning and sinking sharp claws into him. And for some reason he couldn't stop thinking about the way she'd reached for his hand, her fingers holding onto him, not wanting him to leave. Almost as if she'd needed him...

His chest constricted, an insistence pulling at him, and he had the horrible suspicion that in fact it would matter to him if she got sex from somewhere else. And that he would *not* like it one little bit.

There came a soft sound from one end of the room and

he lifted his head sharply to find Stella standing in the doorway to the living area.

She had one of the plush, white towelling hotel robes wrapped around her slight figure, her golden hair cascading in a straight, gleaming fall of gold over her shoulders, and there was a strangely hesitant look on her lovely face.

He made a mental note to get one of his assistants to look into getting some clothes for her, as she had nothing but the jeans and ripped T-shirt that she'd been wearing when he'd taken her from the apartment.

Her gaze met his, something he didn't recognise moving in the depths of her blue eyes. A kind of agitation.

He hadn't seen her since that morning, having let her have some space to process what he'd told her while he'd got on with viewing houses and making arrangements. But maybe that had been a mistake. Was she having second thoughts?

'Good evening, kitten.' He pushed the laptop closed and gave her his full attention, studying her face. 'Is there something wrong?'

'No, not at all. I just…wondered what was happening for dinner.' Her gaze flickered away from his before coming back again, as if she didn't want to hold it for long.

How odd.

'I see.' He put his hands on the couch in preparation for rising to his feet and going over to her. 'Then perhaps—'

'Oh no, don't get up,' she interrupted hurriedly, taking a few quick steps toward him. 'Is that the menu I see? I'll come and sit next to you.'

He stared at her in surprise as she closed the distance between them, sidling around the coffee table and sitting down beside him. She looked meaningfully at the menu sitting on top of the coffee table. 'Can I…have a look at that, please?'

She was very close, her thigh brushing his, and he was very aware that the white robe gaped at the neck, giving him a glimpse of bare, pink skin.

Underneath, she appeared to be naked.

Desire welled up inside him, thick and hot and demanding, and he suddenly wanted to pull the tie at her waist and uncover all those silky curves, bare her to his touch. She smelled of the shower gel he'd used the night before, a fresh scent, along with something feminine and musky that made his mouth water.

You really think you can do a marriage in name only?

Dio, he hadn't thought this would be difficult. He'd thought that perhaps, after the night before, the desire would have faded. And it should have. So why had the simple act of her sitting close and wearing nothing but a robe got him so hard?

It shouldn't. He'd made a decision about his child. And that was more important than sex. He didn't need to sleep with her again so he wouldn't.

It was that simple.

Yet her blue gaze was very wide, looking up into his, and her lips were slightly parted in the most gorgeous, sexy little pout. The look on her face reminded him of that night in Monte Carlo, when she'd tried her hardest to seduce him.

Before he'd ended up drugged and handcuffed to the bed.

A premonition gripped him.

Her hand was in the pocket of her robe and he could see the tension in her arm. In fact, now that he looked, there was tension in her whole posture. Her entire body was vibrating with it and in the depths of her silver-blue eyes, behind the glow of desire, was that strange agitation again.

Except he knew what it was now.

Fear.

The tight thing in his chest clenched even tighter, though it wasn't with anger, not this time. 'Kitten,' he said quietly, staying quite still. 'I already told you. You're not going to kill me. You didn't do it back in Monte Carlo and you're not going to do it now.'

Stella's gaze flared silver with shock. 'What? I don't know—'

He didn't let her finish, instead reaching for the hand she had jammed into her pocket. She resisted, but he was stronger than she was, drawing her hand out despite how she pulled against him.

There was nothing in it. No knife. No gun.

She wasn't here to hurt him.

A sudden and intense relief gripped him, not for himself but for her. For the path that she clearly *hadn't* chosen. Because, while he'd always been certain that she'd never go through with hurting him, he hadn't been sure she wouldn't make another attempt.

There was pain in her eyes and she was breathing fast. 'You thought I was coming to kill you, didn't you?'

'I thought you might try.' He held her gaze so she could see the truth in his eyes. 'But I never thought you'd go through with it. I still don't.'

The narrow wrist he was holding began to tremble, but she didn't look away. 'So what would you have done if I'd actually had a knife?'

'Nothing.' He watched the fierce currents of her emotions shift over her delicate features. 'Because you wouldn't have done anything.'

'You don't know that.' Her voice was husky and threaded through with a very real pain. 'You expected that I would h-hurt you.'

He shouldn't care about this. He shouldn't care about her. Yet for some reason his assumption that she was here to make another attempt on his life had hurt her and he found he cared about that very much indeed.

You know she's not capable of it. But does she?

Dante stared into her eyes, noting the pain she couldn't quite hide and, beneath that, the fear.

It was clear that she'd come to him intending to do something but, as she didn't have a weapon, it wasn't to hurt him.

Except she was still afraid.

Was that because she thought she might? That she was afraid she *would have* gone through with it if she'd had a weapon?

He didn't like that thought. He didn't like that she was afraid, especially when she had no reason to be.

And there was only one way to prove it.

He let go her wrist, got up from the couch and went over to the large sideboard that stood against one wall, pulling open one of the drawers.

'Dante?' Stella sounded bewildered.

He didn't answer. Instead he picked up the long, sharp antique letter opener from the drawer and turned, coming back over to the couch with it.

She watched him, her quickened breathing audible in the quiet of the room, her gaze flaring as she saw what he was carrying. 'What are you doing?' she asked, her voice edged with alarm.

He ignored her. Sitting down next to her, he grabbed her wrist before she could move and slapped the letter opener into her palm. Then he curled her fingers around the handle.

Her gaze darkened as it met his and he could see fear stark in the depths. And his chest tightened, a deep sadness moving through him. Because the fact that she was afraid told its own story.

'Please,' she whispered. 'Don't...'

Without taking his gaze from hers, Dante slowly undid the buttons of his shirt and drew aside the fabric. Then he took her hand in his, guiding the point of the letter opener to his bare chest. 'My heart is here, kitten.'

Her breathing was fast in the silence of the room, the expression on her face stricken. The light flashed off the sharp blade of the letter opener as her hand shook. 'Why are you doing this?'

Reaching out, he stroked the silky, soft skin of her jaw. 'Because you're afraid. And I want to know why.'

She shuddered as he touched her, glancing down at the letter opener in her shaking hand. 'You shouldn't...trust me with this.'

'Do you want to tell me why not?'

'I might...hurt you.'

'No, you won't.' Gently, he followed the line of her jaw with his fingertips, using his touch to soothe her. 'You didn't back in Monte Carlo and you're not going to now. I wouldn't have given you a weapon if I thought you were even remotely capable.'

'But I was going to. That's what I came here to do now. Hurt you, I mean.'

His thumb touched her full lower lip very gently. 'How, kitten?'

A flush of colour flowed over her skin. 'I was going to seduce you. I was going to make you care for me, fall in love with me. And then I was going to leave.'

Part of him wanted to smile at the sheer naivety of that idea, but that would be unnecessarily cruel, and he wasn't a cruel man. And certainly not to a woman sitting there holding a blade to his heart, her eyes full of tears.

'That isn't possible,' he said. 'You can't make me do anything. And I'm famous for not caring about anyone.

But what I am curious about is why you're so very determined to go through with this.'

'My brother—'

'No, I know about your family and why they wanted me dead. What I'm asking is why *you're* so set on taking any kind of revenge you can. Especially when it's obvious you don't actually want to.'

'I have to.' She was looking up at him, her expression full of that strange desperation. As if she was drowning and she was looking to him to save her. 'You don't understand.'

'Try me.'

'It's my fault.' She took a shaken breath. 'It's my fault Matteo died. I betrayed him. And so I owe it to my family and to his memory to go through with this. To be strong for once in my life and not...' She stopped abruptly, her voice cracking.

The tightness in Dante's chest constricted even further. 'Not what?' He cupped her cheek, her skin warm against his palm, encouraging her to go on.

Her throat convulsed as she swallowed. 'Weak.'

'Weak?' he echoed, frowning. 'Why would you think that?'

Her gaze glittered, more pain glowing in the depths. 'I told Papa I was strong enough to do this, that he shouldn't hire someone because it should be one of the family. It should be me, since I got Matteo captured. I promised him I wouldn't let him down again, but...'

The point of the letter opener moved and Dante felt the slightest nick of pain.

A horrified look flickered over Stella's face and she made a soft noise of distress, dropping the letter opener onto the floor as if it had burned her.

He looked down to see blood welling from the tiny cut

she'd given him. 'It's just a scratch,' he said easily, ignoring the cut and reaching out to her.

But she jerked away, trembling all over. 'I can't do it,' she said hoarsely. 'I thought I could. But I can't. I can't do *any* of it.'

Dante caught her slender fingers in his. They were icy cold. 'Hush, kitten. Be still. It's okay.'

But she only looked at him, something naked and terribly vulnerable in her eyes. 'I should have had the strength to go through with it and I didn't. Papa was right. All along he was right. I'm weak, Dante. I'm nothing but flawed.'

Stella felt cold all over, as if she would never be warm again, and she was certain it was only Dante's large, warm hands holding hers that was keeping her from freezing to death right where she sat.

She knew she should pull away, try to recover what she could of yet another failure, but that void in her soul yawned wide and she couldn't seem to move.

It was true. It was all true. She was as weak as she'd always feared. As flawed as her father had always told her she was. She'd tried to be strong, to prove that she was equal to the task she'd taken on, to redeem her brother and assuage her guilt at her part in his capture. But, just as she hadn't been able to pull that trigger, she hadn't been able to cold-bloodedly seduce him either.

Instead she'd ended up telling him everything.

And all because she hadn't been able to stand the fact that he'd thought she was carrying a weapon and intended to hurt him with it.

That he'd been sure she'd never use it hadn't mattered.

He'd really thought she'd come to take his life again and there had been a very deep part of her that had found that terrifying. Because she couldn't blame him for thinking that. After all, she'd been the one to volunteer to kill him, no one else. Who was to say that if the opportunity presented itself she wouldn't do it?

Then he'd given her that opportunity. He'd held that blade to his own chest and invited her to do it, all the while stroking her gently, his dark eyes full of a terrible understanding that had undermined her in a way she'd never expected.

And all she'd been able to think about as she'd looked up into his beautiful face was him taking care of her the night before—washing her body and her hair so gently before tucking her into bed. Staying with her when she'd asked, wrapping her up in his powerful arms and holding her against his chest.

She never should have let him get under her skin the way she had, let the way he touched her and the things he'd said about his life matter to her. But somehow it had happened. And somehow he'd become more than the target he was supposed to be, more than the selfish playboy she'd only read about.

More than the vehicle of her own redemption.

He'd become a man. An actual person.

And she couldn't do it. Just as she hadn't been able to take his life back in that hotel room, she hadn't been able to stand the thought of hurting him at all.

Especially not when all her reasons for doing so were selfish ones.

Dante's hands tightened on hers. 'Not hurting a man doesn't make you weak,' he said forcefully. 'Who told you that nonsense?'

She couldn't tear her gaze away from the blood welling up on his skin where she'd nicked him. It made her feel sick, knowing she'd hurt him, even if it had been accidental.

Yet more evidence of her flaw.

'You're bleeding.' She tried to tug her hands from his, suddenly feeling frantic. 'I need to clean it. You might need stitches.'

His grip on her tightened, the look in his dark eyes intensifying. 'I'm fine. What I want to know is why you think you're weak.'

But there was a sick feeling in her gut, her own heart beating hard in her chest like a bird trying to escape a cage, and she barely heard him. 'Please. The knife was sharp. It could have gone deep and then...'

Dante made an impatient sound. He let her go, shrugged out of his shirt, balled up the cotton in one hand then negligently wiped the blood away with it. The tiny cut began to clot almost instantly.

'There,' he said. 'Satisfied?'

But Stella couldn't stop from reaching out and putting one trembling hand on his hard chest near the cut, wanting to feel for herself that he was still warm. Still breathing. That his heart was still beating the way it should.

And it was. And he wasn't just warm, he was hot. Like a furnace. And there was so much strength beneath all that smooth, bronzed skin. So much power. So much intense, vibrant life.

How had she *ever* thought she could take that from him? Or that she could enact such a stupid, ridiculous substitute plan as making him fall in love with her?

She'd been naïve. So sure that she was as hard and as cold as she'd needed to be. Yet in the end all she'd been was selfish, thinking only of her own need for redemption.

She hadn't even thought about her baby.

Her eyes prickled, full of sudden tears, and she spread her palm out, pressing it hard against him, as if she could absorb that strength, take it for herself. As if the strength in him could heal the flaw in her, make her feel less self-ish, less weak, less broken.

'Kitten,' he murmured. 'Talk to me.'

But she didn't want to talk, not right now, so she shook her head and bent, very gently kissing the cut she'd made instead. His skin burned against her lips, making her shiver, and she pressed her mouth to an unmarked part of his chest, wanting to taste him. Salty and hot and gloriously alive.

He went very still and then she felt his hand in her hair, stroking gently. 'I'm not sure that's a good idea.'

But she didn't want to be soothed or gentled. And she didn't want to be refused. 'Please,' she murmured hoarsely against his skin, desperation coiling inside her. 'I need you.'

His fingers tightened in her hair. 'Kitten...'

She ignored him, making her way up his chest to his throat, kissing him, tasting the powerful beat of his pulse. But it wasn't enough. She wanted more. She wanted his bare skin against hers, his heat melting the cold places inside herself, the places that had frozen the day her brother had been dragged away.

Dante's grip on her hair was too powerful to resist as he gently tugged her head up, the velvet darkness of his gaze meeting hers.

'Please, Dante.' She couldn't hide the desperation and didn't bother. 'I need this. I need *you*.'

And something in his expression shifted, gold glimmering in the inky depths of his eyes.

He didn't speak, yet her breath caught all the same as his grip on her changed and he drew her into his lap, urging her thighs on either side of his lean hips. Then he let go her hair, his hands at the tie of her robe, pulling it open, slipping it from her shoulders and off, baring her.

She reached for him as the fabric fell away, frantic for the touch of his skin on hers, and he responded, gathering her to him, and she gasped at the heat of his body. It was a glory, like the first touch of sun on a land ravaged by winter, and she arched against him, pressing the softness of her breasts to the hardness of his chest.

He made a rough sound, then his hands were on her and he was taking control, bringing them both down on the couch and turning so she was under him, and she moaned at the pleasure that stretched out inside her in response, loving his power and his heat. At how safe and protected she felt.

She lifted her hands and scratched them down his chest, feeling each hard, cut muscle, but then his mouth was on hers and his hips were between her thighs, and he was shoving his trousers down, getting rid of the fabric between them.

She gripped his shoulders, kissing him back feverishly, desperate and aching, need building higher and higher. But his kiss in return was slow and sweet, his hands moving on her gently, stroking, soothing her until she felt unexpected tears pricking the backs of her eyes.

Then his hands were beneath her, lifting her hips, and he was sliding into her, slow and deep, making her moan against his mouth. And he stopped there, deep inside, stroking her, his kisses becoming small nips and gentle licks, easing a part of her she hadn't realised was drawn so tight.

Then he began to move, slowly and carefully, as if she was precious. Her throat closed up and, no matter how hard she blinked, she couldn't make the tears go away. And she couldn't stop them as they slid down her cheeks.

She didn't want to cry, not in front of him. Not while he was deep inside her, the evidence of his strength and power outlined in every muscle, while she was weak and soft and so very broken.

But he didn't say a word, only kissed away the tears and held her tight beneath him, moving in a gentle rhythm that had her gasping his name as the pleasure began to build.

And then she wasn't crying any more, only staring up into his eyes, watching the gold bleed through the darkness until there was no darkness at all, only brilliant light.

Light inside her too, blinding her, a heat so intense it was going to burn her right here on the couch. And she wanted to burn. She wanted to blaze until there was nothing left of her.

She called his name as the fire became too bright to contain, too intense, pleasure flaming out of control. And he held her, kept her safe as she burned to ashes in his arms, before following her into the blaze himself.

Afterwards Stella didn't want to open her eyes. She wanted to lie for ever under Dante's powerful body and never move again. But she could feel him shifting as he drew out of her, the brush of his bare skin on hers making her shiver.

Was he leaving her here? She didn't think she could bear it if he did.

'You should call the police,' she said, trying for bravado. 'Get them to take me into custody. I did try to kill you a month ago, after all.'

'Don't be ridiculous,' Dante said. 'You're not going anywhere.' He sat up then slid his arms around her, gathering her into his lap so she was leaning against his chest, her head on his shoulder.

She didn't have the energy to make a fuss, so she didn't, content to sit there against his warmth, the afterglow of the orgasm, not to mention the aftermath of her own emotional breakdown, making her feel sleepy.

'Now.' Dante's voice was very firm. 'What you are going to do is talk to me. I want to know why you think your brother's death is your fault.'

Stella swallowed. She didn't want to talk about it. Then again, she did owe him some kind of explanation. 'It's a long story.'

Dante settled them both back against the couch. 'I have time and nowhere to be.'

His bare skin under her cheek was warm, his heartbeat strong and steady in her ear. It calmed her.

'My brother died in prison,' she said after a moment. 'He was stabbed in a brawl a few years after he was imprisoned.'

'Yes. I know. It read about it in your file.'

'What you don't know is that it was my fault he was in prison in the first place.'

'Oh? And why is that?'

It was painful to talk about this but she forced the words out. 'Papa and Matteo were plotting to get your father back his throne and the police got wind of it. Somehow Papa knew before they came and he and Matteo managed to get away. Only Mama and I were home and they…interrogated her.'

A shiver moved through her and she concentrated on the sound of Dante's heartbeat rather than the memory of her mother's sobs. 'She was fragile and the police weren't very nice. They made her cry. I was scared for her. Scared that they'd hurt her. Papa told me not to give the police anything, but I…couldn't be quiet. I'd seen Matteo go down to the caves near the beach near our house, so I… told them where he'd gone. So they would leave my mother alone.'

'Of course you did,' Dante said quietly. 'You wanted to protect her.'

He made it sound so reasonable, almost noble, when it was anything but.

'No.' Her voice had gone scratchy. 'It was wrong. Papa told me that I couldn't say a word to the police. He made me promise. He told me that Matteo was the most important person in our family and that he had to be protected. But…they were hurting my mother. And I was scared. And I thought that Matteo would get away—' She stopped abruptly, not wanting to voice it.

'But?' Dante asked after a moment.

The flaw inside her felt suddenly stark and jagged. 'I wanted them to love me. I wanted them to protect me. But they never did. They loved him more. And there was a part of me that wanted him…'

'Gone,' Dante finished with unaccustomed gentleness. 'Part of you wanted him gone.'

She closed her eyes again, unable to bear it, the guilt crushing. 'They took him and Papa was so angry with me. He knew why I'd betrayed my own brother—of course he knew. He told me I was weak, that if I'd truly wanted his love I would have done my duty to my family and not said a word.' Her throat closed and she had to force the rest of it out. 'And then Matteo died and Papa blamed me. He couldn't take it out on me, of course, so when he decided he'd take it out on the Cardinalis I volunteered to do the job.'

Dante reached for her discarded white robe, drawing it around her shoulders. 'Because you wanted to redeem yourself?'

'Yes. And because I wanted to prove to Papa that I was strong.' She tried to blink away the tears, shivering under the robe even though it was warm and Dante's bare chest even warmer. 'That I was worthy of his love.' A tear slid down her cheek. 'It's a flaw in me, Dante. And it caused my brother's death.'

But Dante's fingers were beneath her chin, tilting her head back, and she had no choice but to meet his dark eyes. There was something fierce and utterly sure in them. 'You didn't cause your brother's death, Stella Montefiore. It was his choice to plot against the government, not yours. The police wouldn't even have been after him if he hadn't and you wouldn't have been in that situation.'

'But—'

'And, as for wanting your father's love, that isn't a weakness or a flaw. That's a basic human necessity.' Something in his gaze shifted. 'My mother preferred the bottle to me, no matter how many times I tried to wean her away from it, so I understand what it's like to want something from someone who's never going to give it.'

She took a little breath. 'You didn't try to kill anyone for it, though.'

'No, I simply walked away.' There was a bitter note in his voice. 'And she died anyway.'

Stella stared at him, distracted for a second. 'What happened?'

But he shook his head. 'We're not talking about me. We're talking about you. And you're not flawed, Stella. You're not weak. It takes strength to push through with something you know is wrong, just as it takes strength *not* to do it too.'

'What do you mean?'

'I mean, you were very determined to carry out some kind of revenge.'

'And I couldn't.'

'No, you couldn't. But that's not a weakness. That was your strength. The strength to hold back when everything in you is telling you to do it.'

She wasn't sure he was right about that. But in this moment she couldn't find it in herself to argue. His dark eyes were very certain and there was a deep part of her that craved that certainty.

'You always knew I wouldn't,' she said, staring up him. 'Even back in Monte Carlo. Why?'

'I told you. I saw your soul that night. And it's not the soul of a killer.' His mouth curved very slightly. 'It's the soul of a lover.'

She couldn't stop looking at that mouth. Couldn't stop feeling the heat of the hard-muscled body beneath hers and the ache building between her thighs. An ache that was far more interesting to explore than talking. 'When you said that ours would be a marriage in name only…'

Dante's beautiful mouth curved more. 'Yes? What about it?'

She swallowed. 'Does that start now?'

'Well, seeing as how we're not married yet, no, it doesn't.'

'Good.' Stella reached up and slid her fingers into his thick, dark hair. 'Because you know what I really want?'

Gold flamed bright in his dark eyes. 'Tell me, kitten.'

'You,' she said thickly. 'I want you.'

And she drew his mouth down on hers.

CHAPTER EIGHT

DANTE SAT IN the waiting room of the high-end clinic he'd taken Stella to for her first doctor's appointment. The doctor had wanted a few minutes with Stella alone, which had made Dante want to protest for no good reason that he could see. But he'd held his peace and pretended he was absolutely fine with it.

He was not absolutely fine with it.

Restlessness coiled inside him, a feral sort of feeling that had grown deeper in the past couple of days. Oddly enough, ever since that incident with the letter opener.

He tried to tell himself it had nothing to do with how Stella had told him of her fears then reached for him as if he'd been the air she needed to breathe. Nothing to do with that at all.

Yes, he was continuing to sleep with her, but that was because she wanted it too, and why not? Work out this chemistry now, while they had a chance, because after the wedding that would be it.

Are you sure you want that?

Dante growled under his breath and shoved the thought away. He shouldn't be concentrating on these ridiculous feelings anyway. What he should be concentrating on was the conversation they'd had about where they potentially might want to live.

By mutual unspoken agreement, they'd steered clear of personal subjects, keeping any discussions they did have firmly about the baby.

They'd agreed that since the child would be Italian they would need to live in Italy, but they'd had a minor argument about where. Stella had wanted a house in the countryside, while he'd preferred the city.

He'd shown her the list his assistant had given him and they'd eventually compromised by settling on a couple of places to view—one a *palazzo* uncomfortably near his brother's in Milan and a penthouse in Milan itself.

Dante thought he'd probably end up purchasing both anyway—he was going to need a place to himself, after all, especially to bring any potential lovers he might want to spend the night with—but he didn't want to have that discussion with Stella just yet.

The thought of sleeping with other women left him feeling unenthused and he wasn't sure what to do about it. He'd always planned to stick to his insistence that once they were married they would stop sleeping together, but celibacy wasn't an option for him either.

You could just keep on having sex with your wife.

His whole body tightened at that idea, yet there was something in him that also shied away from it. The sex was good—better than good, truth be told—but there was an intensity to it that made him uneasy.

Maybe because she's starting to matter to you?

Dante shifted in his seat then got up, unable to sit still any more, pacing around the waiting room.

Where the hell was that damn doctor?

His phone vibrated, thankfully distracting him from his thoughts. However, the thankful feelings drained away almost immediately when he saw a text from Enzo pop up on his screen:

Matilda told me you had a conversation with her about pregnancy. What's going on?

Dante sighed. *Dio*, what was he going to tell his brother? Enzo would no doubt find it extremely amusing that his playboy brother's past had finally caught up to him. Except that Enzo had no idea that the woman expecting Dante's baby had tried to kill him and was an enemy of the Cardinalis. And, if his brother ever found out, he'd probably have an aneurysm.

Which meant that until he had Stella safely as his wife Dante was better off not telling him anything at all.

He stared at his phone for a second then quickly typed in a response:

The usual private life drama. You don't want to know.

It's not a problem now, anyway.

That should be enough for Enzo not to enquire further. He usually found Dante's preoccupation with the opposite sex quite dull.

Enzo, however, clearly had other thoughts.

It's not that 'romantic entanglement' is it?

Damn. Why couldn't his brother be uninterested, like he normally was?

Do you really want me to go into laborious detail? Dante texted back. *Or would you rather I work on that PR plan for the new office?*

There was a brief pause and then Enzo finally texted back:

Good point. Carry on.

It should have satisfied Dante that his brother—surprisingly for Enzo—had dropped the subject. But it didn't. It was almost as though Dante actually wanted to talk to Enzo about things child-related, which a couple of weeks ago Dante would have died rather than suffer through.

Things have changed.

Yes. As much as he wanted them not to, they had.

He was going to be a father and he wanted a different life for his child from the one he'd had. A life where his child would be safe, cared for and protected.

And loved.

A hot and painful feeling lanced through him, as though he'd been stabbed.

'You can come in now, Mr Cardinali.'

Dante ignored the sensation, grateful for the doctor's interruption.

Inside the doctor's office, Stella was lying on a special padded bed, dressed in a loose white hospital gown. She looked small and delicate and very pale, her golden hair in a cloud around her head. There was uncertainty in her blue eyes and, when they met his, he thought he saw a small flicker of fear that she quickly masked.

Understandable that she would be afraid. He wasn't exactly feeling calm himself, not when they were going to be getting the first glimpse of the child they'd created together and had no idea what to expect.

But he'd thought, after that night when she'd confessed to him and let him hold her as she'd cried, that she'd trust him at least a little with her fears, not try to hide them. Because she was going to have to trust him at some point, wasn't she?

He wanted her to. They were in this together, after all, and if they were going to be parents they had to trust one another. At least, they were if they were going to give their baby a better childhood than either of them had had.

Crossing the room to where she lay, he reached for her hand, ignoring the sudden surprised look that crossed her face as he did so.

Her fingers were cold so he enfolded them into his palm to warm them up.

Emotions he couldn't read flickered through her eyes and he could feel a degree of tension in her hand, though she didn't pull it away from his.

'You don't need to be scared,' he murmured when she didn't say anything.

'I'm not.' But she wouldn't quite meet his gaze.

'Don't try to hide it from me, kitten. You know I can see that you are.'

Colour stole through her pale cheeks. She kept her gaze averted, watching the doctor bustling around, remaining silent.

But her hand stayed enfolded in his, making the tight feeling in his chest deepen.

'Our baby will be fine,' he went on softly. 'I have you, kitten.'

She stared fixedly at the doctor, doing a good impression of ignoring him entirely. Then her fingers tightened around his, as if she found his presence reassuring, and the protective instinct inside him wound deep into his bones, making him ache.

She thought she was weak, yet she wasn't. She was strong. Yet even so, right now, right here, whether she acknowledged it or not, she needed him.

No one had needed him in a very long time, if anyone had ever needed him at all.

Mama certainly didn't, no matter what she said.

But now was not the time to be thinking of his mother, so he ignored the thought, keeping hold of Stella's hand as the doctor sat down beside the bed and prepared her for the scan.

The doctor talked soothingly about how everything was looking fine and there was no need for concern, and Dante wanted to tell her that he was not concerned at all, but the moment she put the wand on Stella's stomach his throat closed.

Then there was silence as the doctor shifted the wand around, all of them looking at the tiny screen on the ultrasound machine.

'Ah,' the doctor said at last, smiling. 'There is your baby.'

The sound of a heartbeat, fast and regular, filled the small room, and Dante found himself staring into the impossible silvery blue of Stella's eyes. She was looking straight at him this time, everything he'd been thinking himself reflected back in her gaze.

No, they hadn't looked for this. Hadn't wanted it. But it had happened, and now both of them would do anything and everything for the life they'd created between them.

'Give us a moment please, doctor,' Dante ordered, not letting go of Stella's hand or looking away from her.

'Of course.' The doctor rose to her feet. 'Take all the time you need.'

The door closed softly after her and then there was a long moment of silence as he and Stella stared at each other, the baby's heartbeat still echoing in Dante's head, Stella's small hand completely enfolded in his.

'I've decided something,' she said after a moment. 'If our child is a boy, I want him to be called Matteo. For my brother.' There was pain in her eyes, but a proud, strong determination was there too. 'Maybe his death wasn't my fault, yet I'd like to remember him all the same.'

Dante felt something in his chest shift, like sand under his feet, making him feel off-balance in some strange way. He couldn't tear his eyes away from her, feeling the words she'd said inexplicably resonating inside him. 'Yes,' he heard himself say. 'Matteo Cardinali. It has a good ring to it. And, if it's a girl, we can name her for your mother, perhaps?

Her eyes glittered and her grip on his hand tightened. 'What about you? Your family? Don't you have anyone you want to remember?'

His family. His terrible, dysfunctional family.

No, he had no one he wanted to remember, no one female anyway. There was only Sofia, his mother. His lovely, manipulative mother.

Why not her, though? It was a long time ago. You mourned her and then you moved on.

Naturally he'd moved on. But he did not want that tiny life to have her name, to be saddled with the weight of all that history.

Nothing to do with how angry you are at her?

No, he wasn't angry. Not any more. He'd washed his hands of her years ago and when she'd died…well…he'd grieved. But she was the one who'd chosen the path that she'd ended up taking. He'd tried to change her mind, to get her to stop drinking, stop seeing Roberto, but she'd ignored him. And then, on the eve of his sixteenth birthday, she'd told him that if he didn't like it he could leave.

So he had, thinking she'd come after him eventually. That she'd contact him, at least. That she wouldn't just… let him go.

Except that was exactly what she'd done. And the next time he'd seen her she'd been in hospital with a head injury that she'd never woken up from.

She didn't care about you. You've always known that.

The thick, hot anger he'd always tried to deny seemed to come out of nowhere, burning inside him like a flow of lava, but as always he forced it down, pretended that it didn't exist. Because anger meant that he cared, and he didn't. Not in the slightest.

If you truly didn't care, then it doesn't matter what you call your child.

'Dante?' Stella was sitting up now and he was conscious that she was holding him tightly, as if he was the one who needed reassurance.

Ridiculous. He was fine.

'There's no one in my family I want to remember. In fact, I would rather our child *not* have a name associated with that kind of history.' Gently but firmly he loosened her hold and rose to his feet because he wasn't going to have this discussion, not now. 'Get dressed. Time we went back to the hotel. I have a few properties I want to show you.' Then, without waiting for a response, he strode to the door and went through it.

Stella got out of the bath that Dante had run for her, drying herself off before pulling on the soft, blue silk robe he'd bought for her a couple of days ago and belting it tightly at the waist. Then she moved over to the doorway and went out into the living area of the suite.

Dante was sitting at the stone table on the terrace, concentrating fiercely on whatever was on the screen of his laptop. He'd been like that all afternoon since they'd returned from the doctor's office—working, apparently.

She'd found it all a bit overwhelming, the reality of seeing their baby's heartbeat on the ultrasound screen still resonating inside her, along with all the emotions that brought with it. Emotions she'd been trying very hard to deny since she'd first discovered her pregnancy, using her mission as an excuse not to think about it.

But, as she'd well and truly let go of that mission, she had no excuses now.

This was happening. She would be a mother.

It terrified her. She had no idea how she was going

to do this, none at all, especially when her own parents hadn't exactly set her a good example. How did a woman who'd been determined to kill a man transform into a good mother? How could she do the right thing for a child when she'd been so set on doing the wrong thing for so long?

All she knew was that the moment Dante's dark eyes had found hers in the doctor's office she hadn't felt alone. She'd tried to hide how uncertain and scared she was, tried to hold onto the vestiges of her hard armour, but he'd seemed to see her fears anyway. Then he'd taken her hand, wrapping hers in his big, warm palm, and she'd felt that strength of his flow into her and all her fear and uncertainty had simply melted away. Almost as if nothing bad would happen now that he was here.

Stella leaned against the doorframe, studying the man on the terrace. He was in a plain white business shirt and dark-blue suit trousers, the sleeves of his shirt rolled up to expose the strong bones of his wrists and the long line of his muscled forearms. He had his elbows on the table, a line between his straight dark brows as he concentrated.

She was going to have to contemplate all the other bits and pieces of reality that she'd been avoiding, such as the fact that he intended to marry her and buy a house for them to live in together as a family.

An ache collected in her chest.

The past few days he'd been full of plans, showing her potential houses and talking about the kind of life they would build for their child together. She hadn't argued with any of it. Mainly because she had nowhere else to go.

She couldn't go back to Monte Santa Maria, not when her father was still expecting her to return triumphantly, the honour of the Montefiores safely intact.

He'd texted her requesting an update and she'd told him everything was going according to plan. She couldn't tell him the truth, not when she knew he'd only send someone else after Dante to do what she wasn't able to.

He'd discover that she had no intention of following through with his revenge plans eventually, of course, but she wanted to put that discovery off for as long as possible. To give her time to think about how to handle it.

Her only alternative to Dante's plan would be to insist on going her own way, find her own apartment and get a job, a task made even more difficult by the fact that her only work experience to date was waitressing. And then what would she do when her father found out she hadn't completed the task he'd set for her? And, worse, that she'd had Dante's child? He wouldn't welcome his grandchild with open arms, that was for sure.

No, marrying the billionaire and living in the house he'd bought for them, while he ensured their child got the very best of everything and kept them safe, was obviously going to be the best route forward.

The ache in her chest intensified, though she didn't really understand why, not when this outcome was the best for all of them.

You know why. He'll take care of you, but nothing more.

But she didn't want anything more, did she? Yet she could feel the pieces of that jagged flaw shifting around in her chest, the need for someone to put their arms around her, tell her that she was loved, still raw inside her.

Ah, but it didn't matter what she wanted. She was done with being selfish. The only thing that mattered was that their child would have the best start in life and right now that start was with Dante.

She him watched as he worked for a second longer, wondering at the journey he'd made in her head from being a target, to a media caricature, to a man. A warm, protective man. And yet somehow he'd still remained a mystery.

A mystery she wanted to know more about.

Did he really have no one from his family he wanted to remember? She hadn't asked him about his mother's name for their child, because he'd sounded so angry every time he'd talked about her. But there had to be someone else, surely?

His past was clearly a painful story, but he knew her guilty secret. About her brother's death and her role in it. So shouldn't she know at least a little about his? He would be her husband. They would be living together and bringing up their child. Shouldn't she know something of his family history?

Stella stepped out onto the terrace.

'How was your bath?' Dante asked, not looking up.

'Very nice. Thank you for running it for me.'

'No problem. By the way, I've organised a viewing of the *palazzo* in Milan for tomorrow. I'll get one of the helicopters to take us.'

'Okay.' She came over and leaned against the edge of the table and looked down. His face was set as he stared at the screen, the neck of his shirt open, and he wore no tie.

He was so incredibly attractive, so overwhelmingly beautiful.

Her mouth watered and she very much wanted to bend and kiss his throat, taste his skin.

How are you going to cope with this sexless marriage he's insisting on?

The thought arrowed through her, unexpectedly painful. Another thing she hadn't thought about because she'd assumed it wasn't going to happen. But it was going to happen. Regardless of how many nights she'd spent in his bed, he'd continue to insist that once they were married it would stop. That he wouldn't demand anything further from her physically and that he would find his satisfaction elsewhere.

She did not like that one bit.

But that was a discussion that would lead to uncomfortable places and she didn't want to have that conversation with him. Not now. First she was here to learn more about his family.

Her heartbeat sped up, her palms sweaty. 'I've been thinking about what you said in the doctor's office,' she said hesitantly. 'About not wanting to name our child after anyone in your family.'

His gaze remained on the screen. 'I haven't changed my mind, if that's what you're expecting.'

'I'm not. I just… What happened? With your family, I mean?'

'I told you. I was taken away by my alcoholic mother to live in Naples. She died years ago there.'

'How?'

Dante finally looked up at her, his expression guarded. 'Why do you want to know? It's not a very pleasant story.'

Very clearly, it was not, considering how obvious it was that he didn't want to tell her.

'My brother's story isn't very pleasant either,' she said. 'But I still told you.'

His gaze darkened. 'What is this? A quid pro quo? You tell me a secret and now I have to tell you one of mine?'

Stella didn't flinch. 'I'm going to marry you, Dante. Is it wrong to want to know something about the man who's going to be my husband?'

'It won't be a typical marriage, need I remind you?'

She ignored the slight, fleeting pain that pulled inside her at the words. 'I realise that. But I want to know more about you and your past. About what kind of father you're likely to be.'

A fierce, hot spark leapt to life in Dante's eyes. 'You think I would do anything to hurt our baby?' The question was soft but there was a whole world of threat in his deep, rich voice.

Stella refused to look away. 'No. And that's not what I was implying. Don't be so touchy.'

He made an impatient sound and, strangely, it was he who finally glanced away. 'You want to know what happened to me and my mother? Fine. She never quite recovered from my father losing his throne and so, when we were exiled from Monte Santa Maria to Milan, she started drinking. My father didn't care about anything but being king again, and he certainly didn't care about her. So after a couple of months she decided that she'd had enough. She left and took me with her.'

Bitterness laced his beautiful voice, like arsenic in hot chocolate. 'I didn't want to go. I'd already lost my country, and I didn't want to lose my family, and especially not my brother. But she didn't care what I wanted. All that mattered was that she wasn't alone. We ended up in some dirty tenement in Naples, surviving on nothing because she couldn't hold down a job.' He paused, gold gleaming hot in his eyes. 'You want to hear more or is that enough? It doesn't get any better, I warn you.'

She held his gaze, fascinated by that hot glow, the raw emotion he kept locked inside the darkness of his gaze like a candle flame in a dark room. It reminded her of the way he looked at her in bed sometimes when he thought she was asleep, as if she had something he wanted that he didn't know how to get.

'Yes, more,' she said. 'I can handle it.'

He let out a long breath, then closed the laptop and sat back on the seat. A smile was playing around his mouth, but there was no amusement in it. It looked forced. 'Of course you can. You were going to kill me, after all.'

There was a bite to the words that she was sure was supposed to hurt her, but she ignored it. He was angry because she was pushing him and he didn't want to be pushed. But too bad. Underneath anger there was always pain, as she knew all too well, and she wanted to understand it.

Why? So you can heal him?

The ache in her chest deepened. Well, why not? He'd helped her with the pain of her own guilt. Couldn't she help him in return?

No, she wasn't supposed to care about him. But somehow she did all the same.

'Perhaps I should have,' she said coolly. 'Apparently attempting to kill you is easier than getting you to talk.'

A flicker of emotion crossed his face, the gold in his eyes glowing hotter.

She wasn't surprised. If she'd learned anything about Dante Cardinali, it was that he preferred a fight to honest discussion. Which she had too—at least up until she'd seen her baby's heartbeat on that monitor.

He gave a low, mirthless laugh. 'You're a hard woman, kitten. You don't let me get away with anything do you?'

'Why should I? You didn't let me get away at all.'

His smile this time was more natural, and he got up, moving to where she leaned against the table and standing in front of her. Then he settled his hands on her hips and lifted her onto the table top, pushing himself between her thighs and fitting her against him. He was hard, the heat of him seeping through the fabric of their clothing, and she shivered, loving the delicious press of him against her. But she didn't look away, keeping her gaze on his.

Dante shook his head. 'You're not going to let this go, are you?'

'No.'

'Okay. So, we moved around Naples a lot,' he went on, his tone casual, stripping the words of any emotion. 'Since my mother couldn't stay in any one job too long, it meant she couldn't pay rent. Eventually she took up with a series of men who would help her out sometimes. Her favourite was a bastard called Roberto, who beat her when he was drunk. But for some reason she loved him and when I finally grew big enough to put a stop to him taking out his moods on her—and sometimes on me as well—she blamed me for hurting him. And for us subsequently moving again, because Roberto stopped the money he was giving her.'

Stella's heart squeezed. He sounded as if he'd told this story a hundred times and was bored of it. But she could hear the tension in his voice, an undercurrent of anger and of pain. It made her want to do something for him, but she wasn't sure what, so she put her hands his forearms, her fingers on his bare skin, hoping the contact would give him some comfort.

'I tried to make her stop drinking,' Dante went on, his voice becoming harder and more edged. 'Tried to get her to leave Roberto. I did everything I could think of, telling her that it would kill her if she went on like she was, but she wasn't interested in stopping, or changing what she was doing. So in the end I gave her an ultimatum—told her it was either the bottle or me. I was just sixteen, old enough to look after myself—though, to be frank, I'd been doing that since she dragged me away from Milan—so when she said that she wasn't going to stop, that I should go if I couldn't handle it, that's exactly what I did.'

He smiled, sharp and white. 'I walked out, thinking she'd come after me. That she'd change her mind. But she didn't. For six months I heard nothing and then I got a call from a hospital saying that she was in Intensive Care with a head injury. She'd fallen over after a night drinking with Roberto and had hit her head on the pavement.' A muscle ticked in his jaw. 'I spent a month sitting beside her, watching her slowly die. She never regained consciousness and so she never knew that I'd come back.'

The anger in his gaze gleamed, his fingers gripping her tighter, though she didn't think he was aware of it. 'I never got to ask her why she'd dragged me around Italy with her, since it was obvious she preferred the bottle to me. Or why she wouldn't stop drinking, even when I begged her to. She just died and left me with nothing. Just like she always did.'

Stella swallowed, grief closing her throat. For Dante and the pain that was obviously still raw inside him. 'Dante,' she said thickly, not sure what else to say or what else to offer. Her own parents hadn't left her with anything either.

His mouth twisted in another of those terrible smiles. 'So now you know exactly what kind of man you're marrying, kitten. Stateless. Rootless. A man who'd rather walk away from a problem than have to deal with it, because it's easier to not give a damn.'

Of course. The 'problem' he'd walked away from had been his mother.

'You blame yourself,' she said, before she could think better of it. 'Don't you?'

'What? For the way she died? No, of course not.' Dull anger glittered in his eyes. 'She chose that path herself. I had nothing to do with it.'

'If you truly believe that, then why are you so angry about it?'

'Angry? I'm not angry.' He laughed, but there was no amusement in the sound. 'That would imply that I care. And I don't. Not any more.'

But he was lying, that was obvious. Of course he cared.

He cared deeply and she could see the depth of it in the pain that lay underneath all that anger.

'Yes, you do.' She lifted her hand and touched the warmth of his cheek. 'And that's the problem, isn't it? You care too much.'

The smile on his face vanished. 'Is there a point to this?' His hands firmed on her, his hips flexing slightly, the ridge of his erection nudging against the soft, sensitive place between her thighs. 'Because there are things I'd rather be doing.'

Stella fought back the shiver of pleasure that whispered over her skin. It would be easy to surrender, to let him distract her in the way he was so good at, and part of her wanted to. She wouldn't have this for ever, after all.

But this was important.

'The point is that you're angry,' she said quietly, looking straight up into his eyes. 'And I want to help you the way you helped me.'

His mouth twisted. 'Don't care about me, kitten. That would be a mistake.'

'And is that what you'll say to your child when they tell you that they love you? That it's a mistake? That they shouldn't?'

It was a low blow and she knew it. But, whether he liked it or not, this mattered. For the baby's sake if nothing else.

His gaze went dark, any flickers of gold vanishing from it entirely. 'Don't use our child to manipulate me,' he said, low and hard. 'I won't allow it.'

Stella stared back. 'I'm not. I don't care what you feel for me, but I need to know that you'll care for our child.'

Liar. You care what he feels for you.

She ignored the thought, meeting Dante's black gaze head-on, keeping her fingers pressed to his cheek, letting her know how serious she was.

'Do you really think I wouldn't?' he demanded roughly. 'Why do you think I offered to marry you? Why do you think I'm buying a house for us to live in?'

'You're doing those things to take care of us, Dante. But that is not the same as love and you know it.'

'Love?' The word was a sneer, sharp-edged and painful. 'Since when does love have anything to do with it?'

Her heart gave one hard beat in her chest. She refused to look away. 'Since now.'

Stella's fingertips on his skin were light, her body against his soft and warm, and he felt as if he was holding a sunbeam in his hands; all he wanted to do was bask in her heat.

He most certainly didn't want to look into the relentless silver-blue of her eyes and talk about the farce that was love. He'd already given her more of himself than he'd wanted, more than he'd given anyone in his entire life, including his brother.

And he wasn't sure why. He'd never felt obligated to be honest with another person simply because they'd been honest with him. In fact, he'd tried never to feel obligated to anyone at all. He didn't want to give any more pieces of his soul away than he had already.

He'd been in a foul mood since they'd got back from the doctor's office and when she'd brought up his family his temper had become even fouler.

Nevertheless, there had been something direct and honest in her gaze that he hadn't been able to refuse. That had made him want to give her something in return for what she'd given him: her secrets and her pain the night he'd made her hold a blade to his chest. The way she'd clutched onto his hand as they'd seen their baby on the monitor. Her pleasure, every time he touched her at night.

Those had all meant something to him, especially when

his mother hadn't wanted anything at all from him. She'd ignored what he'd tried to do for her, had thrown all his offers to help her back in his face. And when he'd attempted to help anyway she'd told him that he didn't care. That, if he truly loved her, he'd leave her alone.

Even in dying she'd refused him.

But Stella hadn't. She'd accepted his help, let him take care of her. Let him give her strength and hold her. Stella had never refused him anything. Which meant he hadn't been able to refuse telling her about the life he'd had with his mother. But he'd hoped that, once he'd finished, she'd leave the subject alone.

Apparently not.

'What is it exactly that you're asking?' he demanded, trying to sound like his normal, casual self and knowing he'd failed. 'Because, if you're wanting me to fall on my knees and tell you that I'm madly in love with you, you're going to be disappointed.'

'I know that,' she said without a flicker, full of a quiet dignity that made an inexplicable sense of shame creep through him. 'I'm not talking about me. I'm talking about our child.'

Anger burned sullenly inside him, a dull flame that never seemed to go out no matter how many times he tried to ignore it.

He didn't want to talk about love. He didn't even want to think about it.

Love was his mother throwing a glass at his head when he'd tried to call a doctor for her after a hard night on the tiles. Love was her threatening him with the police after he'd punched Roberto in the face after the bastard had hurt her.

Love was her telling him that she was done with him and he should leave her alone.

Love was her dying in that hospital bed without ever regaining consciousness, denying him his last opportunity to talk to her.

He'd been there, done that and he wanted no part of it ever again.

'Our child will have everything in my power to give,' Dante said, trying to dismiss the subject. 'Call it what you want.'

Yet there was something in Stella's gaze that felt like a hand closing around his heart. 'And if he or she wants to love you?'

The hand squeezed harder. 'I won't stop them.'

'But you won't give them anything back?'

The words twisted inside him like a barb on a fish-hook, tearing and painful. 'Do I need to?' He squeezed her gently, flexing his hips, sliding his erection against the softness between her thighs, the delicious ache easing the agony of his memories. 'When they'll get all the love they might want from you?'

Stella's gaze darkened. Gilt curls still damp from her bath stuck to her forehead. She smelled of lavender and musk, and he wanted to bury his face between her breasts, breathe her in. Then maybe lick a long path down between her thighs too, make her scream instead of asking him questions he didn't want to answer, or make him talk about things that should have been left in the past.

Things such as the knowledge that maybe, if he hadn't walked away from his mother, he might have been able to save her.

That she wouldn't have died the way she had.

Because it's your fault. It's always been your fault.

'You don't mean that,' Stella said.

'How would you know? You don't know a thing about me.'

'Wrong.' Her fingertips moved lightly along his cheekbone. 'I know that you care about this baby, whether you like it or not. And I know you want to do the right thing by it.' Her touch moved to his jaw. Why he was letting her touch him like this he didn't have any idea, but he didn't stop her. 'I know you've done nothing but look after me since you brought me here, despite the fact that I wanted to kill you. And I know you're angry. You're very, *very* angry about your mother and, Dante…' She touched his mouth gently, meeting his gaze. 'You have a right to be angry. You needed her and she wasn't there for you, and there is no excuse for that. None at all.'

Tension crawled through him, tugging at his instinct to pull away violently, to turn and leave, no matter how that would hurt her.

But he couldn't do that.

Colour had risen in her skin, making her eyes look bluer. A perfect, pale white-and-gold china shepherdess of a woman. Not a woman he'd ever have picked to hold a gun to his head or end up carrying his child. Not a woman he'd have picked to fight him, challenge him on just about every level there was. Yet she'd done all of those things.

A vulnerable woman too—he couldn't forget that. One who'd been hurt by her past, and whose feelings had been twisted and denied, yet despite that she still had an open heart. She wasn't like him. She would never *not* care.

Which made her the most perfect parent for their child. *Unlike you.*

But he didn't want to think about that, still less talk about it. He was done with anger and guilt. He was done with caring. And he was done with love.

Especially now he had Stella, warm and lush and naked under that thin blue silk robe.

'I think we've done the topic of me to death.' He flexed

his hips again, pressing himself against her damp heat. 'I'm more interested in other things.'

Her fingers gripped his forearms tightly, the expression on her face making that fist around his heart squeeze like a vice. 'You can trust me, Dante. I know that sounds strange, coming from the person who held you at gunpoint a month or so ago, but you can. I will never turn you away.'

The tight, painful feeling in his chest grew stronger and he had to grit his teeth against it. 'I don't want your trust,' he growled, knowing he was being a bastard and not caring, because not caring was supposed to be what he did. 'What I want is your body, understand?'

'Yes.' Her gaze was too sharp, too knowing. 'And you can have it. I told you I will never refuse you and I meant it.'

She wasn't supposed to do that. She wasn't supposed just to…give in to him.

His heart rate began to climb, adrenaline pouring through him. 'Bad idea, kitten.' His voice was low and much rougher than he'd intended. 'I'm not in a gentle mood.'

'I don't care. Do your worst. I'm stronger than I look, remember?'

Oh, yes, he remembered.

He lifted her into his arms, because he wasn't going to take her on the stone table like an animal, not again. He could at least be an animal in the comfort of the bedroom where there was something soft to ravage her on.

Bending his head, he took her mouth in a hard kiss, letting her know that he most certainly would take whatever he wanted from her. But she only wrapped her legs around his waist and gripped him tightly, opening her mouth, letting him kiss her harder, deeper. Showing him the truth— that she would never turn him away. Never refuse him. She challenged him and pushed him, gave him the fight that he wanted, and then she opened her arms and took him in, giving him the surrender he craved.

His heartbeat was wild and out of control, the familiar, intense desperation winding around his soul. He didn't know why it was like this with her every time. He couldn't understand it. But he couldn't stop the feeling that was rising inside him, a desperation, a need. To get close to her, have her warmth and softness all over him, under him.

The feeling pushed at him, battered against his heart, and he couldn't wait, not even to get to the bedroom. He stopped in the living area and laid her down on the thick, white carpet that wasn't as soft as he wanted it to be, but her scent and her heat were affecting him so badly that he just couldn't stop.

Pulling open her robe, he exposed her naked body to the late-afternoon sunlight pouring through the window. She was all golden hair and creamy white skin and soft shell-pink nipples. Her gaze was jewel-bright as she looked up at him, full of desire and need. Need for him.

'You want me?' he heard himself growl as he knelt between her thighs and leaned over her, putting his hands on the floor on either side of her head. 'You want me, Stella Montefiore?'

'Yes.' Her chest rose and fell, fast and hard in time with her quickened breathing. 'I do. So much.'

'And only me.' He didn't know why he was demanding this from her, especially when he was still intending their marriage to be a sexless one. But that didn't change the roaring need inside him, the hunger for something he didn't understand. Something only she, with her pride and stubborn determination, with her warmth and her surrender, could give him.

You can't go anywhere else for this. And you don't want her to either.

No. He damn well didn't.

'I've changed my mind,' he said roughly, deciding right there and then. 'Once we're married, you're mine. There will be no one else for you, understand me?'

Her hands came up, her fingers threading through his hair, her eyes blazing into his. 'Yes, I understand. And there will be no one else for you either.'

He almost laughed, because of course she would demand the same thing from him. Not that he was going to argue.

'I don't need anyone else.' He let her see the truth in his gaze. 'Not when you can give me everything I need.'

A fleeting brightness moved through her face, then she was tugging his head down, her lips meeting his, hungry and wanton.

And he was kissing her, a desperate, hot kiss, the heat of her mouth lighting a fire inside him that he didn't think would ever go out.

That should have been a warning, but he was too far gone to notice. He kissed her, taking what he wanted from her, feverish and desperate, tracking kisses down her neck before lingering in the soft hollow of her throat, tasting her frantic pulse. He wanted to spend more time tasting her, making her even hotter for him, even more desperate, but he couldn't wait. He'd never been able to wait, not with her.

He clawed open his trousers and spread her thighs, pushed himself deep inside her. She gave a soft cry of delight, lifting her hips to meet his thrusts, and he stared down into her face, into those shattered sky eyes, unable to look away. Her body was slick around him, her inner muscles gripping him as tightly as her thighs around his waist. As if she wanted to hold him close and never let him go.

And he shouldn't want her to. He shouldn't like it. It shouldn't feel as if he was somehow home.

But it did. And the feeling didn't go away as the pleasure inside him began to get more intense, more demanding. As he watched the same pleasure rise in her too.

So he eased back on his thrusts, pushing into her in a long, lazy glide then sliding out. Deep and slow. As if there was nothing better to do but this. As if he could do it all day. And he wanted to. He wanted it not to end.

Time slowed down to a pinpoint, to this one eternal moment. To her lying beneath him, her hips moving with his, her fingers twined in his hair, her gaze locked with his. Full of desire, full of need.

For him. Just for him.

'You're amazing,' she whispered, her brilliant gaze on his. 'You're the most amazing man I've ever met.'

It felt like an arrow to the chest, the pain bittersweet and intense.

Because right now, in her arms, for the first time in his life, he felt like he could possibly be that man. The man she thought was amazing instead of the man who'd walked away from a woman he was supposed to be there for. A man who'd let his own mother die, who'd wasted his entire life trying to drown in his own self-loathing, telling himself that he didn't care, not about anything.

But Stella was right, and that was the problem. He did care. He cared about *everything*.

And he thought he probably cared about her most of all.

'Dante,' she murmured, her hands twisting tighter in his hair. 'Take me home.'

So he did, reaching down between them, stroking the

sensitive place between her thighs as he thrust, watching
her eyes turn pure silver as the climax exploded through
her.

Crushing his own cry of release against the softness
of her mouth.

Knowing that, one way or another, he was going to end
up hurting her.

And trying to tell himself it didn't matter.

CHAPTER NINE

STELLA GAZED AT the magnificent view out of the long, elegant windows of the *palazzo*, over rolling green lawns and terraced gardens surrounding a lavishly tiled pool area, to the small wood that lay beyond all that green.

It was so very beautiful. The perfect family home.

She and Dante were viewing the property he'd chosen near Milan, an old *palazzo* near his brother's, though Enzo and his family spent most of their time on the little island Enzo had bought the year before.

Stella had wanted to know more about Enzo—important, considering the man was going to be uncle to their child—but Dante hadn't been interested in telling her much about him.

In fact, since that evening on the terrace at the hotel in Rome, he hadn't seemed interested in talking to her much at all. It had been at least a week since then and he'd spent the majority of it at his computer or on the phone, organising various things. He was having to deal with a few issues with his business interests—or at least that was what he'd told her—as well as preparations for their wedding.

He'd told her he wanted her input on aspects of it, but she found that sitting down and talking about it made her feel…uneasy. All this talk of love and the importance of vows when both of them knew it wouldn't be a marriage based on anything more than shared parentage. It made her ache. For herself and for their child. For the kind of life that they would have, which sounded so very wonderful on paper, and yet…

Stella stared sightlessly at the lawns that stretched into the distance beyond the windows, trying to ignore the bleakness that gathered inside her.

Dante cared, she knew he did, but he wasn't going to admit it. And she couldn't force him to if he didn't want to. So what would that mean for their baby? What would it mean for their child to grow up with a father who wouldn't admit to the possibility of love?

She'd grown up without that in her life and it was her need for it that had propelled her to pick up the gun and point it at Dante's face. Her weakness, her fatal flaw. She would do everything in her own power to make sure her son or daughter grew up knowing they were loved, but would the love of one parent be enough?

Dante's was a magnetic, charismatic presence. He would have a massive influence on their child, especially given how involved he wanted to be in their life. But how would that child feel to have a father who never told them he loved them?

Pain echoed inside her, a vibration that shuddered through her, reflecting off the empty places in her soul and reverberating like an echo.

She knew how that felt. Never to have someone hold her or tell her that they loved her. That they were proud of her.

It hurt. It hurt so much.

A footstep echoed in the empty room, and then warm arms slid around her waist, drawing her in close to the hot, hard strength of the man behind her.

She should have felt comforted and reassured by those arms, by the power in that body. But right now it didn't feel enough. Like a perfect fantasy that only half came true, the rest of it out of reach for ever.

Her child would feel like that. Wanting something from its father he was never going to give it. Oh, Dante might, at some point, admit to himself what his refusal to deal with his past was doing to him and to their child—because it was definitely his past that was holding him back.

Or he might not. He might never admit it.

You will have to hope that your love alone will be enough for your baby. Because what other option do you have?

She could leave. That was another option. But then where would she go? How would she provide for their child? And would Dante even let her? He wouldn't. Of course he wouldn't.

Can you walk away from him? That's the real question.

The thought sat inside her, a cold, hard reality she'd been trying to ignore for days now.

'What do you think?' Dante murmured, nuzzling against her ear. 'Do you like it?'

He was talking about the *palazzo*, of course, but she liked his arms around her, the feeling of his strength at her back, the warmth of his breath against her skin.

He'd changed his mind about marriage in name only. He'd told her that she was his and that they would find physical satisfaction with each other, and every night he proved it to her over and over.

But her doubts weren't about him and whether a playboy would ever be faithful—she knew he would be. He was a man of determination and he'd promised her that if she wouldn't get satisfaction elsewhere then neither would he. She believed he meant it.

No, her doubts were about herself. Whether sex would be enough of a stand-in for the hunger that lay in her soul.

Whether a child would fill up that need and whether it was fair to expect a child to do that.

'I do like it,' she said, staring out the windows, conscious of the warmth of the man at her back and the hunger inside her that would go unsatisfied for ever. 'Perhaps it would be good to be close to your brother. Our little one will have a cousin to play with.'

He made a noncommittal sound. 'I'm not sure whether being close to Enzo would be a good thing or not. If you think I'm controlling, you haven't met him.'

'And will I?' She put her hands over his where they rested on her stomach, trying to ignore the doubts. 'Meet him, I mean?'

'You will. At our engagement party.'

Of course. Dante had made sure not a breath of what was happening between them made it into the media. He hadn't wanted anyone to know, or at least not until he was ready. Luckily it had only been a week, so no one had noticed his absence from the entertainment circuit.

She didn't much care about the media—wouldn't a press release do the job? But he'd told her to let him handle it his way. He'd decided on an engagement party as the best way to announce their circumstances, as the media tended to be less intrusive when they thought they were being given the whole story rather than a carefully selected portion of it. He'd made the observation that it would allow news of what was happening between them to reach her family, so she wouldn't have to deal with them.

She appreciated that. She'd told him about her worries concerning her father and what he might do once he'd found out she wasn't going through with his revenge plans. Dante's response had been to send a couple of his representatives to Monte Santa Maria to inform her parents that she was now under his protection, as she would be marrying him. He'd also included a payment of a ridiculous sum of money to keep Santo quiet, plus a warning that if he tried to contact Stella again the police would be called and he would be taken into custody.

Stella was fine with that. She didn't want to hear from her father. She'd made peace with Matteo's memory as much as she could and with her own failure to go through with her father's vendetta.

Except that weakness, that need for love, is still there.

'You are going to invite him, aren't you?' She kept her tone neutral, hiding the doubt that tugged at her.

'Of course I will. He's my brother.' Dante nuzzled her neck, pressing a kiss below her ear and making her shiver deliciously. 'Except we might keep the fact that we met while you were trying to kill me to ourselves for a while, hmm? Enzo's very protective.'

And so was Dante—she knew that for a fact.

'Are you afraid he'll do something to me?' she asked, curious.

Dante gave a low laugh. 'No. He'd be dead before he hit the floor if he tried to hurt you.'

Stella thought he was probably only a little serious. 'So why not just tell him?'

'He'll be angry and we really don't want an angry Enzo. We need to build up to that.'

Her heart ached at the affectionate warmth in Dante's voice. Yet another reminder that, despite what he'd told her, he cared. He cared about his brother, for example, and quite deeply. Why else would he have chosen to look at this *palazzo*—the one near Enzo's?

But he won't ever care about you.

Emotion clogged her throat. She didn't need him to care about her, though, did she? He was going to give her everything else: a place to live, financial support, help in bringing up their child and all the physical pleasure she might want. Did she really need him to care about her too?

You know the answer to that question.

Yes. She did. That was all she'd wanted all her life: someone to care about her. Someone she mattered to. But her parents had only ever wanted Matteo, not her. No one had ever really wanted her.

And now she was going to tie herself for life to a man who didn't really want her either.

Restlessness filled her and suddenly she didn't want to stand there with the warmth of his arms around her like the promise of something she was never going to get. She pushed his hands away and stepped out of his arms, moving over to the window and looking out.

Her heart thumped painfully in her ears and she felt oddly cold.

A silence fell, though she could feel the pressure of Dante's gaze from behind her.

'Kitten?' he asked after a moment. 'Is there something wrong? Something to do with my brother?'

'You care about him.' Stella turned from the view and looked at the man she was supposed to marry. 'Don't you?'

Dante stood there in one of his expensively tailored suits—no jacket today, and no tie either, his black shirt casually open at the neck, his sleeves rolled to his elbows. Her favourite look on him.

He had his hands in the pockets of his trousers and the look on his handsome face was guarded. 'He's my brother,' he said, frowning, as if that was all the explanation required. 'Why do you ask?'

Stella swallowed, not quite sure herself why she was asking. It was just…she couldn't stop thinking about his refusal to acknowledge the fact that he did care. About quite a lot of things. Was it only her he denied that to? Did he ever say that to his brother too?

'So you can care about people, Dante.'

'If you're wanting—'

'Will you ever care about me?' The words slipped from her before she could stop them and she knew she shouldn't have asked as soon as they were out.

But she couldn't take them back even though, as his expression hardened the way it had back on the terrace in Rome, the darkness of his eyes becoming absolute, she desperately wished she could.

It was a door shutting in her face.

No, he wouldn't care about her.

But you want him to.

The realisation opening up inside her was like a sunflower blooming, shining in her heart, bright and beautiful and golden, reflecting glory everywhere.

She'd always wanted someone to care for her, wanted an acknowledgement that she mattered to somebody. But she hadn't known she'd wanted that acknowledgement from Dante. No one else. Just him.

Dante, who wasn't the irresponsible playboy she'd first assumed, but who was warm and caring and protective. Who'd taken care of her, no matter that she'd tried to kill him. Who'd challenged her and pushed her. Who'd held her when she'd been vulnerable and broken, and who'd given her strength when she'd needed it. Not to mention the indescribable pleasure he also gave her every night.

Dante, who didn't want to care, not about anyone.

The sunflower began to wither inside her, its golden brightness fading as cold whispered through her, the icy breath of winter.

'It's okay,' she said suddenly, before he could speak, because she didn't want to hear him say the words out loud. She didn't think she could bear it. 'Forget I said anything.'

But he didn't look away and the set expression on his face didn't fade. His gaze was dark, his beautiful mouth hard, tension gathered in every line of his powerful body. 'Then why did you ask?'

He was angry with her, of course, and why wouldn't he be? They were here to view a house, not have a deep and meaningful discussion about their relationship.

Stella glanced out of the window again, not wanting to meet the anger in his gaze, wishing she'd never said anything. 'It doesn't matter.'

'It's about what I said to you in Rome, isn't it?'

'I don't need you to—'

'Because if you want the truth then here it is. I will care for you, Stella.' His voice was nothing but cold, hard steel. 'But, no. I can never care about you.'

The words felt like stones thrown at her, each one jagged and sharp, leaving a bruise where they landed. And the fact that they were the truth only made the pain worse.

Did you really expect anything different? He told you not to care about him.

He had. Yet she cared anyway.

No, it was more than that, wasn't it? More than simple caring.

She loved him. Because that glory inside her, the warmth, the brightness she felt whenever she looked at him, was love. The pain she experienced herself whenever he hurt, that was love too. The longing to touch him, have his arms around her, have him be the one to fill the void inside her...

What else could it be?

Only love.

Nothing else would hurt as much.

She stared hard out of the window at the cypresses that lined the grand, sweeping driveway, trying to force away the prickle of tears. 'You won't, you mean.'

'Can't, won't. What does it matter?'

'It matters to me.'

'Fine.' His voice was expressionless. 'I won't.'

The trees wavered in her vision as she lost the battle. Two weeks ago she would have blinked the tears back, pretended they weren't there, but now she made no effort to hide them. What was the point when she'd already given her own feelings away?

'I'm not your mother,' she said, though why she was arguing with him she didn't know. Was she hoping to change his mind? 'I'm not an alcoholic battling addiction. I'm just a woman who wants someone to care about her. You do understand that, don't you?'

'Of course I understand that.' Anger threaded through his voice. 'But this isn't about my mother. This isn't about the past. It's about the choice I made for the future years ago and I'm not about to change it.'

The tears ran down her cheek, but she made no attempt to brush them away. She wanted to ask him whether he would change it for their baby's sake, except they'd already had that discussion, and besides she couldn't—wouldn't—use their child that way.

So all she said was, 'Not even for me?'

There was a heavy silence and then footsteps came from behind her. Dante's hands were suddenly on her shoulders, turning her round to face him, his expression tightening as he saw the tears running down her face.

'Stella,' he demanded roughly, something that looked like pain in the depths of his eyes. 'Why does this matter to you so very much?'

She looked up at him, lifting her chin, because even

now, even here, she couldn't resist the challenge. 'Why do you think? Because you matter, Dante. You matter to me.'

His expression tightened, his fingers digging into her shoulders almost painfully. 'I told you not to care, kitten. Remember? I *told* you not to.'

She swallowed, her throat aching, everything aching. 'Too late.'

Dante could hear his own heartbeat loud and heavy in his ears, and something was cracking right down the middle of his chest, breaking him in two.

Who knew a woman's tears had the power to do that? His mother had been able to turn hers off and on, depending on what she wanted to get him to do. But there was nothing feigned about Stella's. They rolled slowly down her cheeks, one after the other, pain glowing in her silver-blue eyes.

Silly, *silly* kitten. She cared about him. *Dio*, why on earth would she go and do that? After the warning he'd given her back in Rome? After he'd dismissed all that caring nonsense and showed her that their physical connection could bridge any gap?

It was her own fault, of course. Not his. He'd been very clear about his feelings on the subject. He wasn't going to care about anyone or anything, not again, and he'd told her he wouldn't. She'd known that from the beginning.

So why the sight of her tears and the anguish in her gaze made him feel as if she really had taken that letter opener and plunged it into the centre of his chest, he had no idea.

He tried to dismiss the pain, but it wouldn't go away, and that made him angry. Made him want to crush her to him, cover her lovely, vulnerable mouth with his, make her forget her ridiculous decision to care about him, to give her pleasure instead.

But almost as soon as the impulse occurred to him and he began to pull her close her hands came up and she pushed them hard against his chest, holding herself away.

'No, Dante,' she said, hoarse and shaken. 'Not this time.'

Tension coiled in him, the sharp, restless need to do something—anything—to stop her from saying the words he so desperately did not want to hear. To take away her pain. 'You said you'd never turn me away.' His own voice sounded as rough as hers. 'That you'd never refuse me.'

'I know.' Bright determination glowed in her eyes despite the tracks of her tears. 'But that was before I knew I was in love with you, Dante Cardinali.'

Love. That damn word again. The word he'd tried to strip down over the years so that it had lost all meaning, become nothing. But he hadn't been successful, had he? Because of course it meant something.

Guilt. Pain.

'I don't want you to be in love with me,' he said viciously. 'I didn't ask for it.'

'I didn't ask for it either.' Her chin lifted higher, a challenge. 'And quite frankly the last thing in the world I want is to be in love with a man who doesn't give a damn. And yet here we are.'

His jaw was tight, his whole body stiff with tension. She was so warm against him, and so soft. All it would take would be the right touch, a kiss, and she'd melt the way she always did. He knew how to do it. He knew how to make her forget.

'So?' He slid his hands down over the delicious curve of her bottom, fitting her more closely against his hardening groin. 'It doesn't change anything.' And it wouldn't. Because he wouldn't let it.

'Dante, no.' Stella pushed harder against his chest, her palms little points of heat on him. 'You don't understand. It changes *everything*.'

A growl escaped him. He didn't want to let her go. He wanted to keep holding her, because he had the awful suspicion that if he let her go he'd never get to hold her again. 'Why?'

Colour had risen in her cheeks, flushing her pale skin a delicate rose. She was so beautiful and yet the pain in her eyes hurt him in ways he didn't understand. 'Let me go.'

'You're going to leave, aren't you?' He couldn't stop himself from asking stupid questions, when what he should have been doing was crushing her mouth under his. 'As soon as I let you go, you're going to walk away.'

She looked vulnerable and yet there was something strong in her too, a determination he'd seen the night she'd tried to take his life. Only this time it wasn't the brittle strength of a woman forcing herself to do something she knew was wrong, it was the enduring strength of a woman knowing she would do the right thing, no matter the cost to herself. No matter her own pain.

'All I wanted was for someone to put their arms around me.' Her voice was very soft, the edges of it frayed and ragged like torn silk. 'To hold me and tell me that I was loved. But no one ever did.' Her gaze remained steady on his, a terrible knowledge glowing there. 'And Dante, if I marry you, no one ever will.'

Such simple words to have such power. It felt as if she'd plunged not just a knife into his heart but a sword sharp enough to cut through stone.

But she was right. If he married her, if he tied her to him, she would never have that. Because he could never give it to her.

Would *never give it to her.*

No. He wouldn't. And it was a choice. He understood that much.

He'd had a choice back when he'd been a teenager and his mother had told him to go, to leave her alone. And he had. Because he'd been done with her and her constant refusal of everything he tried to do for her. Done with trying to love a woman who'd only dragged him with her because she hadn't wanted to be alone.

Who had never wanted *him*.

Because, if she had, she would have tried, wouldn't she? She would have made some kind of effort to be the kind of mother he'd needed, surely?

Ah, but that was useless to think about. Those questions had no answers and he'd never get them, because she was dead, denying him to the last.

If you hadn't walked away, things might have been different.

And that was the hell of it, wasn't it? Because he *had* walked away. And he would never know if he could have changed things if he'd stayed.

He'd never know if he could have saved her.

Guilt twisted in his heart, but he shoved it away, buried it deep.

This wasn't the same situation and Stella wasn't a fragile, bitter addict, but the choice he had to make was still the same. And he knew he would make the same decision, because he knew exactly how this little story played out.

He would give her everything she wanted, everything that was in his power to give, except that one little piece of himself. And it wouldn't be enough for her. And eventually that would turn to bitterness and anger. It would turn to pain. It would destroy what relationship they did have, and it wouldn't only involve him and her, it would involve their child as well.

The anger inside him, the fire that never went out, flared hot and bitter.

Yes, this was her fault. She was ruining what they had with her constant need for more. And she was ruining it for their child too.

That's right. Blame her for your own cowardice. Remind you of anyone?

Dante ignored the snide voice in his head. Instead he opened his arms, letting her go and stepping back, the warmth of her body lingering against him in a way that nearly broke him.

'There,' he said, his tone acid. 'If you want to go, go. I won't stop you.'

She looked so small standing there by herself, the silky dress she wore his favourite colour, a pale, silvery blue the exact same shade as her eyes. 'So that's really the way it's going to end?' she asked quietly. 'You walking away again?'

'Does it look like I'm walking away?' His voice echoed with a bitterness and he couldn't hide it. 'No, darling, you're the one who doesn't want what I have to give.'

Her mouth trembled. 'I do want it. I just want *all* of it. I want to be loved, Dante. I want to be loved by you.'

It felt as if she'd swung that sword again, cutting through his chest, through sinew and bone, right into his heart.

'Why?' He ignored the pain, reaching for his anger instead. 'Why can't you be happy with what we have now? I'll give you everything you want. Every damn thing, Stella.'

'I know you will,' she said sadly. 'And maybe that would have been enough for me a week or so ago. But it's not enough for me now.'

'Why not?' He'd taken a step towards her before he realised what he was doing, his hands in fists at his sides. 'Why can't that be enough?'

She was framed by the window, the green of the view behind her, and there was something about it that made her seem very isolated and alone, yet at the same time it highlighted her quiet strength.

He didn't understand how she could ever have thought herself weak.

'Because I'm not the same person I was a week ago. You changed me, Dante. You made me want more. You made me think I deserve more. And I…don't want to live the rest of my life simply being content with whatever you choose to give me.' Her shoulders straightened, her jaw firmed. 'I need to be loved. I *need* it. And I don't want to have to earn it or be forever trying to change your mind to get it. I did that with my father and I don't want to do it again.'

Of course she had. And the fact that he understood her made everything worse somehow.

He felt as though he was trying to hold onto something precious that was slipping through his fingers and it took every atom of will he possessed not to go to her and take her in his arms again, to physically hold onto her so she didn't disappear. 'You'll have the baby,' he forced out through gritted teeth. 'You don't need love from me.'

But she only shook her head slowly. 'No, I won't put that on our baby. It's not fair.' Another tear rolled down her cheek. 'I'm sorry, Dante. I can't do this. I can't spend my life waiting for love from another man who'll never give it to me. I don't want that for our child either.'

Everything was slipping out of his grasp and he had no idea how to get it back. Because to get it back would mean admitting that he cared, and he didn't. He just damn well didn't.

He couldn't afford to.

He had nothing more of his heart left to give anyway.

Not even for your son or daughter?

But anger raged inside him like a bonfire, scorching everything in sight, and he didn't want to think about his child right now. What he wanted was to tell her all this was her fault, that she was the one ruining everything, that he expected better from her than ultimatums.

But he locked the furious words safely away. Smothered the bonfire with indifference. Deprived it of oxygen by slamming the door on every single feeling he had.

And it was easy. Easier than he'd expected.

'Fine.' He tried to sound lazy and casual, the way he always did. 'It's up to you, of course. But this is turning out to be more trouble than it's worth, so you'll forgive me if perhaps we put this marriage situation on hold for the time being.'

Pain flashed across her face; she knew what that tone of his meant as much as he did. And it hurt him. It flayed him alive.

But he ignored that too. Because did she seriously expect him to cave in to her demands simply because she loved him? Ridiculous.

'I understand.' Her voice was level and yet he could hear the hurt laced through it like a crack in a perfect windowpane. 'And the baby?'

'I'll buy this *palazzo*.' He gestured at the empty room, taking care not to look too closely at it as he took a hammer to the fantasies he'd been constructing about it in his head. 'You can live here until the child is born. Then we'll have to work out some other arrangements.'

Her mouth trembled as if her strength was coming to an end. 'I thought you wanted two parents for our child, Dante. I thought you wanted to live with us.'

'So did I.' He held her gaze, let her see the utter indifference in his. Because she was right about one thing: his child was better off without him. 'Seems I was mistaken.'

Sadness filled her eyes. 'So that's your response? You're going to walk away from us? Oh, Dante...'

The disappointment and hurt in her voice made him want to howl in agony. Instead, he gave a hollow laugh. 'What? You really thought I'd do anything different? Come now, kitten. You know what kind of man I am. As you've already pointed out, my child is going to suffer having me for a father anyway. Might as well live the part.' He forced himself to turn away, because he wasn't going to stand there looking at the pain on Stella's face a second longer. 'I'll get a car back to Milan. I think I'll stay there a couple of days, in fact. You can stay in Rome until the purchase of this house comes through.' He began to walk towards the exit, having to force himself to take every step. 'Don't worry, everything will be taken care of.'

'I *do* know what kind of man you are, Dante Cardinali,' Stella said from behind him, her voice echoing in the empty room. 'I only wish you did too.'

Pain reverberated through him, but he didn't turn. 'I'm sorry, kitten. That man doesn't exist.'

He didn't expect her to call after him as he walked through the door and, when she didn't, he tried not to tell himself he was disappointed.

CHAPTER TEN

DANTE SAT IN the rooftop garden of his newly bought penthouse in Milan, where he'd once envisaged putting a luxurious day-bed so he and Stella could spend some 'adult' time in any spare moments they might have while looking after their child.

But as he lolled on one of the white couches under the pergola, yet another glass of wine on the table at his elbow as the sun set over Milan, he decided that perhaps one wasn't enough. He'd get in two. After all, he'd need more than one for all the lovely women he'd be bringing up here, because of course he'd be bringing lots of women up here.

Since he wasn't getting married now, he wouldn't need to be faithful, which meant he could sleep around the way he always had.

It would have been a reassuring thought if it also hadn't filled him with a weary kind of distaste. Perhaps it meant he was getting old.

Or perhaps it means you only want her.

No, that would be ridiculous. Why would he? Stella was gone anyway, back to Rome and the penthouse suite they'd stayed at initially, just as he'd told her to. She was, after all, still pregnant with his child and the *palazzo* wasn't quite ready to accommodate her just yet.

Pain shifted in his chest so he lifted his wine glass and took another sip. Sometimes alcohol helped and sometimes it didn't.

Looked like it was going to be another day where it didn't.

A footstep made him look up from his contemplation of the view and he frowned as the tall figure of his brother stepped out from the living area and onto the rooftop.

'How did you get in?' Dante demanded.

'The front door was open.' Enzo casually strolled over and sat down on the chair opposite him.

'Nonsense. The front door has a keypad and a lock that automatically engages.'

'Fine. I had someone dismantle the lock.' There was not one ounce of shame in Enzo's expression. 'You weren't answering the door.'

Dante took a sip of his wine and scowled. 'Seems like overkill.'

'It's been five days, Dante. I was worried.'

'Why? I'm fine.' He gestured with his glass at the rooftop around them. 'As you can see.'

Enzo's golden eyes narrowed. 'You are not fine. You look like you haven't slept in days.'

'I haven't.' Dante shrugged. 'A small bout of insomnia. It's nothing.'

But his brother's gaze was sharp and Dante had the uncomfortable sensation that Enzo could read every thought in his head.

'I had a call,' Enzo said after a moment. 'From a woman.'

Dante went very still, something clutching tightly in his chest. 'What woman?'

'I think you know which woman I mean.' His brother looked steadily at him. 'The woman expecting your child.

Who's been very worried about you, regardless of the way you walked out on her.'

A spike of pain welled up inside him, leaking through the cracks in the denial he'd laid over the top of it. A denial that had been working very well the whole of the past week until now.

Probably meant he needed to drink some more.

'I don't know what woman you're talking about,' he said flatly, taking another sip.

Enzo's expression darkened. 'I thought you were a man, Dante. Not a coward.'

The denial cracked a little more and this time it was anger leaking out, a hot wave of it. And suddenly Dante lifted his glass and threw it hard against the stone wall of the parapet that bounded the garden.

It shattered, wine dripping onto the stone floor.

There was a silence, broken only by the sound of his breathing, fast and hard, as though he'd been running for days. Which he had been.

Running from the sound of Stella's voice telling him she knew what kind of man he was.

Running from the sound of his own cowardice as he'd told her that man didn't exist.

'Feel better?' Enzo asked mildly.

'No,' Dante said.

'Well.' His brother leaned back in his chair and eyed him. 'This is familiar.'

Oh, yes, he supposed it was. He remembered having a talk with Enzo just like this one when his brother had nearly lost the woman he loved. How ironic that it should be Enzo coming to talk to him now.

'Best to go away, brother mine,' Dante growled. 'I'm not in the mood.'

'Don't be ridiculous,' Enzo said, ignoring him. 'Stella

is going to have your child and you're here sulking like Simon does when he's having one of his tantrums. I thought you'd at least behave better than my five-year-old.'

The sound of her name reverberated through him, striking sparks of pain through his entire body. 'Don't,' he said dangerously. 'Don't you dare say her name.'

'Why? Because it hurts you?' Enzo ignored the warning. 'You're a fool, little brother. She told me what went on—and don't worry, she only told me after I demanded she tell me everything. And I can read between the lines. You fell in love with her, and you didn't know how to deal with it, so you pushed her away.'

You fell in love with her...

The words dropped into a quiet space in Dante's head, echoing.

'You're wrong,' he forced out. 'I'm not in love with her. I'm indifferent to her.'

'Is that right? So why did you walk away? Why are you sitting here in an apparently unfurnished apartment, drinking by yourself and refusing to answer the door?' Enzo shook his head. 'You told me once that Mama had her own issues. And I can guess what they might be.' Something in his face flickered. 'I will never forgive myself for the fact that you had to deal with them alone, that I didn't come after you when Mama dragged you away.'

Another crack ran through Dante's denial, jagged and raw. 'You were young. And I coped. I was fine—'

'No,' Enzo said forcefully. 'You didn't cope. And you're not fine. If you were fine, you would be with the woman you loved and readying yourself for the birth of your first child. Instead, you're sitting here drinking, pretending you don't care when any fool can see that you care so deeply you can't deal with it.'

Dante didn't know what to say. He sat there staring at his brother, feeling the denial start to break apart inside him, and he could do nothing at all to stop it.

'She died, Enzo,' he heard himself say. 'And I couldn't save her. I walked away and let her die.'

Enzo didn't ask who he was talking about. 'Mama chose her own path and you know it. So don't let her choices dictate yours.' He paused, his golden gaze steady and sure. 'You're doing exactly what she used to do, you know that, don't you? Drowning your own pain with alcohol and pushing away the people who love you.'

Dante stared at his brother, conscious of a trickle of ice water dripping down his back. A trickle that became a flood as understanding broke over him.

Because of course Enzo was right. He *was* doing exactly what his mother had done. Drinking away the pain, refusing help. Denying the people who loved him. Hurting them, blaming them…

The way he'd hurt and blamed Stella for the simple crime of loving him and wanting to be loved in return. *Dio*, would he do the same thing to his child too?

Shame swept over him.

'I hurt her,' he said, hoarse and a bit desperate. 'I told her not to care about me and then I…blamed her for wanting more. I blamed her for ruining what we had.' He took a breath. 'It's not her fault. It's mine.'

His brother's gaze softened. 'That's a start. So what are you going to do about it?'

Dante's whole body felt tight. All he could see was the pain in Stella's lovely blue eyes and the tears on her cheeks. Tears *he'd* put there. 'What *can* I do? I walked away from her. I pretended I didn't care and then just left.'

'There's one thing you can do,' Enzo said. 'Accept that

you do care and then spend every second of your life showing her exactly how much.'

Dante stared at his brother, into the face of the only
other person in his life he'd ever cared about. 'How did
you do it with Matilda?' he asked. 'How did you just…put
everything aside and make that decision?'

Enzo lifted a shoulder. 'It was easy. I finally understood that I loved her. That her pain was more important
than my own.'

'Easy.' Dante echoed mirthlessly.

But Enzo only shook his head. 'It's about acceptance,
brother. Not that river in Egypt.'

It was a lame joke, but then his brother had never been
very good at humour.

Just as Dante had never been very good at acceptance.

*'All I ever wanted was for someone to put their arms
around me and tell me I was loved…'*

She'd told him that and it was such a simple thing to
give her. Only his heart. And what did his heart matter
anyway? Who was he holding onto it for? There was no
one else he wanted to give it to but her and, if she took it
and ripped it into shreds, what of it? There would be pain
and he'd had pain before.

Besides, he owed it to her for the way he'd walked out.
He owed her an apology. And if she threw it back in his
face it wouldn't be anything he didn't deserve.

And, apart from anything else, he wanted to see her
shattered sky eyes just once more.

'I think,' he said. 'That I suddenly need to be in Rome.
Urgently.'

Enzo eyed him. 'It's nearly midnight.'

Dante surged up out of his chair. The denial had cracked
apart and melted away as if it had never been, leaving noth-

ing but an intense, aching hunger he knew was never going to go away. 'I don't care. I have to go now.'

Enzo snorted. 'Good thing I got the helicopter ready to go, then, isn't it?'

Stella was asleep and dreaming. It was one of the lovely and yet terribly painful dreams that had been plaguing her for the past week, where she would feel strong arms around her and a muscular, powerful body at her back keeping her warm. And a rich, dark voice would whisper in her ear, except she could never hear the words. There were too indistinct.

The dream hurt and always ended the same way, with her waking up alone, a deep, intense yearning in her heart for something she was never going to have.

She hated those dreams.

In fact, as she lay curled up in the bed she'd once shared with Dante, she thought she was having one now, because warm arms slid around her, drawing her against an achingly familiar body. Hot, muscular and smelling of sandalwood, folding around her and keeping her safe.

She gave a little moan of resistance and shivered as she felt lips nuzzle her ear, her whole body falling into longing as that dark voice began to whisper the words she never seemed to hear.

Except right now, alone in her bed, she heard them.

'Stella Montefiore,' the dream said. 'I have something to tell you.' Those arms tightened around her, holding her fast. 'You are wanted. You are loved. And you are loved by me.'

Stella trembled. Was she awake? Or was this still a dream? Because, if it was a dream, she didn't want to wake up.

But the voice was still speaking, that familiar voice

that made her want to cry. 'I'm sorry, kitten,' Dante murmured. 'I'm so sorry for the way I left you. For all the terrible things I said to you. I've got no excuse for them other than the one you probably already know. I was afraid. I didn't want to feel anything, I didn't want to care. But I did care. I cared about you.'

She shuddered, not wanting move or speak in case the dream disappeared, a sob collecting in her throat.

'You told me you knew what kind of man I am,' he went on, 'but all I knew was that I was the man who'd walked out on his mother because she wouldn't give me even one single sign that she loved me. And then she died. And maybe if I hadn't walked out, if I hadn't wanted to be loved so badly, I might have been there to save her.'

Stella couldn't keep still any more.

She turned over, heart bursting in her chest, half-terrified of what she would see—that it wouldn't be the man she wanted, just that awful dream again, and she'd be left with nothing.

But it wasn't a dream.

Dante was lying in the bed, his eyes gleaming and black in the dim room, his expression stripped bare. He was in his usual suit trousers and shirt, yet his shirt was creased and had clearly seen better days, and his normally clean-shaven jaw was dark with stubble.

He looked tired and worn and desperate, and still the most beautiful man she'd ever seen.

'You're here,' she croaked, reaching out a shaking hand to touch his beloved face. 'How did you get here?'

Dante didn't smile, only looked into her eyes. 'I had a visit from my brother. He told me that you'd called him because you were worried about me.'

She was still shaking and she couldn't stop. Couldn't stop from running her fingers along his cheekbone either, his skin warm and real beneath her fingertips. 'I did and I was. And I'm not sorry I called him.'

'I'm not sorry either.' Dante's gaze was dark, fathomless. 'Enzo told me I was doing exactly what my mother had done, sitting there blaming everyone else for my pain and pushing away the people I loved. Hurting them...' He stopped. 'You wanted more from me and I hurt you. I was selfish and I blamed you.'

'Dante—'

'No, you were right to want more, Stella. Do you understand? You were right.' He lifted his hand and caught hers where it was pressed to his cheek and held it there. 'I needed to stop pretending I didn't care. To accept that I did. I needed to stop thinking only of myself, stop turning into my own damn mother.' Gently he lowered her hand and kissed the tips of her fingers. 'And, most important of all, I needed to realise that I was in love with you. Because I am, Stella Montefiore. I think I've been in love with you since the moment I woke up to find you pointing a gun at my head.'

Her chest went tight, her heart so full it felt as though it was pressing on the sides of her ribs. 'Is that why you're here?'

'Yes. I wanted to apologise.' The ghost of his charming smile turned his mouth, but there was something desperate in his dark eyes. 'And to tell you that I will love our child too, with the same desperation with which I love you. And also that my heart is yours, if you want it. But, if you don't, I'll leave you in peace. I won't ever bother you with it again.'

A tear leaked out despite her best intentions and, because her voice didn't work, she leaned forward and gave him her answer by brushing her mouth over his instead.

And instantly he moved, his arms going around her, holding her hard against him and then rolling her beneath him.

'You know that's it, don't you?' he growled, intense gold flames burning in the depths of his eyes. 'That means I'm never letting you go.'

Stella got her arms free then raised them and wound them around his neck, holding onto him as tightly as he was holding on to her. 'I don't want you to let me go. I want you to hold me for ever, Dante Cardinali.'

'And if I don't?'

Stella thought about it. 'Then I might be forced to kill you.'

Dante gave her a sudden fierce, brilliant smile. 'Don't kill me, kitten. Love me instead.'

So that was what she did.

EPILOGUE

'WHERE IS MY COUSIN?' Simon Cardinali demanded, fixing his uncle with a fierce stare.

Enzo, who was standing outside Stella's hospital door and holding Simon's hand, frowned. 'Simon, where are your manners? You know better than that.'

The little boy pulled a face. 'Sorry, Papa,' he muttered. 'But…where is my cousin, *please*?'

Dante gazed down at his small nephew and grinned. 'She's asleep.'

'But I've got a present,' Simon complained.

'She's still a baby,' Dante explained reasonably. 'And she needs her sleep. She can see your present tomorrow.'

'Tomorrow?' Simon looked aghast. 'But that's *for ever*!'

An exasperated expression crossed Enzo's face. 'I'm going to take you back to your mother.' He gave Dante a glance—he'd already congratulated his brother on the new addition to the Cardinali family. 'How is Stella?'

'She's doing well,' Dante said, and she was. The birth had been tough going, but his kitten had been strong. Stronger than he'd been, at any rate.

'And Sofia?'

Dante thought about his daughter and grinned like a lunatic. 'She's perfect.'

Enzo gave a brisk nod. 'Well, you get some rest too. You look like hell.'

Dante didn't feel like hell. He felt incredible. As if he could do anything.

After his brother and nephew had gone, he went silently back into the private hospital room where Stella and their new daughter were sleeping.

Sofia was awake in her crib, her dark eyes—that he knew would end up being silver-blue, just like her mother's—staring up into his. And he found he could only look at her for a couple of moments at a time because it was either that or his heart would burst out of sheer joy.

He was going to have to learn how to deal with that.

Dante made sure the soft blanket was pulled snugly around his daughter and that she was quiet before moving over to the bed where his wife lay.

Stella blinked sleepily as he sat down beside her and smiled, her hand reaching for his.

He took it, the joy inside him becoming complete.

'You were amazing, my kitten,' he said quietly. 'I never knew how much strength it took to bring a new life into the world.'

Stella's smile deepened. 'You were pretty amazing yourself.'

Dante gave a rueful laugh. 'I did not handle it well.'

'You only swore and shouted twice. And you didn't threaten anyone with death, not once.'

Stella was being kind. Being with his wife while she'd been in pain and he'd been unable to help her had been one of the most difficult things he'd ever had to do.

'You set me a great example,' he said. 'I got my strength from you.'

'Because you were with me.' Her fingers tightened around his. 'We got our strength from each other.'

And she was right, they had. Because they loved each other.

Dante lifted his wife's hand to his mouth and kissed it. 'I love you, Stella Cardinali.'

Her smile was the one she kept for him and him alone. 'I will never get tired of hearing you say that.'

He turned her hand over and kissed her palm, staring into her shattered sky eyes. 'That's good, because I plan to keep saying it every day for the rest of our lives.'

And he did.

Because, as dedicated as he'd once been to being a reckless playboy who didn't feel a thing, he was even more dedicated to being a loving husband and father.

And, as it turned out, he was very good at that.

He was very good indeed.

* * * * *

COMING SOON!

We really hope you enjoyed reading this book. If you're looking for more romance, be sure to head to the shops when new books are available on

Thursday 22nd August

MILLS & BOON

Coming next month

CONSEQUENCES OF A HOT HAVANA NIGHT
Louise Fuller

She looked up at César. 'It's positive.'

His expression didn't change by so much as a tremor.

'I'm pregnant.'

She knew that these tests were ninety-nine per cent accurate, but somehow saying the words out loud made it feel more real. It was there—in her hand. She was going to have a baby.

Only the person who was supposed to be the father, supposed to be there with her, was no longer around.

Her heartbeat had slowed; she felt as if she was in a dream. 'I'm pregnant,' she said again.

César's grip tightened around her hand, and as she met his gaze she felt her legs wilt. His eyes were so very green, and for a moment all she could think was that they should be brown.

Her head was swimming. It had taken five years, but most days she was content with her life. She still regretted Jimmy's death, but the acute pain, that hollowed-out ache of despair, had faded a few years ago. Only now this news had reawakened old emotions.

He caught her arm. 'You need to sit down.'

Still holding her hand, he led her into the living room. She sat down on the sofa. The first shock was starting to wear off and panic was starting to ripple over her skin.

'I don't understand how this could happen.'

When she and Jimmy had started trying for a baby he had been so keen he'd taken a fertility test and everything had been normal. She'd been about to get herself checked out when he fell ill, and then there had been too much going on, other more urgent tests to take and so each time she wasn't pregnant she had blamed herself— her periods had always been irregular. Only now it seemed as though it hadn't been her.

César sat down beside her. 'I'm pretty sure it happened the usual way.'

She stared at him dazedly. Her head was a muddle of emotions, but he was so calm. So reasonable.

'You haven't asked me,' she said slowly, 'if the baby could be someone else's.'

In a way, that was more of a shock than her pregnancy. With hindsight—her late period, her sudden craving for fruit juice, her heightened relentless fatigue—all pointed to one obvious explanation, but she knew it was a question most men in his situation would have asked.

He leaned back a little, studying her face. There was an expression in his eyes that she couldn't fathom.

For a moment he didn't reply, and then he shrugged. 'What happened between us isn't something I've found easy to forget. I'd like to believe that you feel the same way. But if you think there's any question over my paternity now would be a good time to say so.'

She shook her head. 'There hasn't been anyone but you.' Her eyes flicked to his face. 'And, yes, I feel the same way.'

As she spoke some of the tension in her shoulders lifted. They hadn't planned for this to happen, to bring new life into the world, and they might not love one another, but those few heated moments had been fierce and important for both of them, and she was glad that this child had been conceived out of such extraordinary mutual passion.

'I don't regret it,' she said abruptly. 'What we did or what's happened.'

Her heart swelled. She had wanted and waited for this baby for so long, and suddenly all those other tests, with their accusatory ghostly white rectangles, seemed to grow vague and unsubstantial.

'Well, it's a little late for regrets.' He paused. 'This baby isn't going anywhere. What matters now is what happens next.'

Continue reading
CONSEQUENCES OF A HOT HAVANA NIGHT
Louise Fuller

Available next month
www.millsandboon.co.uk

MILLS & BOON

MODERN

Power and Passion

Prepare to be swept off your feet by sophisticated, sexy and seductive heroes, in some of the world's most glamourous and romantic locations, where power and passion collide.

LET'S TALK
Romance

For exclusive extracts, competitions
and special offers, find us online:

MILLS & BOON
DARE

Sexy. Passionate. Bold.

Sensual love stories featuring smart, sassy heroines you'd want as a best friend, and compelling intense heroes who are worthy of them.